THE TAPESTRY OF TTEN

BOOK 1. DAWN OF DARKNESS

JULIA CÆSAR

Published 2010 by arima publishing

www.arimapublishing.com

ISBN 978 1 84549 433 9

© Julia Cæsar 2010

Printed and bound in the United Kingdom

Typeset in Garamond 12/16

Swirl is an imprint of arima publishing.

arima publishing
ASK House, Northgate Avenue
Bury St Edmunds, Suffolk IP32 6BB
t: (+44) 01284 700321

www.arimapublishing.com

Dedication

To the Voice that inspired the dream.
Andrea Bocelli
and to those who heard the dream, and helped to make it come true.
My long - suffering family. Teri, Jez, Ken and Jay. Jacquie & Maurice, not forgetting
Duncan for being a prototype. (He knows which one!).
and my dear friends on the "High Council", whose editing, feedback, advice and
artwork, has made this possible.

Terry Brady and Rebecca Johnson, (Editorial team).
Carol Leather, (Webmaster).
Jacqueline Barnes, (P.A and chief Lion Tamer).
Pete Turner (I.T. Technician).
Jenn Barkell (Map Designer)
Hilly Dunsdon (Book Jacket Designs & Artwork)
Jez Cæsar (Technical Research)
Shän Harris (Medieval Textile Techniques).

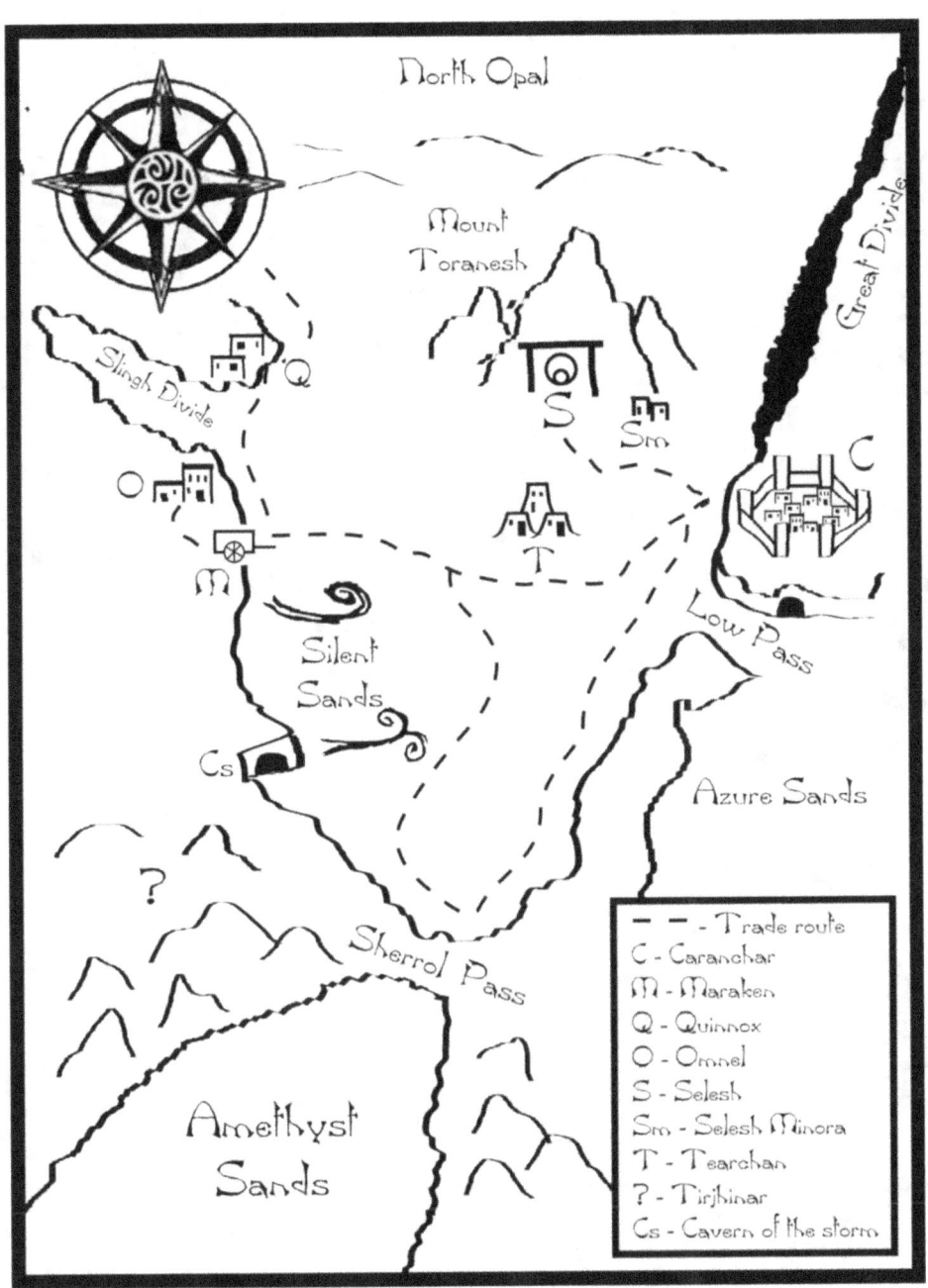

North Opal

Mount Toranesh

Slingh Divide

Great Divide

Q

S

Sm

C

O

M

T

Low Pass

Silent
Sands

Cs

Azure Sands

?

Sherrol Pass

Amethyst
Sands

- - - - Trade route
C - Caranchar
M - Maraken
Q - Quinnox
O - Omnel
S - Selesh
Sm - Selesh Minora
T - Tearchan
? - Tirjhinar
Cs - Cavern of the storm

CONTENTS

Pronunciations

Note: Emphasis or stress should be placed on the underlined syllables. Characters shown **bold** should be hard, e.g. **g** as in **g**o, rather than g as in gesture.
Syllables in brackets are soft. e.g. (g) as in gesture.

Word	Pronunciation	Description
Ahnell	Are <u>nell</u>	Daro's foster brother
Adruna	A <u>droon</u> a	Sorceress Elect (Amethyst)
Anempor	Ann em <u>paw</u>	Capital of the Azure Sands
Arriera	Arry erra	Daro's birth mother
Ashgenar	<u>Ash</u> **g**enn are	Wilderness
Beneva	<u>Ben</u> evver	Guardian of Knowledge
Buerchan	<u>Booer</u> Chann	Capital of the Amethyst Sands
Caranchar	<u>Caran</u> Char	The Town above the Low Pass
Carolus	<u>Carol</u> us	A wandering Apothecary
Czerezin	<u>Cherra</u> Zin	Clan of the Cynabarr Sands
Colonth	Cuh <u>Lonth</u>	Large town
Cynabarr	Sinna Barr	4th Sand of Pelshar
Dinajh	Dinnar(g)e	Invisible water tracts in the Sands
Diras	<u>Deera</u>ss	Daro's bodyguard
Djellim	Jellim	Library established in Selesh
Errish	Ehrrish	The Master Builder of Selesh
Gresshe	Gresh	Clan of the Malachite Sands
Greeeyn	Gree <u>yain</u>	Academic caste, city dwellers
Guaradeign	**G**arra<u>dane</u>	Governor
Hukvah	Huckva	Head dress similar to traditional Arab keffiya
Ikella	<u>Eye</u> kella	Sorceress Ruler of the Opal Sands
Inahana	inner harna	Member of the Council of Nine
Inesh	In <u>Nesh</u>	Second Clan of the Opal Sands
Irix	<u>Eye</u> rix	Antelope like creature
Ivinish	<u>Eye</u> vinnish	Beast Master
Jhirrelle	<u>Jirrelle</u>	Clan of the Amber Sands
Kora-Mai	Corra My	Clan of the Onyx Sands

Malos	Mal oze	Capital of the Malachite Sands
Maraken	Marra ken	Trail stop where the story starts
Mihort	My Hort	Bear-like creature addicted to berries
Miokinish	My ock innish	Boy killed at Tearchan
Myst Cat	Mist Cat	Puma-sized feline which can disappear
Nahamida	Nuh Hamm idda	Sorceress of the Onyx Sands
Nishanawa	nih SHANN awa	Mysterious sect of the Ashgenar
Nishan	Nishun	Dedicated to the Guardians as warriors
Opalwear	Opal wear	Specially woven clothes worn only by the Shalhanhi
Othervoice	Other voice	Magically empowered voice
Patris	Pattriss	Felmin Wagon Master
Sandsinger	Sand Singer	Extinct class of mage
Seobra	See o brah	Wolverine native to the Opal Sands
Skythe	Skyth	Flowering herb which promotes fertility
Shadushantesh	Shaddu Shanntesh	Ritual mask of a Sorceress
Shalhanhi	Shallarni	Ruling clan of the Opal Sands
Shenamai	Shenna my	Caverns with strange crystal roof
Shiarjha	She ara	Sorceress Elect of the Opal Sands
Soiveign	Soy vain	Placed under martial law
Sybillsce	Sibillsh	Clan of the Amethyst Sands
Tearchan	Tier shann	Hospice at the crossing below Maraken.
Tirjhinar	Tier rinn are	Fabled lost city of the Sandsingers
Tuennis	Tue enniss	Inesh woman Guaradeign of Caranchar
Vitali	Vitt arly	Trifoliate plant with magical properties
Zeglurs	Zegglures	Donkeylike Pack animal
Zephryn	Zefrin	Legendary single horned storm horses
Zurias	Zurry ass	Clan of the Azure Sands

Terms of Reference	Definition

Planetary System

Seleus	Solar Body
Pelshar	The world of this series
Jenta	Primary moon
Gatta	Secondary Moon

Special Characteristics of Pelshar

The Source	A universal field of energy which empowers magic users.

Sands (In order of precedence)

Opal	Predominately white, iridescent
Azure	Grey blue, shade ranges pale to very dark.
Malachite	Deep green with seams of silver
Cynabarr	Luminescent burnt orange to yellow
Onyx	Dark grey to black
Carnelian	Vibrant red
Tourmaline	Pale translucent green
Amethyst	Translucent shades pale to dark purple

Named Wilderness

The Ashgenar	Rough scrub, mineral deposits & mining spoil

Castes

Greeeyn	City dwelling technologists & artisans
Felmin	Traders, farmers, landsmen
Clansmen	Sand Dwellers, (also known (inaccurately) as Sandsworn)

Time

Sector of the Sand-Glass	15 minutes earth time
Turn of the Sand Glass	Hour
Day	Day
Dawn	Dawn or Breakday
Height of Sun	Noon
Evening	Sunfall
Night	Night
Week	Ninenight (referring to the number of nights)
Journight	Two ninenights
Journey of Jenta	Lunar Month
Rotation	Year

Clans (in order of precedence)   Location

Shalhanhi	Opal Sands
Zuraias	Azure Sands
Greshe	Malachite Sands
Czerezin	Cynabarr Sands
Kora-Mai	Onyx Sands
Jedrun	Carnelian
Quexoni	Tourmaline
Sybillsce	Amethyst

Minor Clans or Sub Sets

Inesh	Opal Sands
Nishanawa	The Ashgenar

Centre of High Magic	Location
Sanctuary	The Heights of Surrandel
Selesh	Mount Torrenesh, Opal Sands

Legendary Locations   *Whereabouts Unknown*

Tirjhinar	City of the Sandsingers

Animals

	(Nearest Earth Comparison)
Irix	Antelope
Coatan	Goat
Dolcan	Spider Monkey
Zeglur	Donkey
Mihort	Black Bear
Biron	Bison
Sandrigal	Snake
Cuirax	Giant Snow Raven
Dorrowen	Cattle
Mystcat	Puma

Mythical Beasts

	Depicted in ancient artwork
Drecon	Dragon
Zephryn	Single horned Storm horse

Classes of Character

Guardians	Tutors of all things Historic, Magical or Mysterious.
Sorceress	Magically empowered Rulers of the Nine Sands
Healers	Women who can use the Source to heal
Apothecary	Pharmacist, herbalist. Practitioner of practical medicine.
Guaradeign	Town or regional Governor
Servitors	Domestic Servants
Drudges	Menials

PART ONE - DARKNESS DESCENDS

Prologue

"From the Chronicles of Carolus"

It is the wish of my Master that this record of his travels be kept in secrecy. Therefore I, Brannith, in the hope that these writings might enlighten those who guide our society, write his words in an ancient script understood by few others, using a dye of his own making, which neither fades in light, nor in the passage of time.

I am a traveller. During my travels, I have come to believe that some catastrophe once befell our people (forever altering the nature of our relationship with our world and each other). Though it has taken a lifetime to collate the evidence, I may not have many Rotations left in which to pass on my knowledge. Yet to whom can I entrust such information?

Even as I ponder this problem, I still journey, for the nature of my work takes me far afield, gathering herbs, spices, medications and information, much of which fuels the purpose for my next journey. In this way, I store up bright fragments of interest which I can examine later, but this habit marks me as different from my fellow man as a Myst cat is to a mule!

I have spent my life questioning everything - actions, customs, too many objects - till my Clan (being fearful of things they did not understand) shunned me, saying that I should learn acceptance, that to question was to step aside from the Way and the worship of the One. I, therefore, departed my Hall and Clan and keeping my own counsel, continued in the worship of the One, with both eyes and mind open.

But, enough of me! At the heart of this story lies a world so different from the Pelshar we know, that only a heretic or a fool (like I) could believe them to be the same place.

This "other Pelshar", was a world worthy of its name (which means Beloved). There, the sun shone on fertile lands. Wide plains of grassland alive with creatures shared its promise with men, who spread throughout its varied territories. Great expanses of water once flooded the surface. I have read of journeys across these 'seas" written by men who knew a very different world to the arid wilderness that we have inherited. It is difficult to read of things which no man in living memory has seen. Yet I believe, for I have seen both representations of such things, painted on the walls of a ruined city half the world away, as well as the evidence in the land which bears testament to events which I still struggle to interpret.

I have come to believe that long ago all the peoples of Pelshar lived in harmony. Men toiled to support their families and to better their own societies. Women raised children to follow in their footsteps or to apprentice within the Craft Guilds. These Guilds taught the many Ways of Pelshar and recorded these teachings for others to follow. I, over many Rotations of our world, have travelled in places that others no longer venture and can bear witness to feats of ingenuity far beyond anything that men can achieve today. I have seen with my own eyes the abandoned cities of the Broken Land and followed roads that disappear under mountainous rock falls, scorched by some firestorm of a magnitude beyond my experience. Nothing living remains, though the deserted streets echo strangely around highly polished walls of stone, which bear the brand of dancing shadows as though they had absorbed those they were built to shelter. Where once was a living city now, in absolute solitude, great pylons support broken towers and bridges so high as to defy description, all leading nowhere on a plateau of frozen pitch.

In such a place, I have found a Library full of records which now form the core of my belief, for they tell the story of a time long past in a multitude of scripts, many of which I have yet to decipher.

Just as the scars of physical catastrophe mar the natural beauty of our world, so do the divisions amongst our people. The teachers, technologists, astronomers and engineers of the past have withdrawn to the Highlands, below the Broken Land. Here they have bound themselves together as if from one Clan and hold fast to great walled cities. They neither consult with others, nor invite them in, earning for themselves a new name, that of Greeeyn, which means "the Apart" Whether any of them has more understanding of ancient records I do not know, for they exhibit such fear and antipathy towards outsiders that any such enquiry has not been possible.

Below these Highlands are the plains and low foothills of the Fringes. Some of these areas are still quite fertile, which is as well, for here the Felmin (farmers, miners, weavers) have their place. Where possible, small groups have gathered together to form villages, often committed to one endeavour. It is here that some forms of organised transport are to be found, which permits the landsmen to take their produce to market at the outer gates of the walled cities in trek carts capable of carrying either goods or travellers. Traders occasionally even venture into the settlements of the Sands, travelling with pack animals laden with the fruits of their labour. It is in these market places that I have come to trade my skills for valuable information (for my position of trust enables me to gain insight into my fellow man in a way that often points me to another nugget of knowledge). Being able, in the exchange of remedies and cures, to gain insight into the lives of my patients has given me a peculiar advantage, for they and their families gossip openly in front of me while I work. I hear about illnesses that others might not recognise because they are indigenous to a location, which allows me to map very clearly sickness that is rooted in the deficiency of diet (even to view with suspicion some over-abundance of minerals as being contributory to the nature of death and disease). It is a constant wonder to me that I am able to wander amongst the Greeeyn and the Felmin with my cures so easily - but then perhaps I am so old, so used to living alone, that they do not see me for what I am - for if they did the door of the cities would not be open to me, nor would the villages host me so easily for I am of the third caste of our world - the Sandsworn.

Our Sands are the most beautiful of all places. Some call them wild, others desolate, yet they are full of life and living things. Plants high in medicinal properties grow in many of them, thrusting short flowering shoots through the vividly-hued Sands before the dawn to reach as far as the eye can see in all directions. Each Sand has its own Clan and here again I see echoes of the past, for there is union between the Sands. All Clansmen live in harmony, guided and ruled by the last remnants of true power, the Sisters of Sorcery, who can wield the magical powers of their kind by harnessing the natural energy of our world known as the Source. Lately, I have come upon personal records that trouble me greatly, for if I listen closely to the past it contains prophecies that have already been fulfilled. The records tell of the open water disappearing, of violent changes of weather, even hinting that in some way the natural energy of our world may change. Perhaps it is already damaged, or somehow muted? Nevertheless, although in our time it is channelled by only a Talented few women, I have also found proof that once, ordinary men and women could also tap into this power. Now only the Sandsworn can use the Source: the Sisters of Sorcery and the Guild of Healers are its sole inheritors. For this mercy, I am devoutly grateful. At least these will share their gifts with others not of their caste. One thing has emerged from exploring these records, which I must keep to myself for fear of setting our peoples even further apart. This touches on the Sands again for it seems that once our world, Greeeyn, Felmin and Sandsworn alike looked to the Sands for leadership. In those far off times, we were ruled by the Sandsingers who could use the Source in a very different manner. Of these Mages no record remains! Even the title Sandsinger has gone from popular memory, although long ago I heard a mother chastise her children with the promise that she would send for a Sandsinger if they did not moderate their behaviour! I have diligently followed every trail and have only one record of these magic users, so utterly have they been eradicated from our culture.

I refer to a small, thick, hide-bound record which came to my hand through an old friend, whom I only encounter on rare occasions. I have a presentiment that I shall never see her again and so I have treasured it to me, reading late into the night, my eyes glued to the breathtaking facts revealed within. They are written in the same script in which my good Brannith now writes my thoughts for me! The pages of this ancient thing are cramped, the writing fine and neat with the occasional embellishment of tiny sketches, but its contents are truly terrifying! Here I will read directly from the notes I now hold, for these words are more significant than any I could utter.

> *'Presently we received word of a new phenomenon*
> *in the night sky, many of my fellow astronomers and I*
> *departed to the far snows and clear air of the Frozen*
> *North to study this. We knew this aberration had*
> *been observed by others for we met a company of*
> *Sandsingers on their way to hold Conclave in their*
> *fastness at Sanctuary. Much speculation arose amongst*

us, fuelling our conversation on the way to the remote star watching platform at Istakan, where we were to examine a strange shadow that had appeared on Jenta our moon.

"However, when we bent over the cunning viewer that had been made in the Opal Desert, its lens angled and polished by none other than Darius, Sandsinger of those Sands (whose interest in star-gazing was well known), all conversation came to a sudden halt, for clearly visible was the ominous outline of another moon. Larger and darker than our own bright Jenta, it hung, dominating the lens, to our startled disbelief. Obviously, we gathered ourselves together, uneasily exchanging observations of the phenomena, when a powerful yet melodic voice said slowly,

'Remarkable is it not, my friends?'

"Well, there he was. A tall, hawk-eyed man, bronzed and smiling had somehow materialised in our midst. He was in no way dressed for these northern climes either! He just stood peering over our shoulders. You can imagine the astonished babble of confusion. From where had he come, the others demanded? By what right was he there?" (Here the writing quivers as though the author was chuckling as he wrote.).

"He raised a hand for silence against the protests, till we saw the glitter in the atmosphere around him and fell silent in the presence of the Opal Sandsinger himself.

"His mood seemed sombre. His words did little to reassure us, as he remarked,

'My brother of the Amethyst has already dedicated to this monstrosity, the name Gatta, (The Arrival.)'

"He scowled as he told us,

'His wish is to accord to this dark moon a mystical interpretation, which has aroused dissent amongst my brothers and sisters in magic.'

"He almost whispered,

'That need go no further than this room!'

"A frisson of fear touched us all, for we knew his power was absolute. Any word of this meeting escaping would be borne on the wind back to his ear and, while we knew Darius First among Sandsingers to be gentle and forgiving, there was a compulsion in his manner that promised death for disobedience.

17

"He raised his finger admonishingly, but we were all aware that we were signally honoured by his confidence. There was something in his voice - command, persuasion or magic? I shall never know I suppose!

"Darius told us that he needed us to mount a continuous watch, listing the behaviours of animals, birds and the moods of men as being of interest to him, as well as the usual astronomical observations of our new moon. Relays of messengers were established between us, for we knew that in our actions could lie whatever chance our world had of survival.

"I remember the Sandsingers last words to us clearly as I watch flaming rocks fall from the sky over Istakan and wondered at his composure as he said,

'It is my conjecture that if this Arrival does not achieve synchronous orbit with Jenta, then we bear the knowledge that our world is doomed. Not even I know how we could survive should Gatta continue its journey!'

It was thus that the last months of what I call the First Age of Mystery were recorded. I still have to read many more pages of this diary and my progress is slow, for they are not all in the same hand or script. However, I persevere, for recently I am beset with the idea that some change is upon us again. I believe that the Sandsingers and the scholars were of another thread in the weave of time, all of which passed away with some great Cataclysm which left no-one who could tell us what happened, or why.

I only know that old scrolls occasionally emerge from the ancient places of our world, but man has lost the knowledge, not only of their languages, but of their time and way of life. Now, life is dictated by the ruthless observance of the Way! The nomadic People of the Sands and the landsmen still follow the One, but the city dwellers do not. Each of our tribal communities has withdrawn from the other, no longer do we share each other's company, no longer do we share each others trust or knowledge. The Way is to follow their fathers' footsteps, within their Clans, keeping the Faith. The past lies in the past and the Ways lead us ever onward - and only a heretic would say what was may be again. Only a fool would wish that they understood the scrolls, yet Gatta rises high again and hangs above our shattered world. Some wish they knew what became of the Sandsingers or what the scrolls they find say. Others will again try to record the story of Pelshar and pray to survive the telling!

Chapter 1 - Prophecy.

The wind settled into an uneasy quavering drone as evening fell. Far below the observer a line of moving figures, long dancing shadows streaming behind them, took on a sinister aspect as they crossed the horizon. Clad in the iridescent Colours of their Clan, linked together like a strand of pearls, they pressed onward despite the rising sand which, obscuring them from the waist down, added to the illusion that they were simply melting into the Opal Desert. Here, the sands being neither white, nor silver, nor blue, nor lavender, somehow managed to combine the ingredients of all colours, including a wondrous golden rose which in the morning light of a fair day would suffuse both desert floor and wakening sky. Each of the nine great deserts of Pelshar were dominated by the vivid colouring of their own Sands for which it was rumoured that the Deserts themselves had been named. The Clan Weavers contrived to produce the traditional robes of their own Clans to match the places of their wanderings. The people of the Opal sands wore a wondrous weave that glowed with all the shades of the ground beneath their feet and when the sands were stirred by the evening winds their Colours appeared to become one with the desert. This caused such confusion in the eye of the beholder that sane, sober men swore on oath that the desert dwellers could disappear from view within a hands breadth of the observer and of course the secretive nomads did little to explain the cause of this illusion. Those who walked below were Shalhanhi and indigenous to these sands. The women, tall, slender and tawny skinned, glowed warmly against the paler light of their surroundings. Their easy tempered men, reputed to have an infectious smile to brighten the day, gleamed with well-toned muscle and lustrous hair. They walked this barren landscape impervious to the lack of trails, reading in the small clues from the sand beneath their feet where they could obtain water and from the rocks rising to tower above the deserts, they could determine where they were, but these were also a proud and mysterious clan with many secrets, for deep within their lands were the most holy places of Pelshar.

From this place, long ago it was said, came the power of healing and even now and not so far from here, all the healers of Pelshar trained in the sacred underground complex of Selesh. Little was known about the healers except that their rituals were ancient and arcane, that their power left them greatly long lived and that not all who aspired to learn the skill and the mystery of it succeeded. For those that failed there was but one answer and that was the Sealing, a ritual which denied them access to their former powers and removed the gift, the othervoice, forever. Many of these Sealed women became guides for the trek trains that crossed the sands on their journeys between the high cliffs of the Broken Land and the remote cities of the Greeyeyn. It was also true that few of them could bring themselves to use even their ordinary voices again and chose to remain mute. The most recognisable of the Sealed, these Sergas or Silent

Ones, took to wearing their skin record on their faces in direct disobedience of the Rule, but although they earned their Clan's disapproval, no action was ever taken against them for their suffering was great, their exclusion already total. Rumour had it that others had secretly retained some fragment of their power and, forced to live apart from ordinary folk, they appeared at many of the desert trail stops, using their augmented skills as jongleurs and entertainers to earn a pitiful living. These Wanderers were feared in the Fringes, bands of them roamed at night when no same man or women travelled and it was said that they predated at the edges of the trader settlements stealing food, tools and some said unattended children! Such exaggerated rumours had yet to be proved, for many secretly sympathised with them and looked the other way. With trade settlements scattered across wide, largely uninhabited spaces, the Felmin (landsmen who farmed what vegetation could be persuaded to grow in these increasingly arid times) also provided transport and the markets for all produce. Gaily decorated trek carts carried all the peoples of Pelshar, from the supercilious Greeyeyn city dwellers to the Felmin traders themselves. On rare occasions even the desert dwellers took a seat on the great trek carts and made the long overland journey to townships and cities beyond the Desert Fringe, this being the only safe way to travel, in company and sheltered against the weather which of late had been very changeable.

On this particular day, the lowering sky scowled blackly over the Marison Pass above the Opal Desert. The wind had been rising since the Height of Sun. Along the edge of the desert the sands were constantly shifting, the land seemed troubled and the sky was uneasy. Lightening storms were frequent and even in the Fringe in comparative safety the ferocity of these dry storms was unbelievable, great licks of light flaring from the sky, sometimes accompanied by thunder but, more frighteningly, often not. It was common knowledge that the one subject that dominated all trader talk was the weather, which of the last ten Rotations had been getting worse. This night however, looked like being exceptional. Half way down the great escarpment from the high plateau above, several of the great trek trains were waiting impatiently for guides to take them across a part of the desert below, that reached like a finger between Omnel to the South and Quinnox in the North. Here, the trade stop of Maraken had grown, huddling against the great cliff, in the shadow of the natural caverns that many settlers favoured as storage barns. Built in a semi circle at the base of the Upper Cliff the small stone and wooden houses made a natural corral in which traders ascending and descending from the Opal desert below, could draw up. Above, the natural fortress of the Upper cliff soared, with its wide and carefully maintained track ascending in several shallow sweeps to the Highlands above. Wreathed in dust, there was seldom a chance to see the desert floor clearly from the heights of the Upper Cliff, but from the trade stop, perched halfway between the desert and the Highlands, the view was of a wild and savage untamed place, unique and stunning. From the great pillars of natural rock Opal jutting upward like savage, bronzed teeth from the desert floor, an aching sweep of glittering opal sand curling into the distance between the darkling Lower Cliffs and rolling hills of the Marison Pass, was a strange combination of angles and colours dizzying to the eye, dazzling to the brain, once seen never forgotten. At the heart of it all stood Maraken, bustling quietly about its business supporting the travellers of this region. Of those there were many for, apart from one short crossing, here there was little to slow the progress of the traders who could travel the entire return trip in a week, permitting the rare luxury of settled homes and families and many of the Wagoneers had established these along the Fringe and plied this route in exception of all others. Amongst them a wagon train from Dirjiven, far to the south in the lush hills bordering the Amber desert, had arrived. Even now, its master stood poised at the rails of one of the many beast corrals lining the small centre street of the village overlooking the desert, trying in vain to pick out the sight of his appointed guides from the whirls of billowing sand below. He was not alone in his frustration, for along the villages strung out at the base of the High Pass several wagon trains waited in vain. The great trade beasts shuffled and moaned, impatient to be on the trek and rid of their burdens, the wagon masters fretted and roared at the men who tended the animals and a few travellers stamped about impatient to be off. It was an hour past the Height of Sun and with the wind already starting to lick steadily across the dimly visible desert floor, the wagon master stood stony-faced his heart sinking as he finally accepted that there would be no travel that day. Patris was a powerful looking man in his prime: he stood head and shoulders above many of his crew, a useful factor out on the trail and one that made him distinctive at trail stops where people often needed to pick him out quickly. He had corralled the wagon train and paused to wait for the guides, anxiously eyeing a sky that was sullen, roiling with energy. Surely not a lightening storm, he prayed, but the guides did not arrive and the wind was now too high to risk leaving a safe haven in the hope of meeting them on the trail.

Sighing with frustration he called out, dismissing the group of men that hired out for crossings, telling them to return for the following day and soon travellers were being advised to seek shelter in their wagons or in local inns and the Wagoneers began to unload their beasts and store their goods once more in the huge caverns of the undercliff, when, into the middle of the confusion, the one passenger that Patris had taken to on sight appeared. The woman had joined the trek train two villages back. Wrapped in a blue travelling cloak, with the hood up against the occasional flurry of sand, she had ventured below Patris'' own wagon. He was busy and deliberately held himself aloof from most passengers, but she had stood quietly studying him, which is what had drawn his attention. He had glanced down at her a little impatiently and she let her hood fall back, revealing the most flawless of golden skin and dark gold hair, cut short and curling on to her neck like some summer-bronzed urchin. Despite her tiny frame, her first movement revealed she was no child, for she was heavily pregnant, hardly the right point in time for a woman to be travelling alone.

Patris had taken pity on her and where the other passengers from that stop had pushed past her to bargain for seats on the transports, he had lighted easily from the lead wagon and had swept her an elaborate bow, which had startled a giggle from her worried-looking face.

"Can I offer you a seat aboard my wagon mistress?" he had enquired, putting a hand out for the pathetically small bundle that she was treasuring to her. Taking it gently, he handed it up to Somner his driver, enquiring lightly, "Will your house Staff be bringing the rest of your effects when they join you my lady?"

He carefully held out a hand to assist her, leading her to the stepping block and chaffing her gently, treating her as a lady of high fashion with lands and a household and she, wearing as she was the Colours of the Amber Sands beneath her worn travelling cloak knew it, but readily joined in his humour, responding in kind, "Oh, I imagine that I shall simply refurbish my needs in the next town Harmeister." She gave him his proper and full title to his utter amazement, speaking in fluent Darvish, the language of the far south, making Patris for a moment unbearably homesick for a land he had left years before. He shook his head, wondering how she had unerringly chosen to speak to him in a patois that came from a tiny province a hundred seilengs away from this place. She had stepped up on to the runner board, but had needed more assistance to gain a seat on the swaying wagon, so far gone was she and for a moment her golden skin had paled and her mouth looked tense.

She recovered her poise slowly as they drew out of the stop and across the plain above Maraken and Patris observed her sympathetically as she shifted trying to find a comfortable position. She made no fuss, though he could tell that her time was near from the sudden stilling of her features and the worried pinched look that told of the early pains. However, she was quiet and dignified, giving him a grateful smile as he tucked a soft fleece pillow behind her, saying only, "My name is Arriera. Thank you for carrying me, good master." and then the beasts were being shouted into their lumbering gait and the noise of the creaking wagon and the rattling of the stones against the wheels drowned all thought of conversation and when next he glanced at his nomad passenger she was leaning against a package of bedding rolls and was drifting into sleep. For a little while she had rested, but her anxiety to get to Quinnox was obvious and she had confided that she was due in the next ninenight and had made arrangements to be confined at her sister's home in the town. Patris had said nothing, but his experienced eyes had noted her restlessness and he thought privately that she would be lucky to reach the town in time. Yet he knew his duty, the Way dictated that the Peoples of the Sands asked help of no man unless they really needed that help and that to transport her in his own wagon was his own business, though he had noted the disparaging looks of some of the other passengers as he had assisted Arriera into his wagon. Now, with the weather closing in and no sight of their guides she was almost frantic, and Patris sighed as he turned to face her.

"It is surely no good for her to be so agitated at this stage!" he thought.

However, there was little he could he do.

"Harmeister, see!"

The girl pointed dramatically and Patris turned to see a group of local Clanswomen sweeping into the village towards him. Immediately realising that these were not his guides, Patris narrowed his eyes and shielded them against the prevailing wind with his hand, for never had he seen another group like this. They processed rather than walked, chanting happily, a liquid fluting sound which seemed to ripple right through their gathering which he noted included men and children. Patris gazed in amazement as they came towards him for they sparkled, every Sand represented in the myriad Colours of each Kind. This must indeed be a group of some importance he decided, noting the respectful bobs and smiling nods from the beast-handlers in the corrals who despite their own hurried preparations against the weather caught the joyous mood of the Sandsworn who, followed by running children, proceeded along the very track he was standing beside.

It must be some ritual of theirs, Patris decided, noticing that two of the women wore garlands of feathers and herbs. Like their leader, they too wore shimmering Opalwear cloaks and their Colours hurt his eyes as glimmering through the lowering light they made their way towards him.

The leader of the group paused and her glance flickered over him, carried on to see the men unloading the beasts and then slid back to meet his eyes. She was a tall, slim, almost stately woman, late in life with her white hair covered with a great cowl that shadowed and made mysterious her face and deep-set eyes. Patris found himself lowering his glance before her, and then she moved and her Staff became visible. Made of precious Hoja wood, black as the night and nearly three spans in length, it swept in a convoluted curve to a silver mount, which held at eye level an enormous stone that glowed in a strange lilac colour. As she paused before him, she locked eyes with him and spoke.

"You should not travel this day." It was not really a statement or command but the advice of an immeasurably wise woman. "You have guides?" She questioned gently.

"Yes, thank you." He spoke awkwardly, unsure if there was a formal title that he should use in speaking with this lady, who was clearly a person of high rank.

"They did not arrive!" Her statement was light, matter of fact but an unusual certainty settled over him, he should remain here till the weather changed. He wondered vaguely if this great lady had some influence over him but decided it was the changing light, or the odd cadences of the singing voices, something in the radiance of the great Opal perhaps?

"No, they did not arrive, " he answered dryly. "But..."

She broke in on him.

"...That is as well, for if you travel now, there will be no arriving."

Her face was serene, her voice distant, trancelike. Patris shuddered, suddenly cold, as she turned away to lead her group down the path to the desert floor. She paused again to remark, "You should not travel for five days and nights.

Remember this if you want to live."

The wind snatched her words away, the sky darkened dramatically and the Shalhanhi were melting away before his eyes as a whispering voice came back to him from the desert below.

"Remember, five days if you want to live."

That was his last sight of them, flickering shadows crossing the horizon, as they disappeared into the keening sands below.

Chapter 2 - Entombed

The storm continued to build. Centred on the desert below, it swept up to the village crouched on the trail, onto the High Plateau and into the cities of the Greeyeyn. Swirling maelstroms struck at every inhabited place. The demented howling force whirled skyward, sweeping inexorably from street to street. Crushing walls, roofs, houses, barns, destroying what stood in its path, building, by building, until nothing but the debris and the bodies remained to tell their story.

In the trail stops, herd beasts and trek beasts died where they stood, caught in the grip of the breath sucking winds or smothered in the choking dust and sand. There was no water other than that drawn or bottled against emergency. In the Sands below, no mortal could survive without deep shelter. On the narrow trails, there was no way of getting to safety so, with main routes impassable, the Fringe towns along with desert settlements were cut off. In Maraken, the Wagoneers, passengers and villagers cowered where they could. Herdsmen and trek crews huddled in store caverns. Any cellar became a refuge until, on the fifth day, the winds fell. Patris and his crew, emerging cautiously, found that their world had been altered beyond recognition. Half of the buildings had been razed to the ground. The immense cavern entrances (from which they had dug themselves) were almost completely buried beneath fallen rocks and sand. Beyond that, only the brutal truth greeted them. Though the wagons were safe, the trek beasts were dead, felled where they had been turned out to graze. They stood wearily looking around at the devastation, numbly, noting that homes stood only where there had been shelter from the surrounding cliffs, elsewhere they were collapsed or buried and their people along with them. Opal sand drifts concealed the precipitous route to the Sands below. The upper cliff route was covered by landslips of a magnitude that caught the breath in the throat of Patris and his workers, as they realised that Maraken was marooned.

The very air was thick with dust. It clung to the throat, to the nostrils, filling their vision with a swirling mist. As one, trained to sand storms, they adjusted their traditional hukvahs (the loose flowing headdress of the desert). Drawing the upper hem down to shield their eyes, instinctively they raised loose scarves to cover nose and mouths against the penetrating flurries of sand and the stench of putrefaction, as they stumbled out into what had been a bustling community. Grimly they rolled back sleeves, tucked tunics into pants and adjusted heavy work belts, casting about for more survivors.

After the tumult of the storm, the silence in the trail stop was oppressive. Only the soft serration as sand slid off a damaged roof could be heard. There was no more shouting of running children, no bellowing of affronted herd beasts, no parting calls of passengers departing. The silence was ominous and Patris sighed heavily as they approached the place where he estimated the village inn once stood.

Sombrely they stared at the devastation, their sight limited in the milky, lilac-tinged light that swirled uneasily like mist between the shadows of the shattered village. In the silent corrals, great sand drifts showed where their beasts had perished. Patris stared bleakly at the wreckage of his life. His throat ached and his eyes blurred as he thought of Karmeck, his lead beast. He had assisted at Karmeck's birth, as was custom amongst traders and he remembered his overwhelming joy when the newborn had been gifted to him to train for his own. He had lost beast's before this, for the life of a trek beast was hard and there were many dangers on the trail, but "Karmeck, Karmeck!" He thought that the grief would unman him till he caught sight of Ivinish, his beast handler, face impassive below tormented eyes, and knew that he was not alone in his suffering.

He thrust the thought from his mind. He knew that without water, shelter and food, any survivors could not last long and set about deploying his men. Ivinish was soon pulling at a door sunken in the sand below him, resisting all efforts to open it as Patris and the others hastened to help. They worked furiously, scooping broken slates and wooden struts away, from under what seemed like half the contents of the Opal Sands! Wordlessly watching as the glittering grains slid back into their excavation, they worked on, piling it away from what appeared to be a doorway to the local inn. Now, it lay far below ground level, the entire building had been enveloped by sand, stone and other debris to a depth beyond normal experience. They were conscious of thin, hopeless cries below them. Soon, Somner reported that he could see men, women and children huddled together. As they finally persuaded the door to open, the faces of their passengers, together with some of the local people, came blinking into view. Amidst the babble of bewilderment and relief, Patris found himself searching for Arriera and was startled when there was no sign of her. He worried about it even as he assisted Rowbet to clear a window so that what light there was could penetrate into the large stone-built tavern. He helped those within to emerge into the strange, twilight atmosphere above. He continued his enquiry, asking several local women if they knew where she had gone. Although none had not seen Arriera, they nevertheless made helpful suggestions, before busying themselves clearing away the sand at their neighbours' doors.

Patris and Rowbet searched with them, Somner and Ivinish took on the sad duties of laying out the dead as they were discovered, but many of the local men stayed huddled, some of them looking decidedly unwell and most of them blinking blearily, helplessly rubbing at their eyes. Patris thought despairingly that if only some of those trapped were sand-blind the community would be helpless, but as more of them emerged from what must have been a crowded sanctuary, it became obvious that a good percentage were in extreme difficulty. Strangely, there had been very little sand penetration here, no-one had been exposed to the main causes of sand-blindness and even more oddly only the local men were affected. He sighed heavily, thinking, "Perhaps their Sands have turned against them?"

He struggled not to let superstition envelop him, but there was still no sign of the girl and his level of apprehension rose as he considered the likelihood of finding her. Hope dwindled when they found Maraken's Healer buried in the wreckage of her home, along with her knowledge and her herbal medications. Dibinish the Headman, his wife and three children, lay along with others awaiting burial. There were still upward of fifteen men missing, and as some of them had been out on the trail and others minding herd beasts, not a lot of hope was held out for their safe return. However, thankfully none of his passengers or crew had perished, only Arriera was still nowhere to be found.

As the dark, dust-choked day wound its way to an exhausted evening. Patris found himself supervising the entire rescue operation. In the absence of the Headman and in the face of so many sand-blind men he had taken charge and found that as long as he continued organising the removal of the dead to the now empty winter food store and the apportioning of foodstuffs, glows and water to the survivors, he was able to carry on in the face of his own irreparable losses. Nevertheless, the missing girl bothered him and as night descended he repeated his enquiries amongst his other passengers, who all denied having seen her. Once the winds had risen they had cowered in the tavern with no thought for anyone but themselves. To his disgust, Patris found that the same attitude prevailed. None of them had stirred themselves to assist the rescue efforts of the day. They had suffered no injury (other than fright and inconvenience) while they had waited the storm out. None of them were affected by whatever had blinded the local men and without exception they wanted to leave, and now! They sat in comfortable chairs, glows burning in stone dishes on the tables around them, many of them with drinks in their hands, muttering discontentedly. He (Patris) had been paid to take them to Quinnox, or Omnel. Maraken was just a way point, why were they still here? This was followed by a chorus of disapproval. Why was he doing nothing to further that contract? What was one Sandsworn girl to them?

Patris found himself defending her.

'Should her origin have anything to do with her survival?" he questioned hotly and the Greeyeyn making all the fuss said shortly, "These landless people should not weigh so heavily with you Master. They are of little consequence in the greater Way. If she chooses to go with her own kind, why should you be put to the worry of finding her?"

Patris drew breath.

"I have no way of knowing where she went majheer, " he said scornfully, according the narrow-faced man the lowest possible rank used amongst the Greeyeyn, in retaliation to the plain accolade of Master, a rank far below that which Patris held. He heard the hiss as his insult struck home, but continued smoothly, 'she could be in need of a woman's help. She said she was on her way to Quinnox to stay at her sister's home for her confinement, due in the next ninenight."

The Greeyeyn's lip curled derisively as he responded, 'Say you so Master? Then she is not only landless, but a liar, for we would never allow her kind to pollute our cities. We do not permit these Sandsworn into our communities. Not by day, never by night, in fair weather or foul!"

He turned to the other city dwellers at his table who, bolstered with the bravado of survival, nodded muttering agreement under their breath as their spokesman continued stridently.

"They would be expelled by the City Watch if ever they entered our gates. I tell you, no man, or woman living could change that! I fully expect even this storm will have left no mark on our cities, for we know how to build! Our houses don't fall down when a few winds blow!"

He threw the Wagon Master a supercilious glance, saying firmly, "This landless one, she should have done as she was told and gone to the caves to shelter!"

Patris, thunderstruck, stared at them speechlessly. He had told Arriera to go to this inn. He knew they had rooms. Had these arrogant people turned her away?

Sickened and ashamed by their ignorance, he wearily withdrew from their querulous company to continue the search on his own. In his mind's eye he remembered her, standing at the edge of the track leading to the Sands below, one hand clasping her cloak over the swell of her belly, the other raised to her mouth in dismay. Below her, sweeping away down to the desert, he recalled the group of Shalhanhi Healers they had encountered. His brow furrowed as he tried to remember seeing her again before the storm struck, but he was left with a troubling image of her, poised at the very edge of the track, her small bundle at her feet and nothing else. He sighed deeply and Rowbet, coming level with him at that precise moment caught the drift of his mind clearly. The driver touched his hand to his head in a gesture of disgusted dismissal as the rising tide of dissent was heard from the group of rescued travellers and said quietly, "Harmeister, there is no shame in this, you did not have any way of knowing about a storm of this intensity. I must age you by ten Rotations and I have never seen the like of this, and nor had my father of respected memory, for he would have told me or my brother before ever he let us out on the trail. I know you fear for the girl. Ivinish and I will help you search, anything is better to occupy ourselves away from that lot." With a snort of disgust he stalked past Patris just as Somner came out of the room where the other passengers had gathered, with a scowl across his normally attractive features. He shut the door behind him vehemently, just as a voice was heard saying, "No beasts? What does he mean no beasts.? Oh I suppose they were so diseased that they could not stand a small sand-storm? Well he must get others, I have to be in Quinnox by the end of this ninenight and none shall stop me getting there, none I assure you. No so-called Master Waggoner, no diseased beast, and certainly no little sand-storm!"

The condemnatory words rang out into one of those inconvenient silences that stand witness to many a foul slander and, in the passageway beyond, Patris stood utterly still.

With a howl of fury he spun on his heels and hurled himself toward the parlour. How dare these indolent Greeyeyn impugn his character, doubt his honesty, doubt his intent, or doubt his beasts! All coherent thought fled as he thought of Karmeck lying out in the pasturage, great eyes dull in death, great heart stilled forever and all in the service of such an unworthy cause. Hot, angry tears that he had forbidden himself the luxury of all day spilled and his throat clenched on a sob of distress as he moved, but suddenly something, someone had got in his way as his men grabbed him, anxious to prevent him from injuring himself or another. He found himself being borne back against his will as Ivinish and Somner took him firmly by the arms and somehow bundled him back down the passageway to the door. His breath came shortly and his body trembled with the sudden rush of emotion. His nostrils flared in anger and the blood rushed and boiled in his ears till he could hardly hear, yet he knew Ivinish was saying something important, soothing his anger and he forced himself to stand still and listen.

"Harmeister, do not lower yourself to their standards, " he entreated, forcing Patris to lower a raised arm, encouraging him with a gentle paternal touch to draw breath and remain still.

"Do not abandon our Way, I beg of you. We must maintain the peace of our vannage, that much is our bounden duty. We have the right to dismiss them only if they do not pay, we may not use force unless they act against the safety of the trek. They will say that they did not know the losses we have sustained, for they have not stirred from this place, so used to their creature comforts are these Greeyeyn."

He almost spat the last word out and Patris looked at this normally taciturn man in astonishment, as Ivinish went on.

"They do not see beyond the size and the shape and the smell of animals to their strength, their nobility, their selflessness, their sacrifice. Pah! Somner, you had better take both of us away from that ignorant one before I forsake the Way and kill him myself!" Together Patris and Ivinish, followed by a bewildered Somner, forced their way out of the buried inn into the shattered village square, before making towards the cavern in which they had sheltered for the duration of the storm, leaving their passengers and the locals to settle down for the night while they continued their self-imposed search for Arriera in the caverns of the undercliff.

They found a spring in one of the caves, the water was good and plentiful but there was still no sign of the girl, and in the morning, which dawned if anything darker than before, Patris reluctantly faced the fact that she had disappeared into the storm, and must lie with her unborn babe somewhere in the choking death that they called the Opal Desert.

Chapter 3 - Storm Song

Below Maraken, in the bewildering spectrum of sand known as the Opal Desert, the group that had warned Patris to stay in shelter gathered together. Their children were moved gently but firmly into the centre of the group followed by the men. Theirs was a matriarchal society and, practised at looking after the young ones, the men were looking carefully into the faces of each child, checking to make sure that they had remembered to lower their rehenas, the strange clear inner eyelid of the Sand Sworn, which not unlike the nictating membrane of a cat protected the delicate structure of the eye from sand damage.

Ikella, their leader and Sorceress stood firm, her garments plastered against her gaunt frame by the screaming winds, her Staff firmly planted in the ground. She seemed anchored to the desert itself, braced as though deep rooted in the sands that threatened to sweep her off her feet. She paused, looking around the huddle and seeing that her fellow healers were ringing the group with hands firmly clasped to their immediate neighbours she raised her Staff a fraction and called on her powers.

"Anachthin moyen, anachthin ministrall, anachthin moyen!" She intoned the words of power, in a clear bell-like voice, that rang out piercing through the squall around them. As she struck her Staff's hilt to the sand once more, the huge Opal at its head blazed forth in a flare of colour, which seemed to reflect off a solid wall of opal. A glow permeated the air and around the small group sprang a shield, an iridescent aura, emanating from Ikella herself. The effect was instant. The winds roared futilely around them, even the buffeting Sands remained still within the encompassing glow, where the men were checking their packs for water and food. There was a gentle musical sound as the women continued to stabilise the magical weave by singing quietly, using the othervoice of the trained healer to augment the shield. In the midst of the sand squall they camped seemingly impervious to the chaos around them. Food was eaten, water shared, but this night was like no other and still the Storm raged. Ikella, having held the weave for several hours, was visibly tiring. One of the healers spoke against the rising scream of the winds.

"My Deshun." She addressed the Sorceress as the Head of the Guild of Healers. "We must leave here, before your strength and ours gives out! Perhaps we can find the Lower Cliff edge? We could shelter in the caves there. You plainly can't hold the weave longer, and the children need to sleep." The Sorceress considered her words, grimly noting the almost incandescent fury of the Sands, as they battered at her weakened defences. She nodded shortly, her mouth twisted bitterly as she decided, her exhaustion written clearly on her face. They gathered their goods, hefted packs, tied bands around the children's faces to protect their eyes, and encouraged them to hold their hoods across their mouths with one hand and grasp the sash of the adult in front of them with the other. Ikella and Mina inspected the preparations, Mina took up the rear position and Ikella resumed her place at the head of the group. As she raised her Staff the glow in the stone faded, and with the weave dissipating, they stumbled back along the trail. They could not have walked more than forty paces, when Ikella's Staff blazed into life without warning. She stopped still, gazing at the Opal mounted at its head, then she carefully probed the sand near her feet, as the group closed up on her. As one, without command, they joined the search until one of the men stood up. Ikella crouched, excavating the sand at his feet, uncovering cloth first, then a small, delicately boned hand came into view.

Immediately raising her Staff she called out, spell casting, even as the Storm screamed its defiance at her. Slowly, a whirling motion, echoing the movement of her free hand, deflected the battering winds, extracting the sand that had entombed this traveller long enough for the men to raise the body of a woman, shielding her from the children's view with their own cloaks

Soberly, the Healers clustered around the victim of the storm, talking animatedly amongst themselves. The men and children withdrew, standing near Ikella, who was still holding the storm at bay. Hanna, now serving her term as Infirmarian at Selesh, reported tersely.

'she is not Shalhanhi. By appearance she is from the Amber Sands, though what she does here, in her condition I cannot tell. She is heavily pregnant, ready to deliver, but no babe could survive in this! We need to find shelter or we will all be lost to the Sands!"

Ikella, barely acknowledging their plight, turned as her Senior Healer called out. "Deshun! I can see a track, though it seems old. Do you think it safe? Should we follow it?" Easing herself to her feet, the Sorceress joined Mina, observing through the bitter swirls of biting wind what her companion had noted with interest. A path, devoid of any recent marks, was dimly visible, glittering against the darkening desert floor. It twisted and turned ahead of them, obscured now and again by the encroaching sand drifts. In these conditions it might not remain visible for long, she must make a decision before their only chance faded from view. Her mouth thinned, hooded eyes glinting suspiciously. It was not a path she knew. It was ancient, unused and it ran too close to the Silent Sands, an area forbidden to all during her lifetime. She considered the options grimly. Stay here and hope her powers could sustain them? Move on and hope to find shelter? She swept a glance round the group, and found her eyes drawn to the cocoon of cloaks that sheltered the unknown woman, and knew that she had no choice. They must seek shelter. She glowered irritably at the trail ahead, realising that in this, no woman, man, or Sorceress could survive long.

Mina supervised as they slung the girl between the two strongest men. Rianic and Beven, both recently widowed, had undertaken this Walk in memory of their late wives, who had been Healers. Thinking dourly that now the group would have no runners to fetch help if they needed it, Ikella stared down at the hapless traveller, her mouth set in grim lines. They all knew into what danger they walked. Yet they could not leave her, no matter what the outcome. It was the first Law of the Sands. Help fellow travellers, abandon no one, not even your enemy, on pain of death. The protective weave dissipated into the howling maelstrom, and slowly, painfully, bent almost double against the pitiless winds, they moved on. The children were herded in between the adults, without protest. They struggled onward, the collapsed woman murmuring broken fragments snatched by the demented howl of the wind before they could catch what she said. Ikella led on, her Staff supporting almost her entire weight between staggering steps, as they lurched their way through sands that seemed to roll against their legs in some never-ending tide of death.

The Sorceress gasped for breath. Forged in this wilderness, hardened on its relentless plains, and tempered in the fire of its daytime heat, she had never feared it, until this night. She had, as every other of their kind, experienced the death of friends, family and fellow healers in this bleak but beautiful place and had never once thought of her own death with anything other than a remote acceptance, that one day, would be her last. She had never thought the desert cruel or unmerciful or even harsh, it was simply the desert. Now, this night, she found herself thinking that the Opal, the desert of her people, had ranged itself against her in some screaming fury and angered at this rebellion, she found herself screaming back into the wind in defiance.

'Serash, inshalhanish, serash moyen ichshong nachlic! Serash." (Be still, we are your people, I am your Sorceress, I command you, be still!) Even her Staff spoke a long, bell-like chime, before the great Opal flared, green, gold, rose and lavender sparks showered the Sands with her rage.

For a moment there was silence, a long beam of light licked forward across the Sands ahead of her and touched something dark. It was only a brief lull, an even briefer glimpse of some structure, a tannish tree, a stone bush perhaps? Whatever it was, it gave her the direction she needed and as the storm lashed at them again, completely unaware of the astonished faces around her, Ikella headed determinedly towards the patch of dark ahead.

It seemed to her that she was wading waist-deep in the Sands. Perhaps some sand monster had her by the feet? Her arms ached so that she could barely hold her Staff, but she dug deep into her reserves and found herself crying out to the Sacred Wind of her Sands.

"Mirayen, sel moyen, Mirayen toshiminen." (Mirayen guide us, Mirayen save us!) Her mind rebelled for a moment as she thought, 'How strange that I should think of that.' It was the start of the funeral rites of her own people, her own Sand, addressed to the First Wind of Pelshar.

She doggedly went on raising each foot against the sucking pull of the sands beneath her feet, and chanting, now to the second Wind.

"Gurayen sek moyen, Gurayen noi shominen." (Gurayen shelter us, Gurayen defend us.)

The prayer for the dead of the Azure Sands flickered across her lips and fled. She found herself thinking briefly, 'At least when death comes we will all be prepared.'

As she struggled forward another step, her Staff gleaming fitfully blue, azure, turquoise, she raised her *othervoice* in chant once more.

"surayen doue moyen Surayen torinimen." (Surayen watch over us, Surayen receive us.)

Her exhausted thoughts strayed briefly to the depths of the Malachite desert and the wind of the Greshe. Her Staff chimed deeply and ahead she thought she heard an echo. She paused struggling for breath, feeling the despair wash over her as she suddenly realised that she could no longer hear the battering winds.

"Deo protect us," she whispered.

"We are in the Silent Sands."

Still the storm lashed them from every side. She lurched as she dragged her feet free of the cloying drifts and struggled to keep upright.

'To fall here would spell instant Death, ' she thought bitterly.

Her Staff flickered eerily green and in the light, dimly through the driving sand and wind, Ikella saw that they were closing on the darkness ahead. At her feet the pathway Gleamed suddenly, lit by her Staff, leading directly to the source of her interest.

She recovered her balance and strode forward with renewed hope, glancing up at her Staff from time to time. Reassured by its glow in the dark, she chanted, "Verayen anoi moyen, Verayen tellathe tore." (Verayen support us, Verayen guide our path.)

She heard the flicker of appreciation from Nadara immediately behind her as her Staff glowed crimson, gold, the colours of the Cynabarr Sands, and she launched herself into the next chant.

"Amayen tirish moyen, Amayen giren dow." (Amayen feed us, Amayen accept our fear.)

There was a groan from the group behind her as the Staff boomed a low note and then turned dark, gleaming eerily black, silver flickers showing around the dark heart of it. In the depths of her cowl, Inahana's eyes flashed, whites iridescent against her midnight, bronzed skin.

Ikella paused, the storm seemed to have slightly abated. Were they going to get through this strangely silent but ferocious battering? She raised her head a little, narrowed eyes appraising the situation, considering.

'Was it simply drawing back, all the better to attack again?' She gathered herself. 'We cannot die here!' she decided. 'Not with only a hundred paces to whatever that is!' Shrouded in its protective cloak of chaos, she began the chant of the Jhirelle, to find herself eerily echoed in the despairing moan of the woman they carried.

"Perayen moi moyen, Perayen divin duoe duxos." (Perayen take me. Perayen guard my child.)

Ikella stared. Could she believe her eyes?

In the lambent golden flare from her Staff, not fifty paces from her, was the entrance to a cave. At the base of a sheer rock Opal cliff, the billowing sands hardly showed. All contrast was impossible in this cauldron of debris. She forced herself forward staggering into the entrance, daunted by the height of the cavern. The others crowded round her, the men passing their precious burden and the children into safety. However, as the men pushed forward, their joy was dampened by the discovery that the cave was incredibly shallow, offering little protection from the raging elements outside. The sand was already infiltrating as they arrived and the only shelter was a shallow basin, three spans wide by two hands deep. In the centre of the cavern, it lay below what appeared to be a cascading waterfall but water it was not, for it was still, hard, suspended mysteriously, perhaps in time itself and at that thought, the Sorceress had to control the urge to giggle hysterically. Ikella had never seen anything like it in her life. She reached up to see if touch would identify the strange material, but it could not and she felt nothing from it, no magic here she decided, glancing at the basin shape below. It seemed to be full of the substance, like some strange pool, frozen but not cold. She knelt at the edge. There would be some shelter here she determined, though not a lot, they might just save the baby though she thought the mother already doomed. With a heavy heart Ikella watched them laying their patient into the shallow basin. Two of the healers attended her, as Mina returned to her side.

"Deshun, forgive me, but we will not survive long in here," she commented. Ikella rallied, forcing her leaden legs to work once more, examining the back of the shallow cave seeking more shelter in vain. The Sorceress turned away, thinking.

'We are going to die! Here, in the Silent Sands, and that is my fault!'

She watched as the woman, clearly now in labour, rolled in agony, seeing with pity the paling, golden skin as the Healers stripped her blue cloak from her. At that moment, the woman arched as another spasm seized her, her eyes flew open and her gaze locked on Ikella's.

"My baby."

She groaned deeply, seizing Andria's hand as the Healer bent to assist. With her gaze burning into Ikella's she whispered.

"Look after my baby!" paling as the next pain took her, only just able to force the words.

"He is all I can give you!" she cried out then, and as the healers clustered around her, Ikella stood protectively in the entrance, watching the grim struggle between life and death within the body of their patient.

Hearing the Healers chanting for pain control inspired the Sorceress to continue her own prayers. Her Staff firmly planted in the ground, blazing Opal now, all the shades visibly flickering, she shouldered the task.

"Imrayen jhi moyen, Imrayen gesh shomahen." (Imrayen strengthen me, Imrayen comfort those I love.)

Sanra, midwife of the Carnelian Sands, was totally engaged in her work but flushed with recognition and pleasure as the Wind of her Sands was named.

"Quexayen stuo moyen, Quexayen impto hebri honoyen." (Quexayen cleanse me, Quexayen accept my heart.)

The light from her Staff flickered pale green as Tourmaline Healer Andria bowed her head and closed her eyes in recognition of her imminent death. Again, the bell-like tones echoed strangely around the cavern.

"Brochayen deri moyen, Brochayen niri desol." (Brochayen comfort us, Brochayen never leave us.)

As the last of the Nine Sacred Winds of Pelshar was invoked, Ikella's Staff gleamed eerily lilac, amethyst, deep purple, echoed by the clear stone in an ancient ring on Ikella's hand. It brought to her mind one of the lasting impressions of a long ago childhood and her eyes narrowed, her mind returning to the Inner Hall at Sanctuary where once she had trained in the magical arts of her kind. She gazed at her Healers, at least one representative of each Clan, knowing that unless she took the greatest risk they would not leave this place alive. She drew a long breath, her eyes strayed to the great Opal at the head of her Staff, then to her ring and knew she must act. Now, they were ready. Ready to die, but almost as the thought bloomed, she thought she herd a voice ask quietly, "Yet, are you ready to live in a different Way?"

The stone at the head of her Staff and in her ring cleared to crystal as the distant memory surged to the forefront of Ikella's attention. Subconsciously, she recognised that time was behaving very oddly: it seemed that she had more than enough to spare and yet she knew, somehow, that only seconds were passing as she remembered.

With growing clarity she recalled a spell, carved into the edge of an ancient table at Sanctuary, the Mother House of the Sister's of Sorcery. She had amused herself memorising it one long afternoon as, when denied the company of the other novices, she had been closeted with a lesson she had failed to learn. She remembered the precise wording and the warning of the Guardian who had caught her whispering the words to herself.

"Ikella!" Beneva had regarded her anxiously.

"That spell has never been used in our time. It may only be wielded by the person who was intended to wield it, at the right time and in the right place. You are only a novice and the First Rule of Magic is not about power! It is about Obedience to the Rule. Understand this: you may NEVER repeat any words without questioning their origin! Not even in a whisper to yourself!" The Guardian considered for a moment, then said softly, her face remote and guarded, "If you can write this down for me, I will give you a reward for a prodigious feat of memory, but you can only pray you never have to use that spell. It is ancient, older even than I, and can only be used when ritual prayer to the Nine Winds has failed. If you are in the presence of each Clan, if all the Peoples of the Sand are represented and in peril of their lives, you might benefit. Otherwise it could mean your death - all your deaths!"

Beneva's words rang in her ears. The stone in the ring that had been her reward glowed and the Sorceress watched without speaking as her Healers joined hands, bowing heads in acceptance of their fate. Suddenly enraged with the situation, with the unfairness of it all, the Sorceress made up her mind.

She seized her Staff, turning her back on the cave. Braced against the elements, with lightning flickering in her eyes, she summoned every scrap of magic, every fibre of energy and struck her Staff against the Storm itself, opening herself to the Source of all souls, from whence magical power was drawn. From whence came the words she would thereafter never know, but they came and, as the others reported later, it seemed that as her othervoice rang out it was accompanied by some mystical chorus. Ikella, who had only thought to meet her death challenging the Storm, focussed on that fragment of memory. Her fingers twitched as they remembered the strange shapes carved around the edges of the ancient table. Her tongue cleaved to the top of her mouth as she formulated the pronunciation of the forbidden inscription seen oh so many years ago and so far away. Feeling that she teetered on the brink of some great and unknown precipice, she finally raised her voice in desperation. Praying that the words she recalled were correct in every strange syllable, she began to chant.

"Darayen initia moyen, Darayen receffi Arriera issayen." (Darayen renew us, Darayen receive this soul.")

It seemed as if the cliff face above her rang, her Staff chimed and her ghostly chorus lifted, swelled, with voices like no other she had ever heard. Beneath her feet the desert trembled and the furious winds recoiled, bubbling and boiling at arms length, visible and yet impotent. She stared amazed as around her like some incandescent bubble, sprang a luminous shield. It covered the mouth of the cavern, shielding all within from the Storm outside. It settled on them, light as a feather, no colour, no sound, no scent, no sensation, just a gentle, crystal clear glow. Their eyes grew heavy, their breathing deepened and without alarm, as one body, they slipped from terror to tranquil sleep.

In the cavern, there was peace and in the heart of the desert, a baby cried.

Chapter 4 - Visions

In her sleep, it seemed to Ikella that there were people all around them. Dressed in the colours of the Nine Sands, they wandered amongst her small party of sleepers, tending to them. Here a child was stirred, lifted from its father's arms, then settled more comfortably. There, faces were bathed, fluid dripped into dry mouths, almost as though these people were Healer-trained. They crowded around the birthing basin now, gazing at something beyond her view. Ikella struggled in vain to focus on their faces, but somehow, just as she was about to glimpse one clearly, another would stand in the way. It was most frustrating, she thought without rancour, languidly drifting towards a deeper sleep.

In her dream, the strangers formed a double line stretching to the back of the cave. The shimmering waterfall splashed down, though she could not see where the water was flowing to and an air of expectancy roused her befuddled mind. A tall man walked in procession from deep shadows at the back of the cavern and, as he passed, he touched each of the others lightly on the head as if in blessing. He was carrying some gleaming object in his hand as he came to bend over Ikella, who gazed up into a lean, tanned face.

She saw dark, waving hair, a neat beard and wonderful eyes. Fathomless dark pools lit with opalescent flickers, caught and held hers helpless, imprisoned in his gaze like an insect in amber. He looked solemn, yet there was a great deal of humour in the curve of his mouth, and she found herself smiling as he gently raised her to a sitting position. Then his lips parted and a Voice sounded in her head.

"Honoured Mother."

The deep melodic tones poured over her in a honeyed wave, soothing her trembling limbs, comforting her dream-bound bewilderment.

"sorceress of the Shalhanhi, Bearer of the Opal Staff, Warden of the Nine Winds, I greet you."

He spoke again, voice grave.

"Our world is in danger, and only you can save it. You must protect this child, and you must find the 'Tapestry of Tten'. Without that, Pelshar, my beloved world is doomed!" He smiled ruefully, "You have inherited a world on the brink of disaster, but there is hope for all of you, just find the Tapestry of Tten, you will be told how to use it." He stood and turned away.

Ikella, her dreaming brain trying frantically to escape, could not take in what was happening. Whirling thoughts flickered too quickly to grasp before fluttering away like fly-bys before snow and she felt herself slipping into safety, into sleep, but it eluded her curious mind. She watched silently. Lifting her Staff reverently, the leader of the Visitors, for she thought of him as such, kissed the opal at its head, in a strange echo of her own daily ritual obeisance to the stone. She relaxed at last, knowing she was safe, with those who knew that it represented the desert itself to the Bearers of the Staff and all those Sandsworn to these Sands, past, present and future. His hand lifted, raised something to the finial at the tip of the Staff above the great stone and then he laid the Staff down again, turning to kneel before the strange, pool-like structure. He gazed long at the gentle death that lay there, curled protectively around her babe and then he lifted a glowing spectral shape for a second, until there was a shimmer and the outlines of her body coalesced into something like the living image of the girl. As Ikella drifted inexorably back down to unconsciousness once more, her lasting impression was that the girl murmured something to her companion, who gently cupped her face in his hand, before turning to the dreaming Sorceress. His Voice echoed in her mind once more.

"Take care of this child, for he represents the future. His name is Daro."

Holding the hand of the spectral image, he walked into a shimmering mist at the back of the cavern and followed by his attendants, disappeared from view.

Desperate to know more, Ikella struggled to her feet, but her head was spinning, there was a roaring in her ears and everything paled into insignificance as Ikella, Sorceress of the Opal Sands, most powerful and revered of magic users, fainted clean away.

Chapter 5 - Dawn of Darkness.

Ikella stirred, something brushed her face then stroked her hair. She blinked the sleep from her eyes and tried to focus, but she was drowsy, warm and comfortable. A damp cloth was passed over her face, a little moisture was trickled into her mouth, and she remembered. Shakily she sat up and Tisanna the Amethyst Healer respectfully gave her room to stretch and re-orientate herself. She rose to her knees, wavering a little, then to her feet, gazing around her in astonishment, for it seemed from the light as if night was about to fall and yet there was heat, almost like that felt in the Height of Sun when to walk in the deserts was to court death from dehydration. Silently handing the Sorceress a waterskin to drink from, Tisanna padded away to tend the others. Ikella drank, carefully filling her mouth once and letting the moisture permeate through the tissues of her mouth and tongue before swallowing. Her throat was dry, her chest ached and she could have wished for less pain in her exhausted body, but the storm was over, the winds dissipated and the desert lay calm and still around them.

She took another mouthful of water, revelling in the relief of living when death seemed certain for all of them, and then she remembered Midara's hopeless fight for the life of the girl and a single thought seized her waking mind. What had become of the child? Even though her legs shook with fatigue and her body seemed gripped by a strange lassitude, she hastened back to stand gazing with infinite pity at the sorrowful scene in the centre of this mysterious cavern. The girl lay as if sleeping, one arm curled under her head, the other curved about her child. Her entire body seemed focussed on the babe, who slept, blissfully unaware of his mother's death. It seemed to Ikella that she had died gazing at the child, there was a look of wonder on her face still and, although she was not known for fantasising, it pleased Ikella to think that she had left this plain of sorrows at the happiest time of her life. She gently lifted the sleeping child from his mother's arms and wrapped him more firmly in the cloth that someone had used to cover him, balancing him on her hip as she turned to her group once more. The entire company of women was gathered around the men and children. As she walked towards them, she realised that there was a frantic buzz of conversation going on in their midst. Penetrating the circle almost unnoticed, she found them anxiously questioning their families and her ears sharpened as she heard Sanra pressing her son to give her an answer.

"Timmin, listen to me carefully now. I want you to look at Mina and tell me how many fingers she is holding up?"

The boy, eldest of the children at about nine or ten namedays old, looked bewildered, but gazed across the width of the cave to where Mina stood. Timmin cleared his throat and counted uncertainly.

"Elka, Leos, Driat, Vivil."

As Mina flicked up the fingers of her left hand one by one, keeping her thumb carefully folded into the palm, he grinned at Mina's nod and slipped back into the small gaggle of children, unaware of the growing tension amongst the worried adults.

Silently Ikella observed and as Sanra positioned Derun her mate, turning him gently to face Mina, she noticed that Derun's eyes seemed painful: he squinted in the direction of the other Healer.

"Derun, how many fingers is Mina holding up?" Sanra quietly asked, shaking her head at Mina who folded her arms across her chest, gazing steadily at Derun who, with bravado, hazarded a guess.

"serlap is that Mina?" he called, his normally cheery voice sounding strained. Sanra looked into Ikella's knowledgeable eyes unflinchingly.

"Deshun, it is the same for Dovid, Nadara's man. All the boys seemed to have escaped, but Derun and Dovid are blind!" Suddenly even stoical Sanra struggled for control, her arms protectively cradling her devastated partner.

"They could be suffering some sand blindness," she hesitated, her voice cracking, "But I think not. This is something different. There is perception of light but no detail in what they see. They have strange blurring in their eyes, severe pain with light and there is no truesight left for either of them." She stroked her man's arm protectively, saying softly, "Why has this happened to us, why now and how?"

Derun chuckled bitterly, calling into the shadows that would dominate the rest of his life: "Hey Dovid, here's one for you. They should have asked how many Minas they were holding up. We might have been able to see that!" His grim humour broke suddenly and he wept, pillowed against Sanra's ample bosom.

In the face of such distress, Ikella busied herself with small menial tasks: gathering the children together, eyeing the group of solemn faces with some trepidation. Her position demanded a remoteness, a detachment from the many peoples that fell under her protection, for if she was too close to any one of them that might make her unresponsive to the needs of another. So, for a moment, they looked at each other nervously, the group of children all between seven and ten name days old and the great Sorceress of the Shalhanhi, at the height of her powers, in the middle years of an extensive lifespan, virginal as her position demanded and utterly unpractised in the maternal crafts.

It was the baby who broke the ice, for he murmured suddenly and Timmin, child of Sanra and Derun, smiled at him, confidently reaching out to touch the babe gently. Then they all swarmed around, begging to see this miraculous survivor of the storm and Ikella knelt in an unusually graceful move, sinking into the sand with the youngsters crowding her for the opportunity to look with astonished eyes into the face of the orphan. She hefted the baby into the crook of one arm and organised the children in an unpractised but effective move.

"Line up, one at a time, " she ordered gruffly and the children hastened to obey. To their surprise and hers, the next few moments were comparatively pleasurable: the baby wide awake but not fearful of the children hanging over him. The children, delighted with this small, new life, gave him a finger to hold, clustering around the Sorceress, their faces alight with pleasure. For long moments, Ikella bathed in the warmth of their interest, but all too soon, one of the men made a move to stand, nearly fell, and the reality of their situation dawned on her.

They were a comparatively large party, so their reserves were all but used up. They had intended to sleep at the hospice of Tearchan before travelling back to Selesh by way of the market town of Caranchar the following day. Now, all that she had planned paled into insignificance in the face of their current situation, Ikella thought wearily, gazing down at the baby nestling in her arms. With her was the entire Council of Nine, who had gathered in Conference at Selesh only two ninenights ago. She heaved a sigh. What madness had prompted her to invite them to join the student Healers completing their ritual Song Walk? It was normal for the Sorceress to accompany students in this last stage of the ritual training journey, undertaken before they sang their Oath to the Guild of Healers. However, 'This is no longer a formal ritual, it is turning into a veritable battle for survival, ' she thought grimly. They had to get back from this strangely Silent Sand to Tearchan.

'That in itself is a formidable challenge with a new-born!' she thought, peering into the dimness surrounding their shelter.

'In this strange twilight, there will be no Sight of Sun. How can I estimate the time? How can I feed the baby? Even we will struggle to survive, ' she considered dully, an ache growing behind her eyes as she peered at the baby.

'What did his mother call him? Or was his name part of her strange vision?'

The others saw her brow furrow as she cast her mind back. 'Ah yes, he was Daro.' She glanced down at him. The baby did not seem hungry at the moment, in fact he slept totally relaxed, his tiny arms above his head, hands facing upwards, his mouth gently suckling in the reflex action of the newborn. At that moment, Mina intervened. Shooing the children back to their parents and relieving the now aching arm that cradled Daro, she handed him to Midara, midwife of the Cynabarr Sands, who had supervised his birth. As she did so, Andria, their Soul Searcher, swept forward placing in Ikella's hand a leathern travel cup filled to the brim with (if she could believe her eyes) warm, fresh milk!

Thunderstruck, Ikella, her voice unsteady, exclaimed, "How in the Nine Sands?" to which Andria pointed silently through the great cavern entrance, to where, poised against the backdrop of a lowering sky, stood an Irix and its calf. The Sorceress gazed out on to some short, stubby grazing land commonly found in the desert fringes. She saw several Irix standing in small family groups, utterly unafraid of this human intrusion into their territory. This behaviour, so unlike their normal shyness, left her entranced and deeply thankful. She thought somewhat warily, 'At least for this moment, Daro won't follow his mother to the Sands from hunger!'

Steadily the Irix stared back at her, somehow communicating reassurance. Serenely, it walked forward into the cavern, its calf trotting alongside, and Ikella held up a hand to silence the babble of excitement from her companions. She reached out and the Irix drew near, sniffing her hand daintily. It was not large, something like a cross between the Benage of the High Forests and their own desert Coatan, which they milked when a mother's breast's were dry. The Irix seemed interested in the baby and sniffed towards Andria, who was encouraging the hungry child to suckle using the end of a clean cloth dipped in the milk. Ikella leant back against a rock wall, relief flooding through her, as the Irix and her calf trotted calmly from the cave into the desert beyond. In a voice designed to carry to her companions, she said as confidently as she could, "Well, we won't starve and neither will the baby." a note of satisfaction audible as she continued briskly, "What we need is a good nights sleep. I will leave it to Mina to set guards, though I think we have little to fear here. Derun and Dovid must have treatment if they are to travel in the morning. Perhaps tomorrow the sky will have cleared for I need Sight of Sun to take our bearings. I swore by the Winds to get you all back to safety, to Selesh, even if I have to wait and take a reckoning from the stars!" There was a muted chorus but, ignoring this, she continued quietly, "To refresh my memory of the old trails, I shall meditate alone, thanking the One for our survival."

She rose purposefully, intending to set her Staff against the wall so that she could, as was her habit, focus her inner mind on the Opal, both the symbol and source of her commitment. However as she swung it clear of the Sand where it had lain all night, her gasp of surprise attracted the attention of her companions, to where, clasped to the top of the silver finial above the great Opal stone, soared an utterly perfect pair of wings.

They were almost translucent in their delicacy, shimmering with small, but palpable waves of energy. They sent out an eerily crystalline noise as they fluttered and danced for her, power shuddering down the shaft of midnight black Hojawood. Ikella nearly dropped it in shock.

'Where had these come from?' she questioned herself wildly, her mind skittering away from the obvious because it seemed too incredible to consider. Relapsing into the habits of a long lifetime, as the most powerful of her kind, the Sorceress brought the Staff closer to examine it. Seeing a strange inscription running around the band that secured the wings to the Staff, she paused, considering. She fingered it nervously, for these looked similar to the ancient words of power that had saved them from the Storm. She stared silently at the soaring grace embodied in the shimmering wings. Her very stillness communicated alarm to the others, who crowded around, anxious to see this change to the sacred Staff of the Opal Sands.

Mina, Senior Healer of the Guild, was the first to speak.

"My Deshun, " she started respectfully.

"Can I tell you about a dream? I had it while we slept out the Storm."

Unusually, she did not wait for permission, but continued impulsively.

"It seemed to me that we were visited by many strangers, all clad in the weaves of our world, " she began and a chorus of agreement, which included the men and children, rang through the cave. Ikella stared. This behaviour was unlike her calm Clansmen! She stood abruptly and, moving apart from them, lifted her Staff with its new crown of wings, before striking it to the Sand of the Desert she ruled. Instantly, cloaking herself and the Staff in her protective aura, she traced the words carved in the new part of the finial, they seemed strange and yet oddly familiar, as if this was a language she should know. Yet her waking brain knew that she did not, leaving her wondering how she could translate them, safely, adequately? She had already accepted the vision of the visitors as a true happening for how else could the others have seen her dream and how could her Staff have been so altered?

She found herself staring at the inscription blankly. With an enormous effort, she cleared her mind and the words spoken by the man of her vision came to her.

"Honoured Mother, Warden of the Nine Winds of Pelshar." Her eyes flew open in terror. 'Deo! Had she spoken aloud?' Or had the words of the stranger somehow been repeated through the cavern, which certainly reverberated to the power pulsing through the Staff. Through the shimmer of her aura she saw the sand blow gently, almost reverently to her feet where it formed distinct ripples. She silently counted the rings. 'serlap, octivo, noightan." Then all doubt fled as she dropped to one knee, honouring all Nine Winds of Pelshar.

Her aura fading, she took note that in the cave her followers knelt with awe on their faces. So, had they seen the rapid beat of the magical wings atop her Staff still as the Winds dropped? The last thing she needed was superstitions about strange caverns, strange happenings in her life. She thought sourly, 'A baby will be bad enough!' She was beginning to suspect that there might be much more to face, when and if they joined the outside world.

Deliberately relaxing her body, feeling the tension leave, washed away by the knowledge that she could not pursue the myriad questions that needed answering there, she wrapped herself in her cloak and rested, back to the wall of the shallow cave, to await the dawn of a new day.

She woke to darkness and rolling out of her blanket, took up her Staff and walked carefully out of the shallow cavern into the dawn desert. She stretched deeply, looking up into the clouded skies. Her eyes cried out for light. Pacing, she discovered how unfriendly, how hostile her Sands appeared in this unrelieved gloom, where it was hard to tell night from day. Sitting huddled in her cloak, back against the cliff in which the cave had been formed, she watched carefully for the light to grow, taking note of the direction from which it came. The normal glittering of the Opal Sand was reduced to a greyed shimmer. The shadows streaked the dunes, making a pattern like no other she had ever seen.

'One could believe the ground itself was drowned.'

She thought the sand seemed to ripple like the bottom of a river she remembered, from long ago. The subtle shifting light made her feel unsteady on her feet, nervous and shamefully uncertain of the Sands she had ruled for so long, and reluctantly she admitted to herself that she was grateful to be sitting.

Slowly, from the east, came a sickly lavender-hued light, flickering across the clouds that stretched like some pallid textile overhead. This eerily dark dawn reduced the healthy colour of her own hands to a ghastly hue, like some dead thing. She wondered what her Clansmen would make of this sickened sky, thankful that civilisation was at least four good walking days away and that none else would suffer the storm ravaged skies or feel the wrath of the Silent Sands into which she had wandered.

Her musings turned to Selesh, the heart of the Opal Sands, the most sacred place on all Pelshar. It was incredibly ancient, built as an underground fortress city and ruled by rituals older than time. It was rumoured to hold many more levels than those in which her community had been established. Used extensively by the Healer Guild, she longed to be able to extend it, train others, and she shivered as she thought how lucky they had been to even survive the Storm. She wondered if they even knew about the Storm and longed for it. She leant against her rock, while Seleus rose hidden from her by the cloud, through which only fitful gleams of light could be glimpsed. She continued to brood, reluctant to return and pick up the reins of command in a way that she had never before experienced.

The others woke, gathering into family groups. The inevitable questioning from the Healers about the men's eyes seemed to occupy their daybreak conversation, and Ikella remained where she was, anxious not to intrude. The men though stoical, were unable to stand even this low light and Sanra, Tisanna and Derana soaked pads in the remains of yesterday's Irix milk to dress their eyes, before bandaging them shut. Although this relieved the pain, they appeared to be listless and hot and Ikella, taking report from Mina, recommended sithin bark to crush into the next drink they took, saying with gruff sympathy, "That will reduce inflammation and control fever. If their rehenas are sore, they will need to be bandaged for the walk or I cannot guarantee that they will even make Tearchan."

Her voice became more thoughtful.

"Do we have neshroot salve with us?" she questioned, already suspecting that the answer was in the negative even as she spoke, for the root was difficult to grow, harder to preserve and travelled badly. She hesitated then said decisively.

"We should have been at Tearchan last night, so they will be alarmed, may already have sent to Maraken to see what became of us. We cannot hope to get Dovid and Derun back to Selesh without more medication. We will need water before two days walk, so we will head for Tearchan first. Are we agreed?" She caught a look of bewilderment in the eyes of her two student Healers and inwardly smiled to herself. They were not used to being consulted on anything she did, for she was Sorceress and they had not yet ascended to the privileges of full Guild membership, but they saw that the others agreed and bowed their heads meekly.

"Well then, now that's decided, I will attempt to work out a journey plan to

Tearchan from here, " she said briskly adding sotto voce, "That is if I can work out where here is!" and left the others preparing to travel. Returning outside, Ikella sat studying the desert with brows drawn together and eyes straining as she searched the horizon in vain for familiar landmarks.

It was difficult to concentrate her mind on one problem and before long she found herself wondering what she should do with the body of the child's mother.

They could not put their entire party at risk by attempting to carry her with them. At best she could plan to retrieve the body later she mused, ignoring the persistent inner voice that told her she would never pass this way again in her lifetime.

The cavern was dry and would preserve the girl from the elements. She finally permitted herself to accept that perhaps this was the right thing to do. Acknowledging the fact that it was unlikely that anyone searching for her would stray into these forbidden Sands, she nevertheless planned to leave them a direction to follow. Stretching stiffly she rose to her feet and froze where she stood, for not ten hands from her stood the Irix and her calf. The animal looked her up and down enquiringly and only then did Ikella realise that in the shelter of the cave the foundling of the storm was crying lustily. Davini, one of her students, was anxiously unwrapping him and soon, to Ikella's amusement, the girl's nose wrinkled in disgust as the sodden garments were removed. There were a few chuckles from the older Healers and from Sanra some apparent instruction. A small bag was offered and with the aplomb of a street entertainer, the older woman produced some ointment and another cloth which was soon tied, albeit inexpertly, in place. A gust of laughter came from the men at the rear of the cave, who were plainly being regaled by some domestic story and soon, as the baby was re-wrapped again, Ikella decided to return to the group, only praying that she did not frighten the Irix away as she moved. Far from being afraid, the animal tamely followed her into the cavern, where Mina and Inahana gently milked her streaming udders into a bowl till there was milk for all of them.

The baby, who had ceased crying, was screwing up his face, making suckling movements with his mouth into which he thrust a finger.

Davini lifted him into Ikella's arms. Surprised, the Sorceress turned towards Mina expecting her to take him, but Mina pressed a suckling cloth and a cup of milk into her hand, shamelessly daring her to refuse. The Sorceress was so taken aback, that she actually took the implements and sat somewhat precipitately on a large rock before she realised what she was doing. It was many Rotations since she had helped a dry breasted woman feed her child in this way, and for a few minutes she had absolutely no recollection of what to do next.

Dismay flooded through her as she helplessly hefted the baby to a more comfortable position. Thankfully, this small manoeuvre served to jog her memory and, even as she caught a knowing grin being passed between Inahana, the dusky Kora Mai from the Onyx Sands, and Derana, a pale Greshe from

Malachite Desert, the moment passed. As she relaxed, her hands somehow created a teat shape in the cloth, soaked it in the milk and prepared to feed the child.

At least she was being useful she thought, raising the infant to her shoulder and patting his back awkwardly, letting him rest before trying to dribble the other half of the milk in to him. She bent her head, breathing in the sweet milkiness, his new baby smell and his little head nodded as mildly unsupported he lurched, aiming his mouth at her cheek. For a second, her heart squeezed as his anxious little mouth fastened on her cheek, nuzzling hopefully as if at his mother's breast. In that unguarded moment, Ikella learned that even a childless virgin dedicated to the service of her world could, for a brief second, feel the joy of motherhood.

Then reality returned, as frustrated in his search for food, the baby wailed in desolation. Sanra rescued him, taking the baby, the cup of milk and cloth from her hands and swooping away with him.

Rejoining her family on their blanket, she expertly fed the child, carrying on an animated conversation with her partner, patting him lightly with her free hand as she emphasised a point here and there.

Ikella, for one strange moment, felt a rush of jealousy in their intimacy, the newly blinded man relaxed and confident in his partner's care, the baby nestling contentedly in her practised hands, but then she brushed those thoughts away, stood abruptly and picked up her Staff of Office.

She was lost in thought, staring down into the shallow basin where the shrouded body of the child's mother lay. They had wrapped her as tradition demanded: lying on her back, hands crossed over her breast, face wiped clean of any artifice. Ikella suddenly realised that she knew so little of this girl. Had her hair been long it would have marked her as a Guild member of some kind, but Ikella could not recall seeing her hair at all. They would have braided and fastened it with her Songstones, and suddenly shame flooded her as she realised that she had no idea whether this woman had worn the braids of a fellow Healer, or the skin record of some other Guild, although she knew that she wore the Colours of the Amber Sands.

She lay wrapped in her cloak, shod for the road, so that she could take the Long Walk with the One in accordance with the beliefs of their kind. Had she used a Staff it would have been laid by her as one day, Ikella knew, she herself would lie for another to mourn her thus.

The funeral rites for a magic user of high status would be very different to what they could afford this poor girl however, and she shivered as though something icy cold had touched her with its breath.

Mina moved to her side and held out a hand in which lay a curiously carved stone. It hung from a silver mount and chain and Ikella stared at it uncomprehendingly for a moment till the Healer explained.

'she wore it round her neck my Deshun. I thought to remove it so that, if no-one claims the child, we may try to trace its parentage from the stone."

The Sorceress reached out and touched the beautiful thing wistfully. It resembled a fruit of some kind she thought, with a tiny but perfect hummer sat just under the delicate tracery of leaves that combined to make the mounting for the chain.

"Think you this moonstone?" she enquired, raising an eyebrow at Mina, who peered closely at the piece, humming under her breath quizzically but offering no suggestions.

Ikella spoke thoughtfully, "I cannot be sure and I do not want to cast for it here."

She indicated the proximity to the corpse and Mina nodded agreement. Magic was a strangely powerful thing and although she was used to seeing Ikella at work, neither of them could feel the need to cast a tracing spell so close to the recently deceased owner of the artefact that they would use. Death was a veil that no-one should attempt to penetrate and the atmosphere within the cave was unsettling.

Ikella already felt it had become a tomb, suspecting it hid secrets that they had no time or resource to explore. She bent therefore and, with extreme caution, used a mere trickle of Power with which to inscribe the symbol of Selesh through the thin layer of sand that lay in the bottom of the basin and onto the strangely shimmering substance that lay below. She examined her work, an arch, below which two hands opened to receive a single droplet, poured from a gouche or Apothecary's bottle to signify shelter and healing.

'No-one could possibly misinterpret that,' she thought with satisfaction, turning to call the group to order.

"It is my intention to travel during the Fall of Sun and into the rise of Jenta," she announced, cutting through the resultant buzz of comment, holding up a silencing hand.

"I know that we do not often travel at night, but needs must. Since I am unable to make out any familiar landmarks and the heat is so oppressive, it makes sense. Once out of these Silent Sands and back on the track, we can navigate by consensus, but I am responsible for the first part of the journey. I must close this Song Walk, even though it has taken us along many strange paths!"

She smiled sweetly at the two fourth year student healers, who had coloured gently at the mention of their all important ritual Walk so rudely interrupted in its closing phases by the storm.

They had now experienced things that would live with them for the rest of their lives, she thought, observing their swift, silent obedience to her instructions. When all was ready, they sat or lay resting, as was normal for desert dwellers, waiting for the Height of Sun to pass.

Though they could not see the usual intolerable glare from the iridescent Sands, they could feel the heat and would have perished on the gleaming, flat lands had they ventured forth. So they waited and slept, slept and waited, and at long last, when the baby had fed again and the Irix dam had been milked to provide a last meal for the children, they gathered around the basin and the young woman they were leaving behind. Ikella carefully took the baby in the crook of her arm and raised her Staff with the other and spoke, solemnly, in improvised ritual.

"Farewell, sister of the storm, farewell. We leave you in the hands of the protectors of these sands and depart to our own land, taking with us the gift of your child. He carries with him your love, your gift of life and the treasure stone, which we will use in the manner of our kind to seek you out, to identify you or yours, and to bring your child to his father, or to those of his kind to raise. We, the Shalhanhi, recognise the obligation of travellers to aid one another and we acknowledge before the One, before the Nine Winds of Pelshar, your right to call on us to adopt your child and rear him as our own. Should we fail to find your kin, so shall it be. Thus do we acknowledge our duty and comply with your trust."

It was now late afternoon, in these the Opal Sands and at this time of year the light should be strong, the heat dissipating into the evening. There should easily be time for them to find their way back to the main trail, to see their position and navigate back to Tearchan, a large hospice built on the cross trails below the Marison Pass. Here, though it be dusk, they should be able to find their way easily for the Tearchan settlement had several buildings, storage for animal fodder, a corral for a small number of beasts, a barn for drying the herbs and medicaments that the healers used and the hostel itself. With memories of other journeys to this familiar place and the pleasure anticipated in reaching its safe, walled structure, they turned away from the cavern that had sheltered and saved them and walked forth into a world that had woken to a dawn of darkness.

Chapter 6 - Tested before Tearchan.

As the Council of Nine, with the student healers carrying the baby, stepped out from the protective shadows of their temporary shelter, Ikella found herself lingering. Outside there was no sign of the usually clear sky: all that could be seen above were clouds of livid grey, the day was as dark as late sundown, the normally hot, dry air was damp and full of misery. This eerie twilight with its sombre shadows was forbidding and Ikella was forced to admit that she dreaded setting out into the unknown again. She risked the lives of her companions every time that she ventured into the desert but then she knew that, for she was Opal born, Opal sworn and had ruled here for more years than many ordinary men lived. Today, however, she felt especially burdened by the responsibility of this group, for she had with her the Senior Healers from every one of the nine deserts and if they were all lost that would deal a death blow to Pelshar and her people's way of life. She caught herself worrying her lips with small, white, even teeth and paused to consider. There were no known charts of this area and she could expect no sight of Sun from which to get bearings or estimate the time.

She stared around the shallow cavern noting the great height of it, seeing as if for the first time the encrusted back wall, covered as if by ice. The substance seemed like a shroud, concealing the One knew not what. Feeling somehow as if she should imprint these unusual images on her mind forever, Ikella continued to gaze around her, scarcely believing that they had survived crossing the Silent Sands. Could she believe it really existed? She thought that they might even have passed into the peculiarly dangerous place rumoured amongst magic users to hide Tirjhinar, the last refuge of the Sandsingers, and with the recollection of that name she shivered apprehensively then turned to follow the others.

She could not imagine what mischief stirred the memory but suddenly the dry, precise tones of Jocasta, Chief Guardian of Sanctuary, skittered across her mind and she paused, recalling the graceful outlines of the spiritual home and training centre of her Sisterhood. Memories forged half a lifetime ago echoed across the years, as clear in her mind as if it were yesterday. Jocasta's voice curiously entwined with the melodic tones of the strange man she had seen in her Storm vision. Bemused, she had come to a halt in the entranceway and stood, staring blindly down into the "pool" that contained only a thick film of the ice-like substance and the body of the child's mother, seeing nothing. Supporting herself, one hand on the glassy waterfall over-hanging the pool, the other holding her Staff with its new wings fluttering, she was completely caught up in a random memory. Hearing Jocasta's warning voice once more, she was struggling to regain her equilibrium as she was simultaneously teased with the recollection of her storm vision, that of a handsome man with strangely compelling eyes. The others in the group carried on, unaware of Ikella's distraction, hurrying forward out into the open once more, shaking the dust off their sandaled feet as if overjoyed to be leaving the cavern alone with its burden of death, and yet Ikella lingered, the awakening of a particular memory troubling her. She could not have been more than fifteen name days old when, after finding her in one of the great libraries attempting to read an ancient spell chart, Jocasta had spoken to the young Sorceress in training, the Guardian's voice harsh and quite abrupt.

"I hear your interest in the past and its mysteries is quite unlike anything shown by your Sisters in magic Ikella."

Not quite sure if she had done something wrong, Ikella remembered her face flaming and then Jocasta remarked.

"There are many reasons why such interests can be tolerated as you are Opal elect Ikella, but you are exposing yourself to dangerous things. Beneva will always be your Guardian so be sure to listen to her firstly, then to your Sorceress, and lastly to your own true heart before you pursue any such interest further. The secret of our own power must seem very mysterious and wonderful to those without the gift, but we ourselves are but novices. The true power of this world is beyond our ability to imagine or to control, and that power has been locked away so that we cannot find it, meddle with it, or like the Sandsingers of our distant past, cause cataclysmic damage to our world by not understanding it."

Ikella felt a light touch on her forehead and remembered the Guardian saying softly, "You will not remember this conversation unless you need to." and in her head she felt something unlocking, a musical chime sounded and she caught the mocking glance of her own reflection in the pool as Jocasta's voice continued smoothly.

"Remember only this, walk with the One always, take nothing for yourself, seek only to serve and do not seek the past or any part of what is not yours to understand, and if the One wills it, your path will never cross with that of a Sandsinger."

Ikella gazed around her wonderingly, then lifting her Staff once more she stepped out behind the others and walked into the Silent Sands to begin her journey back to Selesh and a much altered reality.

The desperate journey that had brought them to this place was now only a dim memory, the wind was but a gentle breeze, and unencumbered by the woman they had rescued they walked onwards. It was unnerving to see the mouth of the next in line moving, and not have any idea what they said, and Ikella saw how this affected her healers, their men and more importantly the children. She raised a hand to halt their progress, and relieved they gathered together just a short distance from the cavern, Ikella had barely glanced back since she had followed her companions and now she realised that she could barely make out the deep shadowed aperture of its entrance, but decided not to draw attention to this anomaly, as it would only further unnerve her party.

She searched her memory for a suitable weave that she could use, and found one that allowed her to speak to them, as if to a patient suffering from a brain storm. She cast the weave round the group, and with an unaccustomed familiarity found herself able to instruct the party.

"Mina, we are in the Silent Sands now, and for a while you will not be able to hear anything except my voice. I hold you all under my protection and you will hear my directions, though I am not sure how that will affect the children. Now, do you see that rock?" She indicated a high peak that showed in the distance to the west of them, and the entire group nodded. So, she thought, they could all hear her, she returned to her theme.

"I think that may mark the Highland Gap, and it is my suggestion that we make towards it, Strellin."

She addressed one of the men that she had asked to lead the party, "Can you show directions with your cane?" The man turned obediently, raising his cane high into the air above his head, and after five minutes of agreeing the most important signals, like right, left and stop, the party gathered themselves and strode out into the Silent Sands. Somehow Ikella didn't find it difficult to keep the weave going, reinforcing Strellin's directions, encouraging the newly blinded men in their midst and admonishing the children, to the barely concealed amusement of their mothers.

"Telli, pick up your feet or you will gather stones in your sandals. Timmin, don't pick your nose, it's a disgusting habit, and watch your father, he nearly fell over then!"

She felt unusually invigorated, more in touch with her powers and certainly more confident in her magic than she had been in the many Rotations of her world, since she became Sorceress. She hadn't used this weave since she was a novice herself she thought, asking Mina how Davini faired with the baby, even as she remembered that time.

It was as if some barrier in her brain had rolled away with the storm, she thought briefly and then turned her mind to these remote and dangerous parts of the Opal Sands which others called haunted, a barren mysterious silent region which on many of their ancient charts was simply marked as Forbidden. These wastelands rose above them as they wended their way back along the ancient pathway, alongside which dune upon dune of opalescence, strangely dimmed and tinged with an echo of the sickened skies above, shimmered into the distance. Ikella shivered, recalling the countless tales of her youth, which told of travellers lost forever, whose eerie voices crying out for the help that never came remained their only epitaph. It was still early sundown when one of the children took a tumble and crying out revealed that they had passed beyond the Silent Sands. Able to talk amongst themselves again they gathered for guidance, wives making solicitous enquiries of their mates, mothers talking to tired children. Sanra gather the little one to her, and Davinni brought the baby to Ikella, who releasing the weave, noting with amazement that behind them, the sands stretched to the foothills of the high lands above smoothly, all sign of the ancient pathway that had saved them was gone.

To her astonishment Mina and Inahana were busy milking the Irix, who along with her calf had followed them, and so with the baby suckling on his feeding cloth, and the children refreshed they rested, gazing with apprehension on familiar landmarks barely recognizable in this low and threatening light.

As they prepared to leave again, Mina said softly, her voice barely reaching Ikella.

"I think that when we get to Tearchan, it would be unwise to mention the Silent Sands." And then Strellin remarked "They tell tales of the voices of the lost calling to lure others to those lands!"

Inwardly Ikella considered this as the others stood preparing to depart. She found herself assessing the facts coldly, dispassionately, and coming to a decision, an astonishing decision.

She felt almost as if she was not in the right body, it was as if someone more powerful than she pondered a course of action and made plans that she did not even know if she could carry out... but she did not hesitate for a moment.

They were lined up ready to depart, so giving the baby back to Sanra, she faced the line and declared, "On the subject of the Silent Sands or anything that lies beyond, we shall remain just that, absolutely Silent!" and reaching forward her right index finger she touched the centre of each forehead, both male and female, adult and child (with the exception of the baby), saying softly as she had once heard another say.

"Our powers are wonderful and strange to those without the gift, but we are as children to those who knew about the true power of our world. These things are not for us to know about, to seek out, or meddle in. They are in the past and should remain there for the protection of our people and of our world. You will not remember this unless you need to remember, save that we found a woman dying and saved her child, you must forget..." It seemed to her that she felt something lock under her hand, and she thought that she detected a momentary flicker of resentment in Mina's eyes, but then her own Senior Healer and best friend bowed her head in submission before moving to take up her customary position in the rear of the column. Ikella gathered her travel pack, and moved past the men to take up the lead from Strellin as they walked on, ignoring the dust laden atmosphere and the pain in their travel worn feet and legs in search of Tearchan.

"I think that we are heading in the right direction." Mina had been looking at the outlines of the Broken Lands, high above them and at some distance. "This light is impossible, " she continued almost as an aside to herself. Ikella nodded agreement, for some time she had been conscious of a small determined breeze that was blowing steadily against her right arm and experimentally she tried turning into it and immediately the strength of the breeze increased, as if it tried to prevent her taking that direction. She narrowed her eyes, and looked up at the sparkling wings at the top of her Staff, and as if she had commanded them, they swung and spread like some errant flyby.

She slowed her pace, conscious that she walked fast, and that the others were hampered by two blind men and by the children who were too little to keep up the pace she was setting in her current fractious mood. She watched the wings droop a little, and then picked her course, keeping to the left of the low breeze, vividly aware now of the failing light and the deep gloom of the cloud overhead. Behind them, there was an eerie glow, as if some Greeeyn city's night time lights burned in the wastelands where no city stood, but Ikella restrained herself from pointing it out to her companions, who had already forgotten into what peril they had strayed.

They had already walked for three sectors and the children were tiring when the breeze shifted its position and she turned them toward the cliffs again, finding that here the ground was firmer, their path was not so impeded with dunes, and that they were in fact making really good time. She looked back along the line of her followers, and to her pleasure she saw that they had caught her up, were able to keep to very nearly their normal walking pace, and that even Dovid and Derun were managing. Relieved at this sign of returning normality, she relaxed so much that she nearly missed the signs that told of a breacthin lying in her path, and nearly walked into its maw.

The first she knew of the carnivorous plant was the horrid slithering of the sand falling away at her feet, pouring down and into the gigantic gelatinous feeding tube hidden below her. She knew that breacthin tended to grow lying buried just below the sand and spread out flat until their prey chanced across its sensitive inner leaves, but breacthin were small plants surely? They were used by careful householders to dispose of waste food in times of good harvests and certainly were commonly thought to rid villages of unwanted night crawlers and rodent kind. She had observed them as a child and thought them quite efficient but horrid, for having triggered a reaction that brought the leaves, armed at the tip with poisonous spikes, rearing out of the ground its prey was literally trapped inside, clinging on desperately trying to evade the plant's rippling movements only to be impaled on the lashing spikes, or paralysed by clutching at the secondary hairs which grew along the fleshy edges of those same leaves. Whichever fate befell the victim, the outcome was inevitable. Having lost their footing, they would slide helplessly into the cavernous maw of the plant which exuded a sticky acidic substance which could strip the living flesh from the bones of any small creature which strayed into its path.

To Ikella, all of this knowledge released into her mind like some tidal wave, but instead of paralysing her with fright, it seemed to reinvigorate her, and even as she recognized this plants monumental size, she realised the danger facing her companions and cried out.

"Back! Back! All of you! Now! Run!"

The Council of Nine gathered the party swiftly, and amid a babble of horror they stood, walking Staffs raised to defend themselves, wide eyes fixed on Ikella who had raised the Opal Staff against the plant. For a moment none of them could believe what they saw, as around the Sorceress, spiralling from the sand itself seemed to grow a whirlwind. It struck the great fleshy leaves, forcing them outward, flinging Ikella clear of the dangerous heart of the plant and back out on to the path. The vortex increased, making horrible sucking sounds, as the plant, its huge leaves whipping backward and forward, was wrenched from its lair dismembered, torn apart, and disbursed along the edge of a pathway, which gleamed eerily opal against the darkening shade of the surrounding sand. The whirling winds seemed to be chuckling, the plant was screaming in its death throes, and then there was nothing... no wind, no plant, no noise, just a shaken group of women surrounding the shocked Sorceress and their families. They gathered together for a brief moment of reassurance and then holding hands they swiftly followed the gleaming path scoured by the winds, clutching the baby, children and possessions despite hands that trembled with terror.

As they followed the glimmering path through the increasing gloom, Ikella felt a gentle breeze lift her cloak, it seemed to be tugging at her and raising her eyes she followed the direction in which the gentle pull was guiding her. Not ten feet from them was the Irix and her calf. As she stepped out again the Irix matched her pace, and when the path turned gently, she was not surprised that as their paths converged the foundling of the storm had started to cry, softly but hungrily.

The cliffs which had reared high above them over the last two sectors were dwindling away to a set of low foothills that Ikella thought she recognised, though she could make out nothing like the cheerfully painted barns and corrals of Tearchan. True night had descended during the recent turmoil, even Ikella was exhausted so she was grateful to stop in a small clear area, which had some scrubby bushes for the Irix to feed on, and from which a few twigs could be gleaned to start a fire. The children worked as their mothers directed, the men gathered in the centre of their small group and spread blankets, arranging possessions together, forming family sleeping places. Ikella watched as Mina sang a small spell, creating a soothing for one of the women who had burned her finger starting the meagre little fire. "Let me" she found herself directing a thin stream of power towards the blaze, which steadied and strengthened so that they could at least maintain some warmth for the baby, while he was changed and fed. Derana handed over the child's swaddling cloth to Andria, who was busy containing a pair of happily kicking legs, and as she did so, Ikella came to stand over the child and she found herself thinking 'Young man, if only you knew the danger that we are in, would you still kick as happily?'

She sat to feed the baby on the generous offerings collected from the Irix dam by Mina.

They soon prepared to walk on again, for they could not be that far from Tearchan. She had assessed their distance by the break in the Highlands above, noting that one or two of the obelisk like outcroppings formed a right angle on the path behind her, and lifting her Staff, grimly turned back to what should have been the path to the hospice, which was built at the crossing of four main tracks along the Fringes. It was not as she had known it but it was there, strewn with debris, its defining marks erased, the textures and patterns known only to the Shalhanhi all but invisible. She frowned, her mouth thinning as she thought of the difficulty now facing travellers navigating one of the oldest and best used trails.

She found herself praying silently, as she walked.

'Mirayen, First of the Winds, I am your Woman of Voice, Sorceress of the Opal path, may I speak with you?'

She looked up into the blackening roil of cloud above, anxiously seeking some sign from the sky, from the dimly perceived land around her, from the glimmering path ahead. Seeing nothing obvious, she continued her inward petition as she led the others, more watchfully, more in keeping with their slow pace, through scrubby bush and along the barely perceptible path ahead.

They were out into the open desert now, away from the edges of the land above. She murmured almost to herself.

"Mirayen, it is my petition, that I guide these honoured sisters and their families to safety, that I return the children to their homes."

Sure that she had heard or felt something, she paused for a moment but there was no sound, no movement and she felt fear touch her. It was easy enough to lose your path in daylight, and hard to navigate by the stars. Under this cloud cover, with no landmarks, it was all but impossible. The others, sensing her uncertainty, paused as Ikella looked back.

The Council of Nine, serene and calm, their men trusting, children inquisitive, awed by their first experience of night travel. Her students protecting the baby. Her faith returned to her as she prayed.

"Mirayen." she called as she strode forward, picking up the pace a little, then, "As Warden of the Nine Winds, I summon you."

She stumbled over her new title, but continued more confidently.

"I implore your guidance for the children of your Sand. Guide us safely to the haunts of man, where we can restore Daro to his family."

She had noted that from somewhere ahead of her there were sounds. Were they voices? They faded, and she paused, waiting till the others caught her up. Then, raising her Staff and her voice she called again.

"Mirayen. Protect your children, guide us home."

She held up her Staff, the crystal wings fluttering, palpable waves of power shuddering through the shaft, somehow awakening the great Opal. It blazed forth as she placed her other hand on the baby's face. In the featureless dark of the desert, she saw something reflecting the light of the Opal. She heard a strange thrumming noise, as the wind came at her command.

Gently spinning in a small pillar ahead of them, it whirled up the opalescent Sand in a shimmering tower. It bobbed and weaved, advanced and retreated, as if encouraging them to follow. The wings atop Ikella's Staff turned towards the breeze and struggled to fly, pulling at her. So it was after only another half sector of walking, taking only short breaks to rest the exhausted children, that Ikella witnessed the dark dawn again and in the sickened light of a new day, saw with mounting horror, that ahead of them lay the wreckage of the hospice of Tearchan.

Chapter 7 - Missing

It was lying in a shattered spoil of precious brick. Its gaily painted symbols of hope, offering all who travelled shelter, treatment and safety were now unreadable in the totality of its destruction, and Ikella with the certainty of her magic, knew that nothing here lived and she wept. She wept for Tearchan and the stillness of death that hung over it, not as other women weep perhaps, but her eyes glittered unnaturally and her long slim fingers convulsed on the great Opal headed Staff. Her throat clenched on a storm of angry words that came flooding to the surface, and she struggled for control knowing that she must not inflict her rage on the others. A frisson of fear touched her, for to tell truth she could not remember a time when she had felt so furious for the waste of it all, yet so alive and so in touch with the Source of her power. She stood for a long moment concentrating, then announced in a voice she hardly recognised as her own.

"I will scan for survivors, here in Tearchan, and beyond. Set up camp and prepare to receive the wounded." The harsh voice died away as she turned from the ruins and took a deep breath before allowing her eyes to focus on the Opal at the head of her Staff, slowly calming, attuning herself to the purpose in hand. As she entered a state of meditation the Staff chimed a long sonorous note, the stone blazed forth a shimmering spectrum of colours as surrounding her, blossomed the aura of her power. Sanra, Mina, Inahana and Tirana, assisted by Strellin and the other sighted men braved the ruins, Staffs probing the wreckage of the sleeping halls, the kitchens and storerooms. Without a word Midara steered the others away across what had been a courtyard, and gathered them in an angle of two barn walls. Silently, and without instruction, adults and children alike set about providing shelter and food. Still at their full height the walls gave solidity to the improvised camp and it was not long before nimble Telani slung a trarpe that she found flapping dismally in the wreckage to make temporary roofing, while the others laid out blankets and rolled exhausted children into them. Midara took charge of the baby, slinging him into a shawl and securing him to her body while a small fire was lit, a stray cooking pot retrieved and almost the last of their precious water was set to boil. As some normality was achieved they started a small foraging group to retrieve shards of wood and fill water skins from the stone tank they located in the back of the barn, but as the Sorceress returned to them, the full disaster that had befallen them was revealed in her first stumbling words.

'shiarjha!"

Her hands shook and her teeth chattered on the rim of the mug that they eventually pressed her to take. She looked up unseeing, and blinked at the gathering healers. She turned to Telani and continued, her low voice strained and shaking.

'she so wanted to greet you from Song Walk. So like a fool, I agreed that she could meet up with us here. I suppose she wanted to surprise you."

Horrified they realised that tears were pouring down her face. She cuffed at them impatiently, before continuing.

"I have sought for ten seilings, both in Fringe and out on the trails for any living thing. I have even searched for animals, but the Source is so disturbed, I cannot be sure of what I have found."

Her voice shook ominously as she said flatly.

'Save for our group, nothing here remains alive."

Her eyes strayed to where the rest of the party walked in line, probing the strangely drifted sands close to the fallen buildings with their walking Staffs, before continuing, her voice hoarse with restrained emotion.

"Worse still, I cannot tell if she ever reached here, I could find no trace at all."

Conscious that everyone was gazing at her in total bewilderment, Ikella explained in a whisper.

'shiarjha was to travel a day after we left, bringing ointments and salves for Renna."

Her eyes blurred as she remembered Renna, a particular favourite recently promoted to become the resident Healer, then she thought of her young team and her colour fled.

"I think that we have likely lost all of them, unless they escaped somehow. I knew of at least three patients here."

It was too much to take in, and her eyes flooded as she murmured.

"Oh, Shiarjha, why didn't I bring you with us?"

Mina and the men were now conferring over the pitiful bundles retrieved from the ruins of the main building. They were lying in a neat row, and the men, helped by Derun and Dovid were digging to provide decent burials for the victims. Ikella noted them, silently telling her own songbeads for the lost healers. Those with her withdrew to the other side of the fire leaving the Sorceress in some privacy until the rough burials had been completed. There was no time to perform the rituals. From the way that the healers concerned had donned the shantana, a soft cloth face mask used to prevent the transmission of infection, Midara guessed that the decomposition of the bodies was much advanced. This was borne out by the pale faces of the burial party as they returned to their encampment and set about changing clothes, consigning what they wore to the fire.

The men drank thirstily from fresh water skins as Mina totalled the losses grimly.

'so far we have found eight. Five men including Harran, one of our own doorkeepers who came to get his back fixed. However, we haven't found Renna, nor Nianina, her second year girl."

She eyed the Sorceress warily as she spoke hopefully.

"My Deshun, you know the one that was so good at bone setting?"

She continued, telling off the casualties on her fingers.

"Beshana, Toranna, Siobini our Healers."

Unconsciously she had already accorded to Siobini (a student) the title of full Healer, to which Ikella did not demur, as Mina continued the sombre roll call.

"Patients! Harran of Selesh, Miokinish of Caranchar and his brother Tenash. Haminish (the stores man) and Seshan, one of their Inesh guards."

Her lips turned down as she announced.

"Missing Healers. Annona, Renna and the other Inesh girl Diran, but there could easily be others, including…"

She seemed about to continue but then, shockingly, Ikella broke in harshly.

'shiarjha, Sorceress-elect of the Opal Sands! My Sister in Sorcery. My chosen successor, my responsibility, whom I fear I have failed most grievously."

Aghast, those who did not yet know stared across the leaping flames at Ikella. It was unusual for both the Sorceress and the Sorceress-elect to be away from the clan together, but not unheard of. Usually where only the Sorceress' presence would suffice, her elected successor would remain with the High Council of their sands so that the clan were reassured that in the case of disaster, there would be a smooth transfer of power, not that these precautions had ever been needed in the entire history of the Sisterhood. However, as the Guardians advised, it was better to avoid taking risks, than regret them afterwards.

It was Sanra who ever practical, broke their mood, she stretched and groaned with the pain of over-tired muscles as she did so and Mina leapt to her aid with a pot of salve that she had been treasuring to her, cupped in her hands to warm it.

"Oh, I found a few things we needed!"

She exclaimed.

"I have ambar root for aching backs and feet, as well as salve for Dovid and Derun's eyes!"

She proceeded to delve into her bag, from which she produced clay pots with tanbark stoppers, and stone pots with leathern covers, held in place with a twist of hide. Lastly she produced an expensive flask made from sand paste, which contained a clear fluid on which Ikella pounced.

'Stillglass!"

She hissed and Mina frowned.

"Is it really Stillglass, my Deshun?"

Ikella was forced to admit that till she got back to Selesh it would be impossible to test, but she could not restrain herself from staring at the container. It was truly beautiful, a tall tapering shape, tinged with a shade of green and crowned with a stopper made of the same clear material. It was old, very old she thought, from a time when the Guild Halls included men who could work sand paste till it ran in the heat of their furnaces, till it bubbled to form vessels, till the Song stopped and the paste cooled and cured. It was as though she could see it happening. She yawned, her thoughts drifting as she looked through the flask, and the clear liquid it contained to the fire beyond, where the flickering flames danced hypnotically. Wearied beyond bearing and overwhelmed by the new found intensity of her own emotions, her eyelids drooped, she was only dimly aware of the camp settling down around her and still she gazed into the ancient flask and through it into the firelight beyond, till Mina's voice suggested that she lie down on her blanket, where she slipped into deep and dreamless sleep.

Sometime in the few hours remaining of night, she awakened. Dimly aware of a soft murmuring voice she rolled over and raised herself on one elbow. Midara and Telani were feeding the baby. She must have attracted their attention for they both looked up and Midara smiled reassuringly at her as she wrapped him more firmly, lifting him up and patting his back. Telani took him back to the nest of warm blankets he had been sleeping in and sat with him, watching as he drifted off to sleep.

Midara gestured silently that all was well, and she lay down again, aware of a gentle rasping sound. Her eyes strayed to where the Irix was gently tugging at some dried fodder, her calf curled in sleep beside her. Ikella smiled and slept.

Chapter 8 - Return to Caranchar

When again a darkened dawn revealed the Opal Sands in a greyed shimmer, the travellers had already gathered at the edge of the improvised burial place and the rituals for the dead were performed. The very air seemed thick with sorrow, their voices were muted and they sought in vain for solace. They were ready for the road, bundles packed with only the basic necessities and water skins full, they filed from the small cemetery and turned resolutely on to the track for Caranchar. They could not delay here, for the stone water tank was nearly dry, and they had only crumbs to satisfy the children's hunger.

With Ikella leading they took the trail to Caranchar, and even the most reticent of the party grew hoarse commenting on the changes to their path. When once the inner membranes of their eyes would have been engaged to shield them against the glare from the glittering ground, now, they were able to proceed without lowering them. They were swinging away from the Broken Land, every step taking them deeper into the heart of their desert, nearer to Selesh, the ancestral seat of power. The Sands seemed bare of all others as they followed the trail to Caranchar, to where their missing might have fled for help.

A well populated township, Caranchar was built high on the Zurian pass overlooking the strange blue Sands of its neighbouring desert. With a well-fortified cliff top location and ample supplies of water from springs which ran deep underground, Caranchar was the obvious place from which rescue parties could be launched to aid travellers and smaller, less significant places.

They kept a steady pace, the wings atop Ikella's Staff fluttering as she led the way, taking note of the patterning by which the Shalhanhi travelled the invisible pathways of their Sands. From time to time she stopped, allowing the chain made by her companions to close up on her. They rested in the shadow of a towering pinnacle of rock at the Height of Sun and waited patiently for the heat to disperse, always aware of the rolling cloud above, which dulled the iridescent sand into a pallid representation of its former glory, and subdued the bronzed tinge of the monoliths about them.

They noticed that the tiny "waymarks", left to remind visitors where to turn on the path, were now well more than man height above ground level, and as they walked out onto the pathway for the last part of their journey, they were all puzzled by the sharp incline that they found themselves climbing, for the track seemed to undulate in a most unfamiliar way. To their left the sands stretched, dune after dune into the distance as the wide interior of the desert opened up. To the right as they climbed the ridge that now carried the track to Caranchar, it was as though the land had sunk away, to their curious eyes it seemed that some force had stripped the sand down almost to bedrock, well below its normal level by the height of three men or more. They clustered together peering down at the strange vista revealed below them, for none of them including the Sorceress had seen anything resembling this new scenario.

Regular skeletal outlines jutted from the sand, seemingly clustered at the base of the rocky outcrop that bore the track upward to Caranchar and the Zurian Heights on which it stood. Many of these had a peculiar ovoid outline and the party stared in troubled silence, none of them confident enough to raise a question, none of them wise enough to offer an answer, all of them thankful that the higher the track wound, the nearer they were to Caranchar and comparative safety.

It was getting dark already by the time the weary group made out the walls of the town. The children were flagging and in several cases an adult was forced to carry a little one on his shoulders. Tempers were frayed with exhaustion, and Ikella was glad of the assistance of the two novices, so unsteady had her own legs become, but their arrival was less of a relief than the dawn of another terrible shock. Where gates and gatehouse had stood there was but a splintered heap of spoil. Where guards should have challenged the arrivals, only a sand choked gap remained. Ikella led her group of survivors through the gap in the wall, and simply stood stock still, unable to believe the evidence of her eyes.

All of her energy, her expectation, drained away from her as she halted in what should have been the town square, gazing at the shattered buildings around her. She could see that the level of the land was now changed dramatically, sand had piled up on sand, driven by what could only have been forces beyond her understanding. The walled towns of the deserts were few and far between, usually stationed at vantage points on well travelled trails. Here in Caranchar were the markets of the eastern Desert, not too far from the neighbouring Azure Sands and a route directly to Selesh ensured swift passage for her envoys, and a plentiful source of supply for her Healers. Just below the Drekken Pass only a half days tramp from Selesh, an open trail ran, outward to othersands or to the Highlands of the northern hemisphere. Finally, Ikella understood that the town that she had passed through, less than a ninenight ago, no longer existed. They stood struggling to orientate themselves. Here a heap of rubble was identified as one of the local inns, across the rubble-strewn street, that pile of broken wood and stones was the Headman's house. For once, Ikella was totally silent, and her companions too shocked to speak, drew together and looked after the children and their exhausted men.

Telani uncertainly holding the foundling child, watched while Andria and Davini coaxed milk from the Irix, who had tirelessly paced alongside the strange group of human travellers. The Irix calf was faltering, she noted with sympathy, even their own children were asleep on their feet, and she knew that they could go on no longer.

However, she hid a smile in the shadow of her cloak's hood when Mina, taking the baby from her, handed him to Ikella to feed with the cheerful comment, "Here is something to do, if you want to restore your spirits after such a shock!" Leaving the Sorceress to feed the baby as the others busied themselves finding shelter. That night they lay, curled together where they had arrived and slept the sleep of the dead.

Chapter 9 - Rude Awakening

The babble of voices that roused them the following day was not re-assuring. Children ran about unrestrained, and already the Council of Nine were remonstrating with a half naked woman who had been disturbed as she rifled through their belongings. Taking stock of their situation, yet mindful of her dignity, Ikella rose to her knees and using the cowl of her cloak to conceal her interest, looked carefully about.

The sky was lighter here she thought but still above her head the clouds rolled thickly, menacing in colour, viscous in aspect, and the ghastly lilac-tinged light hurt her eyes. Retrieving her precious Staff from under her blanket she placed the baby down, before rising stiffly to her feet, and attempting to get some idea of the time of day. At a distance groups of local people eyed them suspiciously, staring at the Council of Nine and their families. She saw men being guided by youngsters, who were delving into the rubble around them as they passed her, one of them so bold as to say openly.

"Go away. This is our place. We have no room for strangers. Go."

Lifting the baby to her shoulder in a practiced move, Ikella saw Sanra smile as she returned to the low voiced conversation that she was conducting with Mina. Ever watchful, their eyes turned this way and that, Sanra's returning to see that her child was safe even as the youngsters of the town scavenged nearby.

Ikella gently patted the baby on the back looked to see where their Irix was, and froze in horror. Too late to intervene, she witnessed the Irix, it's throat cut, falling to its knees and with a low moan dying in the sand beside its terrified calf. The women of the town were gathered around, laughing in triumph as the bleating calf ran straight to Ikella, who on regaining her feet, had raised her Staff. Anger flooded through her as the tiny orphan ran straight to her and sheltered, butting her legs and disappearing into her billowing cloak. At that, the baby cried out too, stretching its arms wide, as she cloaked herself in her aura, and turned to deal with those who had destroyed the dam.

The cheering crowd fell back in silence as they perceived her fury. Her aura sizzled and sparked around her and Ikella, enraged beyond words at their needless cruelty, did nothing to allay their fears.

She planted her Staff in the town square, plunging it into the sands and allowing the full chiming tone to ring forth, as it did when she was empowered. The great stone at its head flared into life and in a circle of not less than sixty spans, the light blazed harshly. As the people surged forward into its brilliance, Ikella noted with pity their fatigue, their lack lustre eyes, the air of desperation amongst them. As she drew breath to speak, a woman sank to her knees, a bloody knife clutched in the hand that bore witness to the terrible death of the Irix. The woman bowed her head, speaking in a quick nervous manner, anxious to appease the Sorceress.

"Deshun, forgive us, we should have realised that this Irix was yours to sacrifice, but we are so hungry and our children have had no clean food since the Storm. Many have perished, many are blinded, our stores destroyed or used, our bellies are empty and our breasts are dry, what else could we do?"

The child in her arms wailed suddenly, and Ikella saw what a terrible thing motherhood was. The mothers of the town had either to watch their children die, or kill the Irix dam to feed their own young. Her anger dissipated, the brief flush of energy it had given her waned again, but she maintained her grim aspect and her magical aura as she declared, "The dam was in milk, see her calf is but young, and now you have condemned it to the death that its dam saved us from." She waited for her words to sink in, and then strode forward, showing them the baby. "Had it not been for the Irix, we would not have come to safety. Our own children would have gone to the winds without her milk. I claim the sandrights of this boy child, orphaned in the Storm. How shall I feed him tonight? How shall I feed the other children here with us?" Wearily, she laid the baby on the blanket beside her. As she did so, the Irix calf lay down beside him, and she stood protectively over them considering what she should do. At last she raised her hand imperiously.

"It is my judgement that you exceeded all codes of normal behaviour in slaughtering an animal, plainly in the possession, or in the company of visitors to your town. I will not rule on this now, but I will take advice on the situation here before I do so. We have no need of your hospitality tonight, we will keep to ourselves and call you to account tomorrow!"

The women of the town accepted her judgement, albeit reluctantly, and the Healers drew aside from them, regained their own little shelter, built of blankets and staves of broken wood, and managed to feed the baby, and the orphaned Irix calf on the remaining milk. They needed rest, warmth, and food, but they recoiled sickened from the meat that was offered by the bewildered townsfolk, who plainly thought that Ikella had wanted the Irix for herself. The healers disposed themselves round a small fire, back to back ready to protect each other as the shadows fell, and night drew in. They managed to make a meal from some grain, drank boiled water, and stayed by their own meagre fire, shivering and huddled in exhausted groups, trying between them to soothe the baby who wailed incessantly. Later that night, the orphaned calf bleated piteously for its mother, fitfully staggering to its feet to look for her, butting at Ikella's hands urgently, before falling asleep curled in a heap of misery.

Mina looked at Ikella worry, written in her eyes.

"We will be hard pushed to get back to Selesh with that calf alive" she commented, 'some of the townsfolk would have liked to add it to the stew pot tonight!"

Ikella snorted.

"I don't think that they would dare try anything now," she commented shortly, nestling little Daro close to her protectively, and gazing sympathetically at the orphan calf.

"My main concern is how to feed it... I don't recall it trying herbage, or if it was only suckling. We may have to get the calf back to a herd, but how?" She looked down at the baby, resting against her breast, sleeping restlessly.

"How could they have killed the poor dam, how could they?" Ikella was murmuring to herself, and Mina could have wept with frustration, for it was suddenly very clear to her that the Sorceress, who had command of unimaginable power, could not see how to use that power to solve practical problems. Perhaps she was not able to use magic for those purposes? She suddenly caught herself dreaming of laden tables, magically appearing in the town square…and her empty belly gurgled as she slept.

The Sorceress lay down, rolled in her cloak and prepared for sleep, with the feeling that the whole of Pelshar was weighing her down. How would they feed the child, the older children, themselves? How would they be able to lead the Irix calf, how could they keep it with them, who would it follow with its dam no longer there? Still exhausted from the journey she found herself yawning mightily and, try as she might, she could keep her eyes open no longer… A little warmth seeped into her and she slept, despite her wish to solve just one of the conundrums whirling in her befuddled brain.

The little orphaned calf however solved the problem of caring for it till they reached Selesh, by inexplicably dying in the night. They found it huddled on the sand in the spot where its mother had died, legs curled underneath its body, face tucked in as if it still slept. Daro crying piteously had woken them early. He trembled, clinging to Ikella as she lifted him into her arms, rocking him gently but though wrapped warmly in her cloak, he lurched against her, shuddering and inconsolable. Alarmed by his distress, the Sorceress walked across to where the calf lay only a few paces from her, and then she understood. Death had come so gently, that she found it difficult to believe that never more would those bright eyes open, never more would it butt her hands, seeking food or merely to touch its nose against Daro, its milk brother. Sadly, she touched the soft baby fur of it, straightening and stroking the velvet covered ears whilst she wept, and it was there that Mina found them.

Rallying the others to assist her, Mina covered the little animal from view, for they wanted no more confrontation with the women of the town. Hastily the Council gathered their property, their families and prepared to leave, for now all they wanted to do was to get back to Selesh, the One only knew what damage they could look forward to there. Here the cloud still covered the sun and the light of this new day seemed like that of early winter evening.

As they were packing, some of the women approached, and Ikella paused in rolling her blanket to face them. Her Staff was still planted in the sand where she had left it last night as a clear warning marker. She noted with satisfaction that they approached cautiously, waiting at the clearly defined shadow cast by the Staff, eyeing her apprehensively. Ikella straightened, and faced them, one eyebrow raised enquiringly.

"Yes?"

She gave them little encouragement. However, three women who had clearly been deputed to speak for the group, stepped forward. With them they dragged another, bodily, weeping and terrified. Ikella recognised her as the woman who had slain the Irix dam, and marshalled her features to remain stern, unrelenting.

The crying woman dropped at Ikella's feet her hands covering her face, and here she rocked in a paroxysm of fear, or grief. One of them cleared her throat nervously, and begged humbly.

"Deshun, may we speak with you?"

As Ikella inclined her head graciously, they dropped to their knees in front of her. The elder who had spoken first began.

"We know that we have offended you great Sorceress, but lift, we beg of you, this curse. Take this affliction from our children and restore their health."

She trailed off uncertainly, as Ikella, whose astonishment was plain to see, demanded swiftly.

"What curse, what affliction? Tell me fast, and tell me all of it!"

At Ikella's urgent gesture her most skilled Healers came running to her side, listening aghast to the sorry story. There was a sudden babble, voice upon voice telling of children crying in pain, the distemper running from them, the fever, the vomiting, the cold sweats, the silence of death.

The healers stood listening carefully, till a single look from Ikella sent them running for their packs. Swift explanations made, the men corralled their own children and regained their encampment, as their wives gathered around the Sorceress. She stood for a moment in thought, trying to find some common denominator in which she could devise a cure. When at last she spoke, her voice was harsh, her words encompassing the frightened population were totally uncompromising.

"You must separate those who are sick. Take them to one place to be healed. We are only ten Healers and two novices, but we are sworn to work with you to save your children. We also have children to nurse and feed, and two of our men are also blinded by this plague!" More confidently she instructed the healers. "Separate the sick. Feed them nothing but clean boiled water. Find vessels to boil all water, for the illness likely comes from contamination!"

She paced almost angrily, and Mina nodded as the Sorceress ordered, "Allow no visitors to the infirmary. Healthy people must search for clean bedding, medications, clean sources of water, and vessels not only to boil it in, but to strain and store it." She noted with approbation that her Healers were even now moving amongst the townsfolk, and bent forward to catch hold of the woman who still wept and rocked in her guilt and grief at her feet.

"Come, stand up! There is no curse! It is but an illness, and we are all Healers here."

Ikella could feel waves of misery shaking the other's body but she did not resist the gentle pull, climbing despondently to her feet. Just then another caught at Ikella's arm urgently, shrinking back at the Sorceress's outraged stare, but whispering said "Deshun, forgive me, but her baby died this morning, that is why we thought there was a curse. I just thought you should know."

Her informant slipped away leaving Ikella gazing speculatively at the woman now weeping bitterly in Syrena's arms.

Davini stepped forward, greatly daring, and whispered to Ikella.

"My Deshun, forgive me, but could she feed the baby? Might not that help her also?"

Nodding quietly, Ikella handed Daro, to Davini, who, touching the woman on the arm said quietly.

"What is your name?"

Then, to the woman's whispered reply, added firmly.

"Nadra, we grieve for your loss, but there is a way in which you could earn our Deshun's gratitude."

Nadra raised her head as Davini explained, pointing to Daro, while Ikella held her breath, for grief made people unpredictable.

Davini continued, her low voice coaxing. Then Nadra smiled through her tears and with a sense of satisfaction, Ikella watched her novice help the woman adjust her clothing, till one full breast was exposed, and the hungry baby was offered his first human milk. Ikella watched Nadra closely, seeing her tears sparkling through a tender smile as the wet-nurse looked down, watching Daro's hands open and close in the contented rhythm of a suckling child.

At last as Davini and Nadra, heads together talked in low voices over the sated baby, Ikella, greatly relieved, went to see what devastation could have reduced a township on the Fringe of her Sands to such savagery.

Chapter 10 - Devastation

An Elder, apparently delegated to attend Ikella, respectfully indicated that the Sorceress follow a small group of residents. Mildly amused by this self appointed entourage, Ikella allowed them to precede her as they picked a way through the rubble, into the main street.

The sight that greeted her was pitiful. As she wandered through the shattered street she was reminded of the cheerful melee of multi coloured robes, which had stretched as far as the eye could see when the market bustled. Now, through the hazy lilac light, broken walls begged silently from the sickened sands, pieces of masonry and wood protruding dangerously from the ground. A multitude of tattered remnants replaced the gaily decorated market stalls, and stood in silent testimony to the devastation visited on this town. Ikella looked in consternation at the level of the destruction, for it seemed to her that every human habitation had been levelled. She paused for a second trying to get her bearings, and her lips tightened as her eyes fell on a child's toy buried in the sand. She had barely paused when she saw, with mounting horror, the hand of its owner protruding from the shattered masonry nearby. She called abruptly to her guides, who wearily taking note of the discovery, shrugged and said.

"Deshun, we know! There is not a house untouched, not a family complete, and of the three thousand souls here before, there now remains about three hundred. We have no food, little water, no animals, no hope"

Stunned into silence Ikella allowed them to lead her a short distance away, then rounding a corner, she saw the living area of the shattered town spread before her. In one of the residential squares, all the gaiety and colour of the market was spread where tents had been erected. The townsfolk had sensibly laid out wood for burning to one side, near to a communal cooking area, from where a solemn crowd watched her progress. As Ikella looked around, her nose wrinkled as she caught an assortment of scents. True she had expected the smell of unwashed bodies, these people had little enough to drink, let alone enough for bathing, but there was something else... and her eyes narrowed and her face became chill as she observed an open foul-pit, far too close to the spring that formed their only source of water. A long queue of women waited patiently to fill pots as the water flowed from a broken basin and on to the ground at their feet. As she watched, a small child urinated into the stream, disdaining to use the privy pit which decently shielded, had been dug to handle the towns needs. She glanced at a deserted well on the other side of the square, and her guide noted the direction of her gaze and said hastily.

"Two days after the Storm we found the water level much altered. Our rope and bucket could not reach water on the third day, so we lengthened it, twice!" she added grimly. Folding her arms across her chest defiantly, before she continued, "The Headman went down the well to see what could be done, but it was dry. No water left at all, just some foul smelling muck in the bottom. So he went hunting for water, and the One only knows where he crawled that night, but he found an old water course and the men have kept it running, or we would all have perished!"

Ikella saw the pain in her face and asked curiously, "Your Headman, where is he now?"

The Elder sighed sadly, before answering.

"Lady, our Headman would not rest. He laboured night and day to make us safe. He was ill ever after he went water searching. His scrapes and scratches, gained in climbing in the wreckage festered and would not mend. His fever overcame him and he died on the fourth night. His poor widow being brought to bed of a son only two days before the Storm never saw him again. Donnesh was a good brave man. He was out in the town on the day of the Storm, collecting orphans, the injured, showing us how to raise tents. When he took ill, he went down to the animal pastures and lay in a pen rather than infect anyone else. He would not even let his wife attend him for the sake of his son! Kateya, our Healer of Blessed memory took him drink, food, but he was too far gone, and he never saw his child again!"

Ikella stood, her head bowed as she heard the short sorrowful tale, and the enormity of the situation washed over her, wave on wave. If this was the only township to be affected it would be bad enough, she thought dully, in the certainty that it was not. She touched her fingertips lightly to her forehead, lips, and heart in the gesture of invocation…saying softly.

"So many men to mourn, so many mothers bereaved, so many whose courage we must salute."

She saw the glimmer of proud tears on the faces around her as she spoke, and suddenly she realised that her nervousness had gone.

'These are people like my own at Selesh!'

She thought, and then her heart jolted with sympathy.

'No, these are my people, however misguided and desperate. They are deserving of my respect. Deserving of my care!'

She moved to look at the temporary water source, as it splashed from a greening stone basin. It ran in a sputtering flow, much wasted by sporadic gurgling shudders, which caused great gouts of water to overshoot the bowl. Black silt discoloured the old baked-sand pipe from which the water poured, and even as she watched, a woman lashed out at a small rodent dislodging it from inside the water pipe. Squealing the creature ran amongst the crowd, till a group of cheering children grabbed it, dashing it against a rock. A boy snatched it up and hid it in his scrip, and the sickened Sorceress understood instantly what manner of disease they faced.

Her sombre silence had affected the crowd, who shuffled apprehensively under her gaze, till she crossed to the spring, and the queuing women backed away as she placed a hand on the baked sand pipe.

"This water cannot run clean while rodents infest its course."

She announced scathingly, "Precisely what have you done to clean the outflow? Clear the obstruction that is causing that spluttering."

The crowd shuffled under the severity of her stare, but offered no answer to the mortified Sorceress, who stalked forward and laid her hand on the basin.

Closing her eyes she sent a trickle of power scouring through the stone. Blackened slime erupted from it dripping to the ground in greasy threads. The bowl glowed suddenly red hot. Water hissed and steam rose. The green mould cracked and dried, falling like dust to the flag-stones below the cooling basin. Now, the Sorceress altered the focus of her power, trying to sense the water channels source and strength. Her sharply enquiring mind seemed to follow her tracing spell, and she sensed a hard blockage at a bend in the pipe, to which she applied a gentle thrust. There was a soft scraping sound, a small shower of rubble clattered into the bowl, and the outflow increased dramatically, drenching the front of Ikella's cloak.

She shook it, as a buzz of appreciation rose around her, but she raised a hand, and silence fell again.

"There may be other sources of water." She spoke flatly. "That one is nothing like enough for all of you, besides you have not done enough to keep it clean. My healers will come to you this evening and show you how to clear the area, how to run off the waste so that it can still be used for washing. All water must be boiled from now on, if you have stored water, my healers will give out stoneroot to purify it. No-one must foul that water, be they man, woman, child or animal!"

She scowled blackly for effect and added sonorously, "On pain of instant death!"

Turning abruptly from the relieved, yet shocked crowd, she entered the tented town. One glance showed her that even now her Healers had set aside two large tents and were working with the people to gather the sick and injured for treatment and quarantine.

There was much muttering amongst the populace as she passed between the tents, and she slowly became aware that the crowd had fallen in behind her, and that she was being escorted by most of the survivors. An elderly man leaned forward from his seat outside a tent, craning blind eyes skywards as he tried to work out what was going on. His wife drew him back, and bobbing a curtsey to the Sorceress, she hastily told him.

"Mostaq, our Deshun approaches. Quick you fool... On your feet or she will be angry."

Ikella paused then stopped in front of them. Caught between safety and manners Mostaq leaned heavily on his wife for support. Looking frail, frightened and ill, the woman kept her eyes downcast, plainly fearing that they had committed some terrible indiscretion, and Ikella, seeing with pity their uncertainty, the hunger for acceptance, made a decision. She struck her Staff to the sand, lighting the area with the blaze of the great Opal, before asking with deliberate courtesy, in the time-honoured fashion of her people.

"Honoured Father, Revered Mother, may I share your shelter this day?"

As she sank to the ground in front of their tent the amazed occupants, hardly believing their ears, whispered back shyly.

"Honoured Daughter of our Sands, we welcome you to our home."

Suddenly, Ikella was one amongst many making their resting place in the sandy square. Rugs were brought out of the tents, a richly embroidered blanket was spread for her use, as a simple town square became a court for a visiting Sorceress. As a hush descended on the crowd, Ikella raised her hand in a simple gesture, the Staff chimed deeply, Ikella bowed her head, letting the silence grow amongst her followers before speaking the Ritual words of salutation.

"May the One keep all here in peace, one with another and one with the Sands." As the low murmurs of response were made, Ikella opened her eyes and straightened her back. Now, with the safety of her Healers assured, and the people of Caranchar willing to assist her, she launched into an enquiry the like of which was unknown to Pelshar.

PART TWO - PATH OF SHADOWS

Chapter 11 - Enquiry

She began by asking those assembled to explain what had happened to the town, seeking individual stories, sure that she would find some common interpretation of the event amongst them. The sickly dawn had blossomed into a dry warm day now, and gradually the heat built up around her, until quite gratefully she divested herself of her travel cloak, took up a cushion and made a soft raised seat by piling them together and placing them on the stone steps that marked the place where once a large building had stood. Of the building itself, only one wall remained, and that provided sufficient shelter for the meeting to have congregated naturally at its base. Sitting back to the wall, enthroned on her pillow and cloak the Sorceress could see and be seen by the survivors, who gathered closely around her anxious to tell their tales. One of the resident traders spoke up hesitantly.

"If it please you Lady."

He began, revealing himself as a Clansman by his mode of addressing her. Ikella nodded permission for him to continue.

"My name is Amiz. I serve the town of Caranchar as Senior of the Guild of Weavers. I was in my stall in the main market."

He offered shyly, "I had a good position at the end of the Gathering Square, near to the tavern and near to my house and storeroom."

His face clouded suddenly, and Ikella was hugely embarrassed to see tears welling in his eyes. Giving him time to collect his thoughts, she stood and paced thoughtfully along the steps on which she had placed her seat, until he continued gruffly.

"I sold cloth, good weaving that my son, my wife and two daughters made."

His voice was low, strained with grief. Ikella sat down again, leaning forward, picturing in her minds eye a gaily appointed stall with a Weaver's Guild flag flying proudly. Silver and blue... she thought as Amiz continued, biting back his emotions, his voice guarded.

"Around midday the wind rose suddenly and the sky turned a terrible colour... The visitors melted away, and we were fearful of losing our cloth, it got so windy."

His eyes stared unseeingly into the distance, as if he was viewing another time, another place as he continued.

"My wife went to our home with my daughters, she was ever a one for work! She said that they would make a meal, and weave another length while Abaz my son and I unloaded the stall into our storeroom. When we had finished we were to go home, eat, and plan for the next market."

His voice tailed away for a moment, then, "We never got there! My wife, my daughters died alone! I was not with them."

His wail of grief was so abrupt that it sawed at the listeners nerves as though the town cried out with him. The pain of it was so acute, so shocking that Ikella gasped in empathy as the trader choked back huge unmanly sobs.

"Abaz and I, had just finished. We were locking the store when the winds came, bringing the sand, and anything else that moved with it. I managed to drop the shutter, and turned to see the sky meet the sand, and ..." his voice broke... "It was one Deshun, the sand and the sky... it was one, and it rolled in to us, and buried the town and my family! It took my son six streets and when I found him, he had drowned in the sand, in the winds."

He was weeping openly now and at a nod from Ikella a woman rose and gently led him away.

She stood again, and paced as the stories flowed, walls buried, walls fell, walls crumbled, houses made of stone crushed beneath the weight of sand... it was almost too much to take in, and there was something wrong with the timing of it too. She almost missed that, but one woman strident in her claim to relief from Selesh, the Mother of the Sands as the ancient retreat was known, said something that caught Ikella's attention clearly.

"I want to know where are the relief supplies we were promised? Why is it taking so long?"

She stepped forward frowning angrily, and Ikella, controlling her own tongue with difficulty, nearly missed the most wonderful news she could have wished for.

"Your own elect promised us help. Did she not Bethan?" She directed the question at a tall girl, who nodded emphatically before joining in the conversation.

"somishen Shiarjha, Renna, I think also the one called Annona, and a novice healer came to our stall to buy gifts for students returning from Song Walk." She stated firmly, then as Ikella turned towards her, she added.

"Almost as soon as the Storm settled, they borrowed three Zeglurs to go to Selesh for help, but they have not returned, and we have been left to struggle alone!"

The girls voice although low was vehement, and now the first woman returned to voluble complaint.

"It is no good asking those at Selesh for help." She burst forth bitterly.

"I expect the Clansmen have simply shut the door on us. We are not Sandsworn, we are only Felmin, Fringe settlers. We are only here to provide the markets, the food, the transports. The High and Holy don't have to suffer for it do they? Amid frightened glances and a shocked mutter from the crowd the querulous voice persisted.

"Oh, they can hide behind the Gate in the Rock forever I expect. They have the indoor pastures, they have the deep water supplies while we starve, or die by their winds!"

From somewhere a man's voice rose, soothingly, and Ikella was suddenly aware that she was shaking, afraid. She was unused to facing the people without her Inesh warrior guards she realised, making an effort to mask her consternation at the vindictiveness in the voice of the complainant. She shook her head, wearily, and then saw that a tall gentle-faced man was assisting her combatant, sheltering her against a rising tide of anger from the crowd, and leading her away.

However, everything that she had heard here led her to one inevitable conclusion. Whilst she, and the Council of Nine had been protected by the incantation that she had used to save them in the Silent Sands, others had died. Some unimaginable force had interfered with the passage of time, which seemed to have passed in the outside world at a different pace to that which they had experienced in the Silent Sands. A frown creased her forehead, just how long had they wandered through the Storm? How long had they slept in that strange cavern? The return journey had seemed to take an age, but she had thought that, the illusion of night travel and the peculiarity of not being able to pick out landmarks. Perhaps she should have known better!

She had evidence of it at Tearchan, she realised, remembering the advanced decomposition in the bodies of the dead. Without effort she sought through the crowd for the voice of her tormentor, and heard brief snatches…"No good them thinking that if we can manage two ninenights we can wait four… Why didn't the Healers get here…? We are not even a day's journey away yet they still don't come… Do you think that old woman is a Sorceress really? She is not very magical… And what do you think she can do?"

The muttering of the crowd increased as Ikella paced slowly, aware of argument and counter claims flaring up around her. Feeling every one of her many Rotations of life, aged and wearied by the sorrow of her Sands, she eventually sat cross-legged on her pillows, clapping her hands for silence.

Understanding that those at the back would not be able to hear her clearly, she absently wove a carrying thread into her voice, reaching for the Source more confidently than she ever had before. Startled and pleased by the positivity of response, she began to tell their story.

"There are many things here which I must put before the Winds. There are changes beyond our Sands or understanding, deep changes in the Source itself which I must investigate. Though I grieve that you have waited alone for so long, I could not have come here sooner."

She paused, wondering how much to tell the now attentive people, before continuing decisively.

"I have not been at Selesh in two ninenights at least, I have been accompanying two of my students in the closing of their Song Walk" she smiled shyly at the spontaneous round of applause that this announcement evoked. She continued more soberly.

"Our party has been sand-tranced it would seem, we were certainly lost below Maraken during the Storm." She shamelessly used a term from a popular tale as she spoke, adding as a distraction, the comment. "I have with me the Council of Nine, and it is they who nurse your sick and injured, so they could not be in better hands!"

She proceeded with the story, cautiously taking the nods and smiles at the back of the crowd as indication that the mood of the crowd had not been influenced by the angry despair she had just encountered, "We set out from Maraken on the day of the Storm, and headed for Tearchan. We walked for several hours before we realised that we were not on the trail. The winds were confusing, we thought the sand had shifted in the wind, but as we started to correct our direction we found a traveller, a woman in labour, and we sought to find shelter."

There were sympathetic murmurs from the women at the front of the crowd, and at least one man touched the relics commonly carried around the neck of believers. An awed invocation came whispering through the crowd.

"Mirayen protect us." More confidently Ikella continued her story.

"When we found a small cave, we were exhausted, but worse was to come, for in the night the mother bore her child, and died doing so."

A concerted groan swept the crowd, who shifted, pressing closer to the Sorceress so lost were they in the story she was deftly weaving. She sighed compassionately as she commented. "sadly, she was far beyond help when we found her. It is only by the will of the One that her child survived!"

Reluctantly she delivered the worst of her news.

"We nearly missed Tearchan, so totally has it been destroyed."

A groan swept the crowd. Some of them had friends and relatives there, she remembered listing the dead, names were whispered through the crowd and a woman cried out in agony as she proclaimed.

"Miokinish of Caranchar, his brother Tenash may their names always be held in honoured memory."

She saw a woman weeping bitterly, her friends supporting her, and sighed with true sorrow. She wished there was someone to whom she could relate the whole of her own story, but she had to apply discretion. She knew she had been economical with detail, but the least said about their experience the better. It would only draw unnecessary attention to Daro. She needed to think quietly, and there would be no opportunity for that here.

Just then Mina appeared, to report on the work of the Healers. Welcoming the distraction, she mentally listed the things she must warn them about. The close knit community let the Healer through, and withdrew to allow Ikella and Mina the privacy to confer.

Seating herself two steps below the Sorceress, Mina commented on Ikella's own fatigue, and somewhat to her surprise, Ikella realised that her head throbbed and she rubbed her eyes fretfully.

'This dim light is not enough to see by, ' she thought irritably before she remembered that many of the men could not see at all! She concentrated on taking her Healer's report.

"There are crush injuries my Deshun, but most of them have received adequate aid. They lost their resident healer Kateya when she tried to rescue some of the trapped from a cellar which caved in on them. Someone called Sadorin settled those with the fever, using tilbrin juice, which has reduced the irritation and pain. Sanra has obtained some for Derun and Dovid. Our men are managing at our camp, and Daro is happily nursing."

She lowered her voice conspiratorially.

"My Deshun, we have found a cleaner water source just outside the square. However, the dead bring their taint with them. I don't have to tell you, that with thousands entombed in the ruins, this town is doomed!."

Ikella nodded agreement then Mina said, disparagingly, "There are plenty of sighted men, but they seem apathetic, overwhelmed. I hear that others are unwilling to assist any rescue or recovery!"

At Ikella's uncomprehending stare, she added a token explanation.

"There are few Clansmen living here, most of the survivors are visiting Felmin traders, more worried about their stock and how to get home, than what has happened to Caranchar. Of the Clansmen, one claims to be a wandering Apothecary, on his way from Minchan in the Malachite Sands. He has a clerk and a herd of smelly Zeglurs with him."

As Mina's nose wrinkled expressively, Ikella saw a gleam of mischief, but Mina could hold in her news no longer.

"Deshun, he saw Shiarjha! He even lent her his riding animals to get to Selesh! She had Renna and her trainee with her, possibly even the missing Guard! She is alive, Shiarjha is alive!"

The Sorceress smiled, but said cautiously.

"Until we see her again, we cannot know for sure my Mina!"

To the Healers confusion, she insisted, "Something strange has affected the flow of time I believe. They say four ninenights have passed since the Storm struck Caranchar."

She turned her head, so that no-one watching could read her lips and said, (sotto voce).

Even allowing for inaccuracies, I think that must be correct, or at the least more accurate than our own experience of time."

She raised a silencing hand to quiet Mina's protest.

"Remember the dead of Tearchan? The putrefaction? That was not a day and a half old! Think about it Mina, and keep your own counsel about Shiarjha and the others. I will come and talk to you all later, and we shall pray that they got back to Selesh safely, but if they did, where indeed is the help that was promised?"

A thought struck her.

"What about the children? Is the sickness under control?"

Mina's lips thinned as she replied, "Now we have a clean source of water, and attendants who both know and care about children, they will start to recover. All of them have been cold, neglected and filthy, there are even broken bones that need setting! This town has fallen apart without its headman, its healer and a working Council. The women need to impose order, but they are hopeless! They have no idea of how to prioritise!"

She launched into a mini-diatribe, ticking off her points with her fingers, gesticulating as she spoke and Ikella humoured her friend, affection in her attentive face.

"Cleanliness first, removal of tainted food and water second, and discipline. Get the men to start digging, make a makeshift cemetery to prevent the spread of disease. They don't need to re-invent the wheel! None of it is difficult, all of it is life saving, but this lot have given up!"

Struggling not to laugh at the Healer's outrage, the Sorceress thought.

"Nothing changes my Mina! Give her a sharp stick, with which to stir a snake's nest, and she will be happy for the duration."

The Healer left Ikella gathering her thoughts, as she turned back to her investigation. She did not know from whence the Storm had come, nor why. Perhaps her magic was not powerful enough to remedy this disaster? Perhaps healing and a home at Selesh was all she could offer? However, as she settled down to listen once more, her gaze passed over the wings atop her Staff, and the ghost of an idea flitted through her mind, but retreated before she could grasp it.

"Never mind," she thought, bending her brain to business once more. "It will return when I am ready... When we are all ready."

Chapter 12 - Sand Story

Until the heat in the square signalled the Height of Sun, and the crowd dispersed to sleep until it passed its zenith, Ikella became the focus of attention. Surrounded by the survivors she was shown the pitiful remnants of their lives, in exquisite detail she heard of their losses, saw through their eyes the tragedy unfold, and gradually came the realisation that the whole time that her party had wandered in the Silent Sands time, for them had slowed. Their memories showed them only a few days, even with their journey from Tearchan and yet here, time had passed so slowly that their few days lost had become four ninenights in the outside world. Her heart sank. Selesh must think the whole Council of Nine, together with herself and the students, dead! She must get word to them somehow, if she could find someone willing to take a message!

Deeply troubled, she kept her counsel, and made mental notes to discuss with the others alone, when they could be private, for this smacked of an even greater mystery than those contained in the magic of her practice.

She sat casually amongst the people and gradually she built up a picture of their tragedy, a tower of sand that stretched to the sky, from where the winds had whirled it, into a howling demented pillar of destruction. She heard that the base of this pillar was more than a hundred spans as it screamed across the desert floor, and that it had been powerful enough to lift wagons, trek beasts and whole buildings. She listened with mounting horror to the stories of those who had witnessed this vicious maelstrom, and recoiled with a visible shudder as the man who had been a gatekeeper told her of the end of the storm... his voice gruff, he gave a graphic description of the town's last moments of normality.

"I remember clinging on, Mistress."

Ikella, watching with the diagnostic eye of the trained Healer, saw his hands clenching and unclenching with the convulsive memory of that action.

"The far gatehouse was open to let in a trade train from Darnesh. I suddenly felt cold, frightened, and turned to see it, coming across the Gathering Square straight at me."

His eyes rolled, as if in remembered terror, his hands now describing the height and width of the great pillar of sand. He spoke so softly that Ikella had to lean forward to hear him clearly.

"The winds were taking down walls, ripping buildings apart. I saw the main gate go, my commander and his crew with it."

He hesitated before whispering, "I saw it chase men, women, children. It lifted wagons where they halted, trek beasts flew over my head. Then it hit us!"

His voice failed altogether for a moment, then strengthened, as to a concerted sigh from the crowd, he admitted.

"I hid Mistress, I hid. In the cellar below the watch tower!"

His shame was evident, but Ikella leant forward and touched his hand reassuringly.

"It is natural to fear what one cannot understand."

She soothed, automatically feeding a feather touch of confidence to bolster his courage, adding.

"We hid too, and were grateful that we could!"

The man looked up, relief in his eyes, as he explained.

"It did not start as hiding! The wind snatched up the trap to the cellar, and I thought that someone would fall down into the pit below. I was just lowering it again, when the wind hit the tower so hard that one side of it started to crumble. I saw…"

His voice shook as his emotions surged once more, then strengthened purposefully.

"No Mistress, not just I! We all saw family, friends, homes, our complete lives, torn away."

His voice roughened.

"I was holding on to the ring that lifts the trap."

Ikella closing her eyes, pictured him at the top of the stone watchtower. Set in the walls these towers flanked the impressive pasture gates of the town. They opened out onto carefully tended camping grounds, beside a yard complete with water and fodder, into which visiting traders could put their animals to rest, before applying for a non-residential stall in the market-place. She expanded her memory image now, picturing the scene, the sky darkened with cloud boiling overhead. The fearsome roar of moving sand, the howling of the demented winds. She imagined adding to that sound, the creak and groan of distressed timber, the screams of the doomed and terrified, and shivered as the guard took up his story again.

"Well to be honest, I don't know how it happened. One moment my feet were leaving the floor, and the next, I was falling, head long, and a mountain of sand was falling with me. The trap swung me up and over, and I was hanging inside the cellar, holding on to the rim with one arm wrenched out of its socket. The sand poured in on me."

He took a deep draught from his drink, wiping his mouth with the back of his sleeve.

"Is our Sand cursed Mistress? It was as if the whole of the Opal itself fell on our town! I don't know how I kept breathing, but suddenly it was under my feet, and I could stand and breathe again. The winds dropped, but I was too afraid to come out of the cellar. I was not there for my neighbours, I am shamed, and must live Clanless." These last words fell from his lips as the crowd pressed around consoling him softly.

As Ikella leant back against a wall to consider all that she had heard, a drink was pressed into her hand. She glanced up to meet the calm gaze of Telani, the Amber Sands novice, who had brought baby Daro with her. She sipped the tepid stemmis, and thought that never had a warm drink tasted so good, so reviving. Without thinking, she held out her arms for the child, and Telani gave him to her, smiling as the Sorceress planted a kiss on his head as she took him.

"Forgive me Deshun, but he has been fed, twice, and changed. Now he is awake again, Syrena asked if you could mind him a little. We need to bathe the sick, dispose of soiled linen, without this little one being at risk."

Ikella nodded, distracted by the sweet milky smell of the baby. She found herself relaxing, gently touching Daro's soft baby hair against her cheek, thinking fiercely.

'I could rebuild ten Caranchar's, if only I could bottle and sell that scent.'

She was still distracted as she returned to her place, accepting the loan of another pillow to help support the child, before re-engaging with the topic of conversation.

A woman at the back of the crowd spoke bitterly.

"Did we do some wrong that the winds have punished us so?"

She questioned and Ikella, following the distinctive voice, saw a tall, slender, hollow-eyed woman. Her hair was closely bound by a fine veil, and she wore a black robe, the ragged edge of which proclaimed her a widow. It was the red obesh hanging around her neck that made her stand out, and as she moved, the heavy medallion that the man's sash held was briefly revealed. From the respectful falling back of the crowd, Ikella deduced that she was looking at the widow of the Headman Donnish. However, this was not the time to talk privately with her.

Moreover, the ephemeral idea that had brushed the corner of her mind earlier had returned. It had no shape yet, it was just a glimmer in the dark, and Ikella held her breath, refusing to look at it closely in case it fled again. She rested her head against the baby's, and as his hands reached up to explore her face, the idea locked in place and coalesced into a formula that left her breathless.

'The winds had brought the sands, perhaps she could compel them to take it away again?'

Her attention was caught by further dissension in the crowd, voices were raised as people cried out.

"No-one will go!" and "We hold to Selesh here!"

She looked up to see what was causing so much agitation, and found that a tall, dark Sybillsce clansman was waiting to speak to her. Eyeing him curiously, she could only wonder what had brought him north from the Amethyst Sands to Caranchar before nodding an acknowledgment, tacitly giving him permission to address her directly. The man spoke respectfully enough but Ikella, raising her head, thought his strangely brilliant blue eyes seemed calculating.

"Deshun Ikella, I will take your news to Soloria, your Sister in Sorcery. My Lady would help you were she here. I can travel to the Amethyst Hall at Buerchan to fetch help for Caranchar. It is after all the closest town of your Sands to ours, many of us use the markets here."

Ikella was sure that there was more to this than friendly support, and waited impassively for him to reveal his true purpose. He continued smoothly. "Shall I ask for assistance to prevent the spread of disease? Perhaps the survivors would remove to our Sands temporarily? They must be rehoused while Caranchar is rebuilt!"

Now she could see what he was doing! It took many years to build markets such as those held in Caranchar. They sat close to the Healer Hall at Selesh, and nearly every medication known to their world came here, so that the Healers could try them out. They would eventually teach not only their properties, but their use, even the proper way of growing the plants from which they came. Caranchar depended on this trade for its very existence, and Selesh depended on Caranchar's markets, for without medications what was a Healer Hall? She hissed as she took a deep breath, and the baby whimpered.

There was angry muttering at the back of the crowd. Ikella, looking at the baby, saw his frown, and was suddenly convinced that she had to give Caranchar a chance of survival.

She held up a hand, and the muttering tailed away.

"My respects to my sister in Sorcery, Soloria of the Amethyst."

She spoke diplomatically, anxious not to alienate anyone who could offer assistance.

"I need to see more of the town, before I send for help from anyone. We do not yet know how our Sister Sands fare. However, your offer is appreciated, and will be weighed carefully by the full Clan Council before reply is given."

She straightened her legs, shifted into a position from where she could stand, and carefully supporting the baby with one arm, holding her Staff with the other, she spoke softly to the Headman's widow.

"Will you walk with me? We shall discuss what may be done. My healers will then let those of you with sick relatives see them for a while, before nightfall. I have some ideas, and must meditate on them in peace."

She spoke firmly, reassuring the group that still surrounded her.

"Soon, I shall have some instructions for you. Soon we will know if Caranchar can be saved with or without othersands help. I will consider all offers carefully and I will come back when I have taken some rest."

Nodding her dismissal of her entourage, she returned to the makeshift Infirmary, and ducking into the entrance, regained sanctuary amongst the Council of Nine.

Chapter 13 - Caverns

She returned the baby to Telani, listened to Sanra's account of her days work and walked the Infirmary tent, stopping to lay her hands on each of the small patients, trickling power into their weakened bodies before catching herself in the most enormous yawn. She looked across the bed into Mina's scandalised face, and said soberly.

"I know! I am too tired to maintain my dignity! Honestly Mina, tell me, you who guard my dignity better than I ever could. Of what use is it, to a dying child?"

With the satisfaction of one who has at last said something that she had longed to say, Ikella left her dumbfounded Healer and withdrew to the small Inner sanctum that the students had prepared for her, and slept.

When she woke it was nearly Fall of Sun, and she shook out her crumpled garments crossly. Fastening her cloak, she picked up her Staff, and stepped out to join the Healers. Davini had taken over from Telani, and hastened to tell her that Daro was being fed, that no patients had died, and that the others were resting before the evening meal.

Pausing only a moment, Ikella said briskly, "Then I will walk to the Pasture Walls. If I am to help these people, there is no time to waste. I hear some who will come with me, I will return soon."

Sweeping their awning aside, she departed to rejoin the survivors. They were a large group, headed by Tuennis the Headman's widow, and a slender dark eyed woman dressed in the drab dun colour adopted by Healers. Carrying a sand tablet in one hand and a sharply pointed enscrasure in the other, she respectfully stepped back, lowering her eyes at Ikella's approach, murmuring "Sadorin, if it please you, Deshun."

At this, Ikella paused, raising an interrogative eyebrow.

'If this is the Healer's assistant, she uses a totally unfamiliar name! I don't know it by Clan or by language, which is very odd, but no matter. She looks clean and competent, and I need someone to take notes.'

The Sorceress nodded, noting the bright intelligence of Sadorin's eyes with interest. With the thought that changes were beginning to take place already, Ikella's eyes swept the rest of the crowd.

Consisting of able-bodied men and women, including some teenage boys who carried ropes, they stood waiting her instructions expectantly. She saw that they had all come prepared to work, some carrying digging implements, others makeshift bags for salvage. She paused long enough to gather a few more names and then said briskly, "I want to walk to the pasture walls, so that I can see from the highest point overlooking the Low Pass."

Tuennis, now dressed in working clothes, carried a walking cane and at Ikella's request she turned so abruptly that her husband's badge of office slid on the obesh that held it, so that it hung backwards, down the widows spine. Ikella privately thought was most attractive used that way, as well as useful, in that the bright red of the obesh sash traditionally worn by men of rank, marked her out. In the gathering gloom of early evening, this made it easier to follow her.

They set off behind Tuennis, and at her indication the men began to pull aside leaning timbers, dislodge precariously balanced stonework, leaving the youngsters and the women to begin retrieving usable objects. Ikella, walking with Sadorin in the centre of the work party, watched with interest as Felmin traders laid temporary bridges over gaps in the pathways. She was pleasantly surprised to see that the heavy work was actively directed by Olneth, the Sybillsce clansman who had suggested the wholesale removal of her people to his Sands. Her opinion of him softened a little, for he was not above helping physically either.

She noted his height, his distinctive well-muscled torso, gleaming as he laboured in the ruins. He looked up at her, white teeth gleaming in a broad smile, single-handedly supporting a huge slab of fallen masonry, as his fellows cleared an area for it to safely tumble into.

Her mouth twitched with barely concealed amusement as the slab bounced, landing awkwardly canted against the timbers but Olneth refused to be deflated by this failure and inserted a metalwork rod into a gap, shoving and heaving with easy strength, all the while directing the other men's efforts to achieve their aim. Nodding her approval, Ikella moved on, Sadorin standing near at hand to take notes in the manner of a trained Healer. From time to time her assistant directed the Sorceress's attention to areas of particular interest, saying quietly.

"Excuse me Deshun, but here was an apothecary's shop." as she pointed out a crumpled sign, followed by, "This was a particularly busy inn. We rescued some, but many others are still entombed."

Ikella noted the quick gesture of invocation and hazarded a guess.

"Is this where…?"

She had no need to name Kateya, for quick tears glittered on Sadorin's face as she nodded mutely. Ikella, paused to take out her Song-beads and offer a prayer in the late Healers memory.

They went on together now as the pathway broadened out, Ikella grateful for the local knowledge and the assistance of one who could use notation, making swift decisions. At the sign of the Apothecary's shop she called back down the line of workmen.

"Where is Olneth?"

Seeing the dusty, sweat-stained man approaching, she instructed.

"If your team could dig here first, we might find undamaged medicines that we could use!"

Sadorin took over, listing the things that the Healers especially needed. It was obvious that she knew the shop, for she sketched the layout in the air as she spoke. Around them the crowd chattered with renewed enthusiasm as people found something useful to do. Soon both men and women were gathering the precious containers up in their robes, taking them swiftly to the infirmary to be evaluated.

In this way, Ikella, Sadorin and Tueniss came to the broken outer walls, and stood on the edge of the bluff beside the wreckage of the pasture gatehouse, looking down the valley towards the Azure desert.

Ikella was stunned by the change in the landscape. Where previously the glittering sands had been worn away almost to the bare pink-tinged rock by the constant traffic between the Opal and Azure desert, now there was no visible trail. Dune upon dune of opal sand shimmered dimly into the distance.

She peered down, bothered by the strange shadowing below her (produced by the loss of light she thought grimly) but at least there was still a significant drop, which was essential to the plan slowly forming in her mind.

She struck her Staff to the sand, and the chime echoed down the valley below. The stream of light from the great opal flooded the area, and she saw to her horror that the strange shadows were neither shadows, nor bushes as she had imagined, but bodies. Beasts, men, women and children lying amidst the wreckage of their wagons, and then she recalled that the guard had mentioned letting in travellers.

'So this was what had become of them!'

She thought grimly, peering further over the edge of the cliff, to the anxiety of those who accompanied her, gathering in a shivering group to look at the tragedy as it unfolded below them.

A boy, nearing manhood called out.

"Deshun Ikella, the winds were so bad that the caves are uncovered again."

Intrigued, she retreated from her position and walked along the natural curvature of the cliff to join him. He pointed downward and to his left, and to Ikella's surprise she could see ancient cavern entrances in the rock wall below. She looked closely, peering to see if there was a way into the caverns from the trail, but it the dim lilac light it was impossible.

Standing upright and withdrawing from the edge, she found a shallow depression in the rocky ground and sat down to consider the options. She wasn't sure who or what was responsible for the changes she had seen this Fall of Sun, but by stimulating the townsfolk to help themselves, the process of recovery had begun.

It would not be enough, the destruction here was so complete, the loss of life so great that she doubted her ability to put into practice the plan that she had conceived. She felt a light breeze touch her face, ruffle her hair. It set the wings atop her Staff fluttering.

'Mirayen defend me, for I am surely mad!'

She thought defensively, trying in vain to find a solution that did not involve the use of High magic and, sighing, failed.

Eventually, aware of a groundswell of anxiety amongst her companions, she cleared her throat, and began diffidently.

"There is a way, a difficult and dangerous way to save Caranchar. It is not just a risk to what you have left, I risk my Sands and my life, for in involves the use of High Magic, and powers in which I am unpractised. I will take the risk for you, but you must submit to my will utterly! I need to prepare, will you take the vote on this matter Tueniss?"

The Headman's widow stood slowly, and looked around at those who still accompanied them. A hush had fallen as Ikella spoke, and into that silence Tueniss raised her voice.

"My Deshun, it is not for us to question what you command, or take votes. While my husband lived, he would have struck down any man, woman or child who failed to follow your ruling. He swore his fealty to you when he was appointed, and he took that oath on our behalf. Times change, and in many places towns such as this forget their bonds, abandon their tithes and ignore their Clans, and Clan leaders. Caranchar will not be one of those places. Do I speak for all present here?"

There was a significant murmur of approval from the crowd, and Ikella raised her head, looking around. Everyone seemed ready to follow this woman and yet there was no way that she could permit this, for Tuennis was of the Inesh.

Even as the thought crossed her mind, the woman met her gaze levelly and without fear. She drew herself up, proudly, pushing back the hood of her cloak in open defiance of law, showing her face for all to see, even the men.

She was not young nor was she beautiful, but she had achieved that kind of glowing maturity that comes from inner confidence, the knowledge of love, of life. That she had wept many tears recently showed in the darkness around her eyes, that she had sorrows showed in the furrows in her brow but she stood before them, pride and energy in every line of her body, her face. Ikella nodded permission for her to speak again, and Tuennis continued.

"My Deshun, since the day of the Storm there have been those who came forward to offer help to their neighbours. Many of the visiting dignitaries and othersands traders have put their shoulders under the yoke of Caranchar, but illness, apathy and death has all but defeated us, till you arrived in our midst."

Ikella listened attentively as Tuennis continued, her voice condemnatory.

"As many citizens that worked with us have worked against us."

Her tone grew bitter as she repeated the insults that she had endured.

"I have been called unnatural, deviant! Because I could not leave the dead to lie? I tried to get those in the trade train decently buried, but I was shouted down by those who claim that the traders brought our destruction with them! So I have laboured quietly and at night, to find food, water and solace for orphaned children. Now, I must throw myself on your mercy for exceeding my position."

She bowed her head to Ikella, formally raising her hands in supplication.

"If I have done wrong in directing the town, I am willing to accept your punishment my Deshun."

She began steadily enough.

"I only beg your indulgence for the sake of my fatherless child."

Her voice shook then recovered as she continued.

"My son was born only two days before the Storm, and I had no knowledge of what was occurring in the town, other that it had been destroyed and that Donnesh was struggling to save the survivors. We had guests from Buerchan on trade business, and I was entertaining them when the Storm hit us. It was so quick, one moment I had a husband, a child, a home and a life. The next, the town was gone, along with my husband. Now I have nothing. Directing rescue operations has given me purpose, others see it differently and would cast me out for what I have done." She continued bitterly. "I also know the laws, and as Inesh, I know that I have no rights. That I am forever a slave, and that all I can expect is punishment for adopting my husband's authority!"

Against the mutters from the crowd, her voice, now devoid of emotion, continued.

"Some of the women dug out survivors. Inesh, Shalhanhi, Sybillsce and Zurias have worked together, without question. These women have nursed, comforted, salvaged and protected the men, the children. Others, men and women have laboured against us. I will not name them, they know who they are, the winds know who they are. They have hunted like packs of seobra's, taking by brute force what they wanted."

Her face twisted with sudden hatred.

"Burial parties have been chased away. The dead have been left unburied because of looters. I suspect that potential survivors have died in the wreckage because of this. Although we have no absolute proof, we all know of missing valuables. Dead men have been found without their talismans. Women without their bond rings, too many for it to be coincidence or accident! Is this not so?"

She posed the question to the crowd, and there was a concerted swell of agreement from those around them. Ikella frowned as Tuennis began speaking again.

"I have managed, Deshun Ikella, to find those I can trust to help me. Together, we have dug out the entombed, buried the dead in temporary graves, found food for those orphaned or alone, distributed clothes, made shelters."

She indicated with a brief gesture the tall figure of Olneth standing quietly some distance away from the huddle surrounding the Sorceress.

"I have done as much as any man these last weeks, while my baby went untended, and would have gone unfed to his grave, had it not been for the other mothers who nursed him for me, while I worked. In this I am alone, for I am Inesh. Although of these Sands I have less right to do as I have done, than our othersands visitors."

She put up her hands to her throat and tugged on her husband's obesh, swinging the medallion forward till it hung between her breasts momentarily. Raising it to her lips, she kissed the symbol of her husband's authority solemnly, murmuring, so that the words only came to the Sorceress's augmented hearing.

"I have honoured my promise, my love. I have served your town till your Lady came, and I will meet my death for doing so in pride, knowing that it only brings me to you!"

Ikella was outraged by the depth of despair in the widows voice. Looters were the pariahs of these desert communities. No-one was rich, all lived hand to mouth and unless water and food was earned it was not yours to take. Instantly her tentative plans for Caranchar crystallised in her mind in brilliant detail. She took a deep breath, looking down at the supplicant kneeling at her feet.

"Tuennis, I do not doubt your words, but I must listen to all the survivors before I pronounce judgement. I too have experience of the brutality that desperation can cause, but I must rule for all. I call for a meeting, tonight in the Gathering Square. Go now, feed your child and prepare for tonight. I will see you later."

She beckoned Olneth to her. He came swiftly, dropping on one knee to hear her request, and then gathering the men around him he left her with a courtly bow, disappearing in the direction of the Gathering Square to warn their camp and make arrangements for a Gathering. She watched him depart, eyes narrowed as he gave his orders to his helpers.

'High-born!' she thought.

'Practical and a commander of men, but what is a Sybillsce courtier doing at Caranchar?'

It was no good, her brain could not keep up with any more intrigue!

She stood abruptly, and then pointing her Staff at Sadorin she commanded.

"Bring your notes, I want to go through them."

Turning, she saw that Tueniss still lingered apprehensively. She spoke deliberately, making every word a direct command.

"Make sure that fires are banked, food is eaten, and that everyone is present in the Gathering Square at nightfall! One in ten can remain with the sick or with children, but where possible, the head of every household must attend!"

She turned back on to the path that had brought them to the cliff edge, and then remembering something she spun around, nearly tripping over Sadorin who had followed her.

"Do you know anything about the caves here?"

She demanded abruptly, then seeing their blank faces, "I need to know anything that anyone remembers about the caves on the pasture cliff. How deep do they go? How far in will light penetrate? Has anyone ever been in them? Are there maps. You know the sort of thing."

She raised her eyes to Tueniss, holding the woman's gaze with her own as she commanded. "See what you can find out for me, while I decide the fate of this town!"

She turned on her heel and returned to the Infirmary, Sadorin in tow, to consider a revolutionary approach to ensure the survival of Caranchar.

Chapter 14 - Soiveign

The daylight, such as it was, had almost gone when the Sorceress joined her Healers. In their absence, the students would oversee patient care, volunteers stood ready to assist and a runner stood by. So they gathered in the entrance to the Infirmary tent, cloaked against the chill of the night, waiting for Ikella.

Mina had attended the Sorceress, as she prepared to deliver her plans to the people, and even she was secretly impressed with the trouble that Ikella had gone to, in order to capture the attention of the town.

She gleamed palely opalescent, her skin glowed with the glamour of magic and dressed in her Opalwear cloak, with her Staff empowered, she shimmered as though she was the embodiment of that most dangerous of mistresses, the Opal desert.

She bent her head as the Healers knelt to her, and then spoke, softly, swiftly, as she must, reinforcing her role as Head of the House of Sorcery.

"Well my children, are we determined to rescue this place in spite of itself?" She took their answer seriously, for only they could tell whether the lessons that they had imparted to the people were actually being carried out. Solana, the oldest of the Council assented for them, bowing her head and making the traditional response.

"So must it be!"

Ikella stared down at them broodingly, and Mina saw "the remoteness," as she was wont to describe her Sorceress mood, come over her. Her face chilled, her aura, just a light glow against the night, strengthened and Mina saw that in her left hand, Ikella held the Shadushantesh, the traditional upper face mask of a Sorceress. Her lips tightened for this meant tonight would see the most dire of proclamations and she was filled with a shudder of sympathy for the townspeople of Caranchar.

Silently, Ikella swept aside the hangings and led them out of the Infirmary to join their men and children, who still camped near the main gates, ignoring the curious glances and muttered comments of the towns people streaming towards the Gathering Square.

The light was dimmed with the dust and sand particles of the Storm, the cloud-filled sky a sullen purple, streaked with the onset of true night. Mina, who had stopped to pick up a night glow and several wicks, had to hurry after her Sister Healers, arriving breathlessly to find Ikella huddled in her cloak, staring grimly through a rubble strewn hole in the perimeter wall, looking down the valley towards the Low Pass.

The ground fell away below them, and peering downward into the darkness Mina was reminded of the High Plateau, under which Selesh lay. She looked contemplatively at the sands where Opal and Azure blended and as the light trickled away from the darkening skies she became aware that the Sorceress was chanting softly. The wings atop her Staff fluttered, and suddenly unnerved by the shadowy deserts merging below her, Mina cautiously withdrew and went quietly towards the small fire around which the others sat with their men and children.

As she approached she saw that bowls were being filled by some of the townswomen, and her stomach growled softly. Tueniss ladled a mixture of grain, vegetable and fungi into a clean bowl which she offered to Mina, it smelt delicious and at Sanra's nod she wasted no time in eating. She made sure that Tueniss understood that Ikella would not eat until after the meeting and sat back to back with Syrena and waited for the Sorceress to come to them.

When she finally arrived, she looked gaunt, hollow eyed, and Mina noted with concern that there was an uncertain glitter in her eyes. She watched as the Sorceress sank to the blanket with the others, and saw that Solana had prepared a drink for her which she sipped sparingly. Mina watching solicitously, saw the colour flood back into her leader's face as with the warmth, the restorative power of the drink, she seemed to solidify and step back from the brink of whatever shadowy place she had walked in. Solana's eye caught hers, and Mina nodded her tacit understanding of the unspoken order to watch her Sorceress.

Standing for a brief moment, Ikella gazed around her, looking into the deep shadows where the broken walls stood, taking in the destruction before her hands were raised to her face. When she lowered them she stood, tall and glittering. In the shadows of her cowl was the Shadushantesh, masking her emotions, her reactions from casual inspection.

Awful in the impassivity that the mask granted her, Ikella, Sharall deir Opal, clad in the magical aura of Sorcery, walked slowly into the Gathering Square to decide the fate of the people of Caranchar. Before her, sitting on tiered benches improvised from the rubble of their homes, were the survivors of the storm, ragged, dirty and ill fed. They had nothing but what they could salvage, water was running low and was fast being tainted, and she knew what she was about to impose seemed outrageous, yet she had to command their obedience and respect if any of them were to survive.

She took a deep breath, tilted her head in recognition of their hushed attention and then, with a single graceful move, she extended her left hand and sang a small, trilling cadenza that evoked a soft, swirling movement of the air, a glorious chiming note. From where it rested ten spans away against the rock besides which she had been sitting, the Opal Staff flew into her welcoming hand. The Staff shimmered and at its head the crystal wings fluttered, power visibly emanating from both Staff and Sorceress and as contact was made, a visible aura of power burst from her, clothing her in all the tones of Opal light. It was pure spectacle, drama designed to impress, and it worked! From the packed benches came cries of wonder and a few low moans of fear. There were raised eyebrows amongst the Council. Even they had seldom seen Ikella so empowered, and never in the eye of the people.

She turned slowly before them, her outline glowing luminescent in the night like some bright beacon of hope, blazing against the darkened skies. She was tall for a woman, nearly two spans in height and slender with the strength of one in whom whipcord muscles had been honed over many years of a nomadic existence. Her face, hidden by the Shadushantesh, had a serene yet inhuman loveliness and, as one, the citizens of Caranchar gasped in wonder and lowered their eyes. Beneath the Shadushantesh, Mina knew that slanting green eyes surveyed the scene before her calmly. The Sorceress lifted back the hood of her cloak but, despite the absence of ritual costume which usually served to accentuate her status, this night, the firelight, the play of shadows, the Shadushantesh, made her mysterious. There was no doubt of the power she wielded for the air crackled and hummed around her, burning an impression of unshakeable calm, an oasis of invincibility. Eventually, the light from her dimmed, faded and yet was still there, casting little glows about, and Mina found herself able to breathe once more. Yet she was one of the Council of Nine, she chided herself, but still looked at her friend with a little awe as Ikella, ever imperious, summoned the crowd to draw near to the fire and to listen to her edict.

She planted her Staff in the sand, leaving the Opal glowing, gently streaming light about her as she paced back and forth in the natural space between the audience and the fire. She questioned.

"Do you recognise my right of governance in these Sands?" and from the crowd came a low apprehensive moan of agreement.

The Sorceress let it die away and then enquired.

"Who stands for Caranchar? Who will face my judgement for the life of my Irix and her calf?" She waited for this last question to sink in and followed it swiftly with another.

"What then shall I do with a town that flouts desert law, destroys the property of law abiding visitors, and ignores its basic duty to its own?"

There was a rising tide of terror now, and Mina saw with astonishment that the Gathering Square was ringed by hard-faced men, all with their eyes trained in the direction of the Sorceress, awaiting her orders, but she gave none.

One of the townsmen stood. Clearly unsighted he aimed his voice into the night, trying to gauge where Ikella was, his head tracking, his words made indistinct by his inability to place her.

"Deshun Ikella, we have no-one to speak for us. Our headman is dead, those who were the elders of the town either perished, are injured or missing." His voice trailed away, as another spoke, from the fringes of the crowd.

"We have only old or blind men here" the speaker, hidden from view by the press of the crowd continued.

"If you have power why don't you heal us?"

'A bitter man.' Mina thought anxiously, but Ikella was taking it all in her stride. She was calm, collected, standing still and silent as the crowd called their opinions back and forth, till the noise echoed in the ruined streets. Here a man cried out.

"If I could see, I could and find my family and bury them." Another answered.

"Yes, if Healers you be, heal us, so that we might help ourselves!"

Wave upon wave of suggestion was made, until the whole Council of Nine gathered, just out of the light, ready to support their Sorceress if needed. It seemed however that Ikella was positively feeding on the energy of the argument as it raged around her, and she was glowing with power, as she paced beside the fire, listening to the townspeople. Suddenly, apparently having heard enough she raised a hand, her Staff chimed a deep toned, and oddly warning note that silenced the babble in the square, and Ikella stepped forward to face the crowd.

"I do not rule by committee."

She raised an imperious hand to silence the resultant tumult of sound.

"I rule by right of Sorcery. I do not know what manner of place you come from, or where you journey to, but you are here now by my permission, governed entirely by my law!"

Her last comment cracked out sharply, causing little pinpricks of fear to shudder through the assembly. The Sorceress stood stock-still, and Mina was grateful for the solidity of Syrena to her left, the tangible warmth of Midara to her right and the ample form of Sanra to her rear. Ikella was speaking again, a curious flat calm in her voice which Mina nervously identified as anger.

"In the light of your losses, and since none of the women are blinded, do I assume that most of the labour has been accomplished by those women?"

There was a low voiced rumble, as the men muttered amongst themselves. Ikella's eyes narrowed, as she heard disparaging comments about what had been achieved. Then having apparently made a decision, she performed a complicated pass with her right hand, and a sullen roll of thunder silenced the crowd absolutely.

She summoned a little flush of power, making the air around her hum for an instant, and then she announced in a silkily sweet voice (her dangerous voice) as Mina called it. "In fact, there is no free man of Caranchar, native of these Sands, this town, between thirty and fifty name days old, fit to stand for Caranchar as headman!"

There was a shocked gasp from a crowd that had plainly never realised in what peril they lay. Ikella nodded to herself with satisfaction, as the truth dawned, before facing her audience again.

She spoke crisply, the words intended to be indelibly carved in the memories of all who heard her pronouncement.

'Then for your own protection I will, as is my right, declare Caranchar 'Soiveign! Surrendered to my direct rule, for lack of another to govern a frontier town of enormous strategic importance."

This drew a hiss of disbelief from the assembled townspeople and a low moan of fear rippled through the huddle. A whisper here and there escaped.

'Soiveign? Did she say Soiveign?"

As the whispers reached her sharp ears, Ikella raised her head. Green eyes seemed to glow defiantly, her features sharpened before their eyes. The assembly whimpered fearfully. Men bowed their heads in shame, and the women, tired and anxious, peered at the Sorceress tearfully.

To emphasise the point, Ikella stood away from the fire, the darkness behind her making her magical aura gleam all the more eerily, she tilted her head, raising her arms as if embracing the whole of Caranchar, and the glow from her Staff increased, encompassing the arena in which she stood.

She pitched her voice carefully, making sure that every word reached every ear in Caranchar, and applied her skills to enforcing the bond of fealty sworn by every man, woman and child here. Gradually, as she increased the pressure of her will, the crowd broke. Men kneeling awkwardly in their new blindness, sighted men kneeling resentfully. Some women whimpering in fear. Others cradled children protectively, until only one woman stood. Head bowed, subservient, compliant but unbroken, Tueniss, the headman's widow.

She was ready to obey but unafraid, Mina noted thoughtfully. Certainly Ikella seemed pleased by the confirmation of the woman's character as she nodded, reducing the power that held the crowd in thrall. She noticed as she did so, that the ruins around them were reverberating with a low hum, an echo generated by her own power. She had never noticed that before, and thought with immense satisfaction. "Very effective!"

Seeing how impressed the townspeople were, as they stared around, expectantly she lifted her Staff once more.

"I, Ikella Sharall bin Selesh, Sharall deir Opal, (Sorceress of Selesh, Sorceress Ruler of the Opal sands) declare Caranchar, Soiveign!"

There was a deathly hush, silence swept through the gathering. Ikella lowered her arms, swept the Gathering square with an imperious stare, and turned her back on the assembly. She walked slowly back to the fire, where, as her aura faded a little into the night air, she was to stand warming herself, ignoring the crowd, wrapped in her own thoughts.

What she had done was to rescind the patent that had established the town as independent, under the control of its own inhabitants. Lives spent in husbandry, trading, and crafts were now forfeit to her command as ruler of these sands. She had, by declaring Caranchar Soiveign, taken away their status as freemen and reduced the town to an annexe of Selesh itself. Used more usually to return failed townships to the direct rule of the clan, the stigma of the ruling would cling to these lives for years, and this decision had been difficult. She closed her eyes in a devout prayer that she had made the right choice for those here, for they had already suffered grievously.

As the Sorceress stood, staring into the fire, the townspeople were gathering themselves to their feet, bewildered protests were being made, and some of the women's voices were raised in anger as Ikella, used to complete obedience, turned to face them, the babble faltered and the Council of Nine, waiting hidden in the shadows beyond the circle of light thrown by the fire, stepped forward into the light. A slow, desperate silence fell.

"I am so glad that you accept my decision."

Ikella spoke wryly, looking about her for one person in particular. The woman again knelt in the dust before her.

"Tueniss, stand! I command it!"

As she spoke Mina instantly understood what Ikella had in mind. She found herself murmuring…"Mystcat… you sly, underhand, sneaky…" Her voice tailed away as the Sorceress called the late headman's widow to her.

"Kneel!" The Sorceress looked down broodingly on the woman.

"There are too many people here for me to house at Selesh. I cannot use all of you immediately."

Ikella sounded aloof, a trifle bored as she assumed her feudal rights.

She looked at Tueniss steadily, not a flicker of emotion crossed the woman's face as the Sorceress continued.

"I will bond you as guaradeign for this place, if it pleases you, as a reward for your service to the town since the Storm. "She continued to speak softly.

"For those who do not know, as Guaradeign, Tuennis rules here in my place. She holds in my stead the power of life and death over those she rules, and she has my ear at all times if she doubts the Way that she walks.

"The silence grew ominously as the Sorceress continued.

"My first edict is that all property is forfeit to the town and under the control of my Guaradeign, who will decide its disposition. Water and food, clothing and shelter will be divided so that all have an equal share. No-one shall feast while others go hungry. No-one shall be homeless, while others fight to retain property they do not need. Looters and despoilers of property will be executed, without fear or favour! The first law of the desert is to help and support those who cannot help themselves, and ignorance or abuse of that law is punishable by death!"

She raised her eyes to the crowd once more, lifted the Staff from its place and swinging it parallel to the ground, offered it to the wide-eyed woman kneeling at her feet.

"Tuennis of Caranchar, will you accept my mark?"

Her voice was gentle, the words solemn, the Oath binding should be remembered for all time. Tuennis looked up at the Sorceress trustingly, and then bowed her head meekly.

"So must it be!" Her hands shot skyward between those of the Sorceress grasping the Staff's bare shaft firmly.

As the power surged, Opalescent light flashed along Tuennis's body, sweat beaded her brow as a sparkling band appeared on each forearm. Her eyes widened in awe as the glow faded but not before Mina saw swinging gently against the new Guaradeign's chest, her late husband's medallion glowing.

Mina smiled covertly to herself, how well Ikella had handled this potential crisis she thought. Someone had to take control of Caranchar, before the survivors either died in the ruins or drifted away to other townships, leaving the wreckage behind to disappear into the unforgiving Sands.

Making Tuennis, one of the Inesh, her Guaradeign was inspired. As a member of the second clan of this Sand, Tuennis could not hold property or land herself. She had risked death by defying those looters that she had challenged, and had even risked death by wearing her dead husbands medallion, or taking over his responsibilities. By making her town Guaradeign, Ikella had in one move taken the entire town into protective custody so that her decisions were law, and rendered all its residents powerless.

Now Ikella could decide the fate of the town, make the survivors work together as a community. Now Tuennis would be able to dictate fair division of food and water, authorise security patrols, see to the many burials to come, and Ikella had protected the woman, given her a status and a future. The Healer made the gesture of invocation and paused... suddenly aware of something!

Mina, ever watchful of her mistresses safety, felt the prickling of alarm at the back of her neck. Olneth appeared seconds later, concern on his face, three of his men at his heels. They came to Mina's side and stood scanning the crowd, but it was the Healer who noticed the woman as she scowled at the Sorceress, eyes glittering from the shadows where she stood. Even as Ikella raised Tueniss to her feet, congratulating her and giving her the traditional kiss of peace on each cheek, Mina saw two others join the shadowed one, and in the depths of the portico under which she stood, there was a flash of lilac from a sash or undershirt. Alerting Olneth with a touch Mina hummed softly to herself, increasing her field of vision as she did when cleaning wounds. She looked to the group of three, heads together, mouths stubbornly set, as they gathered in the shadows.

The one with the lilac undershirt was definitely not of these Sands, she thought, seeing wide set eyes above the shana (the half veil favoured by traditionalists). All three wore the hakbah, (a filmy hair covering, popular in many cultures). However, it was the ritual braiding of their hair that identified them as Sybillsce, from the Amethyst Sands and members of an elite cult, banned from open interaction with other Clans!

She froze, her brain racing, but her glance flicked to where Olneth and his men were sliding through the crowd, closing fast on the portico.

Almost immediately, the woman picked up a travel pack and handed it to one of her companions before shouldering her own. Mina drew breath, preparing to shout, when there was a blur at the corner of her vision, and the sight of Tueniss, calling the remaining elders of the town together, distracted her. When she looked back, all three of the women had melted away. Olneth was scouting the shadows opposite, a bewildered frown on his face, but they had gone and the moment was lost.

Mina suppressed a yawn. She was desperately weary, and suddenly longed for a quiet dark place in which to sleep. As she rejoined the Council of Nine, Sanra shot a concerned look at her. As Mina yawned uncontrollably, she began to feel dizzy, weak and tears blurred her sight, until Sanra positioned a vial of some acrid restorative under her nose. Mina's head reeled for a moment, and then cleared once more.

'How strange!' she thought. 'I was doing something, but I can't remember what it was.'

Feeling a lot better, she gathered herself and rose to her feet, thanking Sanra for reviving her, and went to see the new Guaradeign of Caranchar take up her duties to the town, appointing guards to ensure the safety of all before the coming night.

Chapter 15 - Hostage to Fortune

Mina could see that the Sorceress was now sitting alone to one side of the fire. She was watching Tueniss, who had gathered the town before her. Some of the women were eager, pushing forward trying to gain her attention, many of the others however, hung back, looking distinctly nervous and Mina guessed that they had at some point offended or been in conflict with Ikella's new appointee. She watched with interest as Tueniss raised her voice.

"Come forward, all of you" she instructed, and the townspeople shuffled forward reluctantly, for the Guaradeign to recognise.

Immediately Tueniss turned on her heel and faced the Sorceress, dropping to one knee as tradition demanded. She waited, till at a nod from Ikella she spoke, her voice crisp, her manner decisive.

"We have today been given a new direction. I thank you my Deshun for taking us under your shield, for we have no other to protect us. Those present are not all of these Sands, and for our guests and our neighbouring freemen, I accept your protection whilst they remain in your domain, providing that those visitors abide by both desert and town law!

She paused to consider the gaggle of people crowding in behind her, poorly-clad survivors shivering in the night air. She beckoned them forward and they came obediently, drawing closer to crouch in the firelight, warming themselves at Ikella's fire, and Mina saw the Sorceress nod her approval as Tuennis continued.

"We have our regular traders, our Felmin neighbours, our workmen bonded to our craftsmen to consider."

She turned carefully running her eyes over the crowd again, and then catching Ikella's eye, she asked simply.

"What of their status now?"

Ikella stood, and paced thoughtfully. She spoke gravely.

"My judgement was for the freemen and women, the freeborn of Caranchar alone. I have, nor want, any right to alter the status of any freeborn man or woman from othersands."

At the concerted sigh of relief from the assembly she raised her voice a little, and the next statement cracked out like a whip.

"However, I do command their presence at my Gather, so that there will be othersands witness to my decree this night!"

There was a shuffle of retreating feet, and the square seemed to heave as outsiders filtered in to listen. Ikella's tone softened.

"I have no news of othersands to offer you."

She admitted grimly, gesturing to the broken walls, now only dark shadows in the background.

"What we have suffered here, could be reproduced over many of our Sister Sands.

96

Aware of the desperate fear on faces hidden in the dark, she was cautious.

"I regret to say that things could be worse. The town cannot provide normal travel rations, let alone transport, so if you will accept my protection, any and all of you are welcome to stay for the next ninenight. You will be treated as citizens and will get an equal share of the rations we give our own people. You must shelter where you can. If you stay and assist us in our time of sorrow, then no matter where you come from or what your status, your voluntary service will give you the right to remain here if you so wish!"

Ikella sank back on to the 'seat' that someone had created from a pile of rubble and continued to monitor her Guaradeign's progress as Tuennis spoke again.

"We have visitors also and those in particular have supported my efforts to enforce the law of this desert, the rules of this town, although there are those closer to home who have not! It is because of their actions, their attitudes that the name of Caranchar is forfeit, it is not because in our frailty we could not withstand a Storm!"

She bowed her head submissively, as a growl of anger swept the crowd, men and women searching for something or someone who was not there.

The tall Inesh continued, from her position on her knees.

"We are yours." For the first time her voice wavered, then strengthening she spoke imploringly.

"We are but your slaves to command Lady. What is your pleasure?"

Ikella, hidden behind the Shadushantesh seemed impossibly remote, the masked face gazed back at the people impassively but she gave a short nod and raised a hand, which was plainly a pre-arranged signal for Tuennis continued, feeling tentatively for every phrase as she did so.

"I will honour your commands in my new life. For all here there must be a new Way and it will not be easy for any of us. Of this township another nine of our sons and daughters must be given as hostages to Selesh" she announced. Impervious to groans from the crowd she finished tellingly.

"With their lives as surety for our endeavours, it may yet be possible to influence those who have watched others labour, while contributing nothing themselves!"

Watching Ikella, Mina saw her head dip at the malice in the Guaradeign's voice, and knew that behind the mask lurked a smile.

Tuennis spoke emphatically.

"I vow before all, that I will take every step with you. I will only eat when you eat, sleep when you sleep. I will not rest while you work, and to that purpose I offer my own son as first hostage to Selesh!"

A concerted gasp ran round the assembly, as Tueniss turned and taking a baby from the arms of an elderly woman nearby, she handed him to Andria, who was plainly expecting this event, for the Healer held a warm blanket to wrap the child in. Astonished, Mina realised that Nadra now stood in the shadows, and it was to her that Andria passed the child, watching as Daro's wet-nurse settled the baby to her breast. Tuennis glanced at them only once, resolute calm in her face. She spoke slowly. "When my man saw our child born, he said that his life was complete, that he was truly happy. He said he had fulfilled his greatest dream, to turn a haphazard village into a great town with markets for all."

Her voice gentled, her mood poignant, as she recalled Donnesh's dream.

"He wanted to marry and become a father so much. Everything that he had planned was done. I know that he wanted to see it to maturity, and that has been denied all of those we lost, but I swear that these hands will replace his hands."

Her hands were held aloft as she declared in tones of ringing confidence.

"That his child will live to return to a town that once again has free markets, free grant of land, and free men and women as residents!"

She rose to her feet, walked to where Nadra cradled her baby and said huskily, "He is what I plan for, so I give him as hostage to our Deshun as tradition demands. In this way will I serve Selesh!"

She hugged the baby briefly against her heart, then handed him back to Nadra, tears flooding her face, her voice choked as she murmured.

"Take care of my son, my Deshun, his name is Ahnell."

The very air was tense as Tuennis called for Sadorin, who armed with tablet and enscrasure stepped forward to announce the names of the other eight hostages. She named Bethan, niece of Diomid a town elder, who turned out to be the girl who had seen Shiarjha in the market. Next she named a frail looking woman, Sherell wife of Gothath, the town's master builder. Then Yonnath, the tall youngest son of Gorron, the market manager. Dorinn, five Rotation old younger brother of Miokinish and Tenash, who had died at Tearchan. Ikella's face tilted as she listened to a brief aside from Tuennis, and she smiled as a woman slipped past the Healers to stand beside Nadra. Mina consulted her memory, this then was Dorinn's mother, recruited as a nursery attendant possibly, but nevertheless it was a nice charity to a doubly bereaved woman. Three other adults joined the group of hostages, Carrish brother of the town's late Healer, and two women, one of which Mina recognised as Ikella's outspoken critic of the afternoon and wondered in mild astonishment how they had packed in so much into one day. She looked about the Gathering Square, from the small area that seemed now to have filled with new responsibilities for the Sorceress.

'There will be nine more to feed and guide to Selesh.' She thought, watching Ikella, who stared down at Tuennis's baby, speaking quietly to Nadra who smiled tentatively at the Sorceress.

"You have done well Nadra. I thank you for feeding the little ones."

She turned to Mina, and then struck with a sudden thought, looked back to the wet-nurse.

"They tell me that you have no-one left now?"

Ikella spoke sympathetically but with direct bluntness, and Nadra was solemn as she nodded. Mina noted her eyes glisten, and her hands gentle Ahnell closer to her, protecting him inside her cloak as the evening wind blew chilly across the square.

The Sorceress continued, "You have been most repentant for your earlier mistake, and I would reward you in some way. Would you come with us and stay at Selesh to nurse the babies until they are older?"

Mina saw Nadra's face glow with pleasure and the woman nodded, too overcome to speak, as Ikella said briskly.

"Good, that is settled then."

Turning, she walked away from the wet-nurse, leaving Nadra to tell her good fortune to the Healers as they gathered around her. The fire flared as the Sorceress passed her hand over it, and she became the focus of attention again as she formally closed the meeting.

"Let no man or woman doubt my will and my purpose." she stated flatly, "Tuennis rules here in my stead. What she decrees, I decree! No-one shall stand against her decision in any matter regarding the governance of Caranchar. She knows better than to exceed my writ! There shall be a Town Guard under her command to enforce my will! Your families are safe with me, while you obey. If you do not..."

Her voice tailed away meaningfully and Mina felt a wave of fear wash through the crowd.

Now the Sorceress raised the Staff and the Opal glowed gently, warming the crowd's mood, sending a glow of confidence into those who watched with bated breath.

"I will sleep now, and so will you. In the morning, we will all begin a new Way if it be the will of the One."

Her hand raised the Staff one more time. There was a rolling finality to the note it tolled, and as the echoes died away, Tuennis stood. Tall and lithe, garbed in desert pants and dark tunic she was suddenly all Inesh warrior. One hand went to the nape of her neck and pulled away the veil of widowhood, the other held a spear and even Mina's eyes widened as she realised this was a ceremonial spear, the type she was used to seeing in the hands of Ikella's personal guard.

Even as she wondered where that had materialised from, Tuennis spoke again.

"Now have the words of Sharall deir Opal Ikella te Syrene, been spoken. Now have her commands been given! Withdraw to your own place under the protection of her shield." and here Tuennis smiled wolfishly as she continued, her voice and attitude brooking no dissent "In the knowledge that the curfew imposed by the Town Guard will protect you and yours from all forms of predation this night. Curfew ends at first light." she added diffidently.

"Collect water and rations from the Town Square on your way home if you wish, but do not wander outside the perimeter I have established if you value your life!"

There was a crackle and a hiss from the fire, and in the leaping of a flame Mina saw with interest that Olneth and his men were drawn up behind the

Sorceress. She did not doubt the shudder of apprehension that ran through the townspeople as they observed the military precision with which Olneth marched them away to their posts.

Ikella stretched out her free hand, and a steady glow settled around it as Tuennis encouraged the crowd to depart with the single command.

"Go now!"

The Sorceress gently tossed the glow into the leaping flames of the fire, as a child might toss a ball into a pool in play, and the fire went out!

As the Square went cold and dark, Mina watched the crowd stream away silently, and feeling inwardly exhausted, she walked the short distance to where a corner of the town walls had been established as their camp. Their fire still burned, hot sweetdrinks were being handed out, and Midara grinned as Ikella passed a hand over the bowl as it was placed on a hot stone to keep warm for late arrivals.

The men were settling the older children down to sleep, as Mina, Sanra and Sadorin drew apart with Ikella. Sadorin still held the enscrasure and tablet that she had been using to enter all she could of Ikella's observations of the day. Now, she waited calmly for the Sorceress to speak, poised ready to take notes as required.

Mina saw that although Sadorin had worked as assistant to Caranchar's dead Healer, she was capable of so much more, but even as the thought crossed her mind, Ikella raised her head, eyes glowing, as she announced.

"I need to write an edict for the government of Caranchar, do I not Sadorin?"

Startled, Sadorin looked up, and the Sorceress continued.

"Very well, I will improvise. You will take notes. When we have achieved a satisfactory form of words, they shall be delivered to Tueniss to announce."

She paused, finishing her drink and adjusting her cloak as she stood. From the depths of the cowl her voice continued, slightly muffled.

"After that I must interview the old ones, the elders who survive. I must find out more about those caverns!"

She emerged from her hood, one hand holding the folded Shadushantesh, her eyes tired but composed as she announced.

"This night we will work while the town sleeps. To that end I have added sithinbark to your drinks, which should refresh you and keep you fit for duty another few hours, but my stocks are all depleted and I must speak to that Apothecary as well."

She picked up her Staff and turned purposefully, calling back over her shoulder.

"Fetch Tuennis and the Apothecary to the Infirmary tent, I will see you all there!", as she walked away.

This last sentence was directed at her Healers, who used to Ikella's way of doing things departed promptly to find the information and people required.

Ikella, followed at a distance by Mina and Sadorin, made for the Infirmary tents, where Derana and Inahana, inseparable companions, so physically opposite, so spiritually alike had taken over the watch.

Inahana, dark as the night, rose soundlessly to her feet as their small party entered. She inclined her head gracefully, in the direction of a hanging blanket that provided a sectioned area, for private use. Mina, drew it to one side, revealing a table, chairs and cushions for seating, and a bed in a corner. Shielded from the night air by drapes, it was patently for Ikella's use.

Inahana spoke softly.

"Is all as you requested Deshun?"

Ikella nodded her approval, quietly instructing.

"Summon my advisors Inahana.", and Mina, hearing the severity in Ikella's voice, fled to find her sister Healers.

Long into the night, the Council of Nine gathered with Sadorin as clerk, to write the proclamation. Long hours later, two sand tablets were full, and the weary Sorceress was putting the finishing touches to the last stanza, muttering it under her breath as Sadorin sat poised to alter or rewrite the section.

"Let it be known that appeal against their status will be considered one Rotation from now, and in the same week every Rotation thereafter, until the citizens of Caranchar achieve their freedom again by their own efforts and the desire of their own hearts. The hostages will remain at Selesh, but will be treated fairly. Where they need healing it will be found, where they need education it will be provided, and their families will be allowed to see them, ."

Ikella paused, her brow creased concentrating on the next statement. She looked at Sadorin closely as she spoke.

"A new Healer will be appointed. She will advise the Council on public health matters. A new position on the Council is to be created for a Town Recorder, so that a written account of all activity can be kept for Selesh."

Sadorin looked up murmuring.

"My apology Deshun, but there has never been a Recorder at Caranchar, we do not even have a scribe, for Donnesh was a well educated man, who could both read and write his own records. I do know that he also schooled Tuennis, which may have been against one law but they were truly married I was present when they jumped the trave, and I know that he felt he had the right to school his wife, so that she could perform her wifely duties!"

The assistant Healer looked anxious, but Ikella, relieved to find that at least Tuennis would not be so far out of her depth, smiled reassuringly. Sadorin went on.

"Can I ask who is to be the Recorder? They will have a lot to catch up on by the time they have been appointed!"

Her concern was plain, and Ikella enjoying the moment said briskly.

"Who should I appoint as Recorder of Caranchar? You are the only candidate worth considering, woman. Unless you have a concrete reason for refusing, I should consider yourself appointed!"

Tears sprang to the surprised woman's eyes as the Sorceress, witnessed by the assembled healers, stood solemnly, bowing to her. Ikella addressed her formally.

"Sadorin, former assistant Healers of Caranchar. Will you swear to record faithfully for Selesh, all events, meetings, and activities of Caranchar. Will you write without judgement, will you record without fear, those things that fall under our ordinance so that we may govern this place in a manner suited to the health, happiness and future benefit of its inhabitants? Will you consent to become a bondswoman of Selesh and wear the mark?"

Speechless, Sadorin bowed her head in formal assent, and Ikella, lifting her Staff, placed its glowing tip gently between the eyes of the Recorder. Sadorin quivered as a small opalescent drop appeared, as if in place of a third eye on her forehead. Her eyebrows drew together in surprise, and as Ikella removed the Staff her fingers traced the shape gently, to Ikella's immense surprise the woman bowed her head, bringing the fingers that had traced her new adornment to her lips and kissed them reverently murmuring.

"To the honour of the Opal, Mother." In the formal language of High Sorcery, used only by the Guardians of Sanctuary or the Sisters of Sorcery!!

Only then did she catch sight of the pale trace of faint ritual tattoos on the backs of the woman's hands. She paused, and then sat looking at Sadorin curiously and with immense sympathy, for she now knew how this quiet, modest woman had come by her knowledge and training.

Sadorin bowed her head before the Healers and asked softly.

"Would you hear from me how I came here, Mother?" Ikella replied quietly.

"Sister mine, it is for you to decide. We demand nothing of you except that you honour your promise to me."

Sadorin sighed deeply, almost with relief, saying briefly.

"As you know, there are choices to be made in our walk, and I made mine on the night before the Oathtaking."

As she spoke the Healers exhaled in one concerted breath, they had not misunderstood, Sadorin might have become a Sorceress herself... but on the night that she would have been invested with power she had for some reason taken another path, and had left the Sanctuary and training behind.

To do so she had also sacrificed much, for her powers had been Sealed. Her magically gifted *othervoice* had been silenced within her. This for a Sorcery candidate was beyond their comprehension. Even Ikella looked pale at the thought of the total exclusion of her status. However Sadorin, plainly a person of huge integrity, had retained the ability to succeed in whatever walk of life she took.

She did not elaborate, but said simply, "In the course of time I came here, and I remained. No one questioned me, and I pursued my knowledge of medicinery, by growing some herbs that I heard Kateya could not source. She came to buy, and then retained my services as her assistant and record-taker. She knew I was trained and, she also knew I was Outcast, but she didn't question me, and I am happy here."

The Sorceress reached across the battered table, and in the dark there was a sudden glitter, and where their hands touched a dim reflection as if some great golden medallion lay on the table beneath their hands. Sadorin hissed between her teeth as the empowered Sorceress touched her. Ikella held her gaze as the Opal aura licked around them, highlighting the droplet on Sadorin's brow.

"There is no way back to Sanctuary for you."

She commented sympathetically.

"However, know this, your service to Selesh and to Caranchar is recognised in that I grant you freedom of these Sands. You may wander freely and still be at home in the Opal desert, Sister mine. No-one shall call you Outcast again. I decree this bound into silence under the Seal of Selesh. I will bind you to the Clan, an honoured Sister of Selesh from this day forward, if you so will it?"

Sadorin looked up, wide eyed at the Sorceress's generosity, and placing both hands between Ikella's, she murmured brokenly.

"This is an honour too great for me, but I thank you and accept it in gratitude. I will be faithful unto Selesh, and will be silent on my past as sworn. May I assist the new Healer when she is appointed my Deshun?"

Ikella, smiling gravely nodded her approval.

The night drew on. Still together, the Council of Nine Healers, Ikella and Sadorin, discussed, wrote and rewrote a workable order of governance. The first dim light touched the horizon, casting a depressingly lilac pall over these once brilliant Sands. As their night's work was completed, in the outer tent, curled near to her little son, Tueniss slept. The two novice Healers were even now rousing her, to appear before the Sorceress, as the shattered township awoke.

Ikella looked round the group, thinking with bitter satisfaction.

'We have achieved much this night.'

She saw that her Healers had worked through their exhaustion, coming to the table with many new ideas. However, hers would be the authority, and Tuennis would bear the responsibility for ensuring that those ideas were put into practice.

She yawned, stretching her aching back, and realised that in the outer tent, Tueniss did not wait alone, for there was an old man to interview also. A travelling Apothecary by report, who knew something of the caves on the pasture cliff.

Reminding herself that this was her next task, she touched her Source beads, praying that she could make another announcement, one which would keep the town busy for the rest of this day, in preparation for the cleansing of Caranchar.

She reluctantly stirred her aching limbs into action. Her team were gathering themselves to check on their patients, with weary but resolute faces. Ikella held up a hand.

"Let us have Tueniss in now."

She ordered, and Sanra rose in obedience to do her bidding. A brief moment later the tall Guaradeign of Caranchar entered.

Mina saw with approval that she had bound her braided hair back neatly. Her face was freshly washed, and her clothes were clean. Loose pants, tunic caught in at the waist with a sash. She wore a simple sweatband around her forehead. Her forearms were bare and the opalescent bands of her rank glittered, like some outlandish piece of jewellery. She wore no shana, no hakbah, only the mourning tattoo of her late husband's family name adorned one bare shoulder to show that she had not always been single, that she had loved and been loved.

Entered the inner tent, she fell to one knee in front of Ikella, her hands turned upward and outward to show that she was unarmed. Ikella, used to such obeisance from her Inesh Guards, nodded briefly in greeting, indicating that Tueniss should sit at her own right hand, between herself and Sadorin. A stack of sand tablets lay on the table, the vivid golden seal of Selesh visible on each, countersigned by the Sorceress. Ikella indicated the tablets, and smiled grimly at the look of sheer terror on Tueniss' face.

"Don't worry," she said.

"I would not punish you by leaving you to try and read those by yourself. I have appointed Sadorin as your Recorder. She will sit on the Council, take notes, and pass information to Selesh as you need. You will rule as a leader, with nine citizens of Caranchar, selected by vote of the people. Council members do not have to be of these sands by origin, they only have to be fit, willing and resident in Caranchar for the last five Rotations. They will act for the people of the town, they will speak on their behalf and they must report to the Recorder anything that needs to be dealt with, so that she can find out all that you will need to know, and summon the right people to any Gathering that you call."

Mina almost laughed at Tueniss'' expression, she looked quite stunned at the thought that she would be calling Town Council meetings. However, Tuennis recovered herself well, and Mina was impressed by the expression of dogged determination that crossed her face as she listened to the proclamation carefully, and Ikella talked her through their decisions.

They finally stood, allowing Ikella to declare the meeting closed. The great Opal at the head of her Staff blazed forth as she spoke. On the table a golden reflection showed for a moment, and then the image faded, the opal light flickered and was gone. The Sorceress raised a hand in blessing and the Council was dismissed.

Sadorin stood quietly, the proclamation tablets clasped in her hand. She waited till the others had departed, and then made a small sign in the air with her right hand, as Ikella passed her. Immediately, Ikella stopped in her tracks, and waited for the Recorder to join her.

The Sorceress said nothing, but tipped an enquiring look at Sadorin as she came level with her, Sadorin looked down apologetically.

"Forgive me Deshun, but I noticed something rather disquieting."

Shielded from open view within the inner tent, she pointed out a small tattoo on Tueniss'' departing back. It was recent, still raised, and Ikella looked at it curiously before turning back to face the Recorder.

"My Deshun, Tueniss has already added the name of her son to the record of those she mourns."

Sadorin faced Ikella as comprehension dawned.

"In the manner of some people, she has shut her son, and the pain of giving him up, out of her mind. Perhaps it is for the best, for she may otherwise be unable to rule here as you have ordained. Nevertheless, she has, if only in her mind, watched him die. If only in her mind she has buried him, and added his mourning mark to her skin record. With respect my Deshun, it occurred to me, that as guarantee for her loyalty, you might hold nothing!"

With those words ringing in her ears, Ikella swept the curtain aside and followed the newly appointed Guaradeign to the Gathering Square once more.

Chapter 16 - The Apothecary's Tale

Ikella, withdrawn and thoughtful, walked to the shattered ruins of the Gathering Square. She was weary beyond belief she realised, her eyes were sore, even ideas came slowly. Glad that she had directed Sadorin to read her proclamation, she processed with ceremonial dignity, behind her Guaradeign, on legs that would hardly support her. She followed the town dignitaries to a high backed chair, where she was enthroned, sitting in front of the people in full view. The townsfolk had gathered in orderly fashion, and as the Healers filtered into their places behind her, Ikella noted how far they had already come on the long journey to recovery. A table had been set for Tuennis and Sadorin, stools had been provided for them and the two women briefly conferred, arranging sand tablets in stacks for Sadorin's use, then the tall Guaradeign rose to her feet, and faced the crowd. It was time, and from somewhere a strong male voice thundered imperiously.

"Silence, silence for our High, most Holy Ikella te Syrene, Sharall deir Opal, Sorceress Ruler of these Sands. Stand now before Tuennis, Guaradeign of Caranchar!"

The announcement of interminable titles always amused Ikella, but Tuennis looked positively shocked as the crowd obeyed, acknowledging her own name, and position bellowed across the Gathering Square. The Sorceress tipped a mildly malicious nod at Olneth who stood entirely unabashed before raising his voice again, chiding the townsfolk.

"You may be seated as you gather together, and hear the judgement of Caranchar!"

The crowd obediently sat, quietly adjusting their positions, as the improvised ceremony began. Ikella leant back, thrusting the Opal Staff into the sand beside her, listening intently as Tuennis accepted her ruling on behalf of her people stanza by painful stanza, in a firm, carrying voice. The Healers gathered behind Ikella, watching protectively over their exhausted Sorceress, but there was no dissent, and presently Tuennis dismissed the populace, instructing them to discuss amongst themselves who would stand for the Council of Caranchar. Slowly the crowd departed, on the announcement that their votes would be counted and the Council sworn in that evening.

Still with duties awaiting, the Sorceress was about to rise, when she saw Davini shepherding an old man, who stopped in front of her and waited for Ikella to speak.

She cast a glance over him. He was of average height and build with long white hair and beard, but his bearing was erect, his step energetic, his bronzed skin as fresh and youthful as any man of middle Rotations. His attitude intrigued her, for it was respectful but not subservient, this was an assured man who knew his place and worth but also knew hers and did not fear her, or her power. Curiously she raised her eyes to his face, which was one of serenity, firm featured and attractive in a way that made it impossible not to speculate on what he must have looked like as a young man. Even in age he was straight backed, his step firm although she noted wryly that he too, sported an elaborately carved Staff.

He was dressed in a faded blue cloak, ancient Opalwear pants and tunic, and at his belt hung the tools of his trade, sheathed in fine tan hide. Over his shoulder he carried a medicine scrip, and it was with a little start of surprise that Ikella remembered, the Apothecary! She had heard much of this man from her Healers already, he had produced medicines for their patients, interceded many times with those in distress of spirit. Even Ikella found herself hoping that he would offer something to relieve the headache that had suddenly seized her brow. As she raised a shaky hand to her forehead, she heard a voice. Deep as the night, as soothing as honey, it poured over her saying.

"Call yourself Healers? Can you not see imminent collapse? Help your Lady to the Infirmary, I will follow!"

Dimly, through the roaring in her ears, Ikella heard him say.

"Deshun, look up."

Mutely gazing into eyes that seemed to blaze with glowing flickers of fire, like the heart of some ancient Opalstone, Ikella barely felt the shiver in the Source. Her head rang with pain, her senses swam till she felt herself falling effortlessly into a deep swoon.

Aghast the Healers gathered around, fanning her face, patting her hands even waving bayen oil under her nose…to no effect. Carefully lifting the fainting Sorceress they stretchered her to the Infirmary, where she roused briefly as they transferred her to the bed. Hands fluttering to her chest, she lay gasping, till Syrena dismissed everyone except Mina, Telani and the Apothecary.

She spoke swiftly.

"Davini you will run messages to me if needed, the rest of you go! All she needs is peace and quiet, sleep and a restorative!"

She made shooing motions with her hands and the Inner tent emptied leaving Syrena eyeing the arrangements sourly.

"There is not much room, but it must suffice. I'll have that table moved, a Healer cot placed just there, and a chair beside the bed. Where is that restorative?"

Mina shoved the table back to the outer wall, moved a chair and held the separating curtain aside for the student Healer to take unwanted articles into the main tent. They had only just returned, when the curtain was gently pulled aside, and the Apothecary appeared. He had in his hand a small vial containing a draught of some kind, and there was an imperious air about him as he said.

"Other than sheer exhaustion, there is nothing wrong with your Lady! I have prepared a restorative draught for her, it will combat deficiency of diet and give her some strength for the coming days. Who should examine this?"

He held out his hand, and Mina took the small vial carefully, for there was no tanbark stopper. She held it to her nose and sniffed carefully. The faint aroma of tilberry arose from the delicately tinted contents. Curiously, she held the vial to the light. The liquid was amber coloured, clear and bubbling gently at which she raised an inquisitive eyebrow. The old man smiled.

"I once saw dissolving olacda crystals. Seeing that they produce a harmless gas which is known for refreshing tingle on a jaded palate. Now, instead of grinding all the ingredients, I use the crystal itself to work a little magic. Just one dropped into the liquid, allowed to dissolve overnight, will speed the action of any restorative," he confided.

Mina nodded, and taking up a wooden spoon, poured a little from the vial into the hollow, and gasped, for where the liquid was amber in the vial, as it was poured into the air it changed colour to pale blue! She raised her eyes to the Apothecary, as he commented.

"A passing fancy, it assists in encouraging those who think all medicines look and taste nasty. Of course, quite unlike the Healers who provide it."

She blushed as his appreciative eyes flirted briefly with hers, and then reminding herself that he was an old man, she bent her head and dipped her tongue into the liquid.

It was pure, and as it tingled on her tongue, she could taste the mingling of common herbs, berries and something warming full and fruity, but nothing harmful. The Apothecary smiled as she nodded, and motioned to her to drink the little that she had poured out. She did so gladly, and felt the warmth coursing through her veins as she handed it to Inahana.

"It is good!" She commented enthusiastically. "It will help her recover, if you can persuade her to take it!"

Turning, she left the Apothecary to administer the draught to Ikella, who sipped it from the spoon with murmurs of appreciation before falling into a deep sleep.

Gradually the Infirmary tent quietened, the old Apothecary sat in the corner of the outer tent, and Derana passing him paused to speak to him.

"Master Apothecary, nearly everyone of us here is sleeping. I am afraid we have not been very hospitable, but we worked all night, after a very distressing day!"

She murmured quietly, "Can I get you something to drink, or eat before I also retire?"

He peered up at her considering, and then answered her question with another.

Did I hear that your Sorceress has a baby in her care? Where is he? I don't see him here, surely she has not left him in the main Infirmary with the sick children?"

Derana thought for a moment, then she said slowly.

"Daro is a foundling. Our Deshun claims his sand-rights, and is taking him back to Selesh where we will try and find his family if any still live! He is with his wet-nurse and the hostage child, they too have their own area and are quite safe."

Even as she spoke, the outer tent flap was drawn aside, and Davini entered with Nadra in tow. She dipped her head in respect to Derana and said quietly, "Nadra thought that the Deshun might like to have the baby when she wakes. He is fed and sleepy. Shall I lay him down by her, or …?"

As Derana hesitated, the Apothecary held out his arms for the child, lifting him against his chest with a practised hand. He murmured some nonsense to Daro, who relaxing, snuggled against him.

The old man whispered, "That is not a bad idea, if your Deshun has feelings for the child. I will hold him and watch him till she wakes. She asked for information about the old caves, but was too tired to continue the conversation. in the meantime you can all go and sleep."

His voice, strong and deep, was hypnotically calm and somehow the Healers found themselves too tired to speak, too tired to think, as wearily taking themselves to the nearest bed, they curled in sleep.

The Apothecary sat back in his chair, and lifted the baby into the crook of his arm, and gazed down into the child's wide-open eyes.

"So my dear one, it begins…" He murmured. Placing a gentle kiss on the baby's forehead, he breathed the words.

"All hail the Voice."

A soft breeze stirred the air in the sleeping tent, whispering along the awnings.

"The Voice. The voice…"

The day slumbered on. In the tent of the Healers, occasionally there was a change of watcher for the Sorceress, a Healer would arrive stumbling with sleep to take her turn, and would curl on the floor next to the cot bed where Ikella rested. She seemed to be totally relaxed, dreamless, and when Mina came to take her turn, she nodded approvingly at the Apothecary as she went about her chores.

"She is resting well, I think much restored."

She whispered to him, and he looked up into her eyes. For a moment Mina felt that she knew him from somewhere, but the thought went out of her mind, as her glance fell on the sleeping baby. She exclaimed.

"Oh, Daro! Has anyone thought to feed the baby?"

The old man smiled and nodded.

"His nurse came not an hour ago, with another baby. She changed their wrappers and fed the both of them, one to each breast." He grinned, "it was a sight to behold, this one and the other, holding hands and drinking from one who mothered neither of them. Then the one that is Guaradeign here, came and the nurse brought Daro to me and taking the other child, went away. I do not know where!"

He glanced down at Daro who had shifted against his chest, and was now busy suckling a fist.

"It is fitting that the oldest in this place should work to lessen the burden on the women, so that they may do their new duties unfettered."

He murmured and Mina smiled, for although he was definitely not young, he had a vigour and a presence that made his age unimportant.

"Surely not the oldest Grandfather."

She teased lightly, but he looked up, dispelling her humour with the gravity of his gaze.

"Oh yes. I think I am quite the oldest here, though I do not think I am a grandfather, nor am I likely to be one."

Mina taken aback, blushed for her stupidity, stammering an apology, thinking.

'Of course, he could have lost his family! Nearly all the residents of his age group are dead. Oh dear. I wish I could bite my foolish tongue out.'

When to her relief, came the waking voice of the Sorceress saying sleepily.

"Mina, is that you? Who are you talking to? Where is Daro?"

The Apothecary swiftly put a silencing finger to his lips, shaking his head in rebuttal of Mina's sorrow.

"It is alright, give the baby to your Lady and tell her that I wait at her command."

Mina laid the sleeping child over her shoulder. Securing his wrapper more firmly, she turned towards the inner tent, her hand already on the curtain when she hesitated.

"What name should I tell Deshun Ikella?"

She enquired, and for a moment the old man hesitated just a fraction, then he said, "Tell her Carolus of the Nine Sands awaits her pleasure."

Mina had the sudden feeling that another name should have been given. She stood poised in the entrance to the inner tent for a second longer, looking into the old man's eyes which met hers steadily, unblinking.

"I will tell her, " Mina said quietly, then thoughtfully, " Does not the word Carolus mean Singer?"

At her question, the old man's eyes flickered, and Mina knew then that there was something unusual about this man, something strange, but still she did not fear him.

'Perhaps he is a mystic.' She thought to herself. 'Perhaps, a prophet sent to the Sorceress to guide her in her work, perhaps…'

"A friend?"

The old man's voice suggested from somewhere, although Mina could have sworn he had not spoken. The baby moved against her suddenly, and distracted, the Healer ducked inside the inner tent to lay Daro in Ikella's welcoming arms.

Ikella felt strangely languorous, she had woken to the sound of low voices outside the small inner sanctum, and lay for a moment wondering where she was.

The last thing she remembered was a pair of eyes, blazing into hers with some meaning, maybe with some power that she did not recognise. On that thought she sat up abruptly.

"Mina? Where is Daro?" She called out, her voice still small in that strange drowsy atmosphere.

As the curtain was lifted a little she could see her friend silhouetted in the opening, cradling the child over her shoulder and without thinking Ikella held out her arms and the sweet warm weight of the child was transferred to be cradled against her heart. Daro's eyes were open though still with that curious unfocussed gaze of the new born. He held his hands out towards the entrance to her small room, and even as Mina fussed about Ikella, propping a spare sleeping roll behind her back to support her, the curtain parted and an old man appeared on the threshold of her inner sanctum.

Of course, this was the Apothecary she remembered, she must have fainted even as he approached her in the Square! For him to be so familiar in her presence, he must have tended to her. Relaxing she decided that she should treat him as one of her Healers. She sighed, as the weave that smoothed her flesh, brightened her eyes and shimmered on her skin, faded. Her head was filled with pain again, suddenly making her feel nauseated. The baby shifted in her arms, turning his gaze from the Apothecary to look up at Ikella, and to her amazement the pain in her head receded and the nausea fled as she let go of her connection to the Source and faced the Apothecary without the glamour of her magic. Mina nodded towards the stool, caught his eye and said hurriedly.

"Deshun, this man is called Carolus of the Nine Sands."

She fled to do Ikella's bidding.

Carolus sat on the stool and leant forward, taking one of Ikella's wrists between long slim fingers. He rested her hand palm upward on his knee, and laid three fingers across her inner wrist. His eyes closed, he seemed to be counting, and curiosity aroused, Ikella left her hand in his, and was presently rewarded when he smiled saying:

"I think my patient well rested, and much recovered."

The fine lines around his eyes crinkled when he smiled, and Ikella thinking, 'This is ridiculous.'

Found herself smiling back at him. She looked straight into his eyes as she did so, but found nothing of the swimmy headedness that she had previously encountered, true she felt a little weak, but she was unempowered, and that was to be expected after the exertions of the last two days and nights. She absentmindedly reached for her powers, and almost immediately the headache came crashing down on her again. So badly that her grasp on Daro slipped, and the Apothecary took the baby from her, hefting him on to one hip, and supporting the Sorceress as she shrank back on her pillows. She raised a hand to her head, shielding her eyes from what seemed like intolerable levels of light.

The Apothecary had apparently put Daro down for he was soothing her head between both hands, and with relief Ikella heard Mina saying.

"I'll hold Daro. What is wrong with her? She is very pale."

Carolus replied, his deep voice low and comforting.

"It is nothing that will not right itself. She is simply too tired to use her magic at the moment."

A hand slipped under Ikella's head, raising her and supporting her.

"Come Deshun Ikella, sip some of this."

Ikella obeyed wordlessly, the restorative coursing through her, warming her throat 'till at last she was able to catch her breath and speak.

"I'm alright."

She protested and Mina assisted her to sit again, this time allowing her to swing her legs out of the bed and get fully upright. She allowed Mina to adjust her robes, wrap her in a light shawl, and gather the baby back into her arms, and then with Daro safely encircled, she addressed the Apothecary once more.

"Carolus, how came you by such a name", she questioned lightly.

"Carolus of the Nine Sands", that is an unusual designation is it not?"

The Apothecary considered her over the rim of a leather cup, one hand corralled a honey cake that had appeared with Mina, and with amusement Ikella watched the old man enthusiastically cramming in the delicacy. He washed it down with a satisfied sigh, before confiding.

"Carolus was given to me as a name when I was a young apprentice. I used to travel for my master, collecting ingredients, herbs, spices, local remedies... you know the sort of thing. I had no family living, and so I had no family name and my foster father had more love of drink than of his wife or of me. He eventually drank himself to death... and she sold me to an Apothecary in Shilinch, on the borders of the Malachite Sands."

Ikella listened, fascinated by his deep voice, the melodic tone, he continued.

"That was many years ago, and I used as I said to travel for Browen my master... and he sent me out with a zeglur to carry all my purchases, all the things I could gather myself."

Already sensing where this story was going, Ikella found herself grinning at him. Just thinking about zeglurs had that effect on most people, for a more comical animal was hard to imagine.

They stood almost a man's height, four legged and slow moving, with large ponderous feet. They were blue grey in colour, coats marked with odd mottling, which distinguished the zeglurs of regular breeders apart. They had long mournful faces, long ears which twitched wildly when excited, and a manic moaning call, which heard across the sands at night was hideous in the extreme. Carolus looked at her solemnly.

"I think there is nowhere on Pelshar that a man can sing, and yet on a day that offers beautiful sights, beautiful sounds and good weather, who could blame a young man for trying?"

He smiled impishly at her as he confided.

"Was it my fault that every zeglur for miles around heard me and decided to call back?"

Ikella suddenly found herself chuckling, she tried in vain to school her features to severity, but it was impossible.

"Where exactly did this misdemeanour occur?"

She found herself asking, knowing in advance what was coming, and the

Apothecary did not disappoint her, for he looked up, smiling straight into her eyes.

"Just outside Mestos on the border of the Malachite and Azure Sands." He offered with a sweet smile of unholy joy.

"The centre for breeding Zeglurs and the home of the largest herd on Pelshar!"

Ikella buried what threatened to become a serious giggle in taking a dainty bite of honey cake and the old man sipped his drink and reminisced.

"When I returned home, I was no longer 'boy', . I had a name, 'Carolus'. Because I had no one left, only my Colours to tell me where I came from, I named myself for the place that I love best."

From his seated position he sketched her a bow.

"May I present to you, my lady, 'Carolus of the Nine Sands'"

He held out a hand to her, and Ikella a little shyly took it. Looking into the Apothecary's face, she found herself wondering.

'Where have I seen you before?'

The baby crowed suddenly, startling them both, and the curtain parted to admit Nadra, who fetched by Mina, offered to take Daro away for a while. Ikella reluctantly handed him over, and the baby suddenly enraged by parting from her started to wail, louder and louder, till the Apothecary gently touched him with a finger saying.

"You are not being abandoned little one. She will not leave you."

The child quietened as if in understanding, and his wet-nurse bore him away.

They were left alone for all of two brief moments, till Sadorin and Tueniss arrived and the business of the day re-started.

In the outer tent, women worked to lay out the medicines, herbs and remedies, retrieved from the shop in the Long Parade, for Carolus to identify, while he remained in the inner tent with the Sorceress, Tuennis and Sadorin to discuss the history and use of the caves below the town.

"They have been there for as long as I can remember." Sadorin offered.

"Although I cannot remember exactly when or why they went out of use."

She screwed up her face concentrating, trying to remember.

"I remember travellers could come in through the Caverns, before the Pasture Gate was built.", she said musingly. Though I never went into them myself."

It had obviously meant little to her at the time, and Ikella suddenly wondered how old this woman was, even as Tuennis added.

"Many of our men hired out as porters to carry goods up to the Gathering Square. Donnesh, my husband said goods went missing, porters were accused, and the system was unwieldy and slow on market days.

Ikella nodded, tapped her teeth with her fingers and waited for the Apothecary to speak.

"Yes. I remember coming here" he spoke slowly, thoughtfully.

"We took the teams straight in. What I remember is how limited the space was, how crowded it seemed. Worse still, there was a fall in the biggest cave, if I recall it correctly. Animals died and traders threatened to desert the markets.

I think it was your husband who opened up the walls to make the pasture and the gatehouses, (though I never came this way again, until the path was changed)!"

Sadorin wrote industriously, and then she offered an old tablet to Ikella, saying diffidently.

"I don't know if this is anything to do with the subject, but this seems to indicate that somewhere here there are steps, leading down into the cave complex."

Ikella, turned the tablet around in her hands till she could see the sketchy map. Little more than a squiggly line drawn near to a square, but centre to that, the artist seemed to be trying to convey the idea of an entrance, for there was a door, and a man, drawn as if ascending from below.

Puzzled, Ikella handed it to Tuennis, who stared at it blankly. The Apothecary looking over her shoulder, and making comments as they turned the tablet this way and that trying to make sense of it.

The Sorceress clapped her hands, and Mina hurriedly attended her, bringing water and thin biscuits to the table as refreshment. As she stood just behind the Apothecary, serving them, her glance fell on the tablet, and she froze in surprise, for it clearly depicted the place from which she had witnessed the disappearance of the woman that she had called 'the shadowed one'

It was very strange, she couldn't remember even thinking about her experience since it happened. She still hadn't told Ikella about it, she realised guiltily, but now it was clearly in her mind she should do so. She picked up the tablet.

"May I speak Deshun?"

She spoke clearly (and if Ikella heard the note of reluctance in her voice, she gave no indication other than a nod).

Mina still holding the tablet, described carefully what she had seen. She included a description of the women, her opinion of their likely origin, and her reaction when they vanished, ending with a somewhat lame apology.

"I am sorry, I don't know why I didn't remember this before."

Her voice tailed away uncertainly as the Sorceress's thin eyebrows drew together frowning.

The Apothecary spoke carefully, his voice precisely modulated to effect calm, reminding the Sorceress of another voice saying something similar to her, a lifetime ago.

"Quite possibly, It was not important enough for you to remember before now"

Mina found herself nodding in agreement, as did the others. The old man's voice drifted hypnotically into the heat of the afternoon.

"If she was indeed Sybillsce, no good would have come of questioning her. They are past masters of subterfuge"

His voice seemed to Mina as if it filled the room and her head. Her whole attention was focussed on the smooth melody of it, like a river of persuasion it flowed all around them.

Even the Sorceress was nodding, as Carolus drew breath to continue, "But", his voice suddenly changed, snapping their attention to him.

"She almost certainly used the old steps to the caves below to get out of Caranchar unseen. It seems likely she also cast some small magic that would have prevented you from alerting us." Ikella stared at him, shocked.

"That comment seems to imply the involvement of a magic user."

Her voice was low, reluctant and Sadorin and Mina's eyes met at the crackle of electricity in the air. The Apothecary looked from one to the other, and Mina could not resist thinking that he was smiling inwardly at their reaction to his suggestion, although not a trace could be seen on his face. He leant back against a cushion, and as he did so he dropped Mina an enormous wink…she was so disconcerted that she hastily picked up the drinking vessels and loading her makeshift tray nearly missed the next revelation.

"Of course."

He agreed easily enough, "but then she wouldn't be the only high born Sybillsce here either!"

Ikella looked at him severely.

"If you know anything amiss in the Amethyst Sands, then you should tell me, not make hints or mischief."

She said firmly, then she enquired.

"Olneth?" and the old man nodded, taking the last swallow from his drink.

"Mmmm" he mumbled. "Then I had supposed you familiar with the Captain of Soloria's Household Guard!" He said with relish, adding as a private aside, intended for the Sorceress's ears only. "I know, he behaves well, and looks better to most women! That's a dangerous combination." Mina was hard put not to giggle at the outraged expression on Ikella's face. She drew breath.

"Deshun, if I could work out my position in the Square, perhaps I can find the entrance."

She offered hesitantly, and the Apothecary nodded.

"That would be a good idea! I will try and find out what brought Olneth here, and if he knows anything, while I am on my rounds this evening."

He said quietly, turning towards the bemused Sorceress.

"May I speak with you alone for a moment my Deshun?"

Ikella found herself hastening Mina, Sadorin and Tueniss to explore the likely access point in the Gathering Square, while she remained with the Apothecary. He sat quietly for a moment before raising his eyes to hers.

"Olneth is a good man, a good friend to these Sands, and many others, but it suits his work that not many people are aware of his purposes."

"Explain!" Ikella snapped, frowning at him.

Carolus continued quietly:

"Soloria faces difficult choices in the coming Rotation. I travel widely and I have heard that there was much dissent over her choice of Candidate Elect."

Ikella stared at him, it was incomprehensible that a man, a mere Apothecary had heard rumours that she had not. Carefully schooling her features to impassivity she let him continue.

"There were two girls in contention, I know this because one of them fell ill, with some kind of muscle wasting disease, and they sent for me." His face grew solemn, dark and Ikella could not resist demanding.

"What happened?"

Carolus roused himself from an introspective silence and said lightly.

"Oh, she recovered when I discovered that she had been poisoned! However, I never did find out who was behind that, they whisked her away too quickly for me to go into it, but that is how I met Olneth. He determined to find out when and why she was made so ill!" Ikella leaned forward.

"What happened next?" She demanded, and Carolus looked up. He seemed all of a sudden weary, and Ikella thought of his age with sympathy.

"I rather think that will reveal itself in time."

He stated, refusing to be drawn further. He sat back, as Ikella stood, and looked straight up at her. Once again Ikella felt a sweep of power touch her, as if he was connected to the Source himself. She sat down hurriedly.

'Ridiculous!' she thought defiantly. 'Men cannot use power.'

Nevertheless, she sat as if hypnotised, listening as the old man told her in a low monotone of dangers in the caverns. She heard him dimly as from a distance, his voice speaking at great speed, as if he was in a hurry to impart some important information. She could not have said what it was he told her, except that her whole body seemed fixed in concentration on his voice.

Some time later she roused to find that the old man had departed. Tueniss' voice could be heard outside, with Mina sounding excited.

"Deshun Ikella," the separating partition was drawn abruptly as they entered.

"We've found something! We think there may be an entrance still, can you come? We need your help."

Ikella raised a hand to her forehead but the threatening headache was fading, so she slowly rose looking around her for the Apothecary but just as he had come, he had apparently left. In the outer tent, Daro wailed, suddenly sounding bereft, the day jumped back into focus once more and Ikella took up her Staff, her burden of leadership, and prepared to investigate.

As she passed Nadra, Ikella paused briefly to look at Daro. He was in a fury, red faced, screaming and thrusting stiff-limbed against the frustrated wet nurse, as she endeavoured to restore him to dry wrappings. Amused at the disturbance this tiny tyrant was causing, Ikella soothed him.

"Oh, so much temper young man."

The baby's cries changed, from anger to distress, until she gathered him to her and stroked him gently. He cried heartrendingly into her arm, soaking the sleeve of her gown with real tears, until bewildered by the child's misery, Ikella handed him back to Davini who had come to support Nadra.

She watched the confident manner with which the student Healer handled the baby, tucking his wrapper firmly around him, ignoring his attempts to evade her. Davini smiled at Ikella, then glanced down at the angry wriggling baby with amusement.

"He seems to be thriving so far, but he doesn't like being fed on his own and is very strong willed."

Producing a small bottle, she explained.

"I tempted his appetite with honey cream yesterday. There is little left, but a drop should suffice."

Swiftly removing the stopper, Davini used a clean finger to capture a smear which she carefully transferred on to Daro's quivering lips. Ikella watched as he paused in mid-scream and made a contented mumbling sound, tasting the sweet glutinous mixture.

Conscious of Mina and Tuennis agitating in the doorway, Ikella watched fascinated as the baby's fists unclenched, the redness dying from his face. His lips smacked in anticipation as Davini handed him to Nadra, who already had one breast exposed. In no time at all, Daro relaxed, his fingers opening and closing in the rhythmic encouragement of the suckling child. Certain it was now safe to leave him, Ikella and Tuennis, flanked by Mina and Syrena left the Infirmary tents and wandered back to the Gathering Square.

As they walked through the township, receiving the evening salutations from the people, it occurred to Ikella that it was good for her to see how the ordinary people of her sands fared, and how difficult their lives were. She could get used to this new custom of wandering where she wanted, only protected by her Healers, rather than as before, borne aloft by her Inesh guards, distant, unknown to those under her rule. She found herself almost persuaded to look behind her, to see if anyone had observed her unseemly display of enjoyment, as they came upon their family encampment, and stood for a moment observing Midara talking to Dovid, as Solana, the elderly Zurian Healer played with the children. Thinking about these perilous times, induced a pang of guilt in Ikella, for they were few, most of them far from home, and realising that friends and relatives might think them dead, came the understanding that such friends might not have survived either. Who knew what disaster she would find at Selesh? Rigidly controlling a rising sense of panic, she scrutinised the Gathering Square more closely, while she admonished herself for straying so far from the Way.

As these strange new thoughts and emotions came under control, she saw that Mina was waiting to demonstrate the position from which she had observed the mystery woman. Joining her, Ikella took a breath, seeking the Source, even as Mina silently indicated the direction of an imposing wall fronted with a large portico, surmounting a doorway. However, as Ikella drew more power, enhancing her vision, it became clear, that whatever existed before was now long gone, only stones blocked the arch of what had once been an impressive entrance.

"Reaching" for her connection to the Source, she subconsciously registered that it was no longer the faint trickle but a roaring torrent, she paused surprised, then with her lips pursed in a soundless whistle, she turned. Using her Staff much as a compass needle, she sought for the faintest trace of the magic that had been used on her Senior Healer.

Mina was aware from a "thrum" in the atmosphere that Ikella was casting a web, using magic to search the area, and held back a multitude of questions. Tuennis and Sadorin waited impatiently in the shadows, as the Sorceress took her time, prodding the ground with her Staff, looking anywhere but in their direction. Mina maintained her position watching closely, till Ikella started, half smiled, and then headed straight for the portico, as if following a trail.

It was the faintest of traces but Ikella locked on to it, nostrils flaring, her head weaving as if she tracked a faint aroma, just like the great Sorrel hounds of the Carnelian Sands in search of skyth, the rarest of flowering herbs. Suppressing a grin at the thought, Mina began to follow Ikella closely.

The Sorceress, oblivious to everything else, felt uneasy. She had a sense of imminent danger emanating from the area that they were investigating, it was strong, threatening. She slowed her pace and almost immediately became aware of something in the thread she followed, so abhorrent that her skin crawled.

Concentrating her mind on tracing the women Mina had seen, she looked up from the ground, and saw a tenuous line of light drifting in the shadow of her own aura. Mentally reaching for it, she felt a palpable connection with something so cold that she shuddered, but hung on. All at once, she stood again in the firebright circle gazing into the dark, surrounded by the townspeople of Caranchar. In the shadow of the portico a pair of unusually tinted eyes held hers chillingly, then the link broke.

Startled, realising that she had tapped into Mina's memory she saw the line that had drifted aimlessly before her, was now withdrawing purposefully towards the portico. She followed hastily and was led to where the doorway had apparently been concealed. Raising her hand glowing Opal with power to the plastered brickwork, she heard a soft "click" and a panel opened. Amid a chorus of surprised murmurs, Ikella bent to see what it concealed. It appeared to be nothing more than a hole, about the diameter of a woman's forearm. she bent, peering into the shadowy depths beyond but even with her augmented sight there was nothing other than darkness to see, so reluctant to risk either her own hands or that of another of her party, the Sorceress drew back, fumbling in the pouch at her waist. As Ikella stepped back Tuennis crouched in her stead, and would have stretched her arm inside the aperture, if Sadorin had not touched her shoulder, attracting her to where Ikella stood, rolling a sphere of energy between her palms. Mina watched her Sorceress wide eyed, for Ikella had a resolute attitude to the use of magic, preferring to do by her own hands what other people were forced to do for lack of magical ability. Eventually the sphere achieved the shape or consistency that the Sorceress required, for she stepped quickly back to the wall, slid the palm containing the hissing, spluttering ball to the aperture commanding.

"Niactrah!"

At this, the sphere increased the speed of its rotation, till even Ikella's arm shook. It emitted a "whorrling" sound, which echoed weirdly in the depths beyond and sizzling, leapt into the unknown.

For a long moment they stood staring at one another, then there was a soft sigh and a gust of wind came from the aperture, and the Sorceress and her Healers nodded knowledgeably at one another. There was no-one hiding in the darkness beyond!

Tuennis waited for Ikella's nod before thrusting a long arm into the hole, seeking a way of opening what they now believed to be a usable entrance to the ancient caverns below.

Tuennis knelt in the dust, straining to the length of her fingers, as she struggled to see if she could find any irregularity on the inside of the door. Ikella listened lips twitching in barely concealed amusement as the Guaradeign muttered oaths and imprecations at the futility of her struggle.

"Kastiss take the one that sealed this !" followed by a muttered.

"By my oath! No normal woman could undo such a catch!"

Tuennis persevered though, squirming, one arm inserted into the narrow recess to the shoulder. Suddenly she recoiled, shouting.

'Owww!!!'.

Withdrawing the injured limb hastily, she licked a long deep gouge, totally unaware of the sudden stillness, the anxious faces of the Healers, as she returned to her litany of insults.

"If I catch whoever did this, she will die!"

It was Sadorin who finally found her voice, as the others stared mutely, inwardly counting the seconds since Tuennis was injured.

"Tuennis!"

The Recorders voice was severe.

"Never lick an injury until you know what caused it. If that had come from a Drecons claw, even now, your child would be motherless!"

Shamefaced, Tuennis allowed Ikella to send a ribbon of light hissing along the deep gouge. It seethed on her skin for a second, before leaving a line of pinkly-new flesh in its place. Bobbing her head in gratitude, Tuennis returned to her task more circumspectly, her voice muffled as she kept up a running commentary.

"Donnesh told me that this was used by smugglers, bringing destreigned goods to the market. He was glad of the rock fall, because it gave him the excuse to seal the entrance."

Her voice dropped, as she caught Ikella's speculative gaze. However, the Sorceress smiled ruefully, dispelling temporary embarrassment.

"Yours is not the only place subject to such abuse."

She murmured, and Tuennis raised her head, eyes widening as she understood the implication. 'Selesh, ?"

She questioned and Ikella nodded, her expression deterring further comment. Tuennis redoubled her efforts, but the catch remained tantalisingly out of physical reach.

As her Guaradeign probed beyond the aperture, Ikella stepped back, focussing magically enhanced senses through Tuennis' arm. Suddenly, she was aware of a hot, angry tendril, floating just out of her mental grasp, but steeling herself, she reached out again. As she expected, it was the thread of power that she had followed. Even as the hand of her mind caught it up, the thread shrank from her, began to unravel as she tightened her grip. Hardly daring to breathe, so tenuous was this magical hold, the Sorceress, sensing a bolt to one side, "pulled" until, with a low unwilling groan, the panel dropped away. Tuennis, surprised, peered cautiously into the dusty passage they had revealed.

Doing nothing to dispel the illusion that Tuennis had freed the panel alone, Ikella swiftly ducked through the narrow opening and walked boldly into the dark, Staff all aglow. A grim smile greeted the astonished babble behind her, as she called back irritably.

"Oh for the sake of the One, do come along! This is what we have been looking for."

The light from her Staff revealed a vaulted roof sweeping high above them. The pool of light, flickering uncertainly up stone walls of massive proportions. Hefting her spear in one hand, Tuennis, murmuring.

"My life in service to the Opal." followed Ikella, her eyes never wavering from her slender form, as she forged ahead of them. Mina and Sadorin hurried hard on Tueniss' heels, and in their wake came the others, wide-eyed and wondering.

Unable to take notes in the gloom, Sadorin dutifully kept a mental catalogue for later, as they took a shallow descending ramp.

Only ten spans later, the Opal on Ikella's Staff suddenly flared into life like some arcane signal stick. With its new wings beating frantically, the Staff tore itself out of Ikella's hand, rising into the air, trilling an ascending warble of alarm and coming to a halt suspended over a deep chasm.

Ikella stood directly below the Staff, poised at the top of a broad flight of stairs that curved away into the dimness below. Peering downwards, she realised that one supporting wall of the staircase had collapsed. The roof here canted at an extraordinary angle, almost as if some incredible force had crushed the ancient caverns, sheering part of them away into the depths of a titanic void. Cautiously, followed closely by her Guaradeign who again hissed curses under her breath (no doubt calling into question the sanity of magic users) Ikella led the nervous group, shivering in apprehension, downward.

Suddenly, Ikella's gifted *othersenses* intruded. She felt a feather touch at her temples, heard an echo of malicious laughter from some far distant place, as a deep and infinitely threatening note tolled from her Staff.

Just where the staircase turned in a steepening spiral, the floor canted wildly, and only a supreme effort brought her stumbling to a precarious stop as she found herself barely three steps from the edge of the chasm. Gasping with relief, Ikella steadied herself on the remains of a stout barrier, which took only a glance to see had been deliberately destroyed.

She peered into the abyss cautiously, as her frightened Healers caught up with her. Ruefully admitting to Mina that even a Sorceress was not immune to shock, she silently eyed her trembling hands, before she stepped forward once more, sobered out of all excitement.

Sadorin followed her, noting that this passage had been altered, and that a turn led them onto a parallel corridor with unnerving views, evidence that caverns had collapsed, taking with them the original passage up into Caranchar. Here, reassuringly, the rails were solid, unbroken, and to judge by their construction, reasonably modern. Apart from the gap where Ikella had nearly plunged down, a safe passage still existed.

They walked on slowly, looking for signs of recent subsidence until they entered a wide corridor, clearly once inhabited, set with stout wooden doors let into the walls. Mina was fascinated, here and there she saw clear evidence that a people of vastly superior technology had lived here and she longed to break off this downward plunge and investigate. She lingered near the back of the group as they followed Ikella, who seemed tireless, and wondered about the change in the normally formal and unapproachable Sorceress. Since the Storm she seemed progressively more animated, more empathic, more engaged with her people. There was a youthful glow about her, a new sense of purpose, if her reaction to Daro was anything to go by. She stood in the corridor considering the outrageous idea that had crossed her mind.

'Is it possible that there is some change in the Source? Ikella uses magic so rarely it is difficult to tell, but even I thought it easier to heal recently. Thanks be to the One!'.

She drifted along aimlessly, 'till the most alarming thought intruded. She had been thinking that even Ikella's Staff seemed to have a life of its own, when the suspicion dawned on her.

'How dreadful! If Ikella had fallen to her death in that fearful chasm, I might have been blamed for telling her about this horrid place. Shiarjha needs many more years of training before her powers mature.'

She was opposite the last door in the corridor, then that the memory of those hypnotic eyes came back to haunt her.

"Mirayen protect us, we are in a trap!"

She cried out, although she was not aware of doing so as she glanced at the door, looking for a means of escape, and found herself wondering if some plan of these rooms lay inside it. However, even as she raised the latch, she was halted, "Stop!"

Feeling as though she had been physically thrust back from the door, Mina stood gaping as the Sorceress and her entourage reappeared. The light round Mina increased, as Ikella stopped in front of her. The Sorceress spoke warningly, though not unkindly.

"Whatever lured you here Mina, is too dangerous to pursue alone! Besides, we have no time to explore !"

She raised an empowered hand, from which streamed luminous green light. It eddied along the passageway, tracing the outline of each door, sealing it with a hiss that made the latches rattle. She examined her work, then without further comment she turned away briskly, plunging ever deeper into the interior, as Sadorin and Mina shared a glance of mutual frustration before following her ever deeper into the complex.

The light dimmed as the tunnel narrowed. Bronzed rock opal now streaked with seams of paxite, darkened as they approached the black granite outcroppings that continued into the Azure Sands beyond. Ikella forged ahead, till she came to an abrupt halt, only forty spans or so from the last door that she had sealed. There they could all see her problem, for stretching floor to ceiling was an immense rock fall.

With their path blocked by stones twice the size of a man, they turned away with an audible sigh of disappointment. However powerful the Sorceress was, removing, either by hand or by magic, a long established barrier of that kind would leave them vulnerable, as the support of aeons was removed from an unstable roof.

They were about to investigate a distinctly unimpressive tunnel, when they were all startled by a long musical note from the Staff which still hovered in the hallway, suspended, ten steps from the face of the fall.

Ikella's aura sprang into life flashing with an unusual clarity, her Staff issued an unfamiliar cadenza as it began to rotate slowly, scattering flickers of light, which struck reflections off the great wall of loose rock towering above them. In response, Ikella, eyes closed, began repeating the refrain over and over again, until the other Healers present tuned their *othervoices* to the lowest common note in the cadenza, harmonizing with the hovering Staff.

Tuennis stood, spear hefted, ready for anything. Sadorin, silently observing, noted that the wings atop the Staff beat a little faster, as the Staff rotated, they gleaming eerily.

As their harmony stabilised, Ikella withdrawing from the chorus she had established, began to weave a counterpoint to the refrain of the Staff.

Mina, used to acting as observer when new magic was woven, watched carefully, trying to make certain that she could recall the notes exactly. However, the dizzying spin of the Staff, the scattering of light and the blend of *othervoice* was overwhelming even her practised brain, so she was not clear on the precise moment that the great rock fall shimmered, swayed, and disappeared, like the illusion it was, leaving in clear view in its place the entrance to a cavern almost as large as the Audience Hall in Selesh. Ikella visibly started as she saw the illusion dissipate. The other Healers fell silent and the Staff of Selesh floated back to Ikella's hand, as they crowded around her, looking into the cavern which lay down the steep slope of a sandy floor.

Here they could see Azure and Opal sands combined, where countless travellers had made their way between those deserts, for millennia. Here and there animal fodder was still piled high and the great smithed rings still hung on the walls where countless trek beasts had been tethered. They walked down into the dimly lit cavern, while Ikella remained, silently observing the whole arena below her. The group of excited Healers gathered together for a moment, and fell silent, concentrating. Ikella's Staff, even with its enhanced glow, was not enough to light all of this huge cave. Soon, a low chorus of Healer voices chanted, followed by the gleam of light, at which the Sorceress smiled discreetly. She approved of the efficient use of magic at all times and small-magic though it was, suitable only for emergencies, handfire was within the remit of a Healer, and was very effective.

With her own small gleam of dancing light balanced on her palm, Mina caught the eye of the Guaradeign who stared wonderingly at her, till Mina swiftly drew her to one side.

"We need to find the old entranceway."

She confided and together they started scouting the outer perimeter of the cave, where plainly some light was penetrating from outside.

The place was a warren of unused rooms, let into the cavern wall. Hastening from one group to another, as discoveries were made, they soon had an inventory that included pans of a quality and fashion that they had never seen before, stone built ovens with plenty of dry tinder, including snarflin chips and firestone, stacked neatly in great bins. Leaving Midara exclaiming over their finds, and Sadorin making enthusiastic notations on the wax tablet that she invariably wore chained on her belt, Tuennis drew Mina to one side, pointing to a larger source of light, coming from the left side of the cavern. Mina cautiously extinguished her hand fire and saw that there was certainly some more light showing up the copper colour tinges in the rock-opal formation. Carefully using their hands to trace the cavern wall, they made their way over the rough scree that showed where ancient rock falls had occurred and rounding a huge supporting pillar of stone found themselves peering out through the old entranceway, which now stood more than ten men's height above the trail below. Tuennis snorted.

"Too high to lower people down from above, too high above to use the trail, what good is this place to us exactly?"

Her acerbic comment carried clearly to Ikella who had followed them towards the light, and Mina's brows drew together as she realised that the Sorceress was within hearing range. Before she could intervene however Ikella swept forward, and stood silently looking over their shoulders, down into the Low Pass below, she drew a deep breath and then faced her Guaradeign solemnly. Her voice was low, controlled and the hair stood up on the nape of Mina's neck as she spoke for fully ten minutes, outlining her idea on how to rescue the town of Caranchar, sleeping in innocence high above them on the bluff. As Ikella stopped speaking, Mina protested, she had noted the light opal sheen on Ikella's face. She knew the signs that Ikella was supporting some sort of magical weave right now. With the thought that she was in some way protecting their small group, she carefully and respectfully submitted the idea that the Sorceress was trying to do too much, but to no avail. As she stammered to a close with a wail of "But Deshun, " Ikella raised a hand and spoke sharply.

"You must allow me to do what I can Mina, and who knows what I can do now?" She raised her eyes pointedly to where the wings atop her Staff fluttered and Mina, remembering how this indomitable woman had used unknown powers to bring them out of the Silent sands, hung her head in acquiescence. Tuennis eyed the Sorceress steadily as Ikella stood overlooking the Low Pass, one leg braced on the rim of the cavern entrance, her Staff still glowing but palely now against the increased light outside the cavern. She seemed remote and Tuennis was unsure of what she should say to her, if indeed she should speak at all. She knelt in the dust and bowed her head.

"My Deshun, you appointed me to speak for Caranchar, and with your leave I will now speak for Caranchar."

Ikella did not move, not a flicker crossed her face and Tuennis licked suddenly dry lips before taking a deep breath and continuing.

"All that has happened to Caranchar seems overwhelming and when you came we did not see who you were, we only saw a group of Healers and we only saw that amongst your group there was food for our starving children. We did you and yours great harm, and then you showed yourself Sharall deir Opal and you cursed us not, you helped us, and you guided us and you take to yourself only nine of us as hostage to my character, to my willingness to serve. Will you also add your death to the bill of reckoning for Caranchar? Will you use all your power for one place in the sands above all others?" Mina's breath caught in her throat with the wonderment that showed on Ikella's face in reaction to Tuennis' challenge, she saw the resolve strengthen, and inwardly groaned as she realised that far from discouraging Ikella from her plan, the Guaradeign had simply bolstered the Sorceress's confidence. Tuennis continued softly now.

"Deshun, I beg you consider this - if Caranchar has suffered thus, will Selesh, Konomhji, Shadesh, Janmar, Jerigan, to name only those local areas to us here, have escaped? Your duty is to the whole of the Opal, not just to the first place that you come to in your travels! If you kill yourself helping us, you do more harm than good. Leave us to shelter here, and return to Selesh, we have much to occupy us and this place is safe enough."

Her voice quavered as the Sorceress turned to face her, but there was no anger there, only a softened smile, and then Ikella stooped to her Guaradeign and took her hand, raising her to her feet.

"I do not intend to die here Tuennis but I have my plan, I have thought it through and I believe I am right to try. You have suffered enough and I make it my decision to help you in my way, and you shall suffer no harm, no blame if I am wrong."

Her face became remote, her eyes inward looking as she softly repeated the sacred words of her Oath, words that had never been spoken in front of any, other than those Sisters of Sorcery who followed her Rule.

"I write what I write and I weave what I weave, and my weave is my own, sealed in my power for no other to wield."

The Staff blazed forth as the ritual declaration of Power assumed by a Sorceress rang forth and a silenced Tuennis nodded in acceptance of her Deshun's decision and the small party returned from the outer perimeter to the central cavern.

Sadorin appeared strangely pale, but waved her wax tablet at Mina enthusiastically, but Mina could not concentrate. She could feel magic, but she caught the Sorceress's eye and decided that if Ikella had placed some discreet weave here, it must be for the protection of the party, and at Ikella's command the explorers started to return to the ruined town above. Pleased with their discoveries they passed their Sorceress chattering happily, and no-one questioned Ikella's reluctance to leave, nor the direction of the long look that she cast at the vaulted roof above her. On their way into the cavern proper, Ikella's attention had been attracted to a sudden gleam of revealed Opal. Oddly enough no-one else noticed, it only caught her eye as she passed below it, and she had little chance to study until her Healers were otherwise occupied. She had casually returned to the ramp and ascended, just two paces from the outer cavern it had revealed itself again. Just a brief glimmer, but nevertheless it was an image so astonishing that she stood frozen in speculation, but apparently the only one who could see it.

It would have been an imposing sight, the colour of exposed Opal gleaming palely against brilliant gilding, completely dominating the entrance to Caranchar, stamping its authority over her Sands.

As her companions fanned out to search in the dim recesses of the cavern she had (careful not to attract their attention) discreetly increased the light of her Staff until the painting started to reveal itself. It portrayed a figure, surrounded by what seemed to be a circle of rare faceted fire Opal, the hands of the figure were depicted with sparks of gold emanating from the fingers, and as Ikella realised that the portrait was that of a magic user actually spell casting within an aura, the light from her Staff lit up the face of the figure. For once, Ikella was so shocked that for one horrible second she felt as though she had stopped breathing, she felt the colour receding from her face and a sense of unreality pervaded her mind making her feel as if she was walking on legs that felt nothing, supported only by the reality of her own Staff, her own magic. For the face suspended above her, immensely ancient in its mystery, was that of a man!. There was no doubt, here was the full beard of maturity, the flowing hair only worn by the male children of those Outcast, they who became Wanderers. Worst still this one seemed to be singing, depicted as if empowered. Trembling with the shock of such heresy, Ikella did the only thing that she could think of, hastily summoning a dark shadow she sent it streaming upward, totally obscuring the picture from casual observation. Still breathless she had rejoined her companions without a word, only now as the others preceded her on their return, was it safe for her to revisit her discovery. Discreetly dissolving her Weave in order to re-examine the image closely, she saw that the eyes were composed of single polished Opalstone, the whole of the aura seemed to be created by skimming the normal bronze tinged rock face with tiny facetted cuts, revealing costly fire Opal below. The effect of this was stunning, tiny flickers of colour scintillated within its depths, leaving the impression that it shimmered, pulsated even as the living aura of an empowered Sorceress moved.

Crossing her fingers in the superstitious ritual of the SandSworn, she studied the face for a long moment, hastily refreshing her weave, shielding the illustration once more, as anxious voices began to summon her from the ramp above. She was silent and withdrawn as she rejoined the group to begin the long ascent, and thankfully the others left her to her thoughts, Tuennis guided her discreetly, making sure that she took extra care where the stairs fell away, and slowly, thoughtfully, a word, no a phrase turned over and locked into place in her mind. 'Sandsinger? Opal Sandsinger?" and suddenly she did not doubt it, though she did not question too closely how she was to explain it! Her mind raced back to her long Rotations of training at Sanctuary, and in particular a day spent in the Hall of the Past. At Sanctuary, where all Sorceress's trained, there were scrolls that hinted at other classes of mage, above and beyond the understanding of current magic users. These were not accessible to students, only the Guardians of Sanctuary had the ability or the right to read these ancient things, but all students of Sorcery knew that they existed, even what knowledge they contained, because of the last ritual of their training known as the Time of Contemplation. During this period of solitary retreat, a single Guardian, chosen by the Sorceress-Elect concerned, would accompany them for the night and day before they returned to the world. Ikella remembered wandering in silent contemplation round the Hall of the Past, gazing in wonder at the serenity on the faces of the women of High and Ancient Magic, as they were termed by the Guardians. As her weary feet found the steps, she mentally retraced the long night that she had spent in the Hall of the Past. There had been no image of male magic users in the Gallery. Adaria te Syrene, the first Sorceress, had seemed explicit in her teachings-men simply did not use magic (probably lacking some physical characteristic that enabled women to develop and train their othervoice). The voice of her mind stubbornly persisted, was it because in their time there were no male magic users, they assumed that it had always been so? Deeply troubled, she found herself almost at the top of the stairs, light beginning to penetrate the upper corridor, as she turned her feet to the return path.

For some reason beyond her immediate grasp she found the term "Sandsinger," a convincing title, and one that came easily enough to her mind, to her tongue but strangely she could not yet bring herself to reveal what she had found. Aware that Mina at least would return for her if she lingered much longer, she gathered herself and strode out of the concealed entrance to join them at the edge of the Gathering Square. Anxious as she was, not to leave the caverns unguarded, it was a little time before the Town Guard posted themselves to her liking. Her manner affected her party as she pronounced a death sentence on any who defied her to enter the caverns before she was ready, and altogether it was a solemn and thoughtful group that re-entered the infirmary tent to prepare for bed.

Something about the outer tent had changed slightly, and Ikella saw with amusement the small cot bed that had been found for the babies was now positioned hard at hand to her own Inner tent, and as she prepared to enter her small segregated space, she saw that Nadra was sleeping on a mat near her charges. She paused looking down at the babies, sleeping entwined together in a tangle of limbs and wrappings, and thought about her responsibilities. Had she been right to confide in Tuennis and Mina what she was planning to do, she wondered as she stripped to her shift, and used the small amount of water in her ablution bowl to wash. She was bone tired, and needed to sleep on her decision, she thought as she wrapped her sleeping robe about her. Telani, the younger novice entered shyly, eyes downcast and took up the ablutions bowl, leaving a warm sweetdrink in its place, and departed without speaking, aware of the Sorceress's pre-occupation. Ikella sat on her cot bed, her bare feet scrunching into the Opal sand as she sipped the drink thoughtfully. The image on the cavern wall came to her easily. Where had she seen a face like that she wondered, thinking of several places that Wanderers gathered.

Her life made it difficult for her to wander amongst the people openly, like her Healers. She had no access to many places of gathering, perhaps there was a passing resemblance to one of the thousands that she ministered to at Selesh? She pulled her blankets back and swung her legs up onto the bed, it was really quite chilly this evening she noted, absently wondering if the image could be reflected in some clan? Perhaps she had seen it in the market places where the non-conformists made their living. Some of the Sealed retained a fraction of their powers, and illegally wielded it as street entertainers, jugglers, magicians. She had wondered whether their children inherited any such ability? She yawned mightily, reaching out to place her cup on the ground, sliding into the blankets, closing her eyes gratefully.

Her brain still raced, worrying about the morning, about her ability to use the power of the winds as she planned, thinking about the man in the painting. Her memories of the cavern below, her dream vision in the Storm, Carolus. 'Honoured Mother?', 'Warden of the Winds?', Daro, Carolus, the painting, Carolus!'

She slept, dreamlessly and remembered nothing.

Chapter 18 - The Cleansing

The following dawn seemed cold, there was no wind, just an absence of the warmth and light they were used to. Waking stiff, shivering and mildly disorientated, Ikella was conscious of low murmuring voices just beyond the inner tent. She sat, reached for her comb and swiftly dragged it through her hair, plaiting the thick white fall of it into a tight braid, before passing the end through an ingenious smith-worked clip. She coiled the heavy mass of it high and tight at the back of her head fastening it with a long pin, then standing abruptly, shook off her night robe and slipped into her shift, smoothing her underclothes into place, determined to maintain her own standards despite the crisis.

She reached for her outer tunic and paused thoughtfully. No, for this she would wear her ceremonials. The Opalwear long robe and cloak, her Shadushantesh. This close-fitting mask obscured her eyes, face and brow from cheekbones to hairline. Set with the great Opal of her rank, mounted centre forehead like a third eye, her own eyes revealed by gently arched apertures, embellished by tiny opal stones which only added to the glittering inhumanity that the mask imparted to its wearer.

She did not know what material it was made from. It seemed as though it might be metal, Smith-worked at a time when such metals still existed here. She only knew that it epitomised both her segregation and her refuge from her people. That wearing it, she represented the very soul of these Sands, the essence of their beauty, the cold ferocity of their inhumanity. Yet as she opened the side hinges, lifted it to her face, locking it into place behind the great coiled mass of her hair, she came to recognise that it had begun to represent to her, eternal imprisonment.

As taught at Sanctuary, she seldom appeared in public without her mask in place. This guaranteed her safety and privacy, it enforced what had been perceived as a necessary distance between the Sorceress and her people, she supposed. Pausing, hand rising to trace the outline of the Shadushantesh, she wondered if this was why the people did not know that she was their friend, their protector? She knew however, that today she needed to show her people the mystery and the power of magic. She wanted to take back an element of control, demonstrate that there was something that ordinary people could do to restore some normality to their lives, and on this demonstration she understood, depended her own future as the ruler of these Sands. Sighing, she stood, hoping that she could also convey her deep respect for the winds of their world, not only to the people, but to the winds themselves, the winds that today would bring her death if she failed. She gave a cursory glance in the direction of the reflection glass that had somehow been salvaged for her use, and paused. A tall flicker of opal cloth surmounted by her mask was what she expected to see, but today, for the first time she saw the Sorceress. She stood out in the dim light of the inner tent like some glowing beacon in the dark, and yet her aura was not engaged. She gleamed with renewed vigour, with confidence, with excitement, her skin was soft and silky, her hair blending with the Shadushantesh gleamed silvery, and the Opal cloth blazed. Her hands, tattooed with the mystic symbols of Sorcery glittered opalescent, the lacy trail of designs normally so faint that only close examination revealed them, now seemed like close fitting gloves engraved on her skin in fire and ice, and the words "gauntlets of power" occurred to her as she stood silent and marvelling. Her eyes seemed to have opal specks in them she thought, and then dismissing the brief glow of pleasure in her appearance, the satisfaction of presenting a veritable Queen of Sorcery, she picked up her Staff and swept the curtaining of her inner tent aside and entered the outer tent, to stand amongst those gathered there, like the essence of the Opal Desert.

As she emerged from the shadows the gathering outside silenced, and into the shimmering awareness of the new day, the clear bell like tones of the town Guaradeign rang out.

"All hail the Opal, all hail Sharall deir Opal, Ikella of the House Syrene!"

Everyone knelt formally, head bowed before her, save for Tuennis herself, who stood proudly, her bronzed legs revealed below the traditional leather jerkin and short pants of the Inesh guards. She held a spear grounded, point upward, and looked as if an army would have difficulty passing her. Around her brow she wore a circlet of silver and the "bracelets" of her fealty shone glittering opalescent against her dark forearms. Ikella held her eyes for a moment, and then acknowledged her Guaradeign's actions with a brief smile, before turning to her Healers, who mixed with the newly appointed Council of Caranchar, still knelt motionless in the sand.

She addressed them quietly, solemnly.

"You are summoned to undertake a task, which must be completed before the Height of Sun."

Outlining her plans confidently, she gave brisk directions to each group, dismissing them to start work as soon as their part in the strategy had been explained. She spoke at length to Olneth and his men detailing changes that had to be made, and with relief, listened to the orders as the tall Sybillsce organised his men.

"Yes, that is right."

He nodded to the craftsman in front of him.

"You will need tools, and I advise you to take someone to guard them. One of the more able blind could do that. I need to get that doorway opened fully, so that even those we are carrying can be got into safety!"

The craftsman turned away, evidently ready to begin his work, but Ikella found herself intercepting him.

"I also need…" and her voice lowered dramatically. "…a certain drop made safe."

She could not help shivering as she recalled her near miss of the evening before. Olneth to her relief did not ask questions, simply nodded briskly to the workman and said. "Do whatever the Lady requires, but mind your men down there, it is a dangerous place!"

"By your leave?"

He bowed to the Sorceress, obtaining her nodded permission to leave himself, before marching the work party back outside, where he was soon heard issuing orders to those waiting.

The rest remained on their knees eyeing the Sorceress uncertainly, and she hastily dismissed them with a double clap of her hands, saying briskly.

"Go now, there is no time to lose, get everything prepared as though we expect to remain below for a ninenight. Tuennis will tell me when you are all ready."

The Town Council left, a few requests passing between them and their Guaradeign, and then even the sound of Tuennis" voice faded and she was left alone. She raised her voice peremptorily.

"Mina, Inahana, Midara, Andria, attend me."

Keeping her head held high she swept back into her Inner Sanctum once more, followed by those she had summoned, and waited for them to assemble before her. Hands extended palms flattened, she gestured for them to take their seats on the ground, while she paced the ten steps or so across the length of the inner tented area. The room had been stripped of everything except her bed, her blanket roll and her travel pack, and even as she spoke to her group, a silent team of townswomen were at work in the outer tent salvaging the medicaments, the bedding and the washing bowls of the Infirmary.

Ikella raised her eyes and looked at her chosen team. Mina the Senior Healer, Inahana with her special gift of inner calm, Midara the fleet footed, Andria the strong willed, the determined one. She spoke swiftly, decisively.

"I have decided that with the dead still lying buried in the ruins, Caranchar is doomed unless I can persuade the Winds to take the sand away again."

She paused as they eyed her questioningly, she continued.

"Their water is already tainted in places, what is fresh now, will become noxious later. Disease will result from that, have no doubt of it, and the houses here are all crushed or buried, lying well below the level on which we walk. Caranchar is the gateway to the Opal Desert and we need it here, as the filter through which our visitors pass, when they enter the sands on our eastern borders. We need Caranchar to remain crouched on the cliff, where none can overcome it by force, none can surprise it, and no one can enter our Sands by stealth."

She paused, frowning, aware that she sounded defensive. However, after a moment for reflection, she carried on.

"We have two choices here, the long choice which is to make a desert camp, find water or bring water, and only use the strongest men to dig the town out piece by piece, home by home. This will take Rotations, it will breed dissention amongst those native here, who will have to give land to those employed in this dreadful task." She paused, letting her words sink in.

"Have no doubt about it, the Way of the hand in this instance, is beyond consideration, may never be accomplished. Many men here have lost their sight with this 'storm fever" The women have children to feed, the sick to protect, we cannot expect them to dig out the town, bury the dead and rebuild their homes as well."

Her voice though controlled left her audience in no doubt that the Sorceress had already determined the direction that she favoured.

"We have no idea what resources lie elsewhere, who or how many are affected by this calamity, even if Selesh still exists."

She stood silently contemplating this last dreadful statement, palely resolved upon her course. She gathered herself once more, scrutinising her inner circle with a tinge of defiance, as she spoke clearly, deliberately.

"We cannot wait. I must act now, and I have decided that I will attempt to command the Winds to take the sand away and over the cliffs again, so that we can clean Caranchar, bury our dead, and move on!"

That there was an element of challenge in her voice, her Healers did not doubt, but they had no intention of rising to it, so completely convincing was her argument. They simply bowed their heads in acquiescence and the decision was made.

Ikella began disbursing them to their various stations.

"Inahana, will you make sure that Telani looks after Nadra and Daro? You are to take the hostages as your particular responsibility. They can stand with their families 'till all this is over but use them as a work force where you need them. As soon as the way is clear I want you to lead that group to the caverns below, installing them as safely as possible."

The dark Kora-Mai Healer clasped Ikella's hands in her own for a moment, and then departed, silently, purposefully. Ikella turned.

"Midara, there are many blind men here. They will need help and watching. Can you place them amongst people who will watch out for them if they have no family? Also, when all is ready and everyone has gone down to the caves, will you make it your responsibility to send Davini to me alone.? She will be able to pass on any messages at that time, so make sure everyone is aware of that."

Midara nodded, whispering.

"To follow your command my Deshun, will ever be my wish."

They turned tearfully away leaving an indelible impression upon the Sorceress that they really didn't expect her to survive any attempt to enchant the Winds.

She however, found herself growing surer that this was meant, that this was the will of the Way, into which she was being guided. Her resolve grew as she felt a stray breeze stroking her cheek.

She lifted her eyes to her closest friend.

"Mina, if I sing you the weave, can you hold it in your mind? I am going to need the cave entrance sealed, or the sands will bury you alive. Andria, you will have to hold the weave for the doorway in the Square, and somehow we must message between us when all is ready."

She paused thoughtfully.

"I can send the Stone from the cliff! Through that I will be able to see your progress."

She looked at the great stone mounted at the head of her Staff contemplatively before making a complicated pass of her left hand. For a moment the air about her hummed, and the two Healers who were to carry her weave stepped in closely, there was a subdued flicker, as Ikella's aura encompassed them both.

It was as if the three of them were isolated in a shimmering bubble that glistened and gleamed with all the shades of fire opal. They were visible inside the aura, but as the colours swirled and shifted their faces were obscured from time to time. No sound escaped, though plainly all three women were singing. Eventually the aura thinned, dissipated and Ikella's voice was heard clearly saying.

"Mina, can you find something conspicuous that you can use as a signal, if something goes wrong? I must begin my work before the Height of Sun. At that time, I will signal before I begin."

She raised a hand against the babble of questions.

"You will not mistake the signal, now go, we only have a short time before this sullen noon is upon us, and my weave must work. I will send the Stone to you both and when you see it you must echo the weave, remember it is not you that conjures, it is I, and I will have to build my power for this is the greatest enchantment I have ever attempted."

She straightened her back, easing her Staff into a more balanced position, looking thoughtful she murmured.

"I will meditate on this, and take my station on the cliff, from where I will cast."

Her voice quavered just a fraction.

"Take care of Daro for me, if I do not return. Seek his family and make sure that Shiarjha does not undo all my work!"

She handed the beautifully carved token that they had retrieved from the body of Daro's mother to Mina, catching her hand and pressing it in farewell. She caught up her Staff, and before the feeling of isolation overwhelmed her, she drew back the curtain wall and strode out into the hurly-burly of the bustling town.

As she passed amongst them, the people melted away from her, touching their fingers to their lips and bowing in reverence before the Sorceress. Ikella turned her thankfully masked face to the lonely path to the cliffs, and the task that lay before her.

As she made her way to the spot above the Pasture cliff, the town seemed already deserted. She lifted a hand to her eyes, shielding them from the steady breeze that was now blowing against her, and wondered how she was going to summon the nine Sacred Winds. She made an approach to the cliff edge, and as she did so the breeze toying around her face tugged firmly at her Shadushantesh until she was forced to hold it in place.

Turning her back against it, Ikella sank to her knees. She was determined to show the Winds her respect by her ceremonial clothing, by wearing the hated mask, so she attempted to tighten the clasp holding it in position. However the wind, if anything, increased and she thoughtfully reached up, unclasping the mask, laying it carefully at her side.

Kneeling upright, she turned her unmasked face into the wind, but the wind was not there. Only a gentle feather touch at her temples told her where it had been.

She stood, and the breeze lifted her opal encrusted ceremonial long dress, her cloak, twining them around her legs 'till she could not walk another step. She found herself chuckling, thinking. "Can the breeze make me do what no man could?"

She divested herself of her precious ceremonials, and clad only in her shift knelt at the edge of the cliff in a patch of soft Opal sand. She attempted to meditate, but her mind was awhirl, no thought staying still long enough to focus on, all thoughts of the Opal, of the Desert, of her people of Mirayen, the Sacred Wind of these Sands. She found herself loosening her hair, allowing it to tumble around her shoulders like a young girl, and was kneeling there, who knew how much later, when she became aware that she was not alone.

Davini was also kneeling ten paces behind her, hands by her side upright on her knees. The novice's prayer came to Ikella in a low sibilant caress of sound. It seemed that the girl was praying inside Ikella's mind.

"Mirayen, wind of my world, protect us today. Mirayen of my heart, guide our faltering feet. Mirayen, Wind of the Opal Sand accept our prayers."

As Davini's prayer came to an end, Ikella realised that she had already left one task 'till almost too late, and she turned, standing stiffly, aware for the first time how she had drifted into meditation. She picked up her Staff and faced the novice, automatically engaging her connection with the Source as she did so.

"Davini, stand before me."

She murmured, and the surprised novice stood, standing quite still and head bowed as the Sorceress approached her. Ikella wasted no time, she extended the Staff until the trembling girl realised what the Sorceress intended to do. Reaching forward she took the Staff from the Sorceress, holding it fearfully with both hands clasped around the midnight black shaft, looking at the Stone of Selesh which dulled before her eyes to a dim lambency, only just visible in the darkened light of day.

"Now?"

The novice questioned her Sorceress, and Ikella nodded.

"Now!" She stated firmly.

"Or you may wait until the next Sorceress takes power to sing the Drajim, and take your Oath. Are you perhaps not ready?"

Davini's lips quivered momentarily, then she caught the sly gleam in Ikella's eyes and her chin lifted, in response to the Sorceress.

Ikella nodded approvingly as she thought.

'I knew I was not wrong. This girl is more than ready to take the Oath, even here in the open, in full view of her people, she is no coward. I must be the one who confirms her Calling, I could not bear to die before doing so!'.

She raised her arms to begin the process that would take Davini into the Healer Guild as she had so desired. Davini would sing the greatest test of voice, connection to the source and memory, before this day tested her Sorceress in much the same way. Ikella's voice rang out.

"Here stands one at the end of her Walk. Does she think to walk further on this trail of life?" Ikella felt the connection between herself and the Source embrace the novice, and she watched the girls face flush in response.

"I will so walk in the shadow of Syrene, faithful to the Opal sands and true to a Healers calling" the girl murmured. Ikella stepped forward, careful not to touch the novice or her own Staff she engaged her aura about them, and bowing her head commanded.

"Sing then, or be stilled forever."

The aura shimmered and danced as the novice recalled the nine spells that she had collected on her Song Walk. Word perfect, sung in power within the protection of the Sorceress's own aura.

It seemed to Davini as if she sang forever. she had learned these spells over a period of four Rotations of wandering the sands. Some of them she had been able to sing only once before exhaustion had set in, and yet here she had to sing all nine, one after the other, and with all the distraction of being in the open, not in the magically shielded Sacred Circle at Selesh. Eventually it was over, her spells sung, her magically empowered voice stilled, perhaps forever. Into the silence her Sorceress's voice intruded, commandingly.

"Look up girl"

Davini raised her eyes in time to see her success, for the stone atop the Staff had been reignited. Her voice, the spell songs, her own connection to the Source had been validated, for the Opal was glowing, little flickers of blue, gold and rose licking the base of the great stone. Then Ikella was taking the Staff from her suddenly nerveless fingers, raising her to her feet.

"Davina. I, who now use your true name for the first time, celebrate your inclusion into the Guild of Healers."

The sound of the wind blended with Ikella's voice, and the breeze licked at Davina's face, drying her tears of joy, as her full Healer status dawned on her.

The girl raised her eyes to the Sorceress in wonderment, and Ikella met her gaze steadily as their awareness of the wind grew to recognition. Davina spoke quietly.

"Mirayen, Wind of these Sands be forever before me, allowing me to serve my people."

Davina's voice was low and reverent, the Sorceress nodded approval as she bent, retrieving something from the pouch that she had discarded with her ceremonials. Her hands scooped up glittering Opal sand from the patch beneath their feet, then with a glow rising from her empowered hands she leant forward and clasped around the stunned Healers waist a cascade of songbeads.

"Go now, return to your Sisters and show them your beads!"

Ikella ordered, her voice gruff with the response to the joy blazing in the new Healers eyes.

"Tell them that your Walk is complete and that they should use the Seal to write your name in the List. They should write it thus. Davina bin Selesh." She silenced Davina's question with a gentle hug, set the Healers hand on the Great Seal of Selesh that she had woven into the Songbeads, saying only.

"Sssh, don't cry, I will retrieve the Seal myself later, directly from your hand. It is better thus, and is for Shiarjha's protection that I pass it to you now."

She considered for a moment, then added softly.

"If I cannot take the Seal back, then Sadorin will know how. I am glad that your Walk ended with me."

The new Healer saw the determination settle over the Sorceress once more. She watched the withdrawal to some inner place of contemplation, as she went to prepare the others for the cleansing of Caranchar.

As the young Healer left, Ikella turned back to the cliff edge. The wind curled about her body in an intimate caress, teasing at the straps on her shift, toying with the hem of the fine linen. An image flickered through her receptive mind and she knelt, both appalled and intrigued at the idea that had crossed her mind.

'Surely not?'

She questioned inwardly, feeling that her intention to show Caranchar a more human Sorceress had been turned back on her in a way she could never have expected. The wind played with her hair, sending the great volume of it in an icy cascade almost to her hips, and she sighed, putting her shift aside, sliding her sandals off till she stood naked before the Wind of her Sands. It was strange, she thought, at the moment of highest vulnerability she felt more powerful than she ever had.

She stood at the very edge of the high cliff, legs astride, bracing herself against her Staff, she engaged her aura and sent the Stone of Selesh soaring out from the cliff edge, in a low swooping flight, intended to signal her state of readiness to Mina and Midara. She deliberately emptied her mind of all distraction, concentrating on the Stone, empowering it for her Healers to send it back to her.

She waited anxiously, 'till hearing the "zing" that the swooping stone made, she opened her eyes, to see it hovering not half a hand in front of her and reached out to capture it. However, clearly reflected in its surface was the bright red signal band that Mina had set indicating that there was a problem. Seething with frustration Ikella stood down from the cliff edge, whatever happened she had to complete her task! Turning away from the Low Pass, she strained her vision to its limits, trying to see what was going on in the Gathering Square below, aware of movement round the entranceway to the caverns. Soon she could see a Healer approaching, holding something awkwardly and wracked with a horrid premonition, saw that it was Mina. Her worst fears were realised in the embodiment of a very angry screaming baby, being carried in a totally unsympathetic manner by his irate "minder"

The Sorceress had been so engaged in summoning the winds, that stepping back from that process left her shaking. She approached the baby in Mina's arms wonderingly, slipping her finger inside his fist, staring down at his crumpled features, noting the spillage of tears still wetting his face. She could "feel" his rage as he screamed defiance at her, at the world, at anyone who would listen, and she swiftly lifted him into her arms, trying to nestle him into her, to rub his back, thinking to ease whatever pain he was in. The child however was not having any of it. He arched against her, hurting her breasts, both hands rigidly extended. His face turned up, mouth agape shrieking, as if a mortal fear gripped him. His face was reddened and Ikella sat gentling him until he quietened momentarily, as she heard Mina grumbling.

"Scream, upon peal of scream. Unnerved everyone, me included. Couldn't raise the weave, couldn't think or hear my own voice above his. It's unnatural. that's what it is! What should we do?"

Ikella settled the baby against her, then stated, with a firmness that surprised both of them. "He should stay here with me. My aura will protect both of us, if you two can balance the weave below. I must have both hands free though, I cannot hold him!"

She frowned till Mina snorted.

"That's easy then, bind him to you as the gleaning women do with their young."

The Healer eyed her Sorceress sourly.

"You could do with something to cover you up anyway. You'll catch your death of cold, you will! Your sash will make a good harness, and I think I remember how to create such a thing!"

The two women took the sash off Ikella's ceremonial long dress, and carefully wrapping the baby as the women of the Fringes dressed their children, they bound him to Ikella's bosom, face in, hands and feet protected.

Ikella stood, Mina holding the great Staff for her but the baby immediately started fighting the binding, his fists bunched, his face almost blue, he gulped several times and then screamed till Ikella loosened the binding and shook him free.

She held him till he calmed a little, and Mina seeing how he seemed happy and comfortable with his back to Ikella's bosom, his hands and feet free to kick, muttered.

"If he would stay as comfortable that way round, I would bind him there." I

Ikella mindful of the approaching Height of Sun and the need to begin her work, suggested.

"Try it."

To both women's relief, the baby allowed them to bind him in place, and leant back against her bosom, sucking a finger contentedly. Mina started off down the track hurrying to her position in the cave mouth below, Ikella went back to the cliff edge, regained her position and waited. Her mind drifted aimlessly, as she tried to recapture the inner calm she needed, before spell casting.

She thought that she had allowed for everything, everything except the baby of course! Lowering her mouth to nuzzle the soft downy head tucked beneath her chin, she felt in the contact a centring of purpose, a reason for persisting in her efforts. As though the child himself was trying to bolster her confidence, he snuggled into her.

In that instant, Ikella felt the lift of the wings atop her Staff, and concentrated on harvesting every elemental contact that she could. She planted the Staff deep into the ground. With a resounding "thud" it went home, and the great tolling echo of its "homed" chime echoed over the Low pass. Next she loosed the finial that again held the stone known as the Heart of Selesh to the shaft. Using only the hand of her mind, she flipped back the catches and sent the Opal soaring once more. It traversed the entrance to the cave on the cliff wall, and whirring above the heads of the trusting population of Caranchar, it travelled through and up to the group waiting just inside the entrance on the Gathering Square, returning to Ikella with an image of pale faces, solemn eyes and the sound of silence. It hovered briefly before her, and as it did so a stray beam of light touched the horizon and Ikella realised that Height of Sun was upon them and she must spell cast now or never.

She carefully returned the stone to her Staff, sending out a cascade of chimes as she did so, alerting those below that she was about to summon the Winds. Kissing the baby, almost in apology for taking him into such danger, she turned her mind to her task. She drew a deep breath, letting it out through her nostrils, 'shushing" it through her mouth, and framed the words that she had practiced in private so many times. Trickling her power gently, coaxing rather than commanding, she drew the Winds to her by name.

At first, she was not sure if anything was happening. There was an odd flurry in the breeze, as if before. and she resisted with difficulty the desire to call out to Mirayen, to call upon him to identify himself. She continued her soft chant naming the winds, one after another, careful to call them in ritual order, increasing the power, less subtle persuasion now, more command in her, and she slowly became aware of a gentle "thrumming" noise.

No, make that a roaring, hissing, percussion that beat incessantly on the ground at her feet. Opening her eyes, closed in reverence, she saw the Winds towering into the rolling cloud above, revolving slowly, twisting great billows of sand into a spiral pillar that rocked on its heels not ten spans from her.

She clasped the baby to her and he screamed in outrage, fighting her protective hands with thrusts of his whole upper body, till she released him. He gurgled with laughter, waving his hands in glee as the great pillar danced before her, and Ikella, connected to the Source in a way that she had never experienced before, relaxed, concentrating on conveying a picture of Caranchar as it had been before the Storm, to the elements that she apparently controlled.

Try as she might, she could never find adequate words to describe what she saw, what she sensed, as the great whirlwind hovered a moment before sweeping majestically out over Caranchar. She watched in amazement as the colours within the pillar changed as it rotated, and saw within the great whirling mass of it, sand gathering, Opal, Azure, clean sand, dirty sand, and other things that she could not identify. The pillar crossed the buried Gathering Square, with a bubbling sucking sound. It looped and returned to her, leaving a miasma of disturbed sand behind it but as it hovered in front of her, apparently waiting for her command, the baby leapt in her arms and she was forced to steady him as he bucked and kicked in excitement. Without consciously planning what she was going to do, Ikella pictured the great pillar releasing the debris in a heap over the edge of the cliff, and with a low roar the whirlwind complied.

In shocked delight, she caught the baby against her in a hug of pure joy.

'Look what we have done Daro! See how we helped everyone!'.

Caught up in the madness of it, Ikella danced and sang as the Winds worked her will.

'If I am a little mad, who cares? I am wielding my powers for the good of my people, so how can that be against the Way? Sanity can return later!'

Trembling with the sheer exhilaration of having correctly divined a method of cleansing Caranchar, she sang and sang and even the baby was cooing with her as the day grew darker, and the winds still worked. They brought the sands from the town streets, out of the buried buildings, and poured it over the edge of the cliff, into the great scar that was once the Low Pass. She sent the great opal over the edge of the cliff to find that the weave, the opal screen that she had her Healers maintaining from inside the caves, still in place. Relieved, she had just returned the stone to Staff when she became aware that the baby was rubbing his eyes. She was now feeling very tired herself, and the pillar of the Winds was again hovering in front of her.

It was turning more lazily now, and close examination showed her that little sand coloured its sides.

'Was it over?'

She concentrated, sure that she heard a voice within the roaring of the winds, but she could not identify what it said. Her attention was distracted, she was becoming too tired to wield so much power. She glanced down at Daro wondering how she was going safely disburse the Winds, when before her eyes, the immense pillar shrank to a man's height. She held out her hands, and the breezes caressed her for a moment. whispering in many voices.

"All Hail the Voice. All Hail."

Before she could raise two thoughts to question what she had heard, the pillar dissolved completely, and was gone.

The baby whimpered piteously, and Ikella strangely undisturbed by the

139

maelstrom, wrapped the shivering child in her cloak. Then she wrapped herself in her discarded finery, scooping up the Shadushantesh, returning it to her face before wearily making her way on legs that trembled, back along the pathway to the town.

Chapter 19 - Recalled to Reality

Still caught up in the magic that she had wrought, Ikella stood marvelling at the newly revealed Caranchar. Now stripped of the enveloping sand, the houses lay bare, roofless to the gloomy sky above, the evidence of the many personal tragedies of this place revealed for all to see. In accordance with Healer practice she always carried a shantana to mask her mouth and nose from noxious elements. She fumbled one handed in her pouch, prepared to don it immediately as she re-entered the town, for in truth she expected horror, the stench of putrefaction and decay from these homes-turned-tombs, but there was no evidence to support these concerns. Surprised she paused in an open doorway, and narrowing her eyes peered into the darkened room within. Those who once coloured this home with all the shades of shared joy now lay abandoned in a far corner. A man and his wife curled protectively around a child of not more than a few months old. The Sorceress' heart contracted, as she glanced down at the heavy, sweet warmth of the foundling, nestling against her maiden bosom. She turned back to the remains, which should have been in advanced decomposition, noting with surprise that instead they appeared rather to be desiccated, but retaining their essential identifiable nature. Puzzled she stepped into the room, carefully protecting Daro's sleepy head in the crook of her arm, she approached this small huddle of death with reverence, removing from her face the Shadushantesh and closing the mask with a small elaborate gesture, she transformed it to its travel size, and slid it into the concealed pouch on her cloak. She looked down on those who lay there, and then became aware that their features were preserved under what she could only describe as a thin coating of opal. As if the scouring winds had polished their corpses they clung to each other, and even as she turned away, overcome with the grief of her Desert a small girl darted past her, followed by a woman of advanced Rotations who was protesting.

"Moula, wait for me, come back. they will not be there. they have gone to the winds" but the child was chattering in relief.

"Mama.! Noni! I knew I could find you, I knew you would be here."

Fascinated, Ikella stood stock-still, watching the child smooth her hands over the opaline frozen bodies of her parents, her baby brother. She raised huge brimming eyes to the Sorceress.

"Thank you Lady, thank you. I wanted only to say goodbye to them, but I could not find them."

She sobbed suddenly and ran to the older woman who was clearly her grandmother. The elder drew the child to her, but turned her firmly back to face her parents and sibling once more.

"Our Deshun and the winds have found them for us, and have honoured them by dressing them for burial in the Opal of our Sands. See how it was for them. they were together, the ones that were chosen by the Sand. Together and unafraid."

Ikella followed the direction of the woman's shaking finger and saw with amazement that the man's body, was curved around his wife's so that he could look down on her with a smile of love. That the woman gazed down on her child with tenderness. Maybe they simply never knew what hit them, but it seemed unlikely that neither of them recognised death when it faced them. Shaken and awed by her discovery, Ikella shifted the now sleeping baby into a more comfortable position in her arms, and pressed the soft sleepy sweetness of him closer to her.

She dipped in the ritual acknowledgement of the families bereavement, and left the shattered home, aware for the first time of a low muttering sound, thrumming like the winds, vibrating through the soles of her bare feet. She peered anxiously through the shattered buildings, now surrounding her, the sand sufficiently removed to have lowered the pathways of the town to their normal level, so that walls once more towered above her. As she did so, the source of the sound was revealed as the people swept back into their town again, running at full pelt, desperate to see what she had achieved. The difference in the demeanour of the townsfolk was astonishing as they ran towards her, chattering, pointing out what damage, great, little or none had been done to their homes as they came. They swept up to her, passed her and were gone, each determined to get to their own place to see what had been revealed in such a short period of time. The Sorceress, cradling the baby to her stood stock still, protecting her own position with nothing more magical than an averted face and her sheltering body, as they rushed past.

When the first flood was over, and the stream of people emerging from the caverns had died to a steadier trickle of those elderly, blind and very young people in need of assistance, Ikella stood away from the doorway in which she had sheltered, starting towards the infirmary tents once more. All about her was noise, bustle and confusion. Already men and women stood at the doors of their own homes conversing with their neighbours, sharing private moments of joy and sadness, as the town gave up its dead.

She saw the weaver at the door of his house, and remembering that he had lost his family in the storm, paused to see how he fared. His eyes seemed to focus on the past as he hovered there uncertainly, and Ikella saw the outlines of a woman beyond him as she peered at something on the floor. As the Sorceress drew closer it became obvious that they were assisting each other in finding their dead, and she wondered dully how many more of the town would be engaged in such sad duties for the foreseeable future.

Then tall, ever more imposing figure of her town Guaradeign approached her. Tuennis dropped to one knee in front of her, spear lowered and spoke quietly.

"Deshun, I am relieved to see that you and the child are well. I have ten of the Town Guard out looking for you, but the people were desperate to return home, so I let them go. It is for the best, for now they will have things to occupy their minds and hands."

Ikella stood looking down at Tuennis, and raised an eyebrow enquiringly.

"Town guard?"

She questioned and Tuennis flushed.

"It is necessary!"

The Guaradeign raised her eyes and studied Ikella steadily.

"Now will be a time of high emotion, of confusion, people react to death so differently I must enforce the law. I cannot wait to gain obedience through respect." She continued.

"I thought that if we had to leave Caranchar, we would need a Guard for the journey. Then it occurred to me, that if you succeeded we would still need a Guard. There are many more houses and possessions than there are living people to use them. Whatever their status, people are still fallible and nature will out! The result of not being prepared could see the weak being cheated of their inheritance. Even the dead need protecting at times!"

Ikella, poised on shaking legs smiled at Tuennis.

"I think I did well to choose you."

She murmured, shifting the drowsy baby to the opposite arm, then adding quietly to her companion.

"If I do not get some rest, I shall fall down right here and now."

Tuennis, bemused, was suddenly aware that this indomitable woman was on the point of collapse.

Swiftly scooping Daro from Ikella's faltering grasp, she lent the weary Sorceress her arm and they walked the ten short spans from the edge of the Gathering Square to the narrow alley beyond which the strangely untouched tents were visible.

They passed the entrance to a courtyard, and Ikella paused to see a couple lifting a small body on to a bright blue coloured cloth. The man, plainly blind, knelt at one end of the sheet, and as his wife covered the child's body gently, he lifted a hand, and Ikella saw with infinite pity that he was pinching the two layers of fabric together, placing stitches in the child's shroud. She walked forward towards them, and the woman looked up, tears streaking her face.

"Sharafi. Here is our Deshun."

The woman murmured to her husband, and was about to struggle to her feet, but Ikella hastily said.

"No, do not get up, it is alright. What a sad duty you perform."

She bent over the small corpse in its bright blue shroud and raised a hand in blessing, invoking the wind of the Opal, praying softly.

"Mirayen. this child takes his long walk in your name. Take him and guide him ever towards the Source and the peace that he seeks."

The woman clasped her hand, pressing it to her cheek thanking her brokenly, as Ikella asked curiously.

"Is this your child?" The woman sobbed as she answered.

"No my Deshun, it is the child of our neighbours. We have not yet found them, but they too have undoubtedly gone to the Sands as well. We have the others in our safe keeping."

At Ikella's unspoken question she went on.

"There are three of them, and the One only know where we shall house them, or how we shall feed them. My husband was the Dresser of the Dead, but we have no children of our own, only a small house, and he can hardly work now he is blind."

She was plainly overcome with the situation, and Ikella frowned as she began to realise the gravity of the situation, in the wake of such a disaster.

Not so Tuennis. She stepped forward.

"Disna, if you will help him, Sharafi can still work, and there is more than enough work for him right now." Her voice was determined, brisk, and the wife of the undertaker looked up in hope.

Tuennis warmed to her theme, almost ignoring the Sorceress, she continued.

"Your neighbours have no living adult relatives, but the surviving children have a right to their home and property, and as they will have to live with someone 'till they are old enough to inherit, it seems only right that they should live with you. You shall have the use of both houses which the town will help you to repair. If we turn the homes of those who died into town resources we can make an Infirmary a mortuary for Sharafi and a place where he can teach a sighted apprentice to help him."

She raised a hand against the soft protestations of the townswoman.

"Disna, if there is work, there is food. No one has exchange right now, but if they provide you and yours with food, blankets, labour, it will only take a short time before Caranchar recovers."

Ikella nodded approvingly. Disna touched the child's shroud doubtfully, her husband plainly listening intently worked on, his hands less uncertain now as he stitched along the length of the sheets.

"Blue Deshun? Such a bright blue?"

Disna seemed to be struggling with the impropriety of using such a cheerful colour for a such a dismal purpose and Ikella hastened to reassure her.

"Bright blue!" Ikella agreed. "A happy choice for a child don't you think? A celebration of the happiness a child brings. The children should have their lives recognised in such a way! We shall honour them with name plaques on the walls of the Gathering Square, for this generation should never be forgotten."

She straightened and speaking directly to Tuennis she announced.

"All property matters must come before open Council Tuennis." She advised seriously.

"As you say, this will be a time of high emotion, and there will be those who will seek to cheat children out of their inheritance. I think you will need an orphanage or a fostering scheme. There is much to consider. Everyone's loss must be recognised or you will swiftly lose control. I fear that I have given you no ordinary task!"

She paused, conscious of something that she had forgotten and then as she remembered, she turned away from the undertaker and his wife, to return to the Infirmary talking to the Guaradeign as they departed.

"Tuennis, at Selesh there is a custom, that when someone goes to the Sands we carve their names, their name day on the walls of the caverns. It occurred to me that each family here could do the same on the walls of the caverns below. Some of us take a flower or a herb that the dead one loved to that place and leave it there on their name days, others like to light a candle so that for their name days the dead have light once more. You might think that odd, but it is something that brings comfort and there is so much sorrow here"

Tuennis paused in her long stride and looked down at the baby huddling against her.

"Yes, " she agreed her tone even.

"Not just for the dead."

There was no reproach in her voice, but Ikella thought immediately of Ahnell, her child waiting for his companion back in the Infirmary and sighed inwardly.

They passed through the narrow alleyway in silence, each thinking of their own responsibilities and in the surreal landscape of the ruined town here was one more anomaly for the Sorceress to ponder, for the small tented arena was untouched, despite the fact that the towering pillar of the Winds had passed right through this area. Ikella paused as she was about to enter the infirmary, and gently lifting Daro from Tueniss" arms she said quietly.

"Tuennis, hear this. Your child Ahnell will be brought up with Daro. He will be nursed by Nadra and will be treated as my own child. No harm will come to him, he will want for nothing, and in the unlikely event that we find Daro's family, we will return both Nadra and Ahnell to you on the day that Daro leaves our care. When Caranchar can stand alone again, you will be the one to bring me the news and to you I will hand over the keys of the town, and the freedom of all the hostages will be assured. Be it in one Rotation or ten, I will honour the arrangement."

The dim light was fading fast, and in front of her Tuennis was a remote silhouette against the bright hued tents behind her. She stood while the Sorceress spoke and then her voice breaking she said softly.

"I once had a son called Ahnell. I shall never forget that or him. but I cannot be mother to a town and a mother to a child as well. I am not like you Sharall deir Opal, Great Sorceress of the House Syrene. You are Shalhanhi, inheritors of the Opal. I am but Inesh, born of the same Sands but born into the second Clan, into slavery."

She raised a hand to silence the shocked Sorceress.

"I know in speaking thus, I probably forfeit my life or that of my child, but if no-one speaks, how will you know what all Inesh feel?"

Her low bitter voice roughened as she demanded.

"Tell me, is there a name stone for Shamatiss my mother? She who was your personal body guard, slain by a tegrin ten Rotations ago. Will there be a name stone for me or anyone to light a candle at my passing?"

The light caught the planes of her face as she whispered.

"I know it is the Way! The Way that my mother lived, the Way that her mother lived before her but Deshun who decreed the Way? Why is the Way so cruel? Will the Way ever change? What power will make it change?"

Plainly distraught, she fled into the gathering dusk, and Ikella pondering her Guaradeign's words took the baby to Nadra, silently watching as he turned his face away from the proffered breast. Laid beside Ahnell, she watched silently as the foundling and the hostage child twined arms around each other and felt a surge of real jealousy. Would that she could sleep peaceful and warm in the arms of another!

Thoughtfully she made her way into her Inner Sanctum and changed wearily into her tunic and loose pants. Finding soft leather boots she pulled them on, determined to revisit the caverns once more. Noting that she still trembled, she wondered how her legs had held her up so long and was grateful to be left to her own devices, to recover slowly.

Davina, the new Healer came in quietly with a warm sweetdrink, and nodding to her respectfully, would have withdrawn till the Sorceress held up her hand.

"Stay a moment child."

Ikella murmured, and the girl remained settling on the ground as the Sorceress indicated. As Ikella buried her face in the welcome warmth from her cup, she shivered and the young Healer raised her eyes and to the Sorceress's amusement, gently captured her hand, seeking the pulse at her wrist. She waited patiently for Davina to satisfy herself, before gently removing her hand from the Healers grasp.

"Would you like to remain here Davina?" Ikella questioned, and for a moment the Healer's face went utterly blank, then flushed as she divined the Sorceress's intention. The girl stilled, eyes narrowed as she contemplated the question.

"Do you mean me to become the Healer of Caranchar?"

She questioned softly, and Ikella nodded.

"If you wished to do so."

The Sorceress replied sipping her drink, taking in the restorative that had been added to the liquid, feeling her strength returning.

"There is much to do, much of it beyond your experience to date." Ikella confided.

"You will need experienced help and until things change, more than one Healer will be needed here, but it is my intention to give you the living of Caranchar. To that end I would like to leave you here when we return to Selesh tomorrow."

Her own words startled her, for she had spoken even as the thought formed. She had spent so little time with the other Healers since she had arrived, that hard on the heels of her decision came the thought.

'We will have little time to prepare for departure.'.

However, everything of value had already been packed for the caverns, so she could be reasonably confident that arrangements could be made, more or less instantly. She eyed Davina solemnly.

"You need not fear being entirely without help, for Sadorin will be your assistant. Because of her position of trust, working with Kateya who was Healer here for many Rotations, I made her Town Recorder. She will manage both positions well, both Healer knowledge and administration are not unknown to Sadorin."

She paused, and then plunged straight on.

"I will take you into my confidence now, for you will need to know certain things which I am privy to. You may not discuss this with any other, even Sadorin herself, for I would not diminish her dignity in any way. Do you remember that I asked you to carry the Seal of Selesh for me?"

Her hand shot out as she spoke and Davina laid her precious Songbeads into Ikella's palm. With a small tinkle the Seal detached itself and Ikella pocketed it thoughtfully.

"I do not know her Sand of origin, but Sadorin is herself a stilled woman. Once, she too would have entered the House of Sorcery, but her path was swept away by circumstances that are beyond my knowledge. As Head of our House, I have accepted her oath of fealty, she is an honourable woman, with the freedom of our Sands. You may trust her as you trust me."

The astonished look on the girls face would have been laughable under other circumstances, but now Ikella pressed on.

"On my return I will send a detachment of guards back to bring you remedies and to accompany another Healer, who will stay and work with you. Do you want anyone in particular to aid you?" Ikella had noted that the new Healer looked a little forlorn as her position sank in.

Davina however inexperienced, showed maturity of decision as she faced Ikella.

"I would have liked Telani to stay with me, but I do not think that it is time yet!" She replied cautiously, then brightening a little she asked hesitantly.

"Can I have Cara?" and Ikella thought of the plump little Healer from the Tourmaline Sands. Remembering her as the one who could get even the most withered of plants to rejuvenate.

"Good, that is settled then. Cara is a good choice, very calm, happy round children if I recall her correctly, not afraid of hard work. Well done."

To the young Healers surprise she swept the curtain to the outer tent back and called out.

"Andria, Mina, fetch Sadorin for me can you? Do we have any stemmis left with which to celebrate? All of you, come and drink success to Davina, Healer of Caranchar. We leave for Selesh at first light."

Amidst the chatter of congratulation, Ikella picked up her Staff, gently touched Mina on the arm and withdrew from the happy bustle in the Infirmary tent, walked back through the town to the Gathering Square and headed directly for the caverns.

"I have something to show you" she said simply in answer to her companions questions, and presently having used the light from her Staff to illuminate their path, she positioned Mina so that she could see the painting on the roof of the cavern and removed her shielding weave. The Healer looked up inquisitively as the masking dissipated, and saw the painting revealed. She pushed her hood back from her hair and stretched on tiptoe, straining to see the full image, and Ikella prompted her companion.

'Oh, use your powers woman. Widen your sight, he cannot hurt us!'.

Mina closed her eyes briefly, sang a long note then drew on the Source, enhancing her vision of the picture above.

She stood in silent contemplation, before voicing her opinion.

"A pretty fancy that, using the rock face like a colour. If it was cleaned the gilding would be very impressive."

Ikella snorted derisively.

"Mina, look at it closely. Tell me what you see!"

She raised her Staff before impatiently launching it into the air with a single word of command.

"Illuminus!"

The light strengthened, brightened, then flared, bringing the painted magic user to life as the gilded walls glowed and the colours of the opal danced in the blaze. Mina looked at her companion with concern.

"You will kill yourself if you continue to use this much power in a day." She counselled. Ikella looked at her strangely.

"So I have been assured before. However, I have noted many changes lately. The Source feels different to me, as though some dam has been unblocked, the flow, the connection is all different now. Even though I am tired, I never felt so well in my life."

Mina, looking at her closely, observed that indeed there was a healthy glow to her friends skin. She showed none of the dreadful fatigue she had exhibited after the Storm, so she kept her counsel and resumed her study of the picture.

"It is unusual that the magic user has been created in all his power."

She ventured, and the Sorceress said witheringly.

"Exactly. *His* power. *His*? Mina, men cannot wield power and yet he actually seems to have an aura. This is heresy. These caverns must have been used by some Wanderer cult. No wonder they were blocked off. No-one in their right minds would have wanted their children to see such things!"

Mina examined the Sorceress covertly. She looked really worried.

"Forgive me, but are you taking this picture far too seriously? It is far too old to worry about. It is very skilled work, partly carved and gilded I grant you. The face seems to be that of a man. or it could have just been the fancy of the artist. It is only a painting Ikella, it has no power of its own!"

Ikella retorted.

"It may only be a painting in itself, but show that to a Wanderer and he will think it a prophecy that means that a Wandering man with power equal to that of a Sorceress either existed in the past, or will come to exist. Show that to a believer and you shake their belief in the powers that are! Show that to me and you shake MY belief in myself."

Her voice quavered suddenly, and Mina immediately went to her and encircled her with a protective arm.

"You are tired my friend, and we must return to the Infirmary. You need to rest, we need to see what occurs in the town. You must not worry about that silly thing. Hide it again if you must, but come, let us go above again."

Ikella let herself be drawn away, concealing the image as before, and soon they were walking through the streets off the Gathering Square again. Lights shone here and there, where glows had been set in windows. Men were struggling to put up shutters with the help of friends or relatives, and they walked amongst the busy town, unnoticed, unseen.

As they entered the Infirmary tent, it seemed to be in uproar. Ikella had been prepared for busy, purposeful bustle. They were leaving, and she suddenly realised that she would be very glad to do so for she already felt a stranger here. Caranchar was coming back to life again, everyone had work to do and they could all be master of their own Way. She and her kind were no longer needed here and her heart ached for a moment, for she had enjoyed her short time as 'one of the people'. Mina cast her a look as she took up the lead, sweeping aside the awning sheet, anxious to see what was going on within. She paused, a smile brightening her face as she stood framed against the entrance, peering in at the confusion inside.

Almost immediately there was a cry of welcome from the Infirmary, as the echoes died away, Ikella found herself surrounded by tall, athletic young women. Unlike her Healers, these wore their hair tightly braided beneath sombre black headcloths. They were veiled in the same black material, each of them wearing short black jackets, loose black pants, wide smith worked belts that jangled fierce with weaponry. As Ikella ran her eyes over them, noting how their bronzed bodies glowed with the essence of vigour, of strength, they fell to their knees facing her. Spears upright, hilted to the sand in ritual salute. As one, they touched their hands to heart and lips before thundering in unison..

"All hail the Opal, Ikella of the House Syrene."

The Sorceress was once again surrounded by her personal guard. By the tradition of these Sands alone, the Inesh warriors guarded the Sorceress, who rarely journeyed without such an escort. Only a ritual, sacred to the ceremonial life of a Healer was likely to break that pattern, and so it had been that accompanied by the Council of Nine, Ikella had left her personal guard behind at Selesh, when she left to meet Telani and Davini from Song Walk.

She had realised that she would be the subject of some concern at Selesh, but more immediate matters had closed her eyes to the fact that to these women, her safety represented their whole reason for living. In fact they would blame themselves if she had been lost to the Storm and so it was that a very chastened Sorceress took their ritual greeting very much more seriously, aware that in their relief at so doing, several of them were openly weeping.

Mina took up the reigns of her position without faltering once.

"The Deshun must rest now."

She swept the Inesh from her path, as Ikella found herself being shepherded to the small inner tent, disrobed, and wrapped in her sleeping shift firmly. Suddenly aware of deathly fatigue, she lowered herself into her bed, hearing the voices that she had thought never to hear again discussing the situation at Selesh, through a dim roaring in her ears. It was not until then that she realised that she had not eaten that day.

Even as she thought it, some fresh bread was being pressed into her hands, and soon she was protesting that she could eat no more, and not until then would Mina allow Driss, Captain of her Guard into her presence.

"Mina, we leave in the morning at first light remember. We must collect up the families, assist the men."

Her voice tailed away uncertainly at the expression on Mina's face, and realised that the well oiled machinery of her entourage had swung back into gear again, as though it had never stopped. Something in her sighed at the loss of familiarity with her teams working practices. Somehow the return to the remote, distanced existence that her position demanded had little appeal to her, and as Driss entered her presence with a clatter of spear grounding and formal salutations, Ikella found that she had developed a positive distaste for such things.

She buried deep within her this knowledge, as she greeted Driss, turning her thoughts to the next day and all the problems still waiting her attention. Soon enough she discovered that close on Shiarjha's panicked return from Caranchar, Selesh itself had been hit by the Storm. Driss confirmed that almost unable to believe what they heard from the young Sorceress-Elect, they had nevertheless brought everyone in from the outer village, only concluding that activity just before Selesh was Storm-stricken. Before Shiarjha and her team of rescuers could leave, the winds had raced up the Great Divide, where her Guard had been on exercise. Finding shelter in the gorge, they had waited the Storm out, before returning to Selesh where they found the Gate in the Rock immovable.

Although everyone within was safe, food and water plentiful, no-one could leave 'till the Gate in the Rock was freed and so the Guard had made their way to Caranchar, seeking news of Ikella, as well as the manpower to free the Gate.

Ikella chuckled grimly as she heard how the Guards had laboured for several days at the task of digging out Selesh, thinking that if she had chosen that method of restoring a whole town, another Age would have found them still digging. Driss, not knowing how her Sorceress had freed Caranchar, was delighted to find her alive, but very worried about the 'storm tower" that they had witnessed returning to Caranchar from their vantage point on the track from Selesh. Ikella was suddenly shy, leaving Mina to explain how they had contrived to liberate the town from the pall of sand that had buried it. Wonderingly the Guard Commander had taken her women out into the township to inspect the wreckage in awed silence.

She knelt at Ikella's feet again afterward, almost incoherent in her approbation for the Sorceress" achievements and Ikella grew gruffly embarrassed by the praise. Driss bowed her head to the sand and clasped Ikella's foot, raising it till her head was under it in symbolic submission, calling her "Great of these Sands" an ancient honorific reference to Adaria te Syrene, the Founder of the Healer Guild, Discoverer of Sorcery. At this she rebelled, drawing Driss to her feet, aware that she should not dwell on her own power for fear that she might mistake a great success for infallibility.

At last, she dismissed them to sleep while they could, and settled down to think, acutely aware that many back at Selesh thought her dead. Later that night as she talked to Mina, who was sharing her inner tent so cramped was the accommodation now, she sleepily voiced the thought that moving the sand was no problem!

"After all." she chuckled grimly.

"I have moved enough of that today, though it was strange that the winds didn't even seem to have disturbed the Infirmary tent."

She sighed sleepily. Mina said soberly.

"Not as strange as the way in which the sands were moved my Deshun."

She paused saying thoughtfully.

"The baby came out of it quite well, though I would not recommend exposing any young thing to such magic. It is not natural, and it is certainly not right for a male child to be exposed to such power."

Her voice drifted until as if one thought had sparked another, she suddenly said.

"Ikella.? don't you think it strange that the picture on the wall of the cavern is not unlike Carolus the Apothecary?", but Ikella was already asleep.

Chapter 20 - Farewell

The morning dawned dark and threatening as the Council of Nine rose and packed last minute possessions, before leaving Caranchar.

'Even the air seems tired these days.'

Ikella thought as she dressed, one free hand holding her leather cup out for stemmis, (brewed from dry leaves, imported from the High Carnelian Plains). She sat, moodily allowing Telani to braid her hair, and stow small possessions into her travel pack, while she brooded over her plans. She saw little point in waiting for the town to awake, for her particular talents were needed elsewhere. Tuennis, and the other families with hostages would only suffer the longer their farewells were prolonged, and she had no intention of losing the advantage of travelling before the sullen heat grew. She was still thinking this over when outside her Inner Sanctum there was a challenge from the Inesh. Shortly thereafter a flustered Driss arrived in front of the Sorceress. For once she was not carrying a spear. She was pale, wringing her hands together in an agony of uncertainty. Licking dry lips nervously, she seemed unable to find the words she sought, and Ikella stared at her as the woman finally blurted out.

"Deshun, forgive me but there is a woman with a child seeking you.

Her normally deep voice crept up to a veritable squeak as she uttered the words.

"She says this babe is yours!"

Dropping to her knees to wait for the wrath of the Sorceress, an amused chuckle reassured her, even as Ikella realised that she was writing a new chapter in the annals of Selesh. Quickly taking advantage of this chance to adapt the Way to her own purposes, Ikella spoke calmly.

"O, forgive me Driss, I had no time to tell you all my news!"

She explained what had occurred simply.

"In accordance with Sand-law, we have prepared his mother for her Long Walk and rescued her son. I will claim his Sand-rights on our return to Selesh. However, it was his dying mother's last wish that I look after her baby which I will do, provided that there is no prior claim to him!"

Her voice had a hard edge to it as she stated her intentions firmly, and Driss stared at her, wide eyed as Ikella commanded.

"Daro, Nadra his wet-nurse, Ahnell and the other hostages are also under your protection while they are with us. On our return to Selesh, you are to make their safety your prime duty. I have long wished to reward your services in some way, and now comes my chance. You will take whom you wish to create a Household Guard and will eventually retire with that honour, on full pay."

Rising swiftly, she by-passed the bemused Guard Commander and pulled the awning aside, revealing Nadra holding Daro in the doorway. She reached out for the baby, carefully supporting him, cradling him high against her shoulder. She stood silhouetted against the pale flush of first light, eyes aglow as Daro nestled into her body. To the astonishment of all who beheld them, it became obvious that Ikella had finally given in, surrendering her heart to the only man that she could allow that close.

The morning continued to bustle about her, as Ikella sat cradling this tiny addition to her household. She marvelled at the complex turns that her life was taking as she used hands and eyes to examine this miracle of survival, drinking in the perfection of him in a way that she had not been given time to do before. He had dark hair she thought absently, realising that she could remember little of his mothers features even now, wondering if he resembled his father's people more?

Mina, checking the medications she was leaving with Davina, watched silently, as with visible reluctance Ikella tore herself away from the baby, handing him to the nearest member of her Guard with terse instructions.

'Take my son to his nurse, she is in the outer tent.'.

Eyes narrowed, Mina realised their previously peaceful ordered existence was about to be complicated by the presence of a small boy, but she forbore comment, leading the way to the house that had been placed at the disposal of the new Healer.

Close to the Gathering Square, the house was built of stone blocks with a traditional flat roof. This provided a large area for cooking and drying herbs and they looked at it approvingly. It was large enough to provide night nursing for at least three patients, and there was even an area to one side that would accommodate an Infirmary tent to isolate infection.

They could see into the next house where Sadorin was already busy, ordering a team of volunteers to clean, clear and restore both properties. The Sorceress was thankful that the Healer and her new assistant would be close together, central to the town's activities, under the protection of the Guaradeign.

Today however, Tuennis was nowhere to be seen, though there was a small team of her "Town Guard", helping to transport Davina's possessions into her new home. Apart from these and her own entourage, Caranchar slept, and for once Ikella was glad, for she hated prolonged farewells. They must leave soon or the townsfolk would surround them, and to her consternation there was a lump in her throat and her eyes pricked at the thought of that parting. Mina called out to Davina.

"We have come to bid you farewell. Sadorin has the medication safe with the supplies that we don't need. Five of the Inesh will remain here with the Town Guard, so you will not be alone long."

Davina positively flew across the small open yard to the front of her house where Ikella waited. She raised a hand as the young Healer approached and said formally.

"Healer, will you welcome us to your Hall?"

Confusion, then delight crossed the features of the new Healer, as she made the traditional response.

"All are welcome at my Hall. Come, leave your burdens at my door. Enter and share your troubles and your joys with me."

She raised anxious, suddenly shy eyes to the Sorceress, and was rewarded with a smiling acknowledgement, as Ikella and Mina entered the house to stand staring around them.

That the previous occupant had high status was obvious, for there was every luxury. Windows that opened, Sharra wood shutters, a bed raised off the ground with a wooden frame, a mattress stuffed with sweet herbs. Even a Sorceress could not guarantee living like this! They found a small room off the sleeping area with a bathing pool, sadly cracked and dry. They blinked in amazement at an indoor "necessary", marvelled at a larger day room with seating areas covered in brightly hued cloth.

However, even this house had not entirely escaped and there was severe damage along one dividing wall. Sadorin's volunteers were even now shifting large pieces of rubble where supports had fallen, and the young Healer went to see what they had revealed.

"It is another room," she exclaimed.

Aware that there were sand tablets scattered all around she picked one up and turned it over in her hand, looking for some clue as to their purpose, just as Sadorin swept into the day room behind Ikella and Mina. The Town Recorder held out her hand for it, and glancing at the tablet cursorily said.

"More records! I suppose this was Donnesh's tithing room?"

Stricken the young Healers hand went to her mouth.

"But Deshun! Tuennis herself gave me this place. She said it would be ideal. It is central, the owner is dead, there is no family to inherit."

She began to wring her hands in distress. "It is her house, her husband's house. Why?"

Ikella and Mina, glancing at one another knew that they had seen this before, and that Davina would continue to witness such reactions for the foreseeable future. Ikella cleared her throat.

"You will encounter this when dealing with the bereaved." She spoke with sympathy.

"Some cannot bear to be parted from anything that belonged to their loved ones. Others try to deny their pain by shutting the door on their memories. I believe that this is the way Tuennis has chosen. On the night I made her Guaradeign, she chose her own child as first hostage. That night she had his name added to the mortuary list on her skin record!"

Recalling two new tattoos just below the nape of Tuennis" neck, one large, one tiny, she paused, conscious of the shock on the young Healers face.

"In declaring Ahnell dead, she also denies her pain."

Ikella started, and Davina took up her thread of thought uneasily.

"By denying his existence Mother?"

Davina whispered, struck with horror at the unimagined depths of pain that her new friend must be suffering.

Mina added to the conversation.

"In the last few days she has reverted from being the widow of the last headman of Caranchar, the mother of a young baby, to her previous life as Inesh. She has changed her clothing to suit that status. She has become Guaradeign, raised a Town Guard, and in so doing has barricaded her heart against the pain of memory."

Ikella broke in abruptly.

"She told me something that I never knew 'till last night. I was thinking that it also fits the pattern of this weave.

She sat on one of the mattresses, and continued.

"Listen, this is something that you should all know. In the Opal Sands there are two Clans. The Shalhanhi and the Inesh have shared this land for Rotations, but once we fought over it."

There was a concerted hiss from her listeners, for aggression between the peoples of the sand was unheard of. Ikella continued, softly, mindful of the boys working in the small tithing room, only five spans from them.

"Part of my training at Sanctuary, along with my Sisters in Sorcery, was to know at least the background of our Clan. It is necessary knowledge, and not actually proscribed by the Way, just not taught to all. A great wise woman persuaded the two clans not to fight, but to play a game, with the Opal as the prize. She bound the tribes by Sorcery, to abide by the cast of the stone and the will of the winds. In the presence of both Clans, the game started. The chosen players continued, night after day after night, until the final tile was cast. When the nine winds were invoked, the stone fell to the Shalhanhi player. As a result, our Clan took control of the Sands. The Inesh were honour bound (by the rules of the game) to serve us and so it has been through countless generations."

Her listeners locked eyes on her pale, absorbed face, as she continued.

"That great wise woman was none other than Adaria te Syrene, who founded our House, and began training those who could, to take the veil of Sorcery."

Her low voice died away to a whisper.

"I wonder, do we still have the right to continue that path?" she questioned.

Those present looked at her in bewilderment for they had never dared to raise such concerns. Ikella spoke thoughtfully.

"Have you not noticed that there are few Inesh men?"

She demanded suddenly.

"They are a small clan, and getting smaller! Their women train from puberty to form my Inner Guard. We Shalhanhi benefit from our Sands, but we do not train to protect it. That Way falls to the Inesh, whose only benefit is slavery, a dying race."

Her voice was thoughtful, introspective as she considered the fate of her Guards.

"Few of them survive long enough to become wives or mothers. Those that do, only do so by my consent. I can also pick and choose when or even if they may leave the Guard, when and whom they marry. For those who do not have that inclination (and for some reason there are many who do not), they and their 'sister friends' simply go on to train others to follow in their footsteps. What kind of Way is that to tread?"

Mina touched Ikella's arm.

"It is not your fault Deshun, it is tradition. They have followed their path for many Rotations, as have we, never questioning its twists and turns."

Ikella responded bitterly.

"No name stone? No memory candles? No-one to mourn them? If you came from that to the marriage bed of a Shalhanhi male of high status, lived by his name, bore his child, how would you feel under the weight of such loss?"

Davina answered her slowly, her voice roughened with emotion.

"I think I would feel that my time with my mate, was but a dream. Possibly, that now the dream is over, I must pick up my burden again and go back to what I had been. To where I knew what was expected of me. To where dreams were forbidden and could no longer hurt me!"

In the room where Tueniss" dreams had died, there was silence. Eventually Ikella spoke again, slowly.

"It is not my will that they have lives bound by these restrictions. It is their Way, and I have never questioned the Way. I am not sure that I should do so now. However, I shall change what troubles them to live with, and we will have no more of traditions that permit such suffering because it has always been the Way."

Her voice was determined, and Mina saw with clarity that to her sorrow she had been born to a time in which a great and perhaps wise woman took the power of decision again and changed the Way. She murmured deferentially.

"It shall be as you command my Deshun, but this one has a question."

Habitually, she had fallen into the formal pattern of speech used in Selesh, and Ikella's eyes narrowed and her head came up in response.

"Ask your question."She replied suspiciously as Mina said simply.

"Did not Adaria set out our Path in the wake of some Cataclysm?"

She paused, allowing her words to sink in, then slowly, slyly added the comment. "Seek you to alter that path in the wake of this Storm?"

Ikella scrambled to her feet, hoisting her Staff and leaning on it, looking down at the floor for a moment before she said gruffly.

"Some would think it heresy to walk in the footprints of Adaria, or speak my intentions in her name, but I think that the Way for some of us must change. I shall consult with the Guardians before I act." She drew a deep breath.

"I cannot remember another event like this in my life, or in any of my studies at Sanctuary. I can only hope that this Storm was limited to our Sands, for some of my Sisters are old and frail! However, you remind me my Mina, that we cannot know 'till we return to Selesh."

Her hand came up in command.

"Davina, fare you well in your new Hall. I will send Cara to you as arranged. Sadorin will see you safe for now. Tuennis will need your care, mind her for me but do it carefully so that she does not see my hand in this."

She looked about her, as if memorising the scene, and for a moment her eyes bored meaningfully into those of the stilled Sorceress. Then, she turned on her heel and without a backward glance she swept out of the house, Mina tripping in her wake, just catching up in time to hear the Sorceress muttering.

"We must hurry, we should already have left."

Returning to the Infirmary, they found that the Inesh guard had just put the finishing touches to a carrying chair, a shedaris, into which Driss plainly expected the Sorceress to step without comment. Ikella still thoughtful, recoiled from the proposal with ill-concealed horror, and then looking at the bewildered faces of her Inner Guard, was forced to explain herself.

"Driss, thank you, it is a wonderful thought but although interrupted, I am still on Song Walk, and cannot ride aloft. However, Nadra and the babies must be kept well, let them use the shedaris. I must remain with the Council and my Novice."

That was all the explanation she would give, and so Nadra and the babies were placed into the shedaris, as Ikella stood aside with Mina while the last-minute preparations were made.

"I cannot ride aloft in solitary state."

She murmured to the Senior Healer, her voice so low that Mina had to strain to hear Ikella, who seemed almost to be talking to herself.

"How can I know what my people are suffering, the weariness, pain and frustration, if I do not share it with them?"

She paused, looking deep into Mina's eyes.

"Is my reasoning mistaken Mina? I would not challenge the Way without reason, but I feel as if I have walked in a dream all this time. Only now am I able to see the Sands clearly and the pattern of the weave is still confusing to me."

Mina looked about her. She knew exactly what Ikella meant. since the Storm she had the uneasy feeling that something had changed, although she could not have identified what it was. The physical manifestation of the Storm would change many places forever. Lives would have to be rebuilt, like the town they were leaving. For that they needed a guide who could follow the Way, like the Sergas could follow the invisible water paths of the Desert. The Way was only visible to those who had the power to see it. To that end she trusted Ikella implicitly, for it was the possession of that rare talent that had confirmed her not only as the Mother of the Guild of Healers, but also as Sorceress of the Opal Sands. She did not doubt that Ikella had her opponents. Just thinking about that, she shivered at the memory of a pair of darkly haunting, violet tinged eyes. Nevertheless, she dismissed that memory as the Council of Nine, their families, and Ikella's hostages, took their positions to leave.

Ikella's Guard trotted ahead of the small caravan. They ranged four abreast, spears at the ready, parallel to the ground, from where they could swing up to the throw in a heartbeat. In their wake came another four carrying the babies and their nurse atop their shoulders in the shedaris. Mina noted with amusement the terror on the face of the nurse as the chair swayed and bucked beneath her and then it was their turn, the Council of Nine. Hefting her walking cane she slipped into place at the head of her party, walking alongside Ikella who was pensive and clearly wanted to think. Behind the Council came their families, the familiar order of procession reversed, with the children wearing bright hued sashes, onto which, Derun and Dovid, (who had not yet recovered their sight), clung grimly, using makeshift Staffs to probe the ground as they stumbled in the wake of their children.

Ikella's hostages walked with the families, and Mina was pleased to note that although there were backward glances, and the occasional sniff of misery, none of them was inconsolable. Behind the hostages, another four Inesh took up the rear, ready to protect them or lend a hand where necessary, and so it was that they wound their way out of the Gathering Square back into the sands, following the trail to the North, to Selesh.

As if by agreement they walked in silence, each busy with their own thoughts and as the track rose, climbing uncertainly towards Jarran Point (an outcropping of basalt rock that grew above Caranchar), the Sorceress noted with sympathy the backward longing glances of the older hostages. Soon the twin spikes of the Point were casting long shadows across their path, in that shade Ikella called out and the party came to a halt. The Sorceress waited with barely concealed impatience for Driss to reach her, and then the tall Inesh following her awkwardly she walked back down the straggling line approaching the knot of hostages, who huddled together at the rear of the column. As she passed their own family group, she reached out a hand to one child and whispered.

"Are you well Timmin?"

The boy nodded.

"Yes thank you my Deshun, Father is keeping up well now."

Derun's head swung in the Sorceress's direction, as she went on down the track to the hostages. She spoke quietly, firmly.

"Walk with me a little."

The bemused group followed Driss, turning back towards Caranchar, and onto a flat strip of land where they stood looking over the sleeping town. Here and there the first to awaken had lit cooking fires but largely the town was devoid of movement, and apart from the drifting haze of smoke it seemed that Caranchar was deserted. Ikella positioned the group so that all could see and hear her, while Caranchar slept below. Then she spoke. Her voice was perfectly controlled, but not entirely devoid of sympathy as she commanded.

"Look back on your town, look back on your lives, and weep if you must, but weep now for you must never again sorrow for yourselves or Caranchar. You will go back, you will return, you must believe that! Hold that dream to yourselves in times of hardship but do not sorrow or your time in Selesh will be doubly hard."

As one body the hostages looked down at the town. One of them sobbed, another comforted her, a man stretched out a hand longingly as if by so doing he could move the town nearer, see it more clearly.

Ikella stood silently beside them thinking of her responsibilities, feeling as though for the first time, the weight of the Sands on her shoulders. As she stood poised on the brink of the bluff, she noted a solitary figure, kneeling on the roof of one of the houses adjacent to the Gathering Square. Even as her othersight told her 'Tuennis', the figure gathered herself to her feet, took up the prayer mat on which she had knelt and then there was a sudden sparkle, a flicker of light from a reflection glass. As the light touched the rock at her feet, Ikella read in the coded flash the single word, "Farewell" Knowing that Tuennis had not intended that signal for her but for her child, the Sorceress, sighing inwardly for the grief that her Guaradeign was suffering, turned away and led the hostages back to the group and resolutely turning her face toward Selesh marched them forward once more.

Chapter 21 - Selesh

They pressed onward, through the crossing trails below the Pass, glancing only briefly at the tracks to either side of them, noting with mounting concern the changes in the landscape. Mina had taken to wearing a Sand tablet like Sadorin, whose gift for organisation she made little secret of admiring. These tablets, made by mixing salted Sand with grease, could then be fired like bricks, providing a densely packed waxen surface that could have notes scratched on it with a fine sharp smithed tool called an enscrasure. Ordinary brick Sand which occurred in seams near the Fringes, had been used to record all manner of things since builders discovered that the compound could be softened by mixing it with grease rather than water. There was always a stone which bore the builders mark in townships but the ability to carry notes had not been considered until recently, when Sadorin had shown Mina how the Sand, baked into a protective box, worked. The resulting tablet would last for Rotations, and could be cleaned and resurfaced without difficulty.

She had pointed out that it would be better still if the tablet was pierced in the making, a loop of coarse cord could then be threaded through the hole, allowing the user to hang it from a plaited belt. To Mina's huge delight, a belt of Zeglur hide and a bright green braid to attach a new Sand tablet had been lying on her bedroll that morning and seeing that both Sadorin and Davina also wore a matching pair, it had not taken her long to work out who to thank.

Now, she used it to good advantage noting how the land had changed. She fell back to the rear of the column to sketch an outline or note "waypoints" for other travellers, before racing back along the line of figures to re-take her position beside Ikella. It was from here that three hours into their final walk, she spotted Torrenesh, the great high Plateau above Selesh, and she stopped dead in her tracks and raised an arm, pointing the direction of her sight, silently horrified. It seemed to her that Selesh must have sunk into the Sands, for the massif under which the underground cavern complex lay, seemed lower on the horizon.

Ikella seemed to have read her thoughts, murmuring. "The sand Mina, the difference is in the height of the Sands."

Thankfully, Mina grasped this concept quickly, but the magnitude of the change was breathtaking. The Sands had nearly buried the imposing entrance to Selesh, she turned towards the bluff and hurried in the wake of the Inesh, determined to see what had become of the legendary Hall of the Healers.

Ikella was the first to approach the Gate in the Rock, the others hung back anxious not to encroach on the Sorceress who had, almost without thinking, invoked her powers as she came to the huge circular metal door.

Even with the sand drifts reaching to half the height of this Gate, Ikella was dwarfed, her iridescent aura thrown into high relief against the dark metalwork of the immense frame. The party of travellers gathered below, watching, silenced by the enormity of the task. They stared up at Ikella, who stood on a ledge provided by an enormous drift, at least six spans above them. Reluctant to raise the hopes of those within, the Sorceress spent little time examining the Gate itself. That it was solidly locked in place she did not doubt. She could see that any ambition to dig this place out by hand was doomed to disappointment, and turned away having discovered that even the inner trave, (a ceremonial door, used only in marriage celebrations), was jammed. She returned to the party, who were sitting on the sand, desperately trying to keep their spirits up, while shading themselves from the increasing heat of the day. Listening to Driss, complaining bitterly that all their hard work had already been undone, she decided to ascend to the High Plateau above Selesh, where the Healers grew their herbs. Here she could see what other means of access could be found.

She could take no-one with her, for what she sought was secret. Hidden carefully, shielded by magic against accidental discovery, was the entrance that Sashandra, her predecessor had shown her.

Over the many Rotations since, Ikella had never used either this entrance, or the ancient tunnels beyond. These ran deeper than the complex that they used. Everyone knew that many dangerous roof falls had caused the Shalhanhi to all but abandon the complex. She had avoided the use of many secret ways that filtered through Selesh, hoping to remove the memory of them and in so doing, prevent unnecessary accidents. Perhaps she had been too successful, for who knew what lay in the Sands? Who knew when the knowledge of these secret paths might be all the difference between life and death?

She had kept her knowledge secret for so long that she resisted the temptation to squander it, for she knew that there was at least one other way of removing the Sand. What had worked at Caranchar should work here, she decided, and rejoined her people in a much better temper.

The heat was now so intense, that in order to shade the children, her companions had gathered at the broken walls of the small huddle of dwellings that was once the village of Selesh Minoria.

It was clear that the group of Inesh warriors that had found her had used these sad remains before. Already they had started a fire, and the hostages were helping the family group to settle on to their travel packs and prepare food. Nadra was feeding one of the babies, whilst rocking the other who lay in the carrying chair, crying forlornly as his milk brother fed hungrily. Ikella drew Mina and Sanra to one side.

"There is one house that has a roof," she commented.

"From here I cannot see what protection it affords, so before I raise the Winds again, I must go to the harvest ground to see if it is whole, if it offers any safety at all"

Mina, observing the determined set of her friend's mouth, realised that Ikella had already become remote, putting a distance between her ordinary existence and her mystical ability as she drew on her powers. It was with almost a feeling of relief that the Healer group watched the Sorceress walk away, back to the path that led to the High Plateau above, scorning the offer of a guard to protect her.

As instructed, Driss and her troop began to investigate the house with the roof, emerging in fits of giggles, having found one local inn! Of course, everyone else including the hostages volunteered to help promptly and soon, working with a will, they had cleared an area big enough to accommodate all of them.

Travel packs had been raided, the wreckage of other houses put to use, and a safe shelter provided. Driss, with Tiran her Second, hauled themselves up on to the damaged roof, and were busy repairing it. Sanra and the hostage women, helped mind the children, while Nadra and Mina watched the babies.

Ahnell slept, his little tummy full, his face blissful. Daro however, refused the breast and had begun a low thready cry, that made the Healers anxious. It was an irritable, high pitched, querulous squall, and Mina prayed that he was not getting sick, so close to home and safety.

The men of their party kept up a running conversation with the Inesh, discussing with good humoured banter how best the women could repair the roof. At last a cry went up and with relief, Mina saw Ikella returning.

The path to the Heights of Torrenesh wound around the terraces where foodstuffs, herbs and medicinal plants were harvested. The climb had been easier than Ikella had expected, despite the fact that the start to the path had been a little difficult to negotiate. She had made no direct approach to the hidden entranceway above but had discreetly used her Staff and the opal at its head to check the area which had, to her relief, lain undisturbed. She had been careful to use only a trickle of power, for fear that she would alert the Healers below and intrigue them into investigating her activities, but even that covert trickle had been enough to alert Shiarjha, her chosen successor.

Stopping by the ancient water runnel that emerged on the plateau, she dipped a hand cautiously into the stone sink that captured the outflow, intending to see if the water was useable.

Quite suddenly, she felt a tingle in the palm of her hand, and peering into the stained, sand strewn pool, she saw her reflection shiver and shift, as it was replaced by the tear-stained image of the young Sorceress elect. Ikella, being practised in magic, realised that her young acolyte had been desperately searching for her, but Shiarjha had plainly not expected to get such a result! With sympathy, the older woman realised that the great dark smudges under Shiarjha's eyes told of long hours looking into a seeking bowl, and probably long hours of bitter weeping as well. For the length of two long heartbeats, they stared at one another, until Shiarjha found her voice, though it squeaked with the shock of her vision. Timidly she asked. "Speak you from the void beyond this plain of tears Mother?"

Then to Ikella's amused outrage, she discreetly made the crossed fingers sign, used by the superstitious to ward off evil. Swiftly dismissing her acolyte's fears with a snort, in a withering voice she rapidly gave a list of instructions, ending with.

"...and keep your counsel Shiarjha, in fact keep to your rooms for I am about to unleash powers that you have never seen before, the effects of which may be startling. Be discreet about my presence, in fact remain utterly silent, so that you do not raise the hopes of the population. Get everyone away from the gates, for we do not know what will happen to them when I have removed the Sand."

She began to turn away, then as an afterthought added "In addition Shiarjha, take note of the fact that you have more need to fear me alive than dead."

Grimly amused to see the her Elect uncross her fingers, she concluded.

"Wait my signal, it will come to you as a vision for it is necessary that you see what I do. Remember get everyone away from the Gate. Use the Summoning bell, get them all into the Hall. Shut the doors and wait. We will prepare, and then at Height of Sun I will cast. Find a mirror to look into as the Summoning Bell calls the time. Be not afraid, I have used this spell before."

Declining to say more, she swept away purposefully and did not hear the low voice of her acolyte as she stammered.

"But Mother, we have not seen the sun since the Storm."

Shiarjha's voice trembled.

"I have looked in our nearest Sands, where there is only this gloom. I only raised two answers from anywhere. Tirjella, and Deschima both know you were missing, but..."

Her voice trailed away uncertainly, for answer came there none. The Sorceress was headed determinedly towards those who waited below. Mina reached her first, and helped her to make the step down from the broken pathway to the Sands. She noted the drawn look about Ikella's mouth, the severity of expression, and was not surprised when the Sorceress muttered.

"Shiarjha is well enough but I think this confinement is telling on all of them! The girl never even mentioned Caranchar!"

Mina quickened her pace to keep up with Ikella, who seemed to be looking for the position of the sun. She paused in mid-stride, and stood poised on one foot, looking along the edge of the highlands that bordered this part of the Opal desert. The sky seemed lower than usual, heavy Sand-tinged clouds stretched to the horizon on all sides, and apart from the dark fingers of rocky outcrops and the looming mass of Torrenesh above, the scene was featureless. The usual shadows created by the light of the sun were missing, so too were the subtle hints of colour thrown off the opalescent Sands, and it was only by touching her song beads, and humming a long low note that Mina had been able to track the dinajh (the almost invisible water trails across the desert that allowed the nomads to travel their Sands with impunity).

Normally, the special sight of the Shalhanhi would have revealed them, even a child of five or six Rotations could recognise them and knew not to stray from them. They were particularly strong around Selesh because many of them drained into the ancient watercourses below the caverns in which the complex had developed, but in this odd flattened light the dinajh showed only a hint of their existence.

At last Ikella seemed to have focussed on the sun beyond the cloud, and was satisfied that there was time before the Height of Sun to assist her Healers and accordingly she took a bearing on one large pinnacle of dark basalt, then drew a great circle with her Staff, using the hilt of it to gouge the sand. She made one or two notations to one side of the circle and then, Mina in tow headed briskly for the shelter they had prepared.

Nearly all of them were already gathered in the gloomy interior. Those that could huddled near to a fitful fire which Driss had lit, more for comfort and light than warmth. Nadra and the babies dozed on a blanket in one corner, and the hostages sat silently in another, looking around them nervously.

As the shadow of the Sorceress fell across the threshold, the Healers were gently attending to the eyes of the men, all seemed occupied in a most domestic manner. Ikella nodded briskly to Sanra and the Carnelian Healer swiftly disposed of the job in hand and pulled out a battered stool for the Sorceress to sit on.

Ikella paused in the doorway, her nostrils flared as she took in the scent of mixed alcohol and unwashed bodies, baby scents and damaged foodstuffs.

She spluttered.

This place smells like a coven of mihorts. I hope Selesh fares better."

This comment produced a round of appreciative grins and a gurgle of merriment Andria but drew from Inahana only a look of blank bewilderment.

They hastened to explain.

We have an animal here, it lives in between the highlands and the Sands, about the Fringes. It is large, slow, very gentle, but has some annoying habits."

Andria's hands sketched a bear like shape.

"They are very furry, with a long snout! They don't bother people much, but in some of the Fringe villages last Rotation, we had problems with a large group of them."

Her eyes danced as Ikella took the stool and joined them. Andria continued in a musing voice.

"Our Deshun had to intervene when Bayard (the headman at Sibrill), wanted to borrow the Inesh to kill them."

Mina picked up the story, and glad of the distraction Ikella listened, almost as intent on the story as the others were, leaning forward, the ghost of a smile on her face.

"The Horts are no trouble 'till berry time, and then it is as though they can smell them from two Sands away! Then, they have no regard for anything that stands between them and the berries. They simply strip the bushes and trees of anything that they can find."

Inahana, wide eyed-listened in wonderment, for in the Onyx Sands the animal population was small, and she had never heard of mihorts before. Mina surrendered the storytelling again, and the group closed in a familiar warm huddle.

Andria took up the theme, emphasising a point here and there with rapid hand gestures then the Inesh joined in, Driss normally so taciturn and stoic, giggling as the Healer went on. "Bayard was furious. They had stored a good harvest and locked it in a new building, mainly made of Sharrawood in the fashion of the Amber Sands. In the night, the 'Horts' came. At this end of Rotation, they do something quite odd with the berries that they find. They squash them, trampling them on the ground until they have a thick cake of berryfruit stuck on their paws."

The Kora Mai Healer was fascinated, and leaned forward as Driss picked up the story.

"They do not eat the fruit straight away but did you know that minka and belisha berries ferment on their own?"

Inahana nodded, she was beginning to get the picture now, and a small smile tugged and the corner of her mouth.

Driss continued, squatting near the Healers, leaning on her spear for support.

"Bayard was beside himself. The 'Horts' had taken a panel from the back of the storeroom and about ten of them got in. They ruined all the fruit they could find, squashing it onto their feet. Because it was warm, dark and dry in the store shed, they decided to settle down for their winter sleep. No-one knows quite how long they were there but something wakened them, so they started to lick their paws, just as they do to get through the cold months when food is scarce. Of course, by then the berries had fermented, and the 'Horts' gorged themselves silly on the fruitcake! They got helplessly drunk, and then the fruit ran out, so they went looking for more. In the village, in the night!"

The warrior threw back her head and howled with laughter. The tears ran down the faces of the Healers who pictured the huge 'Horts' ambling around the sleeping village in a drunken search for more fruitcake, 'till Nadra came blearily awake to gales of laughter and the walls rocked as they all joined in the tale. Even Ikella was moved to comment.

"I don't know whether they really expected me to kill them, or to order them destroyed but Bayard was very upset when I simply provided more fermenting fruit bushes for the 'Horts and lured them away from Sibrill. He still thinks I rewarded them for stealing the villagers food but luring them was better than hurting them. they are so gentle. And have you seen their lovely long eyelashes?"

Mina was unable to stop herself giggling.

"Daro's eyelashes are nearly as long."

She exclaimed, at which the Sorceress's lips twitched as she said. "What are you inferring Mina?" and picked the baby up, holding him close for a moment, crooning to him reassuringly, before handing him back to Nadra with a brisk.

"We are in danger of forgetting what we came here for."

As she headed straight for the door again she paused seeking Andria and Mina, who came at the command of a beckoning finger. She murmured.

"Can you recall the weave?"

As the Healers merriment dissipated, they saw the light outside had intensified and that the Height of Sun was upon them. As Ikella hefted her

Staff and strode out into the Sands, the Healers crowded to the wide door of the inn, and with Andria one side and Mina the other, they raised their othervoices creating a shield of magical energy that protected them all from the Winds as Ikella began spell casting.

Returning to the ashave that she had inscribed earlier, Ikella laid down her Staff, unbound her hair, stripped naked and knelt, communing with the Sands, before standing to plant her Staff upright. She began to chant, naming the Winds, one after the other in order. She made no call on her powers but suddenly her aura was shining all around her, and at that moment a piercing wail filled the air!

It shocked even Ikella into silence, continuing to rise in volume as Daro filled the air with his outrage. The Sorceress silently gathered her strength, struck her Staff to the Sand and stalked back to where Mina and Andria were lowering the weave that she had invoked.

Not a word was spoken as the Senior Healer took the sash that the Sorceress held out, and bound the baby to her as before. She deftly wove this supporting harness 'till the baby was safe but as the Sorceress returned to perform her ritual, Mina heaved a huge sigh.

There was not a moment to waste. As her Healers raised the weave again, Ikella returned to her position. It was with barely a glance at the child, she steadied herself and summoned her powers. Her aura clothed her in a ripple of iridescence, a vibration began to pulse through her and as certainly as she had known they would the Winds returned and in what seemed like minutes the Sands were peeled away again. Layer by layer away from the Gate, away from the village, revealing the totality of its destruction.

As the pillar of power collapsed and become quiescent in her hands, the baby laid against her sleepily sucking a fist, and Ikella dropped a kiss on his head as she slipped into her shift, slid her cloak over that and covered both of them against a sudden chill. Wondering absently what Shiarjha would have understood from this demonstration of power, she resolved to tell her Elect about the strange visitation in the cavern of the child's birth as soon as she could, and so thinking, she heard a voice saying softly.

"Warden of the Winds."

She saw in her mind's eye the true power and nature of the force that she had summoned, seeing the evidence in the broad plateau that had been worn in front of their Gate. Carved in the bedrock, the symbolic Seal of Selesh.

She was still staring at it, when from inside came running feet, rattling and soft metallic rolling of bolts, then, with the usual bare whisper of sound the Gate in the Rock opened, the gatekeepers replaced by the hands of Jashel and Indeera, her personal guards who knelt at her feet, eyes shining with relief. In their wake the people stumbled out into the Sands, so greatly changed. Out into what was left of their village, so completely destroyed and against the wave of those coming out, Ikella led the way home.

Her face bare of the hated Shadushantesh, she returned. A baby strapped to her body, strangely altered Staff in hand, she made her way to the Hall of the Healers, eyes glowing in relief. The Song Walk party at her heels, she slipped into the Sacred Circle, and knelt to give thanks.

She drank in the exquisite carving of the native rock opal, from which this place was hewn. The light here was as it had always been, and she felt suddenly untouched by the Storm, relaxed, refreshed more aware than she had been in Rotations. Into that awareness came the realisation that she was being watched but the moment passed, as the doors opened and the people joined their Sorceress in thanksgiving.

Chapter 22 -Storm Plague

Three day-breaks passed in a sleepless blur, as the news of every highland, byway, Fringe and Desert, came in on exhausted, starving and in some cases dying feet, to lay the woes of the Freemen, the Felmin and Peoples of the Sands before Ikella. For a while, she was given the strength to ride the blows that were dealt her.

In the Way of magic users, she had long outlived her own family, counting only her sisters in Sorcery, or fellow Healers as the foundation stone of her life. She looked only to them, or to Sanctuary, for advice and ruled her Sands alone. Even Healers, who themselves had unnaturally prolonged lives through their own use of the Source could not equal the lifespan of a Sorceress, therefore only her own kind, or the Guardians of Sanctuary could understand the peculiar loneliness of her position. Like many of her kind Ikella had come to represent a constant. Steady, reassuring, immovable in her very being. With the Opal Staff came the responsibilities for the lesser Sands, and that in itself was a mystery, for no one quite understood why or when the Opal Desert assumed seniority over all Sands.

From time immemorial if a Sister of Sorcery had an unresolved question regarding boundaries, health, or life in general, they consulted with the Sorceress of the Opal, before worrying the Guardians. From Adaria, who founded the House at Selesh, every successor had added to that tradition, and now the responsibilities weighed heavily on Ikella.

She had lived for Rotations as the Sorceress elect here, finally coming to the Staff, into her full power on the death of Sashandra only sixty Rotations ago. She worked hard, quietly developing her own path, but she rarely spent a day without remembering that if she needed guidance, she could confer with those at Sanctuary or delve into the magnificent Djellim, the repository of the Scrolls of Pelshar, now held at the Mother House of Sorcery. She had contemplated raising the link many times but had stayed her hand, waiting till the last of the bad news was in and she could impart the knowledge to the Guardians at one time.

However, with the fourth daybreak since her return the news still rolled in. Whole communities across the Broken Land had been decimated. Many small groups were banding together now, and so the villages of her youth were changing their populations, moving to more sheltered places, and the maps of their world were being redrawn in front of her. From the Highlands of the Opal Desert, came news of small towns completely overwhelmed by the force of the winds. From the far distant Onyx Sands came news of renewed tectonic activity, high lands had sunk, areas of stability had become quicksands. She was weary of it. Nowhere seemed familiar or safe. She was becoming uncertain of her abilities. Retreating to her study, she attempted to busy herself with mundane chores to take her mind off changes almost too big to contemplate.

However, even here, sand tablets spilled from the table, where Mina had piled them for her perusal. Requisitions for medications to one side of her, lists of foodstuffs in store to another. The census of survivors littered the shelves, and a rough telling of herbs still drying were to be found stacked on the floor. She stood up from her desk, easing the ache in her neck with one hand, and absently caught sight of herself in a mirror, placed so that she could observe the Gathering Square below without betraying her presence.

Great dark rings surrounded her eyes, she had patently lost what weight she could spare and, she thought absently, a lot more besides, so that she looked haunted, gaunt, severe. Leaning forward she pinched her cheeks to encourage some colour back into her chalk white face, and peered into the depths of the reflecting glass to observe the effect. Satisfied, she had begun twisting her loosened hair up to get it under some control, when her reflection suddenly blurred, shifted and was replaced by another, one she had not seen since she had left the remote fastness of Sanctuary.

As the image steadied and formed before her, through her very veins came a reverberation in the Source. It shook her to the core of her being and even as she bowed her head in reverence to the image that had replaced hers, she heard the tolling of a long dreaded bell, and knew that the Ways were indeed about to change forever.

Even though this event had been instilled into her, from the start of her training, it had never occurred to her that she might bear witness to the last day of Jocasta, Guardian of the Ways, charged with the training of all candidates entering the Sisterhood of Sorcery. That possibility had never been discussed, not even mentioned, for to do so seemed a betrayal of a loyalty that went to the heart of her being.

In the foreground of her mind, she found herself babbling.

'Not now. Not now!', in some terrified litany of hope.

As her training took over she forced herself to take a deep steadying breath before whispering.

"All hail Jocasta, Guardian of the Way!"

Within her she felt a terrible sinking feeling, she clung to her desk for support, keeping her eyes fixed on the mirror, praying that she was misinterpreting the summons, but knowing she was not.

The image did not fade or alter, but observed her in return and then a light silken whisper filled the room as the woman revealed there began to speak.

"Ikella, last of my House, you know why I call on you thus?"

The Sorceress, feeling every inch a child of only fourteen Rotations before this ancient, nodded, bleak eyed.

'So, who is to become Guardian-designate?'.

The soft voice went on without tremor.

"It is my time, and I greet it without sorrow, for I will depart, glad of heart that I leave Pelshar a better place for having lived here, and having seen you to full power."

Jocasta seemed tired but fully composed, yet in her voice Ikella heard the frailty of great age. The tiny tremor in the voice of the woman who had trained her in the use of her own powers brought tears to sting her eyes.

Jocasta continued softly.

"I sorrow only, that the Way is no more!"

The very words touched Ikella with a thrill of terror.

'The Way no more? No more Sorcery? What did that mean?'

Her thoughts whirling, Ikella had to force herself to look at the mirror image, as Jocasta went on, apparently oblivious to Ikella's soft sob of protest.

"The Way handed down to us changes. You will discover that the Way is for each of you to identify, and make your own. From the Fringe to the Highlands and back to our beloved Sands, each man woman and child has been freed of the yoke placed upon us, to guarantee our survival."

Jocasta's image fixed huge dark eyes on the trembling Sorceress.

"Across the Sands my voice will come to all of you my children of Sorcery, my Sisters in Guardianship, and the little Sisters of Healing. What I say now has taken many Rotations to come to fruition, and may not be questioned or undone, for again Pelshar faces its greatest challenge."

Jocasta's eyes seem to bore meaningfully into Ikella's, and suddenly the Sorceress felt herself shrinking from what she knew was to come. The Guardians voice was grave as she continued.

"Ikella. Adaria herself predicted your next task as Head of the House Syrene. That is inevitable, as you are her last direct descendant. However, I also have the task of passing my particular torch to a worthy successor. To my sorrow, I can think of no other than yourself to fill that role, though I regret the addition of such a burden to the load you already carry."

The image shivered as the Guardian bowed her head, then raised it, eyes blazing with power.

"Let me then greet you on the last of my days. Hail Seris Ikella! Guardian-designate, Warden of all the Ways, Sharall deir Opal, Head of the House Syrene!"

Ikella, reeling under a wash of transferred power, barely heard the codicil, so faint was Jocasta's voice, so loud was the thudding of her own heart.

"For there is no other to follow me!"

A soft rolling thunder sounded seemingly behind Jocasta. Ikella was shaken to feel the reverberation of it under her hand, in the increasingly oppressive atmosphere around her. From somewhere a solemn voice intoned the death roll of Sanctuary, names that pierced the thrall of grief that pinned her in place.

"Seris Miriniva, Guardian of Power, Seris Jocasta, Guardian of the Ways. Derenoba of the Amber Sands Soloria of the Amethyst Sands, Telandra of the Tourmaline."

Reeling Ikella reached for the Source and found it in such turmoil that she was almost rebuffed, pushed away in the torrent of power that was flowing. It was making her dizzy, nauseous, leaving her mouth dry, her stomach churning.

Dimly she heard the ancient voice as from some other place, some other time.

"From today Sanctuary is no more. The Hall itself trembles on its foundations and cannot stand. The House has fallen my child and with it all the hope of Pelshar. Of the deserts only the Opal has a leader, strong in power and will, so I cede my responsibilities to you. The House started in Selesh, it is only right that it continues there, if it is to continue at all!"

The thin voice faltered, and with concern Ikella saw that Jocasta was fading in front of her, with an effort the Guardian rallied.

"Did you save that child?" she asked as if distracted and at that moment there was the sound of feet running outside and Mina entered, ahead of a crowd of others.

She appeared to be suffering also, seemed slightly disorientated and put out a hand for support as she stood, cradling Daro in the crook of her arm whispering.

"Forgive me Deshun, I felt the disturbance in the Source and thought that you were ill. I brought the baby with me as I was feeding him."

Her muttered explanation tailed away as she caught the direction of Ikella's gaze and fixed on the image in the mirror as it faded, recovered, and faded again in front of them.

"Jocasta goes forth on the Winds."

Ikella's brief comment told the Healer all, Ikella beckoned her forward, till the mirror image steadied and Jocasta was again reflected therein. This time the area around her was suffused with a pale glimmering light, and as they watched silently the dying woman caught a glimpse of Daro, nestled into Minas arm sleeping peacefully, head thrown back so that his features were well defined.

"Aah."

Jocasta leant forward. "So, the Ways change again."

She muttered to herself, and then she rallied briefly raising her hand as if in blessing. "Weep not for me. I so long to rest."

She breathed. her eyes fixed on the baby's face, drinking in every feature.

"Weep not for me, but treasure this new life. All of your new lives, for they are very precious."

The image faded slowly from the mirror, and as they watched in a respectful silence, there was a deep subterranean groan, as if the very walls of Selesh were mourning.

They were gripped in a torrent of power, as were every Sorceress and Healer across Pelshar, they felt the death of Jocasta, as Sanctuary fell from its isolated position on the Heights of Surrandel into the rift below. As it ended, even the baby cried out in pain and the mirror shattered.

Somehow, in the sound of that small destruction, the depths of her loss became real to Ikella. She, the indomitable one, the spirited one, crumpled and fell into a helpless weeping fit that nothing could assuage. Mina had no need to summon help, for the Healers and Shiarjha Sorceress elect, had come running to investigate the reason for the disturbance in the Source.

Mina, with baby Daro now fast asleep on her hip, bustled amongst them protesting the numbers present and soon the room was cleared, only Shiarjha, Mina and Sanra remained with the shattered Sorceress, who limp and unresisting was soon lifted on to her bed, gently undressed and covered with warm blankets. Shiarjha, pale and clammy with the shockwaves that still pulsed through the Source, bravely tilted her chin as Mina explained in a low voice what had occurred. As Sanra worked over the prostrated Ikella, rubbing her temples with extracts from her own medicine scrip, Mina noted with approval the determined look on Shiarjha's face as she spoke gravely, smoothing down and turning back firmly the fine sheeting on the bed, working opposite and in partnership with the Carnelian Healer, listening in awe to Sanra's description of the powers wielded and the control exhibited by the Sorceress in recent weeks. Active treatment and bed straightening ceased as the two, adept Healer and Sorceress elect faced each other, looking down with pity on the fitfully dozing woman. Shiarjha spoke thoughtfully, her eyes straying to the over-flowing desk and on to the shattered mirror hanging askew above it.

"It can come as no surprise that this has happened then?"

She paused in mid- sentence, smoothing back the hair from Ikella's face with a practiced hand, soothing her as only a Healer could, she continued.

"We must continue for her, till she is ready to pick up the Staff again."

More thoughtfully, in almost a whisper.

"As I might have had to alone, had she not won through the Storm."

Mina, catching a dangerously depressed note of introspection in the young woman's voice distracted her by absently handing the sleeping child to one of the Inesh guards, who eyed the baby hesitantly before taking up the burden.

"Take Daro to Nadra, in the crèche of the Infirmary."

Mina commanded.

"Tell her that the Sorceress is ill, that she should continue to care for the babies until I can come and speak with her."

The Inesh warrior awkwardly eased the baby into her arms, and Mina asked her curiously. "What is your name?"

Startled the Guard stared at her, for this was not the Way that she knew. "I serve the Deshun."

The embarrassed guard muttered, ducking her head and turning away, but Mina persisted. "Your name?"

The warrior, little more than a girl herself, answered in a low voice.

"If it please you Healer, I am Diras, daughter of Morill of the house Sheshell."

Mina raised her voice. "Hear this then Diras, you are appointed protector of Daro, son of Sharall deir Opal Ikella. You are to guard him well while his mother is ill, sleep at the door of his room, be with him day and night."

Her voice dropped into more conversational tones. "Have you a friend, a sister perhaps who will take a share in such a duty?"

Diras thought for a moment and then nodded. Shiarjha left Ikella's bedside briefly and said to the Inesh warrior and Mina.

"It is essential that our Deshun rest, she is very troubled and distressed, and formal announcements can be left for a few days, but I do agree that the babies and Nadra should be put under special watch, and Diras I want you to listen to Mina in the manner of carrying out your duties."

With the point made that such decisions should be in the province of the Sorceress elect and not with a Senior Healer, she smiled at Mina's discomfort and said sweetly.

"Mina, I thank you for your forethought. Nadra should have her own Healer appointed, as well as at least two guards! I think they should be moved to another apartment, somewhere close at hand, so that the baby can be brought to Ikella if she wants him. Can I leave you to make those arrangements?"

So saying, she returned to Ikella who lay, a solitary tear tracking down her cheek, as the loneliness of her position penetrated beyond the shield of exhausted sleep.

During the next few days Ikella drifted aimlessly. She slept without dreaming, or chose not to comment otherwise (spending many hours in solitary contemplation, kneeling in the Sacred Circle, to which she had access from her private rooms). It seemed to anxious observers, as though it was too much for her to break some secret inner conversation. She was so distracted by her inward thoughts, even Shiarjha found it difficult to gain her full attention but slowly she returned to them and when she did, it was to a greater extent because of the baby.

He had become restive, crying unceasingly, and both Nadra and Telani thought that he must be teething but when he refused the breast, taking no food for a full day, a worried Nadra asked Mina's advice. Only a few minutes earlier the Senior Healer had been delighted to hear Ikella ask Sanra how Daro fared, so feeling that there was little to be lost, they brought the baby to her. The two Healers eyed each other as the wet-nurse handed him over to his foster mother who with an inarticulate murmur, buried her face against him. For a moment they stood, fused together, propped against the edge of Ikella's bed, until she subsided on to it, holding out a hand demanding food for the baby. From her hands he accepted a warmed milta gruel, a type of grass seed dried and ground, mixed to a paste with coatan's milk, though it was far too little in Ikella's opinion.

She sat back, holding him while they told her about the nursery, set up just along the corridor from her own rooms. She, more interested in the baby's progress, suggested that he needed more solid food, observing that he seemed pale, listless, and much lighter than she would have expected.

Then Ikella was herself much changed. In the immediate aftermath of the fall of Sanctuary her Healers had noted the lines of age smoothing from her face, had observed an unusual opalescent streaking in her hair, and now as she sat nursing Daro, Mina realised that Ikella had lost a deal too much weight. She sat willowy and insubstantial, hair and skin gleaming palely iridescent against the brilliant scarlet of her blankets as Mina whispered in Sanra's ear.

"We call the Sorceress the "Mother of the Opal" in our ritual salutation, but with that child in her arms, one could be forgiven for believing it."

Sanra nodded in silent agreement, and that seemed to be all that was said on the matter as some sort of normality returned to Selesh.

Ikella and Shiarjha spent a lot more time together, Shiarjha working quietly in the evenings after fall of night, drafting a map of the immediate changes to the area about Selesh. Mina liked Shiarjha. She was quiet, somehow diminished beside the Sorceress, who surprised them all with a new kind of "glamour" about her.

It seemed as though the air itself was darker around her, making the Opal streaks in her silver hair more distinctive. As she began once more to walk the corridors near her private apartment, others noticed her dramatic new slenderness, her singular return to confidence, as well as the change in her manner.

Since her experience in Caranchar, Ikella wandered alone, often unguarded. She went amongst her own people, pausing to talk to them as the storm damage was righted, and somehow no-one questioned this, for it felt completely right, if different.

The outer village was still uninhabitable, temporary accommodation had to be provided, and despite the bustle of rebuilding room was still very tight indeed. Before the Storm, Selesh was used to pilgrims from other Sands, visiting to consult the Sorceress, or to get advice from the Guild of Healers. Many felt that their health depended on attending the ceremonies held in the Healer Hall, often staying for weeks to give thanks for their recovery. Whereas they had always sought accommodation in and around the large village that clustered about the Gate in the Rock, and even brought goods to trade in the village market, now this busy bustling hive of industry stood silent. Selesh had been a fine place to live near until the Storm took the village, and the inhabitants were forced to seek sanctuary inside the settlement of the Rock. It was only when every bed was filled and there was literally no room to spare, that a plague of epic proportions struck, and the sick began to arrive.

Ikella had put off 'seeking" for any remnant of Daro's family 'till her strength grew. Such an endeavour was a rarely-used, complicated spell sequence, one that would absorb her in many hours of planning, and essential to its success was the health of both the spell caster and the subject of that Seeking Spell. Even now, Ikella found herself tiring early, and Daro was teething to judge by his constant irritable fits of crying and so she continued almost in a void of inaction, for she feared losing her emotional control if she had to give up the child. It was easy to do nothing for her fatigue was bone deep. She worked in the mornings or played with the baby, in the long dimmed afternoon. Ikella slept from the Height of Sun, to the cooler hours before night. On the ninth day from the Fall of Sanctuary, rising from one of these short naps, she became aware of the sound of feet hurrying from the direction of the infirmary. Soon a soft tap on her door alerted her to more trouble. She instinctively reached for the Source within her, finding as did all women of Voice the memory of a note she had once sung, and dwelling on the pure cadence of it felt the feather touch of her Power blossom within. She shrugged into the power as ordinary folk draw on a light shawl, and saw to her own surprise a new and strengthened aura settle around her, but not disposed to question it, she settled back into her chair and called.

"Come!" to the ever more insistent tapping at her door. It swung open and the startled Healer revealed there took one look and backed away murmuring indistinct apology for having disturbed her, but Ikella beckoned her. For a brief moment, Andria stood staring at the Sorceress, and then she advanced, pestle and mortar still in hand, for she had come direct from the Blending Room of the Infirmary. At last she found her voice.

"Deshun, I am sorry that I must intrude but we have received this morning ten more sick into the infirmary, and I fear that we have a pestilence in our midst that we have no means to control. From where it comes we do not know, we have no othersands visitors with us. Those that were here fled home to find out what was left. Try as we might to work out what this sickness is, we cannot, and though I mix a tarifin to reduce the fever as I always have, it does not work!"

She handed the pestle and mortar to Ikella, who bent over it, sniffing and tasting a little of the bitter herb contained within.

"This is fresh still," she commented and then rising to her feet she made for the door, walking swiftly, passing Andria she handed her back the pestle and mortar and then almost as an afterthought she stretched out a hand imperiously, and her Staff streaked across the room, from where it had stood these many days unheeded on its stand. Andria sensed rather than saw the movement, and stopped transfixed as with a shower of tiny chimes the Staff slapped purposefully into the outstretched hand of its rightful owner, who merely raised an eyebrow at the Healer murmuring. "Perhaps I had better look into this," Ikella swept out to investigate with Andria in her wake.

Long after these days the Healers would look back and wonder how any of them survived the relentless tide of admittance to the cramped wards of the Infirmary. If it had not been for the many dedicated relatives of the sick and dying who entered therein, they could not have managed even the most basic of nursing duties, so heavy was the burden. There was little time to prepare for the influx, just simple arrangements were made, rooms long disused were opened up, basic pallets were provided until there was no need to nurse the patient, and then they and their families were moved on again. Those who survived were moved aloft to the old storerooms, those who did not were either taken to the Sands by their families, or if they had none at night the Healers themselves accompanied the pitiful corpses, sewn hastily into the most basic of shrouds and carried by cart on to the much scored track to the Great Divide, where they were committed to the deep rifts below by the Sorceress. For a full fifteen days this lasted, Healers working round the clock. The Sorceress, pared to the bone by her recent illness, grew more impressive as she scoured the Sands for some clue to the plague, devising remedies for those she could save and palliative measures for those she could not, conducting burials when they had the time.

They were returning quietly from one such sad duty, when Ikella, deep in thought suddenly said to Sanra who accompanied her.

"Would you say that we have buried fewer this day?"

Sanra, coming forward at her gesture to walk beside the Sorceress, replied soberly. "We have my Deshun, though thirty dead in a day is hardly a low number."

Ikella paused in mid stride looking at the Carnelian Healer closely.

"Yes, that I know! I also know that your husband is blind, you have the responsibility of a growing child, and that you are tired, dispirited and far from your Sands."

The Sorceress walked on more slowly and Sanra feeling suddenly lonely for her warm homeland, felt the threat of tears and was touched when Ikella reached out her free hand and patted her shoulder encouragingly.

"Deshun?" Sanra offered uncertainly, and Ikella bent her head to listen.

"Deshun, we need more Healers, if at Selesh we cannot stem the flood with nearly all the Healers gathered in one place, what hope is there for other Sands?" Almost as she spoke the words, she bit her lip, for it was not the Way to question what was, but she need not have worried for Ikella was nodding in agreement.

"I agree, we have far too few Healers as it is, and the other Sands have many women of Voice who want to be trained in the craft, we must try and persuade the Sisterhood to set up training halls in their own Sands." She lapsed into silence for a while and then Sanra ventured timidly.

"I can't see Deshun Eshima believing that we need our own foundation."

She suggested hesitantly, "Our Sands have remarkably little illness. Apart from one sandrigal's bite last Rotation, I lost not one patient, so little was I called on! It is possible that with time when Lenora accedes to the Staff she might be approached but—" She lapsed into a reflective silence till Ikella spoke abruptly, chiding the Healer.

"That was before the Storm Sanra, the Ways must change if we are to survive another such impact on our world. Could we not set up a training foundation, here at Selesh? I could invite othersands students to study here. If I also invite trained Healers to come and teach their own methods, not only would the knowledge be saved for countless generations, the knowledge would be spread, so that what causes a sickness in the Carnelian could be recognised and treated elsewhere."

She made an enclosing movement with her hands, as though thought could link the Sands together and Sanra suddenly understood the concept.

"You mean to make a Guild Hall for Healers right here, in Selesh!"

She exclaimed coming to a stop, her hands clasped together in a fervour of excitement.

"Oh, Deshun Ikella. Do you think the Sisters would allow it?"

Ikella spoke softly, her low voice carrying only to the Healers ears.

"If Deschima follows the old Way, she will not oppose the wishes of a Guardian-designate!"

She explained dryly, and Sanra suddenly understood how the Way would change and silently glowed, as Ikella put out a hand to prevent the Healer kneeling to her. They walked on, the Carnelian Healer and the Sorceress of the Opal desert, heads drawn together as they spoke softly, and as the track swung toward Selesh and the Gates opened the Sorceress commented.

"Keep your counsel for I still await the proof of the Fall of Sanctuary, and I have also realised something else lies undone, and I must make haste to put that matter right."

She seemed reluctant to go on, was visibly saddened by her thoughts and as they swept inside the Gates and her entourage surrounded her again, Ikella looked back over her shoulder at the Carnelian Healer.

"Send Mina to me when she is awake, and tell her to bring the seeking stone for I have to find that baby's family before I can turn my mind to anything else!"

Sanra fled, on the thought that if Selesh could be turned into a full Guild Hall, then perhaps she could transform her lowly Hall in Sorjhoi village into the training Hall of the Carnelian Sands.

The subdued Sorceress returned slowly to her study, feeling that for nothing would she want the footsteps of all the Sands turned in her direction, for nothing would she want to take on the responsibility of thousands of young minds, hearts and voices in training to Healer status and for no reason that she could think of, her mind strayed to the baby whom she must give up for this, and she wept.

Later that night as the pieces of the Seeking Spell were put into place and Ikella rested back on her heels to survey the pattern drawn lightly on her study floor, using the white soft stone found along the southern reaches of the Azure Sands, she questioned her stout lieutenant.

"Am I right Mina? Even as Sorceress I should never have contemplated bringing up Daro myself. I already have too many responsibilities with all the other Sands to support. If I allow myself this indulgence, I cannot take on the task that Jocasta has left to me."

She turned her head to look at Mina, who stood in the doorway, observing the spell-plan unfolding in front of her sourly. Ignoring her expression, Ikella carried on, sorting through a number of polished stones in a small box as she spoke.

"We must have more Healers, for we certainly have more ills than we can contain. There cannot be more than ten Healers from other Sands, who have completed training in the last few Rotations. Am I right to turn Daro over to his own, so that I can accomplish this transition?" Giving Mina no time to reply, Ikella continued, plainly wrestling with the problem.

"It feels right from one point of view, many will need our help if this plague is as widespread as the devastation of the storm, but the child needs me too, and I am perhaps being selfish?"

Mina snorted.

"As head of the Healer Guild, you could hardly turn your back on what is staring in your face. We desperately need more Healers, a training centre, and many more untrained helpers as well. We need to reinstate the Funerary Guild, which has sadly fallen into disuse, not many volunteers have a feel for those sort of duties. Perhaps you should consider that as an extension of Healing, seeing as all our Sands, Fringes and even the cities will depend on those skills to keep further pestilence at bay, Deshun."

She bit her lip in frustration as Ikella nodded, filing the last comment to that vast reservoir of ideas she had vowed to investigate further. Mina turned the conversation back on to its original theme.

"As to the child, I am not the one who must ignore his mother's dying wish! Of course she could not have known who you were but I grant you, it is a hard choice, and not one I would want to make!"

She began to pick up scrolls that Ikella had been using to work out her incantations.

'Brisk tidying is useful to occupy the hands whilst the mind works.'

She thought a little inconsequentially, moving a pile of sand tablets and seating herself. She watched the crouching Sorceress studying the lines she had drawn on the floor, her lips moving silently as she thought the incantation through to conclusion. Somewhere there was a slight disturbance, a knocking sound or a drum beating, she couldn't tell. Then Ikella wearily stood, stretching her back and thinking out loud.

"My first duty is to these Sands, and all people therein. Daro is of the Opal born, and so he is my responsibility for I found his mother, however, I am hardly of the age or natural inclination for motherhood. I reason that anyone so inclined can raise a child but not everyone can be Sharall deir Opal, and that Daro is still my responsibility if I can reunite him with his family, for I would choose to make him so."

She paused, listening to the tramp of feet approaching, and Mina was astonished and touched as she brushed away a tear before continuing.

"If what I have been told is only half true, then I can change the Way, so that every mother's child can stand a chance to be raised by their own mother! For those orphaned by the Storm, there are as many mothers bereaved of their children. I, who have never borne a child can only guess at that sorrow! I therefore must make the right choice, a single foster child for me, or a living mother for every child on Pelshar?" She gulped on a seemingly restricted throat before whispering.

"My loss is also my gain, I must remember that, I must!"

A step sounded in the ante-room, followed by a sharp rap demanding attention. Mina stood and went to the door, whilst Ikella lifted some stones and other artefacts, carefully covering the spell-plan against an accidental scuff, which would ruin the intricate lines drawn on the floor.

Mina paused for a second and looked back at Ikella, who was once more seated at her desk, before lifting the latch, thinking to see the Sorceress's Inesh guards waiting for permission to enter.

What faced her was a small troop of female warriors, clad in light travelling armour, with soft short skirting of an indeterminate hue, and plumed headdresses towering imposingly above her. Four of them held firmly to the carrying handles of an immense wooden travelling chest, so large that an adult could have been carried within this mighty artefact, blazoned with the insignia of Sanctuary. Stood behind the chest was a woman of mid height, wearing the distinctive bourka and cloak of a Guardian. Bewildered Mina fell back on the most formal greeting murmuring.

"Welcome traveller. Enter into the presence of Sharall deir Opal, Ikella te Syrene."

She was amazed as the woman threw back the all enveloping veil, as with a cry of welcome her Sorceress past her in a blur of motion, enfolding the visitor in a hug of genuine pleasure.

"Beneva!"

She exclaimed, then more sadly.

"I never thought to see you again on this Plain of Sorrow!"

For a moment the two women clung together, Sorceress and Guardian of Knowledge, Keeper of the Scrolls of Sanctuary, linked by their common loss, united in grief.

The guards fell back and lined the walls, six women of imposing stature, each armed to the teeth and although travel stained and weary, ready to protect the chest and its custodian to the last of their strength if necessary. They stood, eyes unreadable, faces impassive, as Beneva sank willingly into the chair that Ikella drew forward.

"Sit Beneva, you look exhausted, from where have you travelled this day? We thought nothing and no-one had survived the Fall of Sanctuary!"

Mina offering food and drink to Beneva noted with concern the glitter in her eyes, the feverish look around her face, the dryness of her skin. She offered shyly.

"If the Keeper wishes a Healer's services?" but Beneva shook her head saying.

"I am but a little dry, and very tired thank you. I am not ill, thank the One." Mina prepared to withdraw, but Ikella stayed her with a gesture.

"This is Mina, my most trusted friend and Senior Healer here."

Mina bowed her head respectfully for all knew Beneva, the Guardian who travelled the Sands, seeking candidates for Sanctuary, accompanied by her ceremonial guards. For a while there was silence while the weary Beneva sipped a restorative. Ikella seemed lost in thought, staring at the imposing chest, now standing to one side of the entrance, Mina tidying the scattered sand tablets on the low shelf that bordered the room.

Almost as an afterthought the Healer asked quietly.

"Your guard? I can have refreshments brought?"

Beneva shook her head, saying in a heavy voice.

"Thank you Mina, but they are foresworn until I accomplish my task here. I ask you to remain as witness for your Sorceress. If all is as prophesied they will rest all too soon."

With that mysterious statement, she made a subtle movement of her hand and four of the women took hold of the arms that protruded from each end of the chest. They hefted it forward, into the light produced by the glowstone lamp that cast its soft radiance over Ikella, placing the chest so that the Sorceress could examine it more closely.

Beneva stood, slowly, moving stiffly until she placed a hand on the enormous lock that hung from a central hasp mounted on the Torrenwood chest. The hasps glittered golden in the light, the dark wood gleamed as if oiled, it seemed almost alive against the gentle grey of the rugs beneath it.

For a moment it seemed as if the Keeper of the Scrolls was communing with the chest, she stood so still that they could not see her breathing, and then with a wordless glance at her guards she sang a soft low note, followed by an ascending cadenza, each note oddly spaced from the other. As she ceased to sing, there was a soft "click" and the lock dropped into her hand, the hasp sprang free, and the lid of the chest opened slowly, steadily and with no hand set to lift it.

Inside the sheer glitter of the contents made the gathered women gasp, for resting snugly in a tray supported by a filet of midnight blue material, were two extraordinary bracelets, so wide they appeared to be battle gauntlets but these were decorated with the most intricate floral engravings, so narrow and tapering that they had to be intended for a woman. Without touching them, each of the Nishan guards held their hands above the gauntlets for a brief moment, revealing forearms decorated with silvery tattoos, echoing the mystical symbols on the gauntlets. Their stoical features softened as the tattoos flared, then with a sigh, each of them turned away again, taking up their stations around the room.

Wordlessly Ikella looked at Beneva, and as Beneva beckoned her forward she knelt, in the shadow of the mirror that now re-glazed hung over her. For a moment, Mina thought she could sense a swirl of some power. The One only knew that there was a tension in the air, a feeling of being swept along by some unstoppable current as Beneva carefully, reverently lifted one of the gauntlets. Ikella's eyes widened as she divined Beneva's purpose, but she did not resist as first one, then the other gauntlet was opened and clasped on to her wrists. As she stood, looking at the gleaming silver clasped to each arm there was a murmur from Beneva and the Nishan women chanted in unison.

"Ayah! Seris Jocasta, Guardian of the Way past. It is done, your orders are complete! Ikella of the House Syrene accepts her path. We salute you Ikella, Guardian - designate, Warden of the Way henceforth. The prophecy fulfils itself, and our Way on this path ends."

As their voices died away, the leader of the small troop of guards stepped forward and dropped to one knee. Addressing Beneva directly she requested permission to withdraw saying lastly, calmly but sadly.

"Keeper of the Scrolls, it has been my task to bring you here to do the will of Seris Jocasta without fear, without faltering, without failing and this I have done. My Way and yours must now part, we to our promise, you to yours. Will you permit that we depart this night without hindrance as is foretold?"

The great calm eyes met Beneva's steadily, and Mina and Ikella saw a message pass between them, as Beneva drawing a ragged breath said softly, sadly.

"It has been my pleasure to journey with you, to accept your path, your trust and your Way. May the One grant me the courage to send you forth, and to hold you close to my heart until we meet again."

Bewildered, Mina watched silently as each of the Nishan warriors caught Beneva's hands in their own great palms, pressing their foreheads close to hers in some sort of ritual of departure. One by one, they bent the knee to Ikella, who held her hands out to them, still encased in the gauntlets sent by Jocasta. The door opened, and they trooped away quietly, with never a backward glance at Beneva, who clearly distressed watched them steadily, framed in the doorway of Ikella's study.

Ikella sat, looking at the gauntlets that she wore, until Beneva swept back, and carefully removed them, returning them to their place in the lid of the Sanctuary Chest, quietly saying.

"The rest can wait till morning but I have brought you more, much more than most could bear. Ikella, you will need your courage, for it is foretold that you will walk a Way of your own, and we that are left must follow and trust you, for the Ways turn among many strange paths, but none so strange as yours!"

With that she closed the chest, and neither Mina nor Ikella could draw her more on the subject for she was plainly exhausted.

Setting a night Guard at her study door, Ikella handed Beneva to Mina's ministrations and all three retired for the night, but not before Ikella cast one doubtful look at the Sanctuary Chest and wondering where in all Selesh she could find the room to found a new Djellim for Beneva to preside over.

Worrying about what in all Nine Sands they thought she could accomplish alone and without the power of Sanctuary to rely on. she decided that she must call a Conclave of the Sisterhood immediately. Dimming the glow stone lamp she lay down, to troubled dreams in which a small troop of Nishan warriors marched with unwavering steps over the edge of the rift that they called the Great Divide, to certain death on the rocks below.

Chapter 23 - Discoveries

The following morning, Ikella sat in her study waiting for Beneva to tell her what should become of the Sanctuary Chest. It sat where it had been left, squarely atop the rug covering her Seeking Spell, preventing her from using it.

Long experience having taught her to exercise caution around magically charged artefacts, it was with a sense of relief that she watched the Keeper of the Scrolls, directing her own chapter of guards, as they removed the chest to the guest room that Beneva now occupied. In the corridor leading to Ikella's own suite of rooms it could be as safely guarded as Ikella was. Beneva indicated the rugs with a slight smile."

I am sorry Ikella, I should have thought and had it removed last night, before."

Her smile faded to an expression which the Sorceress could not read easily, but Beneva turned the conversation lightly."

I must find a place that I can use to store these sacred artefacts in, until my path becomes clear.

She was obviously tired still, and Ikella had no difficulty in suggesting.

Your path has brought you to our door Beneva, rest awhile with us. The ways from here are hard and cold. End of Rotation and our celebrations of Jentaroth will both be overshadowed by the losses of the Sands. With our future so disrupted I must consult the Sisterhood, I intend to call a Conclave to discuss the changing of the Ways." She looked up at Beneva steadily, "I was always wont to call on your advice Guardian, now I need it more than ever!"

She bent forward and flicked back the rug to show the elaborate lines beneath, and Beneva stood looking over them as Ikella replaced the stones in their original positions, moved a feather from her desk and placed it precisely at the conjunction of several lines. She had turned away to gather some herbs when Beneva said slowly. "Why do you locate the start of your Seeking Spell beyond the Silent Sands?" Ikella turned to look at the Keeper of the Scrolls more closely.

"I thought that Jocasta would have told you about the baby, she seemed to know of his arrival." she ventured defensively, to which Beneva nodded shortly, before muttering.

"The legend might be true then," continuing, "I am sorry my dear, my interest is not in your baby but rather in where he may have been born. We found a statement in a very ancient record at Sanctuary, it was not strong enough to call a prophecy, but it is of great interest. It says that if Pelshar was in great peril, then the lost Hall of Tirjhinar would return to protect us." She frowned at the spell plan, "What did you see?" She listened avidly to Ikella's descriptions of the shallow cavern, the terrible events leading up to its discovery.

"In our search for shelter we could only wander as the winds let us. I can tell you that at the time I truly thought that my death was written in those Winds, but we found a cave, not much of a thing at all" Ikella tilted her head to watch Beneva who had sunk down into a chair and was fumbling to take up a clean sand tablet and an enscrasure from the table. Indicating that Ikella should continue her story, Beneva began to write, swiftly. Ikella told her everything that she could remember how she had prepared them for death, how the men had bravely carried the girl, unable to protect their eyes against the Storm. Eventually, she paused and sat for a moment with her head thrown back, trying to remember what she had noticed about the cave. It seemed so little really for all the momentous events that had occurred there. She could not offer any way points for the storm had obscured everything, and she knew that she could search for many Rotations again without finding the place. She remembered and described for Beneva, now starting on her second sand tablet, the great opal cliff and how the strange light of the storm had disguised it, till Dovid walked almost head on into it, and then that she had realised that the patch of dark they were aiming for had to be a cave.

She had just described the strange waterfall, frozen in time it seemed and the "pool" that they had laid the girl struggling to birth her baby into and looked up to see a strange look on Beneva's face, her hands had stilled as if she could not bear to write. Clearly this was something that the Keeper of Scrolls had recognised.

"What?" demanded the Sorceress. "What now?"

Beneva shook her head and carried on writing. Crossly, Ikella told of the mother's long protracted labour, and of her Healers struggling, and how she had lost her temper with the winds!

"It was so unfair." she declared, echoes of the anger she had felt still in her voice. "And no I don't have any idea of why I did it either!" She stammered to a stop, remembering how it had been, how she had shrieked defiance into the storm, screamed the names of all nine winds and chastised them for stealing the babies life, and the memory of the incantation she had used flickered through her mind. Beneva saw her embarrassment and chided gently.

Sometimes we do our greatest good when roused to fury. We must chronicle this Ikella, you know we must."

Ever so reluctantly the Sorceress explained.

"I remembered the lesser Hall at Sanctuary, you know the one, outside the Djellim where I was often sent to await Jocasta's righteous indignation" The sheer number of times she had awaited the displeasure of Guardian Jocasta, stained her cheeks with colour. Beneva however, chose not to notice, simply raising an interrogatory eyebrow.

"Go on," she murmured encouragingly. Ikella creasing her brow, thought back.

"I used to sit on the floor, under the long table, but one day I found that another small table had replaced it. Sitting under it, I found the carving round the edge. Don't you remember? It was you who told me not to Spell Shape! You even gave me this ring when I could draw the pattern of it. I didn't know it for a language then but when I discovered that it was the old script, I tried to decipher it, for by then I knew it to be a spell."

She coloured to the roots of her hair as she admitted.

"I thought, that as soon as I was a great Sorceress of immense power, I would learn that spell and use it. However, one's dreams at just sixteen Rotations are unlikely to be fulfilled and actually, I simply forgot it!" her voice tailed away as she confessed her ambition but Beneva, writing busily, simply said. "And have you not realised that now you are a great Sorceress of immense power, that you did learn the spell for a reason, that in your sixteenth Rotation you could not divine! Recalling it at the right time, for the correct reason, you were then able to channel that power, and so you used it! If you had not, would any of us still be here?"

Silenced, Ikella fell into a light reverie regarding the birth of the child, and was just recognising that there was some sort of pattern here, when the Keeper of the Scrolls prompted her again."

"Continue."

So the early morning passed with the revelations of her dreams being told to Beneva who, hunched over a growing pile of records, pursed her lips and made soundless whistles of amazement as the story unfolded. When Ikella gradually revealed the powers that she had acquired and unleashed to rescue Caranchar and re-enter Selesh, Beneva came to a stop, casting down her enscrasure and remarking, "Ikella, just listen to what you have told me, and repeat that you cannot understand why Jocasta sent me forth to deliver to you the remainder of the great symbols of Power? You credit yourself with so little my dear friend. You are no longer able to hide behind the scruffy, unconventional image that you convey. You are undoubtedly the one chosen to guide us, to protect that child till he comes of age. Ikella, you always doubted yourself, but doubt no longer for you have the power, the energy and the will to make this succeed. You are indeed Adaria come amongst us again, although the purpose of the child is yet unclear I believe your purpose is entwined with his."

Ikella's eyes flickered and strayed to the spell workings on the floor, and Beneva said comfortably. "That too, you should proceed as you have determined, for even if you let him go you are still linked, are you not?"

Ikella stood abruptly, putting a hand on Beneva's shoulder. She spoke from the heart. "Stay with us Beneva, we could make you a new Djellim here, there is so much you know that I do not. You could advise me, advise the Council of Nine. Please stay! Beneva, stay!"

Ikella knew that she was pleading, sounding unnaturally unnerved by events but she did not care. Beneva smiled serenely as she gathered up the pile of sand tablets, and as she prepared to leave Ikella's study she spoke softly, in reply.

"I always planned to Seris Ikella."

She said, pronouncing the new honorific carefully as the door closed behind her.

As Beneva departed, Ikella was already absorbed in the detail of her spell symmetry. It was true, she had drawn a physical map of the area in which the baby had been born, but had she included all that she could, she wondered. Daro was of the Opal born and under her protection she mused, peering down on her spell plan from her high stool, her right knee supporting her elbow, chin cupped in hand. She flicked out her left hand and rousing herself slid from that wrist her Source beads, given to every Woman of Voice the day their mastery of power was confirmed. Sliding from the stool she crouched down, tracing the line that represented Daro back to where it had begun, and tenderly spreading the simply strung wristband of Opal stones she enclosed the seeking stone within the small circle that it formed. Her hand strayed to that strange carved fruit that they had found hung on a cord around his mothers neck after her death, wondering which side of his family it would compel, but found to her disgust that her eyes were watering at the thought of handing Daro over to some stranger. Abruptly she reached into her pocket, drew out a clean kerchief and blew her nose. Briskly, she dabbed her eyes and turned her attention to the other lines she had drafted.

Plainly his birth mother had been a Jhirelle of the Amber Sands and she thoughtfully held a hand out towards a side table, with a light silken whisper of sound, a sheer thin drift of colour rose from the table and came to her hand. As she laid the narrow ribbon of Jhirelle braiding at the junction of the child's lifeline and the line that represented his mother's house she wondered idly if he would remain within her sands, or would his family insist on taking him away. Who knew from where his father came, although when she thought of it she had a strong feeling that he too was of the Opal. She thought through all the clues that they had regarding the child and decided to go and look at him herself, to see what she could discern from his shape or colouring. She straightened from her studies and was about to approach the door when there came a hesitant tap. Almost before she could invite her visitor in, the latch lifted, and Nadra stood uncertainly at the door.

She was carrying the baby, and something in her posture cried "alarm" to Ikella, who swiftly by-passed her spell plan, reaching for the child in the automatic reflex of a Healer, or mother.

Lifting the child from his nurse the Sorceress confirmed her fears, there was a very significant problem, for Daro was even lighter than she remembered. He was pale and lay gazing at her impassively from dark sunken eyes. She saw his listlessness, his skin translucent with feathery blue veins showing at his temples and wrists, even as she took the child his head rolled weakly against her heart. The Sorceress exclaimed in dismay.

"He is losing weight, not gaining it! What has caused this?"

Nadra wrung her hands in an agony of despair as she explained that every food had been tried on Daro, how Hannah the junior Infirmarian had worked with her daily but now he was even refusing the breast again. Nadra, plainly distressed, reported dully.

"I know my duty Deshun Ikella. I know how to prepare gruel for nurslings who need weaning. I took classes with Kateya to make sure that my children were well nourished, and clean," she ended, her voice tailing off uncertainly as she perceived the Sorceress's concern.

Ikella peered into Daro's face absent-mindedly, saying softly.

"I know Nadra, it is not your fault, I do not blame you for this. I blame myself for not trying the Seeking Spell sooner."

She moved to a low backed chair, seating herself and rocking Daro gently in her arms.

He needs rehydrating as much as anything. Has he been sick recently? The nurse explained that she was about to prepare some watered Irix milk, as Daro had actually stopped vomiting about daybreak. Ikella waved her away to the nursery, settling herself down to cuddle the child, who seemed to her to have regained a little warmth as she held him.

"Poor little man."

She crooned, and the baby's eyes flickered. He sighed and Ikella's heart sank, this apathy was far more dangerous than any Storm-born element. She considered her options and stood abruptly, trilling a chain of notes as she engaged her aura, surrounding both herself and the child in an Opal mist. As she did so the child's chest lifted and he took a deep shuddering breath, seemingly breathing in the very opalescence that surrounded him, to the alarm of the Sorceress who looked down observing his reactions carefully. He seemed more aware second by second, grasping her hands as she lay him carefully on a padded chair, stripping him naked. She reached for a large stone pot, opening it to pour into her hand a few drops of a clear liquid, breathing in the sharp distinct odour of sirris oil she felt her own chill hands warm. Transferring a few drops to the other hand, she began to massage the baby, stroking him deftly while she wove her voice in a low pitched rhythmic chant around him. She steadied him with one hand, whilst she placed on the baby's bare chest a perfect gemstone from each of the nine deserts, the last one of which placed directly over his heart, was a perfect fire opal.

The baby stilled, relaxed and wakeful he stared up at her as she began to sing her incantation, magically linking the spell plan and map on the floor of her study with intricate passes of her hands. As she worked, a subtle glow surrounded the child, it seemed as though a line of light sprang from each of the stones on his chest to link up with what had been the plain soft stone lines on the gleaming rock opal floor, line after line in all the shades of the deserts suddenly glowed brightly across the darkening room but brightest by far was the gleam of the opal next to Daro's heart.

Ikella stood back from the network that she had woven for now was the most difficult part, and she had to make sure that every line was fully and inextricably linked, one with another, in the correct order of precedence. Satisfied, she reached for her Staff, and with a soft whirring sound it floated to her hand, the strange wings atop the Staff beating almost lazily, flickering with a brilliance that she had seen before in the deep caverns of Caranchar. For a long moment, she wondered if the magic of the cleansing had harmed the child, 'till her training took over, and she lifted the Staff and sang. She kept her mind and heart sternly detached enjoining both the winds and sands to reveal any trace of the child's family. She invoked layers of magic that she had not thought to use, and as she sang the seeking stone lifted and hovered for a moment above the encompassing Source beads and then passed to each of the stones laid on the child's chest. It seemed to Ikella that it hovered on tiny wings, replicas of those atop her Staff, as it sped along the lines she had conjured, back and forth from the stones on the child to the lines which indicated his birth. This was as it should be, the stone that linked to child should seek from sand to sand for any living or dead relict of his family. Towards the end of its searching flight, for a second the tiny gemstone fruit hovered by Ikella, then sped again to the child and to Ikella's total astonishment hovered over the Opal laid on the child's heart, before suddenly hurling itself on to the Opal and disappearing into the heart of the glowing stone. As if magically fusing itself to the stone it grew brighter and brighter, causing Ikella to shield her eyes against the incandescence of the moment and then it was gone. With a soft popping noise, it simply vanished, leaving the opal pulsating with light for a second. The baby, who had lain still whilst the seeking spell was cast, suddenly gave a crow of delight, and as the room started to get brighter and the magic dissipated, Ikella abandoned her Staff and snatched him up, anxious to check that he had not suffered any harm from her casting. He seem positively recharged, kicked energetically and made life difficult for her to replace his wrappers, but there was light in his eyes again. The vital spark that she had sensed burning low seemed to be back. She made haste to remove the opal from his hand, which even now he sought to place in his mouth. As she recovered the stone she glanced at it, wondering what had become of the beautiful carved fruit that she had used as a seeking stone. To her amazement, deeply carved in the surface of what had been a natural unpolished opal was a facsimile of the strange fruit carved in the original. She stared deeply into the heart of the Opal, it was darker than many of its kind, tiny fiery flecks flashed green and gold, lighting up the unmistakeable shape of the strange fruit that now embellished the surface. There was no trace of the original stone into which the fruit had been carved but the opal was slick, almost as though it had been dipped in water. She lifted the baby up, cradling him into her left arm, examining the stone she held in her right hand. Yes, it was wet and yet the baby himself was dry as a bone. Puzzled she raised the stone to her nose and sniffed but there was nothing to detect there. She flicked the tip of her tongue out and tasted the stone cautiously, it was strange, hot, sweet and salt at the same time, she filed her impressions away for future thought and turned as Nadra, stumbling in the wake of Mina, came in.

Mina was scolding her wet nurse as she entered. "Excuse me Deshun," she said, surveying the room swiftly, pouncing on Daro and lifting him into practiced arms as Ikella reluctantly relinquished him.

"Come Nadra, let us get young Daro some food"

She passed the baby to Nadra, who retreated towards the nursery, as Mina took possession of the Sorceress. Leaving Ikella poised in the centre of the spell plan, Mina shut the door on the nurse and turned . Noting the sheen on Ikella's forehead, the glitter in her eyes and the discarded Staff lying against the wall, she drew a deep breath, guiding Ikella to one side.

"Spell casting round that child again?"

She queried, but before Ikella could answer her she gathered a flagon pouring a long stream of berry red liquid into a cup, and pressing it against Ikella's lips.

"I wish you had waited for me, " the Healer grumbled.

"You must have worked on Daro before you started, and you are not yet back to full strength yourself! Come, don't go to sleep on me now," she cajoled.

"You must drink this."

Ikella, fighting the inevitable fatigue of spell-casting, said meekly "Yes Mina." and drank.

She had tucked the opal stone safely into a deep pocket on her robe and after she had slept half the afternoon away, she pondered over the incantation she had used. She devoutly hoped that her spell would find his family for the child's sake. They had come to the end of the epidemic she thought, in the past six hours not one patient had died, and no more had been admitted to the Infirmary. In another week, families that had accompanied their sick to her door would be leaving. In another two weeks all the sick would have recovered, by the third, she would be able to open the doors of Selesh again.

She sat brooding, planning her College of Healers, and wondering when she should contact the Sisterhood. Her eyes strayed along the shelves in the corner to where an ornate bowl in shimmering Opal glass stood on it's cast metal stand, her gaze shifted to the matching flagon stood on the same shelf, full of liquid and she gave a start, almost looking over her shoulder although she was alone in the room.

'Of course!' She thought, crossing the room swiftly and lifting down the slender flagon reverently. Removing the stopper, she wetted the tip of her index finger on the clear liquid within, raising it to her mouth. As it touched her lips, she tasted the same sweet salty flavour of the wetted opal stone and her brows drew together, considering. 'Stillglass.' She breathed the word, her whisper dropping into the silent room with shocking impact. Her mind raced.

'How could Stillglass appear on Daro's heartstone? How could the rarest, the most mysterious element on Pelshar come to be transferred to the Opal. What happened to the Seeking Stone which had subtly transformed the child's heartstone?'

Still pondering these questions, she wandered back into the heart of the room and stood looking at her spell plan for a long time, recalling old Janiah who had tutored Sorceress acolytes in "magical properties" at Sanctuary.

They had learned about Stillglass. Where the rare liquid had been found, how it worked. Lost in thought, she began undoing the magical locks and protections she had placed on the spell plan. She found herself recalling the time that Janiah placed a drop of the precious liquid on each students lips to taste for the first time. "There Ladies, this be Stillglass!"

The Guardian had grumbled in her deep rich voice, typical of the Onyx Sands from which she had originated.

"Remember this well, for it be the rarest commodity on Pelshar. Used in ritual it can allow you to view from afar another Sand, or a person far removed from you. It occurs naturally, being harvested by the Nishanawa, who serve the Temple of the Winds in the Ashgenar. Use it very sparingly for it has properties beyond our understanding."

Ikella frowned as she recalled Janiah's last comment.

"Not for nothing is Stillglass called the Tears of the Singers!"

She put the idea of summoning her Sisters in Sorcery immediately to the back of her mind. Daily events dictated that, she decided, knowing that Beneva would advise her when the time was right. For the moment, she had to clear the Infirmary of those who lingered there, start the rebuilding of Selesh Minoria so that when the impending festival of Jentaroth arrived, they would be able to host their usual visitors and await the results of today's spell-casting!

Thoughtfully, Ikella disassembled the remains of the spell plan, smoothing the soft stone lines from the floor and replacing the rugs, putting stones in wooden drawers and returning herbs to drying baskets. She prowled around her room, wondering how long it would be before the Seeking Spell did its work and Daro was claimed by his family.

It was many days before Ikella confided in Beneva. She showed her the alterations to the child's heartstone, swiftly sketching the original carved fruit that she had used as a 'seeking Stone", spoke of the strange melding that had welded it to the opal as she cast the spell. To her immense disappointment, Beneva had never heard of anything like it, but she promised to search her records immediately, and Ikella had to content herself with that.

She was paying her first visit to the largest of the old storerooms, which Beneva had requested both as Library and living quarters for herself. The Sorceress was surprised to find it spacious, comfortable and already furnished with tables and chairs for scholars to use. Along one wall, Beneva was supervising a number of volunteers as they arranged scrolls and artefacts that were currently piled on an ornately carved table. Ikella paused by it for a moment, her hands caressing the elaborate symbols carved along its edges, then raising an eyebrow she turned and stared at the Librarian without a word. Beneva coloured but said nothing, and Ikella simply trailed a hand along the intricately worked edge to the table as she passed, following the librarian to look at some of the artefacts that had been rescued from Sanctuary. At one end of the room the walls narrowed inward and in the resulting alcove Beneva had positioned a large work desk. Three walls lined with shelves stacked with sand tablets, scrolls and smaller artefacts surrounded the desk, and two large and comfortable chairs had been placed for their use. Beneva had arranged for wall hangings to be placed on a wrought pole, drawn closely they produced a level of privacy for the Guardian, who slept in a small room to the rear of this reception area. Ikella admired the way that Beneva arranged things, she seemed already a part of Selesh, almost as well set up as the Sorceress. She sat, her thoughts drifting, until she sensed a hint of magic. Was it sight? Sound? Smell? She could not have said what made her feel the Source so strongly but there was an undoubted tingle along her skin and a feeling of expectancy in the air.

Sensing Ikella's awareness, Beneva said comfortably enough. "So you feel it too do you? It was my reason for asking for these rooms. I seem to sense Sanctuary here. Certainly I am convinced that there is power grounded in these walls, and thought I would ask you to douse the path, when time allows."

Her referral to Ikella's workload wrested an ironic smile from the Sorceress, who stretched herself into a more comfortable position and said in a satisfied way.

"Actually Beneva, as far as the sickness goes our workload is more than bearable. We have decided to take on ten women to work alongside the Healers in the infirmary. They will learn the skills that do not require Talent, bed-making, washing, cooking and the like. The sort of work that can free a Healer for more important tasks."

She placed a hand on the back of her neck and began to rotate her head, plainly trying to loosen some tightness there. Beneva nodded absently, "These are times that will require a new Way if we are to survive!" she murmured, then.

"I am afraid that I too am setting precedents that I should have discussed with you before I did so."

She looked guiltily at Ikella, still soothing her stiff neck and said simply.

"I asked a couple of your Inesh girls to help me find some furniture for the rooms here. They were quick to find a bed and a chest for my clothing, but they didn't know what I meant by books or shelving, so I went exploring and found nearly all you see here in the undercroft, below the kitchen levels."

She regarded Ikella steadily across the desk.

"They warned me that such exploration was forbidden but I could not bother you more, you were so pre-occupied. Please excuse any impropriety that has occurred."

Ikella smiled at the thought of the staid, totally correct Beneva committing 'improprieties', then groaned as she released another knot in her neck.

"If I cannot trust you and your judgement Beneva, then I cannot trust myself, but be careful. The ancient corridors and rooms below are off limits for safety reasons. Because they are unexplored, I have no idea if they are safe to walk in. The Clan have protected Selesh against exploration since long before Adaria." she confided, adding thoughtfully, "One wonders if the dangers from the past that we have all been warned about lie mainly within our own homes?"

She pulled a wry face at that, rubbing at her neck again, stretching it this way and that, and then she stood with a frown.

"Beneva, forgive me, but I think that we must draw one of these curtains a little. There is such a draft on the back of my neck, I must be growing old and stiff!"

She made for the right-hand curtain, aware that the busying people in the main hall of the Djellim were leaving in answer to the Summoning Bell, calling them to their evening meal. As she raised a hand to close the curtain however, she felt a familiar feathery touch of awareness. The slight draft change direction, changed temperature and Ikella knew that what she felt was no ordinary breeze and turned back to see that Beneva was also aware. With a conspiratorial murmur she said "Do you feel that?"

Beneva took Ikella's arm, leading her along the shelf-lined walls, one hand raised, apparently following the draft as it wafted through the high ceilinged room that she had selected as her Library. Ikella followed the Librarian silently checking off in her mind the uses that the room had been put to since she came to Selesh. Ahead of her Beneva slowed, she knew that she could sense old magic here, and turned to see the corresponding flush of excitement on Ikella's face, as she stood rooted in her tracks.

Ikella was vibrating with the strength of the call. It caressed her, tempted her, frightened her because even though residual, it was of a glamour and a style that she could never emulate. It was strangely stilling, making her more aware of her surroundings, making her want to engage her aura and seek it. Beneva saw her hands clench against the temptation, and the Librarian came to a halt, her hand hovering above a shelf on which stood a dusty bowl.

"Here Ikella?" Beneva queried, and Ikella nodded, every inch of her body quivering in anticipation of some terrible trap.

With a shiver she found herself. Looking back into the strangely dimmed Djellim, she saw the table that had been placed centrally there, feeling again the carved symbols running around its edge and remembering, she made a decision.

"Stand back Beneva." She commanded in a gruff voice, and stretching out her hands she intoned."

"Shalonthi, shanushek, adreo opus."

There was a soft 'shushing' noise, as the wall facing the two women slid aside, and they found themselves looking into a huge room, the existence of which had never before been suspected. Wordlessly they looked at each other, Ikella raising an eyebrow at Beneva, who was peering curiously into the hidden chamber. She spoke irritably.

"Well don't blame me! It has been here, in your house for longer than I care to think about, and you didn't find it before! Think you that Sashandra knew of it?"

Ikella stepped right up to the entranceway and looked in over Beneva's shoulder to a dimmed grey room, deeply shadowed in the corners and looking as if it had been used as some sort of repository for furniture, for central to this chamber was an enormous table. She answered Beneva thoughtfully."

"No, I do not think Sashandra, or Idirinha, or even Adaria herself knew of this place, or they would have told someone about it, and the information would have been handed down. In Adaria's day they used only the ground level chambers, in fact when she finally left to found Sanctuary, Selesh was virtually uninhabited for best part of a hundred Rotations. No-one could believe it when she returned with Idirinha, proclaiming her Sorceress. Idirinha had the rooms that we now use for our living area created, and as you know it was she who discovered and re-opened our Central Hall, which Adaria sanctified for worship and secular Gatherings. It was Idirinha who found the Book of Rule and had it moved with its pedestal to the Sacred Circle in the Hall, from which it has never been removed since."

Beneva stood back from the entranceway to which her whole attention had been focussed, she looked at Ikella for a long moment, and then asked quietly."

"Do you know where the Book of Rule was found?" she had a curious expression on her face, and Ikella, sensing that the question was important paused before answering quietly. "No, we do not know where it was found. Idirinha made reference to some place of high magic, said that she thought the artefacts better placed in our Sacred Circle to prevent anyone damaging or misusing them, and no-one questioned that, it was the Way of things then." To which comment Beneva said tartly, "Yes, I know, do not question what does not affect your life. Follow in the path your parents or betters set you. Never seek the unknown for danger lurks there. Never put your foot to an untried path, for fear of bringing down those who make the Ways clear for you to follow." And on the last stanza Ikella, her voice somehow sounding tremulous joined in with.

"Only follow the tried and trusted Way. Walk only the Path that is set for you and question not the paths and ways of the past. What is past has long gone, what is faded from mortal view was not for man to follow, to see or to use as a path. What is done is done, what is done cannot be undone, know only the Way forward for the truth, trust only what you are taught by those who live still and walk that path. Never turn away from the path you are set, dedicate your heart and your hand to a true path and follow only the Way. That is the law and the Way of Pelshar."

The two women eyed each other and then Beneva drew Ikella away from the mysterious hidden entrance, saying.

"Before we stray from the Way, we should discuss this." Ikella nodded and joined her companion who walked back to the centre of the new Djellim and stood looking down at the strangely carved table she had placed there. She turned to face Ikella as the Sorceress approached her.

"When we came into this room we found that there was a light patch here on the floor. It made everyone uncomfortable, a sort of prickly feeling. Nothing would do but we had to cover the place. However, even with a rug put down, somehow the lighter patch showed through and that is why I put the table here. Do you remember the table? I thought to bring that with me, knowing of its significance in your early life, but being totally unaware of its significance in the wider concept!" She bit her lip.

"There was no discernable magic here Ikella, or I would have called you." her voice tailed off thoughtfully and Ikella nodded, looking about her with new eyes, seeing the height and the breadth of the room, the vaulted ceiling, the niche in which Beneva had installed her worktable and lastly the strange hidden room on the opposing wall. At various points along the wall she could see where wooden beams had been inlet and as she noted their strange symmetry, she thought she could discern a purpose in their being. She pointed. "Beneva, do you think that perhaps there was a gallery along that wall, with a staircase near your niche, from which you could ascend to the gallery above?" she questioned her companion. Looking a little bewildered, Beneva drew back from the table and followed the direction of Ikella's pointing finger. She peered up into the vault of the ceiling where the light of the evening glows could not penetrate, and observed for herself the regular height of the beam ends, their spacing and their size, and nodded.

"It is possible." she agreed and made haste to obey Ikella who said suddenly.

"Beneva, go to that end of the room and look carefully to the wall above where I am standing and see what you can from there."

The librarian picked up a torch from a wall sconce and lighting it casually with handfire, conjured so naturally that Ikella blinked, she made her way to the far side of the Djellim. There she stood for a moment and then swiftly returned, her brows drawn together.

"If you are right, then the gallery ran right round the room."

She commented and then to her surprise she saw that Ikella had dragged the table to one side, exposing the ancient floor beneath, where a faintly glowing circle lay, dappled with age but still visible. Ikella drew Beneva to one side, while she tracked the walls with her eyes, seeing in the gathering gloom some familiar markings. She held out a hand to Beneva, peremptorily demanding.

"Enscrasure, tablet." As Beneva hastened to her command, she paced, muttering to herself.

"Seating area for Healers, Way of Challenge, Council chairs, gallery for a speaker."

She quietened as Beneva brought to her the tools she had demanded and then she made a series of marks on the tablet, and handed it back to Beneva saying."

"Do you see what I see?"

As the librarian checked off the floor plan, Ikella could hardly bear to breathe, let alone speak, so great was the sense of excitement. It was a long time before Beneva finally spoke softly. "If you are right, this room just might have been the original Hall. There was one not too dissimilar at Sanctuary once."

She moved to stand in the fading circle on the floor. "This would well have been their Sacred Circle." Ikella whispered hoarsely.

"Whose? Not Adaria's surely?"

Beneva turned calm eyes on the Sorceress.

"No, this is far older than Adaria my dear! This is of the First Age of Mystery, long before our kind. It is old, very old, and thankfully very rare, but I suspect that there is much in Selesh that has never been revealed in our time. It has been waiting for some event, or someone to find it, and now you have!"

She swiftly crossed to the brighter patch roughly central in the circle "and this where the Book of Rule stood on its lectern."

She frowned, plainly displeased by one impression that she had obtained from her investigations.

"Where would the people have sat, how would they have accessed the Hall?" Ikella was silent for a moment and then she said, "I don't think that this Hall was for the use of the people at all, just for the use of the Sorceress and the Healers. Although I suspect an entirely different, higher magic may have been practiced here at some time, for that hidden chamber would be beyond my abilities to construct, to conceal, and am I not supposed to be the most powerful magic user in the whole of Pelshar?" She spoke entirely without pride, just questioning what seemed obvious to her. Seeing something in Beneva's face, she paused and stopped, demanding.

What?" and the other woman grimaced as though uncomfortable with her thoughts.

"What troubles me, is why are we asking these questions now? Why are we so able to digress from the Way ourselves?" She craned her neck round to nod at the unexplored new room still patiently waiting for them.

"Perhaps we can find some answers there."

With a mere whisper of sound from their robes they turned and made their way back to investigate.

Chapter 24 - Feydora

As they approached the silent grey chamber, Ikella found herself growing nervous. She had come to the Staff hearing Sashandra utter dire warnings of the terrible dangers lying in wait for unwary explorers. She knew that rock falls and subsidence had rendered even comparatively modern chambers unusable. Sashandra's secret corridors and hidden entranceways were obviously part of a far older complex, much of it buried beyond restoration, all of it encompassed with an air of subtle menace, good reason to avoid temptation.

This large outer room that she had already designated 'The Djellim', (Library), had lain empty since she came to Selesh. In fact she had forgotten its existence, until Beneva begged to use it. However, she was absolutely sure, no hint of this hidden chamber appeared in any record.

Considering that her intention to enter this hidden chamber constituted a breach of the Way, Ikella paused guiltily, wondering if perhaps she had the right to investigate.

As she stopped Beneva, ever thirsty for more knowledge, reached the opening and stepped across the threshold. Ikella saw the Librarian's outline flicker for an instant. A ripple extending into the atmosphere around her.

As the Sorceress started forward the edges of the doorway glowed, where it supported a transparent field of energy across the threshold. A bright glow outlined Beneva's body, as gently, but inexorably she was repelled.

Ikella hastened to her side.

"Are you alright Beneva?"

Ikella asked anxiously, reassured by Beneva's look of mortification.

"Yes, yes!" Beneva exclaimed testily, remarking.

"That's a very strange sensation. I wonder how we gain access? How did you know it was there?"

Ikella smiled remarking only.

"A little draft told me! Perhaps we don't gain access at all Beneva mine. It only opens to one hand."

She smiled faintly at the Librarian's outraged snort, giving no hint of the fact that she actually didn't know how she had accomplished such a thing. Considering, she engaged her aura and surrounded by a swirl of sparkling light, she stretched a hand into the unknown.

The sensation was very odd, like pressing on a sheet of cool gel. Then the barrier parted in front of her, leaving a cold frisson running over her skin as she crossed the threshold impetuously, just as the field of energy collapsed. Only then did she realise that on taking that step she had firmly shut her eyes, and shamed herself completely when she needed to use her left hand to uncross the fingers on the right. Already Beneva was calling.

"What can you see, what can you see?"

The Librarian hovered at the doorway in an agony of impatience. As Ikella took another pace forward, there was a sighing sound and Beneva literally fell into the room. Ikella looked back to see the softly shimmering outline to the door had disappeared, the barrier was plainly gone. Not only that, but the chamber was being lit from some source unknown. The walls, like those of the Djellim without, were lined with shelves on which were stacked scroll after scroll after scroll. On one side of the room was a flight of three steps, leading to a dais on which was an ornately carved chair, embellished with a huge blaze Opalstone, set into the back panel. Below that, was an unusual table, contrived from a silvery wood. Ikella stared at the table mystified, it resembled the trifoliate petals of vetali, a sweet green plant that grew frequently on the more temperate Fringes of the deserts. Each "leaf" of the table was circular and had seating for three persons, the chairs for each person being slid beneath the table. In the centre connecting the three "leaves" was a great plate of clear sand-paste, wrought to show no mark of firing, no sprue of spinning, in itself a wonder of her Sands, remarkable in its construction.

Ikella carefully pulled a chair out and sat. To her astonishment the sand-paste panel flickered, clouding eerily opalescent. Presently Beneva was persuaded away from the scrolls, to sit opposite Ikella, who was still trying to make sense of what she saw.

"I was not aware from outside how big this room really is!"

Ikella tried to sound casual, though every nerve was tingling. She had discovered that she could swivel her chair around, due to some ingenious mechanism and was enjoying the novelty of that as she explored, using hands, as well as eyes. Casually slipping her hand into a curious holder fixed to the right arm of her chair, she fingered it remarking.

"Some sort of pole went here I think, do you have one on your chair Beneva?"

She glanced at the librarian and was at once aware that Beneva was frozen, staring over her shoulder at something behind her.

"Beneva?" She questioned, feeling the hair stand up on the nape of her neck, as a wide eyed Beneva managed to part dry lips to hiss.

"Why don't you ask her?"

With a tangible shiver of apprehension Ikella turned to face the dais. Sat with one hand loosely clasping the arm of the chair, was the most beautiful woman she had ever beheld. She was fine boned with long palely golden hair and flawless skin. Her delicate tip tilted nose was set above a provocative mouth, but it was her eyes that held the gaze. They were extraordinary, glowing as though imbued with the qualities of fire opal, sparks of turquoise, shimmers of purple swam in their depths, the whites merged with the iris, to make the woman's features appear subtly feline.

She extended a hand in welcome, but the Sorceress saw immediately that she was not actually looking at them, rather she seemed to be looking out into infinity. As they sat mesmerised, the woman's lips parted and she began to speak. Ikella found herself becoming internally still, ultimately focussed, as this strange vision addressed them, shocking Ikella to the core with her first words."

"I am Feydora, Sandsinger of the Opal Sands. From before the dawn of your time, I am come to warn you of great danger."

Feydora's image shivered changed posture slightly. Closing her eyes momentarily she ran a cord through her hands on which a carved fruit swung gently. Ikella was pinioned by the voice which filled every fibre of her being, drowning her own thoughts, subjugating her will, till all she could think, hear, taste or breathe was that Voice.

"It is in the hope that one amongst you has command of power, that I speak."

The hypnotic voice continued.

"Yours is a new age. You must guide the others. You have the responsibility for guarding the secrets of the past, until now sealed from your knowledge or understanding. Your task will be to control the knowledge and use it wisely, you must make changes to the Way, knowing that many will resist such interference."

The Opal drowned eyes turned to Ikella's briefly and she found herself trembling as the voice in her head strengthened, but already the title echoed in Ikella's memory 'Sandsinger, Opal Sandsinger' and the image from the caverns below Caranchar flickered through her mind as the another memory surfaced, locked away, against the day she needed it.

'Sandsingers, incredibly powerful mages who died out long ago, used both paths of Power, male and female, which is possibly why there was such a cataclysmic end to the First Age of Mystery.'

Miriniva's voice sounded incredibly close to her ear, and she looked round, half expecting to see the late Guardian of Power at her elbow. Her eyes sought Beneva's, and though her courage faltered her chin lifted as the Voice continued. It was inexorable, breaking through the distraction of Ikella's revelation.

"This is my last task, to make a record for all time of what was, of what we understood and saw, of what happened to Pelshar, and how we hoped to protect you from making the same errors!"

Beneva, had armed herself with tablets and enscrasures before they entered the room and now, hunched over the table, she was wildly writing, trying for all she was worth to record every last word spoken. Her hands shook with the effort, and Ikella found herself subtly trickling some strength into the librarian, extending her aura to protect her companion, who looked up at her and smiled her thanks.

The all encompassing voice continued.

"As my last act of faith in the Ones great goodness, I have, with the help of another, placed about our world a spell working. I have set a key to undo that spell, which will only take effect when the conditions permit the return of High Magic. I have determined that only one may recognise this key, and only when the need arises. Only they will have the courage to pronounce the unlocking of my work. It is to them that I now bring this warning."

For some reason, Ikella found herself both seeing and feeling under her hands, the ancient inscription on the table that had somehow found its way from Sanctuary, into her Djellim. The words themselves untangled in her head, and she understood at last what she had done. Strangely unafraid, she felt suddenly a kinship with this being, a common bond of purpose. Feydora's face changed subtly, her words now held command, her eyes compelling.

"Yours is a precious charge, for in your hands you hold your world. Time alone will reveal the past of Pelshar. Neither you nor I can speed the progress of the Way your feet are now set upon. You will make changes, though they break your heart, or run counter to your writ. You will discover, as we did, to our great shame and sorrow, that amongst us were those who refused the responsibilities of power, whilst corrupting and perverting its greatest pleasures."

Ikella and Beneva felt an agony of shame, sorrow and weariness overcoming them, leaving them shuddering under the impact of Feydora's emotions.

Beware of seeking power for powers sake, beware of those who seek to control others. Listen, listen for the voice within, but do not follow blindly, look around you for traps, for temptation, for pride in your own power. Above all listen, be still and listen every day. Tell each Hall to listen, for one day they will hear another Voice."

It seemed to Ikella that Feydora's image was growing, her glittering eyes dominated the room and there was a throbbing note of prophecy as she proclaimed.

"One comes, who walking in the night, shall yet lead us from the shadows. He shall move great obstacles from the Way, and walk amongst men as a man himself, though he is as far removed from you in power, as I am in Rotations. In his command all things, from the great sweep of the snows to the far deserts, to the perfume of the airs, to the winds themselves. He shall love and be loved, live beyond the furthest knowledge of man, and in his hands shall be the fate of Pelshar."

For a moment, it seemed as if Feydora was in the room with them, instead of her image-self, and both women reeled under the impact of her eyes.

"Remember me. Remember what I have told you. Listen! Wait. You shall perhaps live long enough to hear his Voice."

Then there was silence. Both women came shaking to their feet but Feydora was gone and it seemed to Ikella that with her departure, the grey dust of eons fell.

Silently the Librarian gathered the tablets she had written together and slowly looked around the room. Ikella rose to her feet, remarking in a low voice.

"It seems to me that we have more questions here than answers my Beneva."

To which Beneva agreed wearily.

"So many questions that I would not know where to start looking for answers."

She stood at the threshold, gazing into the room, saying bitterly.

"I am known to all as the Keeper of the Scrolls, the librarian. You know me as the Guardian of Knowledge, and yet I feel as though I know nothing!"

Her eyes ran over the room, lingered on the scroll shelves possessively, as they prepared to leave. Ikella said thoughtfully.

"It occurs to me my dear friend, that the appearance of this Feydora is too much for others to accept. Even the Sisterhood do not need to know what lies within the remit of Sanctuary. That is only for the Guardians to know! The room itself can be concealed when we are not using it, but I do not think we could or should hide its existence. We must reveal very slowly what we have found until we have read and discussed what we can, and treasure what we cannot until this prophecy is fulfilled."

She held up her hands in mute appeal, and Beneva nodded, as they passed out into the Djellim. On the outside the Sorceress turned to face the doorway.

"Ashrak zorash!"

She commanded and there was a gleam at the edges of the opening where the barrier re-engaged. As it did so, with a click the wall slid forward to conceal it from view, and they returned to Beneva's work alcove to sink into their chairs, staring at each other mutely. Ikella finally spoke.

"I think that we can safely trust our urge to investigate, provided that we keep it strictly to ourselves at first. We can pass anything in the remit of the Healers to them as we stock the Djellim. I am fairly sure that whatever we found in that room was for our eyes, and so I do not think it proscribed, merely lost, and so as we understand it we can use it, though I wish I could think of some explanation for that rooms layout or furnishings!" Her voice brightened."

"You know, that would make a superb Council Chamber for Selesh!" she mused and then electrified, exclaimed excitedly. "In fact, am quite sure that I have solved another problem by providing a stunning, positively sensational place for the Sisterhood when I call Conclave as I soon must:"

Another thought crossing her mind, she jerked upright exclaiming.

"Our Staffs could be supported in those holders on the chair arms! I wonder if that was the original intention?"

Just then Beneva commented.

"We must have missed supper. I am cold, I can feel my belly growl. We were in your 'Council Chamber' for ages!"

As she spoke, they heard the Summoning Bell for evening Gather, and in confused silence they covered the newly scribed sand tablets and went below to eat.

They sat together, each engrossed in their own thoughts, 'till with her last drink, Ikella met Beneva's eyes.

"I think that any action tonight would be precipitate."

She announced quietly, adding in a more normal tone of voice.

"After evening devotions, I will retire to continue some unfinished duties, one of which must be to check on Nadra and the babies!"

This last was addressed to Mina, who had unusually picked up on her mood, and remained silent throughout the meal. The Senior Healer who sat with

Hanna, looked up.

"Nadra is still having a lot of trouble feeding Daro"

She spoke bleakly.

"He seems so sickly that I really fear for him. His weight decreases daily. He tolerates so little in the way of solids, he is not thriving."

The Sorceress felt guilt blossom within her as she volunteered. "Tomorrow I must inspect the new Hall for visitors. I have already promised that I would. However, I will see both babies at their morning feed time. I will feed some solids to Daro myself. He relaxes and takes his feeds from me, when he fights Nadra."

She dragged herself unwillingly to her feet, shocked by how tired she felt, but even with discoveries and revelations to absorb, this worrying trend of Daro's had to be addressed. She turned to her Senior Healer.

"So it is fixed. Mina can you come at daybreak? Hanna will you tell Nadra what we are about on your way to bed, and Beneva, can you seek guidance for us regarding this strange malaise of the child, so that we may keep him well till his family arrive?"

"Will you all join me for evening meditation?"

Ikella turned away, and without checking to see if they followed, she swept out of the refectory, down the corridor to the Hall of the Healers.

She knelt, trying to still her thoughts, but they whirled giddily around her head like busybugs. She found herself comparing the Hall to the Djellim, forcing herself to concentrate on making the correct responses to the chanting voices of the Healers, but all the time hearing Feydora's voice as it transcended the Rotations.

"Be still"

It whispered in her ear.

"Be still and listen."

Chapter 25 - The Master Builder

At the break of a particularly cold, dark, day, Mina, Hanna and Beneva reconvened in Ikella's dayroom, where the glows still burned. The visitors, having brought their drinking bowls, were soon breaking their fast with a rough grained olas cake and a warm sweetdrink. Ikella's only real claim to luxury Trinet, her elderly hand servant, waited on them silently and departed, firmly closing the door behind her, leaving the small group huddled waiting for the glowstone set in the simple hearth to reach full heat.

As the chill finally lifted, Ikella said slowly.

"It is very strange, I have lost track of the Seasons! I apologise for the cold, Trinet will be setting the fire earlier in future."

Beneva cleared her throat uneasily, and Ikella firmly commanded.

"Speak!"

The Librarian, pacing the length of the room, finally marshalled her thoughts, saying.

"It is my belief that this is not true end of Rotation, but some false season brought on us by the Storm. Without the full light of Seleus, the sands are as chilled as in the night, slowly giving up the heat they hold till day brings back the sun to reheat them. We have had no direct sight of Sun since the Storm. Without its light or heat, soon there will come an end of Rotation unlike any we have known. We will be as the deep snows in the far north, though other sands may hold the heat for longer. I fear the best chance of survival lies in the far South, where the Onyx Sands contain hot springs, mountains that boil. Pitch bubbling through the sands, and steam vents! With that activity, they may survive, it is the other sands who may not, us amongst them!"

Ikella was silent, musing over her librarians words and then she stood.

"We have water in plenty, so if we can heat the water where it flows through Selesh, we can use the covered pastures for growing food and herbs. If we can safely open up the area around the bathing pools, to provide a small warm area for the most vulnerable, then we might survive till next Rotation. I will need a Master Builder to help decide how best those precious resources can be used."

She paused, thinking aloud.

"He must be prepared for change, able to copy things that Guardian Beneva has seen or used on her travels"

Her eyes bored into Beneva's meaningfully, as the Guardian nodded placidly, lifting her head to enquire delicately.

"What was it I saw so far to the north, my Deshun?"

A ripple of conspiratorial amusement ran round the room, even Ikella allowed her lips to twitch and then with an air of solemnity she said.

"Well it is good to see that we are at least a Council of War, if not yet enough in number to form a High Council for Selesh!"

At which the others fell silent as the direction of her thoughts became clear to them.

"It occurs to me, that we have a hot spring right here. It has always heated the bathing pools, a gentle heat, but heat just the same. A skilled Builder might know how to channel that heat. Such a possibility might exist don't you think?"

Mina was the first to break the ensuing silence with the comment.

"Even if we do not understand such things my Deshun, I know a man who might!"

Ikella stared at her stalwart lieutenant in surprise, as Mina exclaimed.

"His name is Master Builder Errish. He came from Kathliar, (only days before we left on Song Walk) to install the new facings that you ordered for the Healer Hall doorway. His men are rebuilding our village, while he has taken on repairing a storeroom here so that he could extend it, creating a Hall of Welcome for all visitors. It was also his intention that this would safely quarantine new arrivals, helping us prevent spread of contagion."

As her voice died away with an embarrassed blush, Ikella saw her friend as a woman, teetering on the brink of entirely new emotions for the first time.

"The Ways turn and twist in unpredictable directions indeed!'.

Ikella thought with gentle amusement and swiftly despatched a Guard to the village to find Errish. While they waited, Mina ran through the report of the Infirmary with Hanna. The Healers had created a large functional Infirmary from unused storerooms, and she hazarded the comment that she wished it could be permanent, a real school for the Healer Guild. This was greeted with such enthusiasm that Ikella wondered how she would greet the news that a certain Master Builder's services would be needed for the foreseeable future? At last, her Guard returned announcing.

"Master Builder Errish my Deshun."

At which the object of Mina's interest strode confidently forward, and doffed his burnous. Dropping to one knee in front of Ikella, he startled a nervous giggle from Mina who, silenced by the quelling glance of her Sorceress, blushed furiously, busying her hands in weaving her fingers into the fabric of her robe.

Rising to her feet, the Sorceress indicated a seat for him to take, then using her most beguiling of voices said formally.

"I bid you welcome Master Builder Errish."

The honey silk voice seemed to fill the room, and Errish stole a suspicious glance at her but although her skin glowed, there was no aura, no shimmering of her outline and he relaxed. Ikella smiled internally, like many, he was suspicious of magic, of matters beyond the skill of human hands, but she liked what she saw in him.

He was clean, clothes though patched were both neat and serviceable. He was of that slim, whipcord strong breed, with bright intelligent eyes set in a darkly tanned face, under an unruly head of curly hair. She looked him fully in the face and he tilted his head upwards. As his eyes met hers, a sketch of a smile crossed her face as she resumed pacing thoughtfully. She spoke to him softly.

"Master Errish, we have a matter of the gravest importance to bring before you, and I can only thank the one that you are here, and possessed of the skill of your trade for we undoubtedly need your advice on a matter of solemn confidence"

The man's demeanour altered utterly as she spoke, from the challenging gaze of a healthy male, he lowered his eyes before the leader of his clan and clenching his right fist abruptly he struck it over his heart, repeating the last stanza of a Guild Masters vow.

"In the commission of my articles let me divulge no secret, let me be bound to utter silence regarding the business of my patron, and the execution of my craft. As a Master of this most ancient Guild, so do I swear!"

Mina's head came up, eyes narrowed as she heard the defensive tone of his voice, but even as Ikella crossed swiftly to the Builders side, holding out a hand in the gesture of peace, she relaxed hearing Ikella exclaim.

"Good Master Errish! I do not mean to impugn your integrity, but it is vital that we prevent panic about what we are about to face and that your designs remain secret until the work is tried, tested and ready for others to see and copy."

The Master Builder nodded shortly, the flush that had suffused his cheeks subsided, as he listened intently to what Ikella had to tell him regarding the hot springs and the provision of some means of capturing the heat that was produced. He mused for a moment, pinching his lower lip between two fingers, then said.

"May I have time to draw up some plans Deshun? I would need your permission to explore the hot spring also, perhaps a guide could be provided?"

Ikella studiously ignored the gleam in Mina's eye, and appointed Jervis, the guard who had fetched Errish earlier. The Master Builder, clearly disappointed smiled briefly at Mina before saying.

"We meet later this day to look at the new Hall of Welcome do we not?"

Ikella nodded, her mouth twitching as the man carefully added a mark to a familiar looking sand tablet that he sported. She asked him conversationally.

"Who called the quarantine building the Hall of Welcome?"

She was amused, for some had been against them having such a provision, feeling that the inns of the village would suffer from the loss of earnings. Errish shrugged his shoulders and then grinned up at her mutely 'till Mina intervened, her voice suddenly full of pride as she gazed fondly at the man she so plainly admired.

"If it please you Deshun Ikella. The provision having been arranged by the Healer Guild, of which I am Senior Healer, it was not the place of villagers to argue against it. However, Errish said he would much rather have every resident with us, than against. You were too ill to intervene, so we called a village Gather, and I explained why this was as important to them, as it is to us. Errish provided ale, and after the Gather, the people chose the name! Must it be changed? They are very proud of it."

Errish shuffled under Ikella's astonished glance as Mina continued.

"Once convinced they had misunderstood the need for quarantine, and that the inns were an essential part of the Hall of Welcome, everyone joined in. Errish explained that they, and only they, could run the hostelry, as we can't run the kitchens as well as nurse. Errish designed a warming oven and special boxes for carrying hot food in, and he..."

Mina's voice tailed off in confusion as Ikella raised an eyebrow at her.

"Well..."

The Sorceress broke in comfortably.

"That's alright then. We must allow Master Errish to get on with his work, now I know that his skills and discretion are at my command."

On this last comment, there was a flash of green eyes, and her meaning was made absolutely clear. The Master Builder stood and bowing departed the room and the group of women began to prepare for the day as the morning bell summoned them.

Ikella called Beneva to her study as the librarian prepared to leave. She said only one word as the door closed behind them.

"Shiarjha?"

To which a world of meaning was attached. Similarly reluctant to voice their discovery of the night before, Beneva nodded, emphatically.

"She must definitely be told, everything!"

The Sorceress agreed adding. "I am loathe to tell the others about Feydora yet."

Beneva nodding vehemently, said. "I agree! Superstition runs rife in Selesh anyway. They would be looking over their shoulders all day, every day, and nothing would get done."

She continued. "I had no sense that she was actually there, did you?"

The Sorceress didn't consider that point long.

"No. It felt like we triggered something that had been left for others to find. What it all means I have no idea, and my head aches with all the other things I must deal with. However, there is nothing to stop you trying to find out who she was, what she was and report back to me later. I must go and help with this baby, see Shiarjha, inspect this Hall of Welcome and see what this Errish has come up with! All in a days work, and no magic to help me!"

She walked towards her door, ready to commence her rounds, ushering the librarian out. She followed her 'till they parted at the door of the nursery, but as Beneva left Ikella, she could not help thinking.

"She is too stubborn to see that she could use magic if she wanted to. She battens down her power as though it will run out! I really must complete her education, before she grinds to a stop!'.

The morning progressed with the feeding and bathing of the babes. Ikella was dismayed by the translucency of Daro's skin. He was indeed small, almost puny, against the glowing strength of Ahnell, and after they were laid wrapped in soft rella weavings to kick and stretch, she was forced to admit to her concerns. Nadra was dark of eye, plainly tired from her duties, and with a pang of compassion Ikella recognised that the woman was barely holding on to terror as she watched the large and active Ahnell kicking happily beside his weak and feeble milk brother.

"I am sorry my Deshun. He seems totally unable to tolerate the food Healer Mina suggests."

This humble admission seemed almost wrung from Nadra, and Ikella saw that she was plainly moved by her nursling's plight. The woman continued haltingly.

"Can you tell us anything about where he came from? Perhaps he lacks some mineral that should have been in his mother's milk?"

Ikella nodded thoughtfully.

"That is true Nadra." She admitted.

"When we found his dying mother trying to birth him on the Sands, we knew nothing about them. She was too far gone to tell us anything, and died giving him life. I fear that his strength is running out, that we will bury him before his family can claim him, if any of them roam our sands alive"

She paused, hearing the slap of approaching sandals as Hanna came from the Infirmary to show Nadra how to mix an invalid gruel for the baby. Laying a hand on the startled woman's arm, she said softly.

"We met in anger Nadra. I didn't understand the anguish of your grief or the desperation of Caranchar. I have come to feel grateful for our meeting, for you are helping to ease the burden of my responsibility for the babies. One day it may be that Tuennis will be able to claim her Ahnell, and if he lives, one day my Daro may be able to thank you himself, but you must understand one thing."

As she became more formal in her speech, Nadra raised brimming eyes to those of the Sorceress, as she said firmly.

"If Daro dies, I already know it will not be from lack of care, nor, I think, from lack of love. Please understand that no matter the outcome, I will never blame you for his weakness."

She looked gravely at the baby, who had begun a thin, querulous squalling. As Nadra hastened to bend over her charge, Ikella said clearly.

"If things do not go well, do not fear for your safety. Believe me, you are quite safe here. You have no need to fear my anger, do you understand?"

Nadra dipped her head submissively as the door opened and this conversation, too private to continue, ended.

Ikella sat and watched carefully as Hanna rehearsed the wet-nurse in the scrubbing of hands, the cleaning of bowls and the measuring of the milta grains into a scrupulously clean marble mortar. As the Infirmarian applied the slender pestle vigorously to the grain she explained to Nadra.

"Daro has a weak digestion, so we grind the grains to make a fine powder. This means that all the goodness contained in the grain is quickly released into a broth, or into a custard that conveys nourishment. Today I have fresh egg, beaten in Irix milk. It has been cooked very gently, and run through a fine cloth to take the solids down to a smooth custard. Now we will cook the milta powder in clean boiled water 'till it clears, and add the custard 'till it reduces and thickens. Let it cool in a covered bowl before feeding Daro."

Ikella observed Nadra's fine intelligent face taking this all in, deftly stirring and testing the baby's gruel. She fumbled in her pocket and brought out of her robe the babies heartstone, now strung carefully from a silver clasp, tied to a fine cord. She picked the baby up, and sat with him for a while, holding his heartstone to his small, heaving chest and after a while he relaxed, seemed somehow less stressed and Ikella hummed happily to herself as preparations for his breakfast continued. She gentled his body against her, and he lay, his head resting limply on her lap, 'till Nadra swooped him up and positioning a wrapper firmly about him, swaddled him ready for feeding. The gruel was fetched and Ikella took it doubtfully, sniffing the soft sweet mixture which she then dribbled slowly into the baby's mouth. This did at least attract some attention, for the baby turned his head firmly away from the food, and refused it.

Hanna, seeing the anguished frustration on Ikella's face, took over, making the baby open his mouth. Inserting the tiny wooden spoon half laden with food, she stroked his throat gently to prompt a swallowing reflex, and with gratitude Ikella saw three whole spoons of the custard disappear. Nadra spoke comfortably from the depths of the nursing chair where she was spooning Bievel-broth into Ahnell.

"Some just take longer to wean, my Deshun. The little one has gone through a sandstorm already, I will give him the breast when this terror stops kicking me, then he will sleep. You could come back later this afternoon, or in the even to see how he progresses but at least he has eaten today!"

The Sorceress had been standing by the high window that gave her a view of the Gathering Square, the doors to the Hall and unaccountably felt the pull of her faith drawing her to the place of her greatest sanctuary. With a short acknowledging nod to both the Infirmarian and the wet nurse, she fled the nursery to the Sacred Circle, were she dropped to her knees and prayed earnestly for the child's safety.

She came to her feet slowly after some time spent contemplating the Book of Rule, wishing that she could turn the pages, read the words written there. She shivered as the cold of the stone beneath her feet penetrated her thin sandals, and found herself wishing that she could go back to the nursery, remain with Daro, be an ordinary mother.

She turned to see Errish, standing in the doorway silently looking at the old panels that he had come to replace. Her movement startled the man, who had been totally unaware of her presence. He hastily stepped back and made an apologetic bow saying mildly. "Ah, Deshun Ikella. I hope I did not disturb you?"

As the Master Builder entered the quiet dark depths of their Hall, Ikella stood watching the look of awe, mingled with respect cross his face.

As he beheld how a greater Master of his trade than he, had (many thousand Rotations before), hewn this great treasure out of the living rock of the Opal, his hand raised in the gesture of invocation. He moved with dignity to the central

Way of Challenge as it opened up before him, to stand looking up into the high vaulted roof, its unused gallery hanging at a dizzying sixty spans above the Sacred Circle.

He went to the edge of the metalled plate that divided the place of the people from the path of the Healers and there he knelt, to Ikella's astonishment, and deeply, respectfully, he lowered his head in obeisance to the great Book of Rule as it soared above him, the height of it increased by the steps up to the Circle and by the elaborate plinth on which it rested.

Ikella much moved by her sense of the man's respect and wonder, his obvious regard for the holiness of this dim still place, waited for his devotions to end, and greeted him with a much less wary smile as he gathered himself quietly to his feet.

Almost tiptoeing back to her side, he glanced upward, into the far heights of the roof. He made no move to speak, and Ikella saw that he was far away, pondering the immensity of the Hall and the mechanics of its construction, and a little awed by his obvious appreciation, she respected that silence 'till they left the imposing majesty of the surroundings. They walked a little way out of the entranceway and into the Gathering Square, busy with people about their business.

In seconds without sound or summoning, two of her Guards fell into position, and attracted the rueful interest of her companion, as they walked ten paces behind, spears held ready for action. He indicated their company with a flick of his fingers, and said lightly.

"I suppose that there is no point in my asking you to run away with me then?" to which comment the startled Sorceress chuckled with unaccustomed merriment, replying quite seriously.

"I think that one amongst my Healers would challenge me sooner than allow that" and Errish stopped short and looked at the Sorceress for a long moment, before continuing on his way, catching up with her just before the doorway to the new Hall of Welcome. He stood before her foursquare but plainly he needed to pose a question, so Ikella nodded her permission.

"Lady, forgive me, but do you think that I have a chance?"

This blunt question threw Ikella off guard a little, she was unused to the company and conversation of men, even less used to interfering in secular romances but she replied slowly and evenly.

"Errish, the Ways change, they lead us on paths that we may not recognise as our own but with patience everything is possible, particularly if you want it so much that you are prepared to water the seed of your dream and feed it with love, and watch it bloom under your hand."

The man smiled gently, as if he understood her reticence. He spoke simply.

"I hoped for nothing except my work, my building, and then she was there, and now I cannot think at all. Everything I own is far away and yet I do not miss it, for it is just another Builders aggrea where masons work and brick makers toil and tilers practice. I had a cott there, but it was never a home, not one she could share. I have so little to offer one such as she, that I dare not speak, could not take her from where she is so needed."

His strong normally confident voice faded, and Ikella found herself saying briskly.

"Well, nothing will come of my Senior Healer babbling like a child every time she sees you, and no good can come of a Master Builder who cannot rebuild Selesh or turn it into the Healer Hall for all Pelshar, just because he cannot bring himself to speak his heart! The only thing that will allow you two to move forward is to forget each other and go along the way you always walked or take the courage to admit that the sun shines in the others eyes, and to wait and see how things develop."

The Master Builder bowed his head and held the door ajar for her to enter the Hall of Welcome, and no more of the budding romance was mentioned as Ikella owned herself amazed and pleased with the high standard of workmanship and the speed in which this most important of facilities had been constructed. There was a spacious eating area and three good dormitories, with dividing curtains round each cot. Ikella peered into the unused rooms, noting that much thought had been given to their potential guests accommodations. Errish explained that the three rooms set out on each side of the dining and communal area had been planned for drovers, traders and itinerant workers visiting Selesh. Along one side of the building there were doors, with unusual smithed latches and she indicated her interest in them. Errish blushed, but managed to regain his composure telling her that they led to the necessaries and the ablutions rooms, barely containing his dismay when Ikella insisted on visiting them. She swept around the rooms, looking at tiled floors, exclaiming over sloping depressions where there was drainage supplied below a hanging point.

"What would you call this provision?"

She demanded and Errish said diffidently, "This is a washdown my Deshun, where dusty men can hang a bucket of water above them on that hook. With a rope attached to the pulley here.

He reached up and canted the system, demonstrating it for her.

"The bucket tilts and water pours over the user."

"He seemed conscious of her interest in his design and coloured faintly as she said. "That's brilliant Errish! Our Healers could do with something like that! I could definitely do with such a facility in the wards inside as well."

Still processing all she had seen, Ikella didn't protest as he ushered her into a corridor lined with single rooms all fitted with locks, to which he gestured, saying.

"These rooms are for the use of minor dignitaries, and female guests, who would want more privacy."

He opened a door into a pretty room with two pallet beds and a discreet curtain which he pulled back saying, "Ablution and necessary for each of these rooms" and before she could comment swept her on and out and into another communal room, very differently decorated with much richer colourings in the wall hangings and much more comfortable seating. "This area is for the comfort of your female guests and others who prefer to be quiet in the evenings."

Everywhere was light, bright and welcoming, everything had been thought of, no creature comfort forgotten, and she sighed wistfully commenting that.

"I should move my Healers here and let those who want have the cavern rooms, for here is luxury indeed"

Errish looked confused, but seemed to realise that his work was receiving a great accolade, and he said quietly.

"These accommodations can hold about sixty in comfort, if there was another Storm it would provide emergency accommodation for the villagers or about half of them anyway, and should virulent disease strike again it will give Selesh a place of quarantine. The inner rooms could provide sleeping quarters for Healers."

He opened another door and she passed through at his indication. He continued.

"At the back of the kitchen area there are large store rooms, some of which could be used as stores for herbs and medicines. I took the liberty of making hanging racks for the kitchens, it would be the work of a morning to make the same for the herbs to dry."

He showed her into one of the areas where he had building materials all in store and set up in the middle on a large table a drafting tablet. He pulled aside the damp cloth which had covered the tablet, and revealed a drawing, the like of which Ikella had never before seen.

"This is a hotfloor." He offered and Ikella stared down wordlessly as he took up a long rod and pointed out the details, tapping the large sand tablet, as they slowly walked around it.

"Firing points for firestone hearths." and "breather points for air to carry the heat, and vent points for gases and smoke to escape."

He indicated these, then continued with growing enthusiasm.

"All of it is supported on brick ledges and piers that carry the weight of the upper floor." He explained.

"I have but to source the best materials for the tiles of the upper floor and we can begin."

He waited for her to comment and Ikella found herself wishing that he was the Master Builder of Selesh.

"It will take a long time to construct, will it not?"

She offered and he nodded agreement, saying quietly.

"It is important to make a start before this end of Rotation becomes the end of Selesh and all who dwell there."

Ikella found herself unaccountably shivering at the thought, and questioned him quietly.

"Do you think it will be that bad then Errish?"

The Master Builder said slowly, "Forgive my ignorance, Lady, or my unintended breach of the Way, but it takes much to make a Sorceress walk abroad, without her guard and unmasked. If that is to be the Way, then can I not hope, that maybe these skills will become part of that new Way?"

"Ikella stared at him but said nothing, for there was little she could say. Besides she was losing track of time, there was so much to see, so much to take in. As Errish led the way back through the new complex, she asked him.

"How did you achieve so much in such a short time, without your trained labourers?"

Errish laughed comfortably.

"Well, I employed no magic other than dedication here Lady." He replied easily.

"I simply asked the villagers where I could get labourers from, and they all volunteered. Men blinded made bricks, men with a little sight cut wood, women gathered spelex fibre, children dug for clay mud, and then we all made bricks. Even the Inesh came and helped when they were off duty and I can tell you that I would swap one of those women for twenty trained bricklayers. They have no concept of danger, they run along beams forty spans high without a thought, and will work their fingers to the bone for a draught of mead! I had labourers indeed, every Healer in the place has set more than ten bricks. Even the drudges came to work here, for every cook and linen minder in Selesh volunteered their own drudges without a backward glance."

Ikella stared at him wonderingly, for she had heard nothing of this. He continued beaming with pride.

"Oh I had labourers in plenty, and all of them are now my friends so I have been well rewarded for my work!"

His manner, so correct previously, became slightly truculent as he stated with delight.

"So put away your purse woman, for I have been paid far and beyond what you and your magic can do for me."

'He seems to have achieved full stature as a Master Craftsman.'

Ikella thought in surprise.

'Was there no end to this man's ingenuity?' She wondered as she inspected the kitchens, the cupboards, the emergency shelters for traders and haulers. She found herself wondering if she dared hope that the emerging romance between Mina and her Master Builder could be encouraged, and then gave herself a mental shake and withdrew from that line of thought just as there came a cry from outside.

"Ho the gate, Ho the gatekeeper."

Errish grinned happily at her.

"Well Lady, we seem to have our first customer."

He said, and diplomatically opened the door into the Gathering Square, handing Ikella out and into the arms of her waiting guards. She glanced back over her shoulder to where a man and a whole train of well-laden Zeglurs were being directed in to the compound surrounding the Hall of Welcome and full of the agreeable domesticity of her day she turned her steps toward the door to her private accommodations, thinking only of perhaps peeping in on Daro to see how he fared, before she took the Stillglass bowl and summoned her Sisters to Conclave.

PART THREE - BEYOND THE DOOR

Chapter 26 - Apothecary's Intervention

As the Sorceress crossed the almost deserted Gathering Square, the door she approached opened abruptly and Nadra ran towards her shrieking for help, stark terror written on her face. In one dreadful moment, Ikella focussed on the baby clutched in Nadra's arms, head hanging downwards. Mucus and vomit drained from his mouth and he lay utterly unmoving, his skin already tinged a deathly blue.

Ikella felt as if she too had ceased to breathe, it was like an iron clamp had fastened around her chest, terror seized her mind and her senses swam. She lunged for the child, screaming.

"No-o-o, Daro, no, no!" Then came the most incredible surge of power she had ever experienced. Somehow her bewildered brain caught the shimmer of it but she had not summoned it! She was paralysed with shock yet it was there, lighting her Opal, shielding her frantically beating heart. As her aura encompassed her trembling limbs, it swept the pain from her chest 'till she could thankfully breathe again and she reached out for Daro once more. However, something was holding her back, a man's strong arms reached over her head, and whisked the child away. Incredulously, she recognised the complicated braiding of long white hair and beard. Even as his face came into focus she found herself sobbing.

"Carolus, oh thank the One!"

As Shiarjha reached her side clasping her hands firmly, the Apothecary knelt, gently wiping the child's mouth and tilting his head backward, pinching Daro's nostrils shut as he did so. Silently, gathering Healers watched in amazement as the old man breathed into the child's open mouth. Once, twice, three times vital air was provided 'till the baby's chest rose. Then, the Apothecary turned his head away, and gently pressed the child's chest, using just his fingertips to expel the air, before returning to breathe into Daro's mouth again and again.

Nadra knelt weeping, the Inesh guards gathered about them while Ikella stood frozen hardly daring to breathe, watching Carolus closely till with the first hiccupping breath of the baby he withdrew. Rising stiffly from where he knelt to lay the child into her arms, limp and wheezing, but definitely alive.

Still wrapped by the Source, feeling the child's chest heave under her hand, she carefully slipped the thong carrying Daro's heartstone around his neck, placing it, pulsing dully, on the child's chest. She stood watching him closely, hardly aware of her own trembling, 'till Carolus placed a cloak over her shoulders, saying quietly.

"I would not presume so, but both you and the child are shocked my Deshun. It grows chill here already."

Somehow the door was opened again, Nadra had already been taken by the Inesh to the infirmary and soon, too soon, Ikella was handing Daro to Hanna, who whispered.

"He must have vomited in his sleep. He clearly choked."

She took the Master Apothecary's instructions without comment.

"Bathe and change the child, wrap him in warm clothes. Feed him only Nadra's milk, and watch him. Any change call me, I will be with your Deshun."

As Hanna made her way to the nursery Ikella, pale and shaking was led back to her day room where she collapsed into her chair and to her utter chagrin, burst into an almost incontrollable storm of tears.

Sometime later, she was instructed. "Drink this."

Rousing to find that she had been wrapped in a blanket, a warming stone at her feet. Trinet was regarding her anxiously.

"Deshun, the baby is well. He sleeps in the nursery now, and Nadra with him. Hanna and Mina will keep the night watch. Mina says you can come and see him for yourself, but only when you feel better!"

Ikella, still speechless with shock, nodded mutely, at which Trinet glanced to her left, where the Apothecary sat comfortably warming himself before the glowstone fire. In his hands a text that Ikella had been trying to decipher, an expression of deep absorption on his face. He looked up at Trinet absently and made a face, irritably flapping a hand at her, he said brusquely.

"Oh go girl, I can look after the Deshun, she and I are old friends, she is quite safe with me" and Trinet fled plainly relieved to do so. Carolus leaned back with a comfortable groan and half closed his eyes, resting his head against the back of his chair. He yawned, and Ikella roused herself saying tartly.

"You seem very familiar with our arrangements but don't get too comfortable, I need to know what brought you to my door."

She staggered to her feet, disentangling herself from the wrappers that had been placed about her, and went towards the old man.

He didn't raise his head or move, but focussed on her from under his eyelids as she towered over him.

"I came to replenish the Infirmary with the medicaments that you are running short of." He said directly but Ikella faced him, head on one side enquiringly.

"We sent out no orders yet, how come you know what we need?"

She was hoping beyond reason of hope, that he would say that he felt suddenly compelled to come to Selesh but he looked at her with that strange penetrating gaze that left her baffled, tongue tied and suddenly feeling that besides this old man, she was dwarfed in reasoning power.

"What in the name of Nine dry Sands are you feeding that child?"

He demanded and Ikella, distracted, concentrated on the list. As she recalled that morning's effort, he snorted derisively, repeating after her.

"Milta ground with egg? Bievel broth? What on the Plains of Pelshar do you think you are doing woman? This child cannot tolerate animal products! Look, even I can draw a parallel with his bouts of illness. He is very small, likely born before his time, and without benefit of his own mother's milk. Kept alive on Irix milk and curds, before being put to the breast of a wet-nurse. When someone tried to feed him solids, he reacted to them. However he cannot live at the breast forever. He is underweight, dehydrated through vomiting and he is retreating from life."

Ikella stared into the glowstone.

'He's right! How had they missed the signs?'.

She thought dully, the old man continued slowly.

"We know that he likes honey cream, which thankfully is vegetable. He can tolerate bread in milk. He reacts to meat broth, egg and I hear whole animal milk. Intolerance to animal products seems to be the common factor so far. He cannot eat them in any shape or form, and must not be compelled to do so, or he will likely die! Each and every reaction being more severe than the last."

Ikella sat still, reviewing what the old man had said, and then she passed her hands over her face, rubbing her eyes, trying to stroke away the fatigue of shock, and his voice rolled over her consciousness.

"Have you tried berry broth, hanweed, milta sweetened with honey cream, gan curd?"

The list went on until Ikella said wearily.

"Since the Storm, we have lost contact with many places, many of our Sands are cut off, and no one has travelled to market for ninenights! Most of what you are saying makes sense, but we have not travelled as widely as you. Many of these foods are unknown to us, or unavailable."

She stood abruptly and paced her floor muttering.

"I cannot do this, I cannot be mother to a Sand, as well as a child. What shall I do with him? I can hardly take him back! I wish I knew more about him! Oh why doesn't his father, his family claim him?"

The old man regarded her steadily, saying calmly.

"You can do this. You are mother to the Opal indeed, what is one more child to that? You must do this for you were entrusted with his care! It is clearly your duty to do this, and your will if you will only listen to your heart! Now I know what the problem is, I will devise some medication to assist Daro's digestion, and I will look in my stores for some of the food stuffs I carry. Others we can obtain as time goes by. Now tell me more of this child's birth. It is nearly time for you to visit him and we can talk on the way."

He opened the door and strode out confidently, almost as if he knew the innermost layout of Selesh intimately, but paused outside the door saying.

"Perhaps you had better lead on, I will get us lost."

They walked on into the darkened glow-lit passageway leading to Daro's nursery. Ikella telling Carolus of the finding of Daro's mother, of their fight for life in the Storm, the cavern that had saved them. She told him of the strange waterfall of warm ice, and the place that they had left the child's mother, she recalled her vision, and the realisation that they had indeed stumbled on a truly magical place with the discovery of the winged Staff in the morning. They walked slowly, and yet the corridor seemed to stretch out forever. The way seemed so long that Ikella paused for a moment, feeling disorientated, flustered and Carolus came to her side and said easily.

"I know you are tired, you have far too many worries on your shoulders."

He reached for her arm to support her and Ikella found her gaze locked on his strange compelling eyes again. A voice in her mind said.

'It is nothing, it will pass, there is nothing to fear, nothing to remember, nothing.

She stopped in mid stride, looking about her in surprise and seeing the Apothecary striding away from her, she hastened to catch him up saying "Oh dear, I suppose I must be getting old, what was it we were talking about?", as they reached the door of the nursery.

Inside the room Nadra was tenderly nursing Daro, who seemed to be making up for lost time as he suckled hungrily. Mina was spoon feeding Ahnell who angrily spluttered, reaching for Daro.

Ikella knelt on the ground gently stroking Daro's downy head with a finger, feeling an overpowering swell of emotion as she thought of the baby nearly dying in her arms. Carolus pinned Hanna down with a sand tablet in his hands, jotting down a list of her requirements for the Infirmary, saying.

"Tanbark stoppers? Let me see. I think I have a couple of sacks full, do you need them badly?" and the evening passed on in comparative domesticity.

Eventually when the babies were ready for bed, Carolus stopped Nadra from putting them in the same cottle.

"I think Daro is too frail to leave him sleeping with another child so much larger. It will be better to separate them for a short while, even if they hate it."

He offered his opinion very gently, and Ikella agreed soberly.

"I wondered if he was overheated when he vomited"

She admitted and Nadra swiftly brought out another smaller crib for Daro, who whimpered forlornly for a while before falling asleep, one finger in his mouth. Carolus bent over Ahnell and sniffed carefully.

"That is a healthy baby scent." He said earnestly, and whispered. "Sleep well little man."

As Mina and Ikella talked in low tones, the Apothecary approached Daro's crib.

He bent forward and put his lips to the baby's ear.

"Sleep well, sleep your way back to health."

The baby whimpered, stretching up touching the old man's face with his hand, searching for him with his eyes. Carolus withdrew within himself for a moment then glancing at the women, who seemed quite oblivious of what he was doing, he took a deep breath and whispered again to the child.

"Sssh, Sssh, be still."

A soft breeze seemed to sigh within the room. the glows flickered as he continued. "Be still and stilled within."

As he dropped a kiss on to the baby's head, there seemed to be a minute shiver in the atmosphere but it passed the women unnoticed, as Carolus rose to his feet and left the room without a backward glance.

Chapter 27 - A High Council Convenes

It was a strange, dreamlike time that spanned the next ninenight. Ikella followed Carolus about as he perambulated the complex. She found it impossible to refuse the Apothecary entrance to even the deepest recesses of Selesh, although she was careful not to reveal any of Sashandra's secrets. During these explorations, she could have sworn that he was leading her, for she had no prior memory of any of the convoluted corridors he walked. He asked about the deep waters beneath the caverns, introducing Beneva to a symbol that he swore stood for clean water. Ikella took to spending long hours studying ancient texts, seeing not only the repeat of that symbol but more that she could understand in the records of the new Djellim. Though she had restrained both herself and Beneva from taking any further interest in the scrolls held in what had become known between them as the Council Chamber.

Meanwhile, Errish had recruited a team of itinerant tile makers who had arrived hot on the heels of Carolus, who each day made it his afternoon duty to sit and mind the nursery, which permitted Nadra some time to take for herself. On the seventh day after Daro's near brush with death, Ikella watched Nadra go before slipping along the corridor to see Daro. She did not disturb the old man, who slept with his head thrown back and mouth open on the long bench that stood against the window wall. She tiptoed across the room and looked into the twin cottles, where Daro and Ahnell slept off their morning feed. They lay like bookends, in almost exactly the same position, and with surprise Ikella realised that Daro was catching up with Ahnell so quickly that all traces of his illness had vanished. Daro's hair was thickening to a rich brown black against Ahnell's bronzed brown, he was still fair of skin with fine delicate colouring to Ahnell's ruddy bloom, but he now looked well, was positively thriving despite the strange diet that had been prescribed for him, and to Ikella's relief there seemed to be no ill effects from his close brush with death. She had started to withdraw, had even gently lifted the latch on the nursery door, when Carolus spoke.

"I thought that it was you, my Deshun" he sat up and stretched, glancing at the sleeping babies as he stood easing the crick in his back.

"Bah, I grow old and tired of all this journeying, and it grows so cold here. I am minded to leave and go South, far South to the Onyx Sands, where they have warmth aplenty. How is that young man and his hotfloor coming along? He will have to work swiftly before the ice season is upon you!"

Ikella thought of Errish, who she had watched marking out the Great Hall of the Healers only that morning. He worked methodically, supervising the removal of seating, sweating over the exact placement of brick piers on the base floor, setting out the stone and tile arches that joined them creating massively strong supports for the tiled upper floor.

"He works tirelessly."

She commended the builder quietly, and Carolus, understanding her mood of uncertainty, tried to lighten the subject.

"Although the winds will blow from the deep frozen north, only still water will freeze. Outside there may be frost and snow on the ground but with the hotfloors, the living areas should be warm enough. To go into the lower depths as we did yesterday will be to dance with death, the ground itself will freeze but that is not all bad, my Deshun. You will be able to store foods, meat and vegetables, fruit and drink in the rooms below the kitchens. In the cold they will keep fresh for months, so you will not starve if the preparations begin now!"

Ikella shuddered with the thought of the deep cold, they were not used to it, save at end of Rotation and in the dead of night. She said hopefully.

"If the Master Builder has his way, the largest area in Selesh will be warm enough. The villagers from Selesh Minoria are welcome to share our warmth, Errish has already made provision in the Hall of Welcome for this, it is the other Sands that I worry about."

Carolus nodded, saying simply.

"You will not be able to travel if it gets as bad as I think it could, I should call your Sisterhood quickly and see if you can help each other survive the next season, for I think it will be bad for many."

Ikella looked at him as he moved to rock Ahnell's crib, the movement sending the restive child back to sleep.

"What will you do my friend?"

She asked, curious to hear his plans, but he pursed his lips and shook his head.

"I shall not go until young Daro is much better," he reassured her, continuing, a speculative tone in his voice.

"If the new season falls fair, and foods and medicines are available, then I shall travel back to Caranchar, if they still have markets there. However, plans may change, the future is an uncertain book."

She regarded him in exasperation. He had a habit of leaving conversations without really answering her questions but putting that down to the habit of a solitary life and his age, didn't quite excuse him.

"When will you call your Sisters?"

His casual reference to the other eight Sisters of Sorcery, rulers of the lesser Sands, caught her so unaware that she answered him, before she really thought about it.

"If we have or hear of, no more major disasters, on the day after two more dawns."

She stared at him. "Why do you always seem to answer one question with another? It is very distracting!"

He grinned at her, placed a finger alongside his nose, saying impishly.

"Gets answers though!"

She left him and went away, suspecting that somehow he knew more about the practices of magic users than he ought, but in the fullness of her afternoon she found that she had forgotten these concerns, although she recalled clearly the prediction he had made regarding the weather"

When the halls and corridors went quiet for the long drowsy rest after Height of Sun Ikella went to the Djellim, where Shiarjha still toiled over the massive self-imposed task of mapping the changes to the sands. She had taken to sitting at the great central table where there was a certain increase of light, some of it undoubtedly from the high glows set in the domed roof but some of it almost emanating from the rock itself. Ikella and Beneva had already noted it and Beneva had said softly.

"This is the sort of light that readers much appreciate, I wonder if this place returns to its former use? Wherever we have gone to place shelves there are signs that such were placed here before, you know, the little hooks and dowelling points used by builders to fasten great weights to walls? We found many sheets of wood in one far storeroom, which we are using here, but Errish says it would take an entire forest of trees to provide so much wood, and even in the south where the forests still rise, there is not so much left to use!"

Ikella said little but a thought troubled her throughout the day. Was it possible that Pelshar had been so very different once? She thought of the great highland cities inhabited by the Greeeyn, who refused to share their knowledge with the Felmin or the Peoples of the Sand. What did they know, that she did not? What was the reason for the separation of the people?

The Peoples of the Sand, though very different one from the other, had at least one attribute possessed by no other caste, and that was the command of magic and the use of the Source. She puzzled over this even as she surveyed the bank of scrolls, set aside for Shiarjha's use, instinctively feeling that this was as it had always been. The Way of Healing demanded that they share their skills with anyone needing help but, she considered carefully, could the power be used for things other than healing, or protection? Determined to find out, she went to the shelves and sought a particular scroll, one that she had found some long time back. She had not pursued it then, but she remembered that it seemed to show that there was no limit to the power of the Source. It was not where she expected, so with a nod to Shiarjha, Ikella took herself to the librarians curtained alcove to discover her deep in conversation with Carolus, who had been spared his nursery watch for a while. He sat casually, draped in one of the easy chairs, with just the scroll that Ikella sought lying across his lap. Beneva caught the look on Ikella's face and conversation died as she spoke.

"When you have finished with that scroll, I would appreciate a look at it Carolus, but right now, I think we must discuss matters of immense importance."

Carolus looked up, his eyes seemed to light lambent as he said. "If this is magic users talk, I must away."

He prepared to rise but Ikella pushed away the niggling threads of a headache and said firmly. "No Carolus, stay. It is on my mind that you are something more than you seem but you may only be a tool of the One, and not aware that wherever you appear problems seem to solve themselves. When I see you, suddenly I know that there is less to worry about than before, perhaps it is because of your travels and the good advice you are able to give us, perhaps it is... She paused, aware that the old man was looking straight at her, one eyebrow raised questioningly, as he finished her words for her saying with a chuckle.

"Because of my extreme youth and good looks Deshun?"

Ikella smiled, relieved that he was not offended, saying simply.

"I owe you a great debt Carolus of the Nine Sands and you, you infuriating old man, know it!"

She walked over to Shiarjha's table and interrupted the young Sorceress-elect saying.

"I must have your assistance this afternoon Shiarjha, I have something to discuss with a number of you, will you clear your table? I have need of it."

She turned away from the bemused girl and left the Djellim to summon a small cohort of Inesh guards, stationed in the corridor without.

"Send to the Djellim, Driss, Indeera and Jashell of my guard. Then Healers Mina, Hanna, Dorra, her assistant Satra, and Master Builder Errish. I want the Djellim kept private for a meeting. Let no-one enter other than those named."

She withdrew to let the others work. Beneva to collect sand-tablets and enscrasures, Carolus to help Shiarjha clear away her work. This they accomplished swiftly, leaving the ornately carved table standing in the centre of a growing pool of light. Beneva found chairs and set them round the table, while Ikella went swiftly back to her study, gathering up her Staff, before returning to the Djellim.

Driss, stationed at the doors said simply. "It is as my Deshun required."

Then hefting her spear, she opened the door, intoning as she did so.

"All hail the Opal"

Ikella, strangely flustered by the bowed acknowledgement of the assembled company, paused just inside the doors and said quietly.

"I want no formality here, we all know each other well, our particular roles and positions do not matter to anyone inside this room. Here and in the presence of witnesses we are to convene a meeting the like of which has never been held in my lifetime. You have been selected because of your unique knowledge of administration. There are some here whom you do not know well but as I call you to sit I will explain what I require of each of you.

The gathering shuffled in anticipation then stilled to stand expectantly ranged along the inner wall, near to the doors which were now guarded on the outside, Driss having joined the company.

The Sorceress paced around the glowing circle on the floor of the Djellim, plainly deep in thought then said.

"Guardian Beneva, Librarian of Selesh, to take the records of this Council."

Beneva came to the right hand of the table and sat, taking up writing implements and beginning the notation with her own name. Ikella nodded approval and then called them one at a time.

"Dorra, I wish you to represent the people of Selesh Minoria, and report all we do here to them."

The Healer, who had come to Selesh from no further than the outer village beamed with pride and sat next to Beneva. Mina was called next, and appointed to represent the interests of the Healers, taking her place opposite Beneva with blushing surprise. Next came Hanna who was to represent the interests of any patients within the Infirmary. Slowly the table filled. Satra, their provisioner, appointed to take charge of those resident in the Hall of Welcome. There were only four places left when Ikella caused consternation by calling Driss to sit as head of Security. The Inesh warrior quailed under the imperious gaze of the Sorceress and awkwardly sat perched on the edge of the unfamiliar chair, plainly wishing the floor to open up under her. The Sorceress noted wryly that Indeera and Jashell looked on their senior with envy written on their faces but made no comment and turned her attention on her visitors. She cleared her throat to attract attention, and a subtle buzz at the table died away, as she walked to the table and sat at its head.

"Because this is an appointed Council and not an elected one, I will attend as often as I can, however in my absence or by my command, Somishen Shiarjha will stand in my stead."

She indicated that Shiarjha should sit at the opposite end of the table, and now there were only two places to fill. She marshalled her thoughts, then spoke again.

"Master Builder Errish." She summoned him forward. "It is in my mind that simply to repair the damage of the Storm is not enough. We have seen the quality of your work, listened to the wisdom of your experience and understand that change is forced upon us. We have for many, many Rotations just fixed what already existed but now we must adapt to new Ways and to do so, I will need the services of a Master Builder at Selesh.

She was aware of an intake of breath at the table, but ignoring Mina, continued unflinchingly.

I understand that your aggrea is set to the south of Dunoon, where green stone is plentiful. However, we too have stone aplenty, and room to expand both our development, the village and its associated buildings. Would a permanent aggrea and a full time appointment as Master Builder of Selesh interest you?"

She looked up, catching the blaze of excitement in Errish's eyes and added thoughtfully.

"Your men would also be welcomed here, Master Craftsman Arkneth lacks anyone to follow him, we have so little wood, his Guild has all but died out. It would be a kindness if you could take him into your aggrea as Master Woodsmith. You could build your aggrea beside the village, when all is well we have inns and markets and I guarantee a cott for each family.

It was a generous offer, and Errish didn't hesitate for more than a moment. He looked her straight in the eye as he said gravely.

"I will send for my men immediately, my Deshun. I will hold to Selesh very willingly, setting my seal to your works, in return for a safe place for my men and our families."

He fumbled in a pouch and produced his Masters Seal, laying it on the table before Ikella with gentle pride. She glanced down at it, seeing with genuine astonishment that it was independent, just the symbol of his name and trade, no indication of patronage adorned the impressing plate. She touched it delicately with a forefinger asking curiously.

"No patron? No Guild bondage left?"

With pride Errish replied, his voice ringing out.

"My Guild bondage was discharged ten Rotations ago when I discovered a greenstone deposit, large enough for the Guild to draw on for centuries. I take patrons with interesting work, preferring to supply my own materials. All my workers are free men, for I have purchased their indentures. They hold to me willingly and are paid the price of their work. I have no ties to any particular place, other than Selesh, my Deshun. I am a free man, born of these Sands and willing to enter your service!"

Aware of at least two pairs of hopeful eyes fixed on her, Ikella said softly.

"If your men agree then?"

Beneva slid a sand tablet in front of Ikella and she saw a new symbol sketched there. She frowned in concentration and then saw the Door in the Rock, half opened and a mason working on the door. The complex symbol for Errish's name lay at the threshold, and Ikella's own sigil was used to create a border. Beneva tapped the new Seal, showing Ikella that it should not replace the Master Builders own, but be used beside it and the Sorceress nodded her hand moved over the sand tablet for a moment, there was a subdued glow and the flat plate collapsed, coalesced, then reformed into the impressing plate of a new seal, the basic ingredients of the tablet transformed into the traditional green stone stamp. Beneva picked it up still glowing and pressed it into a wax tablet, holding out the impression to the Master Builder, who gazed at it in stupefied silence for a second before bursting forth.

"That will also be my Seal? I am still a free man? This shows me protected, appointed but not bound to Selesh. But I gave my word willingly, my word is my bond!"

The Sorceress spoke softly.

"Errish, your work is your bond. I find no reason to guard against sharing your work and abilities with others. You are bond to me whatever you do, for am I not the Head of our Clan? As your spiritual leader, I advise that a more valuable bond is created through mutual respect and loyalty! Now sit I pray you, so that we may continue our work."

In a daze Errish joined the table, turning his new Seal over and over in wonderment as he did so.

Ikella's attention turned to Carolus, who stood and approached the table, just short of her chair and waited for her to speak.

She regarded him soberly before declaring.

"Carolus, it is in my mind that you might become a roving Ambassador for us. You have made it clear that you intend to keep travelling the trade routes, and when this Rotation is over and the Ice Season has passed, then would that be something you could undertake?" The Apothecary stood very still considering this silently.

"I would be able to come and go as I wished?" He asked, with a twinkle.

"I might want to stay at Selesh during the cold, I am no longer young enough to take on such a responsibility through every season!" He added hopefully.

"Can I use the underground pastures here for my Zeglurs? I have a clerk of sorts who minds the herd, sells my potions and ointments at fairs, and keeps tally for me, if needed Brannith could be of help in the Infirmary. He is used to blending herbs, can make a fine poultice, and understands notation of a kind!"

Ikella pondered this, it was unusual, for the Apothecary did not call Brannith his apprentice but she could see no harm in it, so she agreed readily enough and the last seat was filled. As Carolus took his place there was a distinct murmur of welcome from the others Ikella glanced around as a buzz of anticipation filled the room, people settled in their chairs and sand tablets were arranged before those who understood notation. However there was still one important task to perform before she turned to other business, she rose to her feet and silence fell as she walked to the other end of the table, besides Shiarjha and stood with one hand casually draped over the high back of the chair in which Carolus sat, the other holding her Staff of office. She made a tall statement of elegance in her flowing robes, her white hair caught back in two opal encrusted combs, and with a gentle pulsation of the crystalline wings atop her Staff, it was certain that no-one could have ignored her. She chose quite deliberately not to engage her powers, for hers had to be an authority not brought about by enforcement, by right of the powers vested in her but one engendered by respect.

She paused for a long moment to let the chatter settle and to gain their attention by the very stillness of her poise, then she signalled to Beneva to join her, and when the librarian came to stand on the other side of the chair where Carolus sat, they began their tale.

Ikella told of the draft on her neck, the seeking of the cause, and as the story unfolded she found they had drawn the others into it with them as they re-enacted the finding of the Council Chamber. Eyes wide and gleaming with excitement, their audience craned forward with bated breath as the wall slid aside at her command. As her aura snapped around her, she and Beneva stood aside to permit a view of the shielded entranceway to their companions, who had left the table anxious not to miss a thing. Carolus, at the rear of the group, watched Ikella so intently that she could feel his gaze on her, as she once more pierced the shimmering barrier to the Council Chamber and revealed it for all to see.

Ikella raised a hand as with a murmur of curiosity her companions clustered around. "Wait!" She held up her hand imperiously and the group subsided as she called. "Indeera, Jashell, attend me!"

The two remaining Inesh called to the meeting stepped forward. Ikella indicated the Chamber with a flourish of her free hand.

"This is one of the Inner Secrets of Selesh, many of which are yet to be revealed. All within must be protected and so, as my most trusted guards I appoint you as Guard Commanders of the Inner Djellim. You will be entrusted with the care and protection of all our treasures. You will both be raised to the rank of Commander and will each have a cohort of Guards, one for the time of day, the other for the night patrol. This is necessary because we approach end of Rotation, the Gathering of the Clan as well as the solemn Conclave of Sands. You too, are to sit on this Council which shall henceforth be known as the High Council of Selesh!"

There was a concerted gasp from those gathered, and the Sorceress smiled grimly to herself. They had heard in recent days of High Councils from the scrolls of Adaria discovered amongst Beneva's treasured trophies. There had been a High Council once before in the time that Adaria had wandered, searching for Sanctuary. Ikella's smile lit them suddenly as she said.

"It is, as it was before, you see. Three advisors."

She indicated Beneva, Shiarjha, herself, as she returned to the table and sat, looking at those she had chosen.

"Three representatives of the Clan."

The three Healers returned to the table.

"Three warriors!"

Her gaze lit on the Inesh Guards, who prowled the entrance to the Council Chamber heads together, hands flickering in the strange silent language they used between them.

A deep voice enquired delicately.

"What of the Master Builder? The provisioner? Myself?"

Ikella looked into Carolus' amused eyes and said smoothly.

"Satra reports to Dorra, and is her understudy. Arguably there are many more areas to cover at this time than the traditional nine members could deal with. Master Builder Errish has an honorary position on the Council, to enable him to advise us directly, and to make sure he is privy to any further discoveries within Selesh. On the other hand Master Apothecary, your appointment as Ambassador creates something that digresses from the Way."

She paused for effect then said slowly.

"The full membership of the High Council shall from this day be one more than usual. Instead of nine, we shall be Tten!"

Down the length of the ancient table, edged with its mysterious inscription, the Sorceress and the Apothecary traded a long level look, then he smiled.

Chapter 28 - Rededication

The rest of the afternoon was spent in earnest conversation, taking decisions over purely administrative matters but as they prepared to depart the Djellim, Ikella rose to her feet and spoke, her manner serious, her voice solemn.

"After this day's work and our preparations here, I have to gather the Clans, speak to the Sisterhood and ready our people for the changes to come."

She laid her Staff of Office carefully centred down the length of the table, its crown of wings for once quiescent under her hand, its hilt near to Shiarjha, who would one day hold it as her own.

"As Members of the High Council, you will all be privy to secrets which must remain under the Seal of the Opal. This is at once a great burden and a privilege. It will set you aside from your fellows, it will even set you aside from anyone not a Member of this Council. If you can shoulder this responsibility it will be my joy and privilege to accept your solemn oath of silence as we depart and go about our duties again. I will announce the appointments tonight."

As one body the new Council rested one hand to the Opal Staff and swore the oath, there was a little silence in the Djellim as the meeting finished during which Ikella retrieved her Staff, quietly satisfied that with such a Council, Selesh would prosper, then the mood lightened as the evening Gather bells rang out an invitation to supper. However as they passed her on their way, Ikella singled out Shiarjha and Beneva, saying quietly.

"I would see you later tonight. Meet me in the Djellim after supper!"

After all the announcements had been made at evening Gather, the new council Members sitting together and eating in silence, Ikella noted sadly that her prediction of a separation from their fellows had taken effect quickly. As usual she sat with Shiarjha, Beneva and Mina, but this night she found herself making room for Carolus and Errish as well, watching the others gather together, bleak-eyed. Ikella, Shiarjha, and Beneva returned to the darkened Djellim separately, slipping in through the newly guarded entrance door and coming each of them in their own time to where Shiarjha sat at the central table working beneath a pool of light, given off by nightglows set into stands. By some unspoken accord they had dressed in warmer clothing under their cloaks, yet they still shivered in the dimly lit high vaulted room and Shiarjha said quietly.

"Why do I suddenly feel a little unnerved, not afraid exactly but aware of something odd in here?"

To which comment Ikella raised an eyebrow at her librarian, before bending to examine the area that Shiarjha was mapping. The Sorceress-elect glanced up nervously as Ikella's long fingers traced the considerable area she had covered already. Shiarjha cleared her throat, describing the area her seniors traced.

"Our closest pass is through the past Caranchar, into the Low Valley and beyond. We are told that great landslips have occurred at the pass. We will need to ascertain if the Highlands to the West are still impassable before we try to get to the Amber Sands in that direction."

She suddenly seemed to have grown immensely in confidence, as taking command of the conversation she slipped swiftly one map after another on to the table, showing the borders of the Opal Desert from all angles explaining as she did so.

"This way, the Sherrol Pass leads into the long narrow valleys that connect with the Amethyst sands. We know that the top end of the Pass is just about negotiable but we have not followed the valley through to the Sands themselves. It was ever a difficult place to negotiate, and the Sybillsce do not welcome visitors! They are a very private people."

She passed on to another map, tracing the long lines of the Opal borders with a slender finger.

"Here is the Fringe to the west and the village of Maraken from where, my Deshun, you met those returning from Song Walk just before the storm. We know that the route to the Highlands there is still impassable but the Felmin traders use that pass regularly to get across the Slingh divide, to the high towns of the Greeeyn."

Her finger tapped the vellum of the map.

"Here at Omnel, here at Quinnox and of course further into the Broken lands at Pinjara, we assume that the Felmin (possibly assisted by the Greeeyn) will have worked to clear the high passes, if they are at all accessible. However, none of us has been summoned to go that way since the Storm and so we have taken care of our own, and must await information to come in once the markets open again."

She paused, chewing a finger uncertainly, then throwing caution to the winds she said decisively.

"What I want to know about is here, on our northern border beyond Selesh, along this corridor where we pick up the trail for Colonth. My scouts have not been able to penetrate so far, and I have no word from our spies either!"

Her chin lifted defiantly as Ikella raised faint objections.

"Spies Shiarjha? Don't you mean the faithful of our Sands?" Shiarjha blushing continued.

"There has been no word from the plain of Aridenis, only silence from the high trail to Sanctuary." She sounded forlorn.

Ikella leant forward with interest to study her acolytes work. She was amazed by the delicacy, the accuracy of the drawings. The symbols transcribed with loving care and embellished with script taken from older maps, detailing the places where fresh water ran, where plants and fungi grew, where people lived or gathered for trade.

She saw the fine flush on Shiarjha's face, noticed the tremble of her hands.

'For the sake of the One!' She thought in amazed irritation.

'This child is afraid that I won't approve of her work!' She spoke approvingly.

"Did you ever see such a thing, Beneva?"

She found herself demanding and the Librarian nodded solemnly, saying slowly.

"Only once, many years ago and that scroll was ancient. Even then, craftsmanship of this kind was unusual! It is I think a skill unique in our time and you are to be commended Shiarjha, for it is rare indeed that such knowledge can be combined with the creation of such beauty."

The Sorceress-elect beamed at them.

"I thought that if I made the drawings tell of what was to be found on the trade routes you would not be displeased?"

The girl was pressing her hands together in earnest supplication as she addressed Ikella and the Sorceress answered in a bewildered voice.

"Displeased, with something this exquisite?"

Ikella looked quite surprised at her own turn of phrase, but went on.

"I promised to show you the Council Chamber did I not? I want you to see it as we did, before it is rededicated tomorrow. I would value your thoughts on it"

This oblique reference to the appearance of Feydora caught Beneva's attention, so summoning the newly formed Inner Guard to attend them, the three magic users went to the far wall and revealed the hidden Council Chamber.

In their stoical manner the Guard positioned themselves, so that they could protect both their Sorceress or her acolyte. Beneva glanced at them doubtfully but followed Ikella and Shiarjha without a word.

Inside the Chamber Shiarjha seemed overwhelmed by the elegance, the functional simplicity, the wealth of knowledge contained in the scrolls and in the sand tablets stacked on the shelves. She stroked the great table lovingly agreeing that it made a wonderful Council Chamber but seemed pensive, withdrawn and confessed herself a little anxious about the place, saying.

"I feel magic here Deshun, but not mine, not yours either. Oh no this is old, very powerful and quite different from ours. My head hurts with it. It echoes with it."

To be true she was pale, her eyes looked troubled and Ikella swiftly pulled out a chair at the great table and sat the young Sorceress elect in it, for it seemed to her that Shiarjha looked likely to faint.

Once seated she seemed to recover swiftly, and with a little colour in her face was just about to ask Beneva something when her eyes widened, her gaze shifted to the dais with its single chair and once more Beneva and Ikella listened in silence as the hypnotically liquid voice of Feydora filled their ears.

It had occurred to Ikella that the message from the Sandsinger might be delivered again and to be honest, she had rather hoped it would. However, the impression she had gained from the first occurrence had not altered, and Shiarjha, once she had recovered from her surprise, was distinctly unmoved.

"It was odd." She commented.

"Very rehearsed, quite theatrical and somehow unreal. I received no indication of power being used to transmit that message from another place. Did you?" She asked, adding "It didn't feel quite real to me!"

They closed the room down carefully. Beneva walking ahead of them welcomed them to her fireside but Ikella said swiftly enough.

"No more tonight Beneva! Shiarjha needs to consider what she has seen, before she organises volunteer cleaners for that room. I need to sleep! Did you note the dust in there? It must be cleaned and censed, perhaps that alone will dispel our phantom, but in any event Shiarjha, Beneva and I have already decided to say nothing of this to anyone outside of Sorcery!"

She yawned abruptly and signalling her guards, she passed through the doors, complaining bitterly as she disappeared down the corridor.

"I feel as though I walked the tar sands at Ishgenard, my feet drag my brain has ceased to function."

Passing through the doors in her wake, Shiarjha grinned conspiratorially at Beneva as the Djellim fell silent.

Ikella woke suddenly in the early hours of the morning. It was cold in her room and she shivered as she washed and robed. Her eyes felt hot, her head throbbed and she felt unaccountably weary and depressed. She thought back to the apparition of Jocasta, comparing that with the appearance of Feydora, and engrossed in that process missed the Summoning Bell and was forced to break her fast in her own rooms.

She threw on a cloak and went out across the Gathering Square to the Hall of Welcome but Carolus was nowhere to be found, so she went directly to the Djellim to discover that she was almost the last to arrive.

She had also forgotten to provide herself with cleaning equipment, and when she entered the library to find that only four people grouped there, she exclaimed in exasperation.

"Oh. I might have known that if I asked for volunteers everyone would assume others had volunteered in their place. Well we must make do as best we can."

She clapped her hands and Driss came at the run, Indeera and Jashell on her heels.

"Driss, send for drudges. They are to come with cleaning rags, warm water, honey wax, sofus grass, soap and strong brushed skirlas. They must not enter the Djellim, they are simply to carry cleaning equipment to the doors. I need a detachment of your Inner Guard for carrying, lifting objects under the direction of Guardian Beneva."

She hitched up her own robes, tucking them firmly into her workbelt as she did so, despite soft protests from the Inesh and turned to face Mina.

"Thank you for volunteering Mina, what we do is simple cleaning and some other small setting of protections around our new Council Chamber. I, of course rely on your utter discretion."

To which request Mina, pinning up her own hair and covering it with a tightly pinned wimple agreed, albeit with an air of amused tolerance.

Beneva was already organised for cleaning, but Shiarjha gave a horrified glance at her Sorceress and said faintly.

"Mother! You cannot mean that we, you and I…"

Her voice died away in the face of Ikella's reaction, for the Sorceress had compressed her lips (mainly to prevent herself smiling at her acolytes naivety) and was frowning at her.

"Of course you and I. Come Shiarjha, just a little menial work will not ruin your reputation. We could dispel dirt and dust, and create a sheen on all things in the Council Chamber but, you said yourself, that the place has a feel of old and high magic. Who knows what we might set in motion, if we use our powers."

The Sorceress was engaged in placing sweet sand into a large bucket that Beneva was holding on to tightly as she spoke.

"I, personally, decided never to use magic when my own two hands would do the job. Only when time does not allow, when safety decrees otherwise, do I use power. and then I am not given to the lure of small magic. Unlike some people I know, who barely comprehend the mixing of herbs or the making of sick beds without it."

She raised a hand to still her acolytes protestations.

"It is of no matter, how something is achieved so long as the result is the same you think but I have learned by the many years of my life that some things are best not tampered with and yes, if I am cold I heat my room myself for I would not trouble a drudge who needed their sleep. If I am hungry or thirsty I can create a meal whilst nursing a dying man, by use of small magic but it is a craft of the past, a thing from another branch of power that does not sit comfortably on my shoulders, and while I have my senses and the use of my hands, it suits me to exercise both."

She finished speaking and turned to Beneva conversationally.

"Do you remember old Ishandra of the Cynabarr?"

She queried, and Beneva grinned impishly at her.

'Wider than the Shenagran plain?' The librarian quoted, laughing.

"Jocasta said, she got that way by small magic but we never understood what she meant! We thought that for some reason, Ishandra who was so fat she could not stand unaided, had used small magic to get that way. We, so young we comprehended little of the story at that time, suspected that she had not been able to reverse the spell again."

The Librarian smiled sympathetically at Shiarjha, "It was much later that we realised that poor Ishandra had been desperately trying to impress her people with her powers and had used small magic for nearly everything, until through lack of exercise she had become too fat to stand and then too ill to save, dying when only just one hundred and two Rotations old, because of her own misuse of magic!"

Ikella 'tutted', under her breath.

"Such a waste, such a waste."

The two older women turned away from the horrified expression on Shiarjha's face, struggling to contain their secret mirth as they entered the

Council Chamber to begin cleaning.

Not long after this, Carolus reappeared to help the Inesh warriors as they removed scrolls from shelves, stacking them neatly on the table. The rest of the party, now swelled by other members of the High Council, dusted, polished and replaced the scrolls where they had been found. Beneva handled the fragile sand tablets, swiftly taking impressions of them with the soft wax produced by busy bugs, then handling them delicately, placing them on rush mats for support. It was back breaking work, but entirely necessary for the dust of aeons had settled in this room. At Height of Sun, Ikella was filthy with tiny smudges all over her face where she had pushed back her wimple from where it had slipped. Her hands ached from washing, rinsing and wringing out cloths, and she thought that waxing the panelling would be an endless job. However the room progressed from ancient dust lined mystery to gleaming sweet smelling Council Chamber, and when the last of the bulk dirt had been swept into a pile for removal, and the skirlas had been shaken and put away, Beneva glanced up from the floor where she was washing the stone slabs and said happily.

"I feel we have earned our midday meal my dears. I ordered Irix curd and fresh beans, some berry bread and milk for all, to be placed in my chamber. Why don't we eat, then go and bathe? When the floor is dry, we can lay down the sofus grass, light the candle glows and cense the room." As the others agreed with alacrity, Carolus said slowly. "If you ladies will permit I must check on my Zeglurs. I have no doubt that you have rituals to perform. We mere men also have our Ways to Walk. I will bathe but will eat my meal in the Hall with the other visitors and then I will peg out the herd in a new pasture before I return. If that is as you permit my Deshun?"

His question somewhat surprised Ikella, for somehow she had forgotten that he was from outside the community here. He seemed to fit so well into the deepest heart of Selesh. It was almost as if he had always been here.

'Very odd!'.

She thought to herself, questioning her vows to make sure that she had not somehow come to hold this man in a dangerous affection. Satisfied that she had not she nodded her dismissal of him, regretting it instantly, for the room seemed somehow diminished as he left. Pensively, she took her meal, making small talk 'till she was thankfully able to escape and bathe in her own private pool, where the steam did much to remove the grime from her skin and the loneliness from her heart.

Swiftly she sped along the corridor to the nursery to spend a few precious moments with Daro, opening the door to see Nadra, encouraging him to hold his head up, supporting his wobbling back with good humoured comments.

"Oh yes. your mother will be so proud of you my boy."

The wet nurse exclaimed as Daro, teetering gently, subsided into her hands after 'sitting" for all of a few seconds. She looked up with a smile as Ikella swept in.

"Did you see that my Deshun?" She lifted Daro up to her shoulder.

"He has control over his head already, and he spends a lot of time just looking around! He is so knowing, an intelligent child."

She hummed happily against the baby who gurgled clutching at her hair.

With an entirely unreasonable sense of jealousy, Ikella held out her arms for the baby and as she took him, she mourned for the youth that might have given her children of her own, had she chosen to walk a different path in life. He was heavier now and stronger much stronger. He gripped her fingers with his hands and looked, really looked up into her face, then he smiled. Not one of those small secretive twitches of new muscles, or the sort of smile that is really a wind-driven grimace of discomfort but a true wide smile of pure joy, pure love, absolute recognition showing in every line of his face. Ikella wept with the surprise of one unused to true emotion.

"He knows me he really sees me!" She found herself babbling.

"Did you see that? he smiled at me."

She smothered the baby with little blissful kisses, saying over and over.

"Hello baby, hello my Daro do you know me? Hello my son!"

Into this joy however came the insistence of the Summoning Bell, 'till sadly she handed Daro back to Nadra, retreating to the doorway with a wistful expression, glancing over her shoulder at the baby, as she regretfully went back to the Djellim and to the task awaiting her.

Going straight to open the Council Chamber, she stood for a moment breathing in the sweet smell of the grasses and herbs that they had heaped on to a burner and placed in a corner. She stretched out a hand and let a little trickle of brilliant blue smoke form above the palm and studied it, as it curled into the far reaches of the high ceiling above her, watching for the eddies that would signify danger. Seeing none, she sat herself down and carefully began to tear the grasses and crush the leaves of the dried herbs between her long narrow hands. She found the scents arising from the growing pile of burnable material soothing and she was engrossed in her task when a footfall in the corridor outside alerted her to the return of the others.

Bathed and cleanly dressed they entered. Shiarjha carried the slim wand that marked her out as Sorceress-Elect in one hand, a terracotta pot, with a carefully shielded glow burning, in the other. Mina holding an amber-coloured container in both hands. Then came Beneva, a new vellum scroll under one arm, carrying a fine brush and an ink pot. Soon they were seated round the great table, preparing for the dedication of this room.

Firstly, Beneva stood announcing that she was ready, then at a nod from the Sorceress she declared in ringing tones that they were intent on dedicating the use of this Chamber to the future of Selesh. There being no intervention, magical or otherwise, Beneva sat and recorded in straight black strokes of the brush the adoption of this room. Mina now stood and carefully went over to the burner, clasping the pot she had brought with her in one hand, wielding a soft spray of white feathers with the other. She shook the feathers, dispensing a pleasant spicy perfume, before marking off nine paces to the left of the burner.

At this point she stopped, refreshing the feathers, scattering the sweet oil from the pot once more. Beneva watched Mina's progress, 'till as the Healer returned silently to her place, she carefully inked another line in what they had all come to recognise as the script most used in Sanctuary. Next Shiarjha stood and holding her wand out at right angles to her body, she came to each of the nine points of progress and prayed softly.

"Mirayen, Wind of the Opal Sands look deep into every recess of our hearts, cleanse them from all things of this world. Let us harbour no evil within. As we have cleansed this room, preparing for your presence within, we beg of you to search out all harmful entities, all residual magic, bearing them out into the purity of the sands that are your domain, and leave this place dedicated in your name to the service of all."

She spoke with conviction. Ikella watched her progress quietly, before rising to take her own place. Emptying her own mind of all thought, other than her duty, before engaging her powers, she lifted her Staff in one hand directing the other, long fingertips extended, towards the incense burner. She spoke no word aloud, just inwardly calling.

'Mirayen, come forth. Make your presence known in the flame, in the sweet scent of the burner, and take from this place every hint of ill doing, past or present.'.

From her hand came a long searing stream of flame, it licked at the dried contents of the burner, leapt to the nine points of progress in an encircling barrier of fire around those gathered at the great table, and returned to the burner in the blink of an eye. From the heart of the small pile of ashes in the centre of the burner came a sweet summery scent, redolent of flowers, fruits and honey and then as quickly as it had come, the fire died, leaving not one trace of its passing except for a little grey ash.

The dedication ceremony was over. During the last moments, hushed footsteps had approached, stopping in the outer Djellim. Beneva raised her eyes to the doorway and smiled in welcome as both the Apothecary and the Master Builder came into view. Noting her glance Ikella looked up, and beckoned the men to join them, which they did, noticeably lacking the diffidence that they had portrayed on earlier occasions. Both were warmly clad, carrying hukvahs, and to Ikella's astonishment they brought with them a small sack, which contained some rare stone blossoms from the Heights of Torrenesh. Plainly they also wanted to make a contribution to the Council Chamber and the Sorceress willingly accepted them, putting them on the corner of a shelf where they shifted into place, settling down to perfume the air with their strange petals widely extended. Ikella sat in one of the chairs and swung it to look down the length of the room.

"I would like to move the table to a more central position" she commented, "And that wall looks so bare."

Beneva leant forward. "I was going to ask a favour on that point Ikella."

The Sorceress frowned a little, looking at the two men who stood just out of earshot, conversing about the stone blossoms and their properties.

"Errish." She commanded.

"I want to move this table a little, but it is plainly too heavy to do it ourselves. Can you two rustle up some helpers?"

As the Apothecary and the Master Builder departed, Ikella relaxed, indicating that the librarian could make her request.

"I had hoped to place the Sanctuary Chest here. It is the most precious relic that we possess, without it, Sanctuary can never be rebuilt. Without it, I could not have saved one scroll for your Djellim. It holds the treasures of that place of precious memory, many artefacts, more memories and not a little magic of its own."

Her voice was low, controlled and yet filled with pain and Ikella and Shiarjha turned to her, comfort in their eyes.

"I will need time to make my own preparations for certain investitures. A shielded room that I might use in privacy to find the articles I need, would be wonderful."

Her voice grew wistful as she explained.

"The Sanctuary Chest is so precious that without anywhere to secure it in, I have endless fears of leaving my library unattended. I do not know why, but recently, even with a Guard posted within and without, I am so nervous that I sleep next to it, using my bedding roll to hide it in the day!"

She confessed, a little self consciously. Mina, and Ikella both groaned in sympathy, sleeping on bedding rolls in the most uncomfortable of surroundings, all too fresh in their memories. The Sorceress looked at Beneva before saying slowly.

"Yet you dismissed your Guards, despite obviously feeling unsure of the safety of the Chest, or your welcome here. Why?"

Beneva closed her eyes, apparently overcome with pain.

"My journey here was the last part of the old Way. Honour bound me to Jocasta's dying wish, and I fulfilled it."

The Guardian's head lifted proudly, and Ikella was astonished and touched to see the tears brimming in her eyes as Beneva continued softly.

"I walked their last walk with them, 'till they brought me here. Until the last I did not know their mission, save that they followed the commands of Guardian Jocasta of revered memory. They were sworn to her will, obedient unto death, and I had no part of the directing of their journey. It was simply their task to deliver me here, with the Sanctuary Chest. Had I not entered here, nor been made welcome, their task would have been to destroy the Chest, the artefacts, me."

Her voice had grown small, lost, she blinked rapidly. Without a word Mina sought her side and slid a comforting arm round her, till presently in a curious and sombre voice Ikella asked.

"The Nishan? It was not a dream then? They are gone?"

Beneva, her lips quivering said with finality.

"Their Way has gone, Sanctuary has gone, the Way of Guardianship is forever changed, and yes Ikella, they are gone!"

She heaved a huge sigh and the Council Chamber echoed her sorrow dully.

As one person Shiarjha and Ikella reached out, encircling the Librarian in a ring of sisterly embraces 'till Ikella said quietly but emphatically.

"Then let our dedication to the service of Sanctuary, the service of Pelshar and its peoples be no less!"

She clasped Beneva's hands in hers, catching the Librarians tear-drenched eyes with her own, she declared.

"Faithful unto death, Beneva?"

A muted echo came back from all present.

"Faithful unto death!"

Chapter 29 - Through a Glass Dimly

In complete contrast to the solemn mood of the room came Mina's voice. Thoughtfully she said. "I think the Sanctuary Chest would look good on that wall Beneva! It would be totally safe in here and your privacy would be guaranteed."

Ikella, blessing her stout lieutenant for the welcome distraction from melancholy, looked at the area that Mina had indicated saying quietly.

"When the men return, we can get the Chest moved as well Beneva, then you shall sleep more soundly."

Shortly thereafter, the tramp of feet could be heard approaching from the corridor outside the Djellim. The librarian stood, and went swiftly out into the darkened library. Shiarjha watched her go curiously, and then said quietly to Ikella.

"She is not as I remember her my Deshun, she was always so, so..." She paused fumbling for words.

"Happy child? Confident?"

Ikella suggested wearily and the young Sorceress-elect looked up, and saw the confusion, fear and uncertainty touching her Sorceress too. She instinctively reached out across the table. With a quiet smile Ikella allowed herself the intimacy of a gentle touch on the arm, a clasped hand.

"I fear that Selesh is changing too rapidly my daughter."

Ikella bowed her head, murmuring.

"All Pelshar is wounded, needs healing, but we must heal ourselves before taking up such a task."

Thus speaking Ikella rose from the table, and to Shiarjha's surprise and mute pleasure, she reached across the table and placed a hand lightly on her acolytes cheek, tilting her face into the light, studying the girl thoroughly. The Sorceress's eyes took in the uncertainty there, but noted the obstinacy of the mouth, the firm gaze of the clear hazel eyes and saw that Jocasta's choice had been good. She nodded encouragingly at the young woman and with a brisk acknowledging.

"You'll do!" She swept out to see what occurred in the outer Djellim.

For a moment Shiarjha sat, her hand pressed to the cheek Ikella had touched, deliberately savouring that blessed moment of acceptance. Then she felt another pair of eyes on her and turned to see Ikella's strange old Apothecary friend. The old man's eyes called hers, and for a long moment, she hung imprisoned by his compelling gaze 'till he shifted, smiled, saying simply.

"Well done, my dear, well done," before patting her on the head and following Ikella.

Shiarjha found herself grinning inanely at a beaming Mina, who simply cupped her hands around those of the Sorceress-elect, dipped her head respectfully and said comfortably.

"Well now, aren't you glad that's over? It took something to make Ikella accept that she needs a successor in place. She had only just acceded to the Sands when Jocasta searched you out. If you had heard her comments about it then, you would never have believed that she would ever accept you or anyone else! However, all that is past now, she welcomed you in her own way, and I think you can look to hold that wand more confidently now, my Somishen. Use your title more willingly and stop using your power to make beds, wash patients. Use it for other things, Higher things. Now she will tutor you herself and you will call her Mother, follow her every command, and thank the One on this day every Rotation, that she has taken to you at last!"

Shortly thereafter, a small troop of Inesh warriors led by Driss and followed by an anxious Beneva, carried the Sanctuary Chest. Four to each side made light work of shuffling it into position, directly opposing the dais at the end of the room.

It sat, the imposing symbol of Sanctuary prominently displayed on the side facing the dais. Beneva fretted and fussed till the Chest was placed exactly to her liking, and then Ikella commandeered the use of the warriors to move the immense table, just a matter of a few paces away from the dais and its centrally placed chair.

She supervised the distribution of chairs around the table once more, and soon they sat looking with great satisfaction around the Council Chamber. Shiarjha spoke seriously from the depths of her chair.

"Deshun, when you call Conclave, this room will become central to all the activity in the complex. With six full adepts of the Sisterhood, as well as three acolytes to raise to the Staff, will we have enough hospitality rooms, food and supplies for all their retinue?" to which Mina added. "Excuse my asking my Deshun but will we be able to hold Conclave before this Ice Season is upon us?"

The Sorceress replied sombrely.

"I wish I knew my friends, what say you?"

Strangely all eyes turned to the Apothecary who sat quietly pleating the sleeve of his tunic, apparently unaware of their scrutiny.

At that moment Beneva, who had been looking at the Sanctuary Chest with a small crease furrowing her brow, suddenly leapt up from her seat muttering.

"No, it still is not back on that wall, nor is it straight."

She went to the chest and shoved at it impatiently until Errish rose smoothly, muscles rippling in his broad chest and back, and joined her. He patiently removed her from her hopeless task and with a courtly.

"Allow me Lady Beneva." As he braced himself and pushed the chest until it suddenly shot back the half finger or so that it had been out of line, and as it did so their was a soft sighing, 'spanghhh' of sound and a shimmer of glass appeared in the corner opposite the incense burner.

The mirror, for that is what it appeared to be, hung above the ground not more than a child's hand span. It was huge, made from a sheet of sand-paste large enough to reflect someone from head to toe. Errish, who had sprung back from the Chest as the mirror appeared, looked a little alarmed at first, but seeing the angle at which the glass was set, simply said sheepishly.

"Sorry, I must have trodden on some sort of lever, or moved the chest against one. That's a fine glass isn't it? So cunningly set that I can see right to the door of the Djellim, long before anyone entering would know I was here, which could be useful."

He hunkered down near the Sanctuary Chest, and ran his hand over the floor, looking for some mechanism he had missed, bearing Beneva's scowling scrutiny with equanimity. However, Ikella had felt a feather touch at the base of her spine and she looked at the mirror with eyes narrowed in suspicious anticipation.

Shiarjha stood, despite Ikella's murmured warning as she approached the glass. "Care child!"

Absentmindedly, Shiarjha pulled a straggle of unruly hair into place, adjusting the polished opal of her rank on her forehead as Ikella passed her giving an impatient snort, raising everyone's awareness that the Sorceress took a dim view of what she was doing.

"Can't you feel that, child?"

Ikella asked her brusquely as she peered at the mirror, so close to it that her nose should have touched the "glass"

"Whatever possesses you to prink and preen in front of an object of such power?"

She demanded then, in a single flowing move, she summoned her Staff from where it had been snapped into the holder on the arm of her chair.

As the opal at its head blazed into life, Ikella enveloped herself in the cloak of her aura. At this the mirror turned milky, then shivered, finally clearing to a soft, swirling, mist held in a frame of light. However through this miasma, Ikella could clearly see the head and ears of a very frightened Zeglur.

For a single heart stopping moment the beast stared at her, and then it reared in fright and with a dreadful moaning 'yehawing' sound it bolted. Ikella who had frozen in surprise, found that she was quite literally stood in the Council Chamber grasping the "frame" where the glass of the "mirror" had hung, but looking through a sort of window into the grazing compound outside the Gate in the Rock!

Slowly closing her eyes, she retreated, dismissing the experience as impossible. Plainly the others had seen what she had, for suddenly she was surrounded. She carefully backed from the "viewing plate" as she found herself calling this artefact and still maintaining her powers for the protection of her companions, she returned to her chair and sat watching them as they commented on what they saw.

"It is amazing, truly an immense discovery."

Shiarjha was saying and Mina, carefully supported by Errish, peeked through squeaking in terror as she discovered she was less than a foot from a nasty, smelly Zeglur!

The Apothecary sat silently while Ikella, who was still shaking, slowly let go of her grip on the Staff. She relaxed backing the power she had summoned down, from full sweep to gentle trickle, and as she did so the image in the mirror changed. With the quieting of the panic in her own blood, she was able to let go of her instinctive seizure of the Source, and the misty swirl in the glass disappeared.

The Apothecary spoke.

"May I go and quieten my Zeglurs now my Deshun?"

He seemed anxious to leave, but Ikella raised a hand forbidding it for a moment.

"Wait, Carolus, are you sure they were your animals? I thought that they were in the pasture outside the Gate?"

The old man nodded.

"Yes my Deshun, they are or rather were. Zeglurs can run for miles when they are scared and you certainly frightened that one! I need my Zeglurs, Lady. Can I go and check on them?"

He was on his feet and Ikella did not have the heart to restrain him further, but she found herself staring at the image of his retreating back, reflecting benignly in the mirror, as he scurried away.

Errish started suddenly, and then he said quietly.

"I have an idea my Deshun, may I speak?"

He rose to his feet.

"With no magic involved, what you have here is a mirror glass which shows us who approaches the Council Chamber, if we are endangered here. With magic at work, it seems it shows the area immediately outside the Gate. This provides a warning of approaching danger, if there were any."

Ikella nodded, seemingly in agreement with that supposition, but as the Summoning Bell sounded for even meal and the party disbursed to their various tasks, Ikella sat thoughtfully at the Council table. To tell the truth she was loathe to move for fear of what she would see, then with a cross shake of her head she stood up, deliberately looking at her right sleeve, where frightened Zeglur teeth had snapped shut, tearing a long thin strip right out of her robe. She uncurled her hand slowly and clenched tightly in the knuckles were the unmistakable feathery hairs from the mane of a baby Zeglur.

Instinctively she found herself bringing that clenched fist to her heart, to her forehead, only just preventing herself from superstitiously kissing the fingers that had strayed to the great Opal that blazed on her forehead. Shocked at her own fearfulness, she carefully unwound the strands from her hand, placing them in a curl on the Council table, but even as she did so, she bowed her head in the acceptance of what was and rising, went to a silent supper, praying earnestly for the return of the reality that she was familiar with.

Chapter 30 - Jocasta's Door

Somehow Ikella was not surprised to find Carolus apparently doing little in the ante-room to the Djellim, as she returned there after even meal. She had refrained from joining the others at prayer, for her mind was too disturbed to concentrate, and she willingly ceded that part of her duty to her acolyte, saying gratefully.

"Somishen Shiarjha will lead your devotions tonight my Healers, for I am reporting myself to the Infirmary with great soreness of hands and knees. These pains have been inflicted on myself in service, so I think you will not begrudge me one night of rest and healing?"

The titter of amusement that swept the table died away naturally as the Healers rose, and followed the tall figure of Shiarjha to the Great Hall and evening prayer. Ikella watched them leave, thinking about the young Sorceress-Elect. Was it only an impression but did that child walk with her head held higher, was that a smile of quiet pride she saw on her face, she hoped so and suddenly a view of the long years of her life, and the years to come for Shiarjha marched away in front of her, and she shuddered. Anxious to dispel this sudden feeling of apprehension, she went swiftly first to Daro's nursery, where he, Ahnell and Nadra slept blissfully unaware of the turmoil of her thoughts, and then to the Djellim.

Entering the ante-room, she saw Jashell and Indeera talking quietly, other Inesh organising their night rota and Carolus, waiting quietly, his face shadowed. Passing him, she caught his eye and he followed her, straight to the Council Chamber. He was dressed for travel, even carrying his carved Staff as though prepared for imminent departure at which she raised an eyebrow, but declined to comment. They scurried through the dimly-lit Library, she with her silvery head of hair framed in the high collar of her gown. He, with his face shadowed in the cowl of a winter cloak, which billowed behind him. They found the Council Chamber open, Beneva seated within, the lid of the Sanctuary Chest raised and various artefacts lying in a pool of light. The librarian was studying a small hand glass intently, turning it this way and that, as they entered the room. She looked up at Ikella, nodded to Carolus and then to Ikella's astonishment, she made a hand gesture and the room's strange magical barrier closed behind them. Ikella, recognising that tonight Beneva had reassumed the authority of a Guardian, came quietly to the table and sat, as did Carolus in a distinctly authoritative manner, snapping his Staff into the holder on the arm of his chair as if he had been used to doing so all his life. Beneva, who had lowered her eyes to the small hand glass looked up at Carolus and said firmly.

"Traveller, speak to us of this!"

She indicated the newly-revealed reflecting panel, which innocently showed the scene from the entrance of the Council Chamber to the guarded doors of the Djellim, despite the energy field being in place. She held out the hand glass to Ikella, who took it wonderingly for framed in its surface, was a view of the pasture and the Zeglurs placidly grazing under the night glows set besides the Gate in the Rock. As he stood Carolus seemed to have grown in stature and Ikella saw that he and Beneva knew each other well. She stared at him openly. He seemed lither, easier in his movements, his voice faintly apologetic as he spoke gravely.

"I am known as Carolus, called by some the Traveller."

He made a sketchy bow in the direction of the Librarian as he continued.

"I have ever been in the service of Sanctuary."

Beneva raised steady eyes to those of the Sorceress, fixing her gaze as she took over.

"He has been our eyes and ears in the outside world, bringing to my Djellim at Sanctuary many strange objects of a power beyond our own. One of those artefacts you now hold in your hand, my dear. Seris Jocasta used that glass as she sought the emergence of power, searched and guided those talents to their Way. With this she kept us safe, protected the world of men from the accidental discovery of powers that they could not control. This, and her ability to use it, allowed Sanctuary to function."

Ikella glanced down at the small apparently innocuous, hand mirror. In her mind a fleeting memory of Jocasta, as she had first met her and with a small cry she saw the scene again, appearing in miniature, swimming in a many shaded mist of colour. Jocasta, smiling at her and she the hot-headed, fiery creature of passion that she had been, crying forlornly against the Guardians knee, because a spell had gone wrong, would not work for her.

Carolus from where he was standing could also see into the mirror and Ikella absorbed in her "viewing" did not see his lips twitch in a smile but she heard his voice saying to Beneva.

"She is the one then! Has she worn the cuffs?"

To which enquiry, Beneva said in a curious tone of voice.

"Yes. It was the first thing I did! The Nishan saw it too. Although not yet invested, she is fully able to harness their power."

Ikella raised her eyes with difficulty from the scene of her childhood and broke in to their conversation abruptly.

"I would thank someone to speak to me of this anomaly!"

So saying, she reached forward to pick up the loose coil of baby Zeglur mane in one hand, laying the flowing sleeve of her robe bare for all to see, complete with teeth marks and tears. Beneva examined both with wonder on her face, leaning forward to touch Ikella's sleeve.

"Truly Jocasta sought one, who as a child, would surpass even her Talent! My dear friend, you have indeed touched that reality beyond the glass!"

Visibly moved, Beneva clasped both hands together and the silver wristlets worn by a Guardian gleamed brightly. Ikella thought, 'In deep satisfaction.'.

Ikella, all the more perplexed, looked at Carolus for explanations and he spoke reluctantly.

"Of course I never saw it done, but revered Jocasta always thought the glass at Sanctuary to be not just a window through which she could reach her Sisters in Sorcery but possibly in the right hands and at the right time, as a door or gateway to some other place. However, each of us has our own limitations and being entirely without power myself, I can only speculate on the properties of these glasses, windows, gateways whatever they are."

There was silence throughout the room as Beneva and Ikella tried to take in what the Apothecary had said. Eventually Ikella found her tongue again, and said, to no-one in particular.

"If that theory is right, then is it a gateway to one place in particular, or could there be many places that it leads to?"

At which, Beneva said suspiciously.

"How would anyone tell if a place seen in such a mirror was real? Could what we see be part of a shadow world?"

Ikella shivered, mindful of children's stories of shadow worlds in which bad or disobedient children were trapped. With her eyes still drawn to the large mirror she presently went to stand in front of it, tapping her fingers irritably, against the hand glass that she still held. As Beneva and Carolus conducted a low-toned conversation behind her, she seemed to come to a decision. Assuming her powers, her glittering aura reflected for a moment in the mirror before the glass faded in front of her, leaving a swirling energy pattern not unlike that of the rooms own barrier.

Through the mist, she saw a movement and soon made out a Zeglur, placidly munching at the sparse grassland near the Gate in the Rock.

"Carolus," she called. "You give your animals names don't you? Can you identify this one?"

Reluctantly the old man came to the glass, and stood silently observing the beast.

"That's Zephryn Seris Ikella."

The new honorific left her totally unmoved, so he explained slowly.

"Named for a legend about a Storm Horse, because he runs a mile when we have lightening storms!"

At that, Beneva raised her head, suspicion dawning in her eyes.

"What mad plan have you hatched now?"

Even as Ikella gave a harsh chuckle and stepped into the mist which shivered and dissolved as she passed right through it, disappearing completely from the Council Chamber. For a long moment Beneva sat frozen in shock, then she cried in outrage.

"Ikella! What have you done now, you dreadful girl?"

Carolus turned toward her saying bleakly.

"Aah well" As he followed the Sorceress through the strangely shimmering haze that now occupied the area that had so recently seemed to be naught but a mirror. Beneva stood, looking toward the "mirror" till she saw the mists settle.

She tentatively walked up to the frame, where to her relief she observed both Ikella and Carolus, calming the startled Zeglurs. Soon afterward there was a fizzing sound from the corner of the room, heralding the return of her companions.

They were enthusiastically discussing all the possible uses and properties of the 'travelling glass', as they returned. Ikella's enthusiasm was only momentarily dampened by Beneva's single quelling look, even as she apologised to the Guardian for her thoughtlessness. The Sorceress was drawing Carolus back to the Council Table, reaching for something to draw on from the pile of vellum scraps, brushes and sand tablets piled where Mina had sat earlier .

As she leant forward chattering to Carolus, she voiced the idea that they should use the travelling glass to transport the Sisters of Sorcery to Conclave, if they could test how far the travelling device allowed them to roam.

Ikella, talking about Nahamida of the Onyx Sands, was still sorting through the scrap vellum when her Source beads, worn fastened around her wrist, touched the glazed panel in the middle of the table. She hardly noticed, so intent was she on reaching for the pen nearest to her, until there was a sudden shiver in the Source. Beneva jumped out of her skin, then glancing down at the table to see the Sorceress of the Onyx Sands staring at her in surprise.

Nahamida, midnight daughter of the Sisterhood, wide eyed with fright, shook as she stared at Ikella, one hand pressed to her heart as she spoke tremulously.

"All hail Sharall deir Opal, Ikella my sister, my guide in Sorcery. How come you to take the path of Jocasta, Guardian of beloved memory?"

Ikella had to use every inch of control, as she realised that she must now appear to the Kora Mai Sorceress, as Jocasta had to her.

'A reflection, dimly seen in some glass? As her own vision of Jocasta had appeared? Perhaps sited above a desk in a study, far to the south in the hot Sands of the Onyx Desert?'

"All hail my sister, I come to you from Selesh, and I bring with me Guardian Beneva, who now resides with us. This is her summoning to Conclave, here in Selesh, at Jentaroth."

Smoothly, Ikella moved to one side and let Beneva look into the glass on the table where more relaxed, with a tentative smile of welcome Nahamida waited.

"All hail Nahamida, Sorceress of the Kora, Mai!"

Beneva slotted easily into place, as if this conversation was planned, the strange properties of the table understood. If it was only Carolus and Ikella who saw her fingers superstitiously crossed behind her back, what did it matter?

"I summon you, all of your Sisters, to Conclave at Selesh. Here we must learn of the sorrows of our Sands, discuss the turning of the Way and prepare three acolytes to accept the Staff of their Sands"

She raised a hand against the storm of questions that hung in the air between them and went on.

"I am charged by Seris Jocasta, with this duty. With her last breath, I was commanded not to reveal more, 'till all are assembled at Selesh. You will stand ready to travel to the Opal Sands on my command."

Ikella listened intently as Beneva continued.

"Prepare for the cold, for an Ice Season is upon us. Bring only your Staff and Ceremonial wear and one trusted body servant. Be prepared to travel immediately when called."

She sounded if possible more remote and mysterious than ever as Ikella slid into place, she engaged her aura, seeing awe in Nahamida's face, she happily terminated the conversation with the reminder.

"Other than letting your own people know that you are travelling as instructed by Guardian Beneva under my protection, it is not necessary to speak of this conversation further."

She allowed a little of the 'glamour' to trickle through, narrowed her eyes and said soberly. "Do I make myself clear?"

Nahamida nodded saying softly. "I will keep the Faith my Sister."

The Kora-Mai Sorceress bowed her head as she spoke and Ikella responded warningly. "I hold your word Nahamida. No word of what is to come must leak out to the people, or there will be panic!"

As Ikella lifted her hand to bless her Sister in Sorcery, her source beads lost contact with the table, there was a soft sighing sound and the connection was severed.

No sooner had the image of Nahamida faded and the "glass" cleared, Ikella and Beneva fell into each others arms, convulsed with mirth, shrilling like novices to the other.

"Did you see her face?" Followed by. "For a moment, I thought she would faint!"

"I could only speak as I have heard, Jocasta, and hope that she would believe me. I am not sure that I believe myself."

As Ikella frowned thoughtfully, trying to remember what she had said in the excitement of the minute, their eyes met in the most sisterly of concord, as they suppressed the giggles that threatened to overwhelm them. Beneva was clutching on to Ikella's arm as they slowly subsided into their chairs.

"I don't believe this room, are we ever going to get to the bottom of all its mysteries?"

Ikella, eyeing the centre panel on the table cautiously, said soberly. "I don't suppose we ever shall, but I am glad that it was you and I that have revealed the most powerful. To call Conclave here, without any idea of what this room, the travelling glass and whatever this table contains would have been very dangerous."

Carolus leant forward to the table and looked carefully at the centre panel. Resting, it was a strange milky white colour, when Ikella laid her source beads on it, it seemed almost to become liquid and now it seemed to be setting again and like some crystalline matter it was clouding. The Apothecary spoke thoughtfully.

"This seems to me to be familiar, it has a scent about it, perhaps a taste."

He leant forward and touched the panel respectfully. Ikella stood carefully and took up her Staff, laying it down on the table, moving the crystal wings atop the finial towards the panel.

As the two surfaces touched, there was a tingle in the air and then the wings shimmered, blurred and melted into the panel on the table and what was left was a contained pool of clear liquid, from which emanated a soft, gentle green light. Ikella and Beneva stood looking down into the swirling depths of the liquid, and with one breath they simultaneously gasped.

'Stillglass!"

They dipped their fingers into it, and raised them to their lips and it was so.

Carolus stood looking at them curiosity on his face, in his eyes and they explained carefully to him about the properties of Stillglass, how rare and precious it was, being the only medium through which they could effect long distance communication. Ikella said gently.

"I may have lost my wings forever here, for we did not know that Stillglass could assume a solid state."

She eyed her Staff curiously, for it now looked and felt bare without its wings.

"It is even stranger that two different solids could melt together like that."

She mused, then in a smaller, sadder voice.

"If my wings are gone, they are gone, I shall manage without. Empowered, liquid Stillglass allows us to communicate between the Sands, but it shrinks each time we use it. I was not in power when my beads touched the table, so it was strange that Nahamida appeared just after I thought of her, don't you think?"

Beneva, who was peering at the pool of liquid Stillglass grunted by way of reply.

"Uh, uh, I fear this may not return to solid, now we have tampered with it. We Guardians call Stillglass, the Tears of the Singers, though I do not know how it came by that name, nor do I know of any other place that I may get more."

Carolus nodded knowingly, saying.

"Then it is lucky that I do, but it is a perilous place, high in the Ashgenar near the place they call Star Weavers Table."

The group fell silent thinking of the strange badlands, to the north of the Azure Sands, and its equally mysterious inhabitants both animal and human. After a long pause, Ikella moved her Staff. With a somehow refreshing jingle, it lifted in her hand and high atop the Opal, they floated, Ikella's wings, and her heart sang, though she said nothing. At her brow the Opal of her rank glowed suddenly and the others smiled at her relief. Glancing around her, well satisfied with the evenings events and a little weary if the truth were told, she was ready for her bed she realised and said so with a small smile adding.

"In fact I do not think that I have been this tired since I first tapped the Source. It feels as though I walked to the Onyx by myself!"

Carolus said cheerfully.

"It is as well that I can make up the wexenberry restorative that I gave you the first time we met. Do you have a headache as well?"

Ikella was forced to admit that she had a low grade throb, which affected her eyes.

"Then…" announced Beneva decisively. "…We shall retire to my area, which is all the more manageable for being rid of the chest."

So speaking she gathered up the artefacts and swept them into the lid of the Sanctuary Chest, which opened and closed at a casual wave of its Guardians hand but not before Ikella has noted the symbol of Sanctuary glow. They silently eyed the Council table, the Sanctuary Chest and the dais with its solitary ceremonial chair and left, walking back into the Djellim proper Ikella could not help remarking.

"I wonder who that chair was for?"

Carolus caused her steady pace to falter for a moment, when he said quietly.

"How can we know whether it was for anyone of the time passed? Perhaps it is intended for one yet to come?"

Leaving her standing, he swept past Ikella and sat himself at Beneva's hearth. By the time the Sorceress had recovered herself and had followed him thoughtfully, he had raised Beneva's kettle to the flames to prepare a hot sweetdrink and was stirring together some powders, to which he added a little of the wexenberry syrup from a large container on the hearth. He listed the ingredients as he put them away for Ikella's edification.

"Farand heart." Ikella nodded, and a memory of the large flowered shrub sprang to mind, the root of one of these was a dense succulent which dried out to make an effective treatment for fevers, ground down it formed the basis of much medication. "Texin bark for pain, and wexenberry syrup to blend the whole and to reduce swelling." He handed the concoction to her with a small bow, and Ikella held it to the light of a glow where it showed a brilliant but dark red shade. "So you really are an Apothecary as well as the spy of Sanctuary?"

She questioned, as she tilted the horn cup to her lips and the restorative slid down. Carolus chuckled as he took the cup from her.

"Happily for me, I am indeed an Apothecary first and foremost. I am a traveller, an itinerant never able to settle for long in one place, and with me I take my trade and my eyes and my ears. If something should spark my interest, well I can always leave a place early to investigate, or stay longer and no-one notices. No man owns me and so I travel freely to carry on my trade and learn my information, and if Sanctuary needed an Apothecary from time to time, who would notice that I travelled there very often after finding something of interest in some other sand?"

His bright eyes caught Ikella's knowingly, and she laughed. "Would you travel that often to Selesh?" She enquired delicately, and Beneva's lips twitched in amusement as the old man nodded, picked up his own Staff and said.

"I have to gather supplies for the Healer Hall at Selesh, do you go that way too my lady?"

Suddenly Ikella ceased to be amused as Carolus seemed to diminish in front of her, becoming more ancient, less of interest, almost shrinking back into the shadows of the library, disappearing into his cloak. Seeing him do that, she nodded saying quietly.

"There are many tales about the Messenger of the Guardians. The legends say he comes and goes, melts through walls at night, or sends his reports on the heels of the Wind. I think that I am looking at him, am I not, Carolus of the Nine Sands?"

He came back to his full height as he answered briskly.

"Yes Seris Ikella."

She looked him fully in the eyes as she said soberly.

"Then your duties are transferred with Beneva to our Djellim, where you will report as before. I also have need of you as an Apothecary, and a gatherer of medicines. I thank you for your restorative, now I must rest and plan on how and when we will call the rest of my Sisters here."

So saying she departed, leaving the others behind her.

As she left Carolus said quietly to Beneva.

"She will rise to her full power very soon, and she will have to come to terms with the fact that her biggest enemy is neither time, nor nature, nor the effects of this Storm, the biggest danger for her lies within."

He subsided on to the settle near the fire, cupped his hands around a beaker and refused to be drawn further on the subject.

The next few ninenights were a blur of checking and planning, seeing that the Master Builder had finished the hotfloors, making sure that all the young people of the village had been set to gather fossil fuel, the outcrops of firestone found in seams along the lower Sands. Visitors from Fringe communities were welcomed, with green foodstuffs to trade for medicine, keeping the Apothecary busy in the infirmaries herbarium making replacements for common medications. From the northern parts of the Opal Sands came builders to bring more materials for Errish and everywhere there seemed to be noise and confusion during the day, and planning committees meeting in every available space throughout the evenings. Ikella wisely took to staying in her own rooms, finding that if she stirred from them she was immediately co-opted to settle arguments, make decisions and rulings, and she was well employed herself, using the hidden rooms and corridors that only she knew of to prepare for the ceremonies of empowerment to take place.

She roamed these during the days when she needed to think and soon found that she had a way of getting from her rooms to the Djellim. Simply entering the hidden swinging door in her study, carefully concealed behind a wall drape, took her to a small flight of steps and a long corridor. In that corridor were several doors, only one of which she had used before and that she knew took her directly to the Hall of the Healers. It was known to the Healers that she had her own private entrance to the Hall, into the Sacred Circle and this was never questioned Ikella prowled, dousing rods in hand, trying to map in her head where the ways led, the ones she had never before explored or questioned and within hours she had found her way through a narrow pivoting stone, into the dark recesses of the Djellim and had given Beneva a nasty fright in so doing. When the little librarian had stopped squeaking in dismay, she carefully showed her the way through which she had come and the two of them had spent the rest of the day sketching the corridors, so that in emergency she could come to Beneva and the librarian could get to her unseen. As the days grew shorter and the winds grew colder, the Healers turned the lower infirmary into the main treatment rooms with access to heated bathing pools which had always been the desire of Ikella's heart and the upper infirmary was made into treatment rooms for dignitaries, senior Staff from Selesh and a private set of rooms for Ikella herself should she need them. Mina, who had wheedled all manner of adaptations for her "hospice" from Errish, showed the Sorceress proudly what she had achieved. Ikella was stunned by the foresight of her Senior Healer and declared herself speechless with gratitude. Proceeding to elaborate in a most uncharacteristic manner over the way water had been channelled into each of the rooms, allowing for cleanliness to be enforced. She waxed lyrical over the enclosed necessaries and washdowns that the Master Builder had achieved, and was presently dumbfounded when the Apothecary showed her round the facilities provided for the manufacturing of medicines. She stood, overcome with emotion, clasping her hands together in the midst of these changes and had just opened her mouth to speak, when Mina burst out with.

"Let the othersands see this, let them open their eyes on the glory of Selesh, let them see the halls of training, the hall of welcome, the hotfloors, the infirmaries above and below, the Djellim, the Council Chamber, the newly appointed Hall of the Healers, the herbarium, our Sorceress, let them look on our glory and weep in envy!"

Struggling not to laugh at her Healers provocative statement, Ikella gulped saying weakly.

"Ah Mina, you have a way with words" and the entire company broke up, laughing.

That night Ikella met Beneva in the Djellim, it was late, Gatta and Jenta the twin moons of Pelshar should have stood high in the heavens and the stars should have been visible, but for the looming clouds that still filled the skies. Silently Ikella indicated the librarian to put on her cloak, she was already dressed for outdoors and Beneva noted that she held her Staff in a gloved hand. The librarian prepared herself swiftly, silently and was not surprised when Ikella took them through the doorway into the Council Chamber.

The Sorceress took no time, crossing the floor of the room in three swift paces. She positioned herself and Beneva in front of the travelling glass and assumed her powers. As the aura formed around her, she drew Beneva into the encompassing glow, and then she held her Staff out in front of her and said one word.

"Sanctuary!"

The "glass" grew milky, opalescent and then cleared to a mist, and the great dark plain of Colonth spread out below them. Ikella stepped forward boldly compelling Beneva almost by force to join her pace for pace. They paused, teetering on the high edge of the cliff top path on which they now stood, and turned to look about them.

To the far north of the Opal Sands, from Selesh to Sanctuary, the great plains stretched almost to the Eternal Snows, rising imperceptibly at first, then more steeply 'till the unwary traveller found himself teetering on the edge of the Djurum Pass. There was no way forward from here save on the path to Sanctuary, and little had been added to the natural fortifications of this place. It was eerily silent now, gone the gentle chimes of the wind bells from the gatekeepers lodge, gone the great wall that hid the treasure of Sanctuary from ordinary eyes. The bare rocks rose around them, and desolation lay before them, framed by an oily rolling mass of cloud, grey and sullen, where once the gentle sun had shone.

Where there should have been a high arched span of bridge only a chasm yawned below, and heart-sore at the devastation they paused, eyes drawn inevitably to the depths where mounds of masonry could be made out far below. On the other side of the chasm, where once had stood the great castellated buildings that housed the order of Syrene there was nothing. Not a stone remained but the natural bedrock of the mountain against which it had stood for five hundred rotations. Nothing marked its passing but a sullen flicker of light licking along the point on which a guard house had stood. The two women stood for a long moment and then Ikella spoke. Her voice harsh she said. "I am sorry Beneva but I had to know, not from report, not from another's eyes, even those of Jocasta herself. I, had, to, know!"

Comfortingly the librarian blinked back her own tears and laid a hand on Ikella's saying.

"I am not surprised. You were always the one that had to know of your own knowledge. It is what made you what you are, it is what will keep the House of Syrene together, come what may."

The two women leant against the rocks for a moment, looking down into the depths of the chasm below, each mourning friends, sisters in Sorcery and the Way that was, and then Ikella spoke wonderingly.

"Beneva, look."

She pointed across the chasm to the foundations of Sanctuary and gathering there was light. Growing from a flicker here, a glimmer there, it seemed as though some mighty crowd, holding torches, gathered at the shattered bridge. As the two women clung to each other on the edge of the precipice, the clear sound of a voice came to them across the divide, and then there were many voices, raised in Song, the otherwordly, othervoices of those departed were heard. Clear and true they came to Beneva, to Ikella, who found herself compelled to lean forward, raise her arms. As she did so there was a humming sound, a great rush of air lifted her long cloak, and Beneva gaped in wonder as the fiery glow of the lights across the chasm gathered, balled and flared, streaming towards Ikella who stood bathed in the eternal glow of the Source, hands lifted to those who passed and at her wrists there was suddenly an incandescence. A great bell tolled, and clearly Beneva heard a voice, stilled though she knew it to be, "The day is done, the torch has passed to its last bearer, our Way ends in the dawning of the new Day for Pelshar. Fare thee well my sisters" and the wind fled, leaving behind it all the remained of the House of Syrene and its Guardians.

Beneva drew a ragged breath, asking.

"How in the Nine Sands did you know that we had to come here?"

Ikella shook her head.

"There was no compulsion, I felt nothing here that will tell us how we change our Way, or who will follow in our path. There is nothing left here for us, my Beneva, nought but the chance to say 'Goodbye' and now we must return."

Beneva saw that the frame of the travelling glass was there again, with the Council Chamber warm and welcoming against the cold lonely whine of the winds where they stood. They stepped back through the threshold, and Beneva watched curiously as Ikella carefully dusted the snow from the hems of their cloaks, removed small pieces of debris they had inadvertently brought with them. They carefully moved the Chest back against the wall, and as the familiar "click" of the mechanism was heard, the mirror vanished once more. Silently Ikella tidied the table, lifted her Staff and inclined her head to Beneva. Plainly she was not going to talk about their experience tonight, and the librarian did not blame her. She felt overwhelmed by all that had happened lately, and this last was no ordinary experience. It was something to hold in contemplation before speaking of it. She withdrew from the Council Chamber, and left Ikella closing its shielded door as she went on her own way to bed.

Ikella left the Djellim silently, sweeping along the corridor to her quarters deep in thought. She paused by the nursery and listened, but could hear only the sound of deep and regular breathing.

"So Nadra and the babies sleep do they? That is good, I won't disturb them."

She smiled wearily, thinking that although temptation beckoned, to go gather the baby into her arms, she also needed to sleep. She made the right turn on to the corridor in which her own quarters lay. At her door, Sorrill, one of the Inesh stood hesitantly, waiting it seemed for the summons from within. At Ikella's approach, she dropped the hand that was about to knock at the door again, and dropped to one knee.

"Forgive me my Deshun, we knocked for you earlier, but thought that you must be about Council business, we could not find you in the nursery or infirmary..."

The unspoken question was there.

'How in this community could the Sorceress disappear for any length of time?'

Ikella ignored it and simply raised a questioning eyebrow at the young guard. Sorill's next words however were like a sword blow to the heart and Ikella felt herself reeling, dizzy and heartsick, though she stood impassive and calm as the woman said.

"A man comes my Deshun, asking for the baby! He has been persuaded to rest in the Hall of Welcome this night with the others of his company. He came seeking a young woman and her child. They say that she was lost from their train at Maraken, on the trail above Tearchan. He says this woman's name is Arriera, he holds a token of hers, which he gave me to put into your hand, and your hand only. Ikella felt as if the ground opened up beneath her feet, but steadily she held out her hand and into it was dropped as she knew it was to be the match to the child's search stone a tiny crystal apple, twin to the symbol now embedded in the opal heart stone, that she carried in her innermost pocket, next to her own heart. She examined the carved fruit impassively, turning it in the light. The Inesh guard looked on, a troubled frown on her face but presently Ikella came to herself and said briefly.

"Did you see this man, yourself Sorrill?"

The woman nodded, "Yes my Deshun, he came asking for audience, almost as soon as the wagons he led came to a halt, he has other men with him, three or four, and they have escorted some traders who come for conclave. Even now there is an encampment of strangers building up outside the village, without the Hall of Welcome we would be hard put to find room for visitors yet to come.

"What is he like?"

Ikella asked feeling curiously detached, already preparing for the pain that was to come. Hadn't she cast the Seeking Spell, why had she thought that no-one would answer to that magical summons?

"He seems to be a man of some substance" Sorrill sensed that her reply was all important to her Sorceress, and picked her words with care.

"He asked if a young woman had made it to our gates, she would either be a new mother with her child, or possibly a bereft woman, childless and perhaps in need of our infirmary skills. He said that she was of the Amber Sands he thought, and that she would have been here sometime." The Inesh woman looked a little hesitant but continued.

"When we realised that you were about Council business and could not be disturbed he then gave us the stone, he said that it was all he had left of the woman to identify her by, he hoped you would recognise it." As Ikella took in these words, she lifted the latch to her rooms and entered, turning to say to Sorrill thoughtfully.

"Very well, it is too late to do anything regarding the baby now, let us sleep and see what the dawn brings. I will keep the stone for now and return it to him, in the morning at Audience." She closed the door, and leant against it trembling, her legs feeling that they could not hold her upright a moment longer.

Late into the night one light burned on, as the Sorceress pored over every scrap of information she had about the child and across the hallway in a room set aside for him, Carolus nodded over a set of stones carved with mystical symbols. Every now and then he would lift one, and transpose its position with another, while he pondered what seemed to be an ever-increasingly difficult equation.

Far below them in a guest room a man paced, till in the cold deep night the lights were snuffed and Selesh slept fitfully, waiting for the dawn of another darkened day.

If you have enjoyed this book, follow the unfolding mystery in:

The Tapestry of Tten - Book 2 by Julia Cæsar

"Curse of Night"

Following the Storm, Jentaroth (the annual Rite of Passage), takes on new significance. Amidst mourning rituals, Ikella must protect the Union of the Sands from treachery within, whilst resisting her growing emotional attachment to the frail orphan she longs to adopt. Beset by premonitions as she gathers her Sisters in Sorcery at Selesh, Ikella is forced to defend the Gathering as one of three new Candidates reveals herself as a practising heretic, with command of Dark Magic. As she confines Adruna and her followers to her own Sands, Ikella cannot prevent her cursing baby Daro, but did her curse have any effect?

As Daro grows up, how many Rotations must Ikella endure his relentless obsession with the ancient mages of the past? Is this something to do with "The Curse of Night? As his obsession leads him into perilous places, can he survive to find "Another Shade of Mystery?"

"The Tapestry of Tten", a gripping series of Fantasy Fiction novels by Julia Caesar is published by Arima Publishing. To order, please visit our website: **www.arimapublishing.co.uk** or write to us at:

Arima publishing
ASK House
Northgate Avenue
Bury St Edmunds
Suffolk
IP32 6BB
UK

The Tapestry of Tten - Book 3 by Julia Cæsar

"Another Shade of Mystery"

Having exiled Daro for his obsession with the ancient mages of their secret past, life is still far from peaceful in Selesh. The aging Sorceress has found no relief from troublesome children, for she has given refuge to Jalni. The girl, hotly pursued into the heart of the community, has an intriguing (though erratic) command of power. Admitted as a novice, Jalni commits a catalogue of crimes, and is on probation when Daro returns empowered, to challenge his foster-mother's long held beliefs.

Determined to ignore the personal price he has paid for his power, the Opal Sandsinger takes Jalni as his guide, and sets out to save the children of Scartel. Encountering Myst-cats, Wanderers, Storm horses and a mysterious mentor, Daro must also find his feet in a strange new world, looking for "Another Shade of Mystery", to help him understand, "The Song of Sorcery"

"The Tapestry of Tten", a gripping series of Fantasy Fiction novels by Julia Caesar is published by Arima Publishing. To order, please visit our website:**www.arimapublishing.co.uk** or write to us at:

Arima publishing
ASK House
Northgate Avenue
Bury St Edmunds
Suffolk
IP32 6BB
UK

The Tapestry of Tten - Book 4 by Julia Cæsar

'Song of Sorcery"

Returning from Scartel to safety, Daro and Jalni are shaken by the death of a child. As Daro questions his faith in magic, Jalni decides that if he can face the past of a world, she can face her own, and slips away unseen. En route to Jerritol, followed by an old friend, she encounters Orto and decides to help him find the Tapestry of Tten. At the Temple of the Winds there's no trace of the relic, but the Oracle predicts Jalni will become "Mother to the Tenth Wind."

Jalni goes into retreat, but when the Sorceress Tirjella is poisoned, she usurps Sandsinger powers and saves her. Returning to Selesh, Jalni can predict Ikella's reaction, but Daro's she couldn't have foreseen in a thousand Rotations!

Empathise with Jalni's struggle to control her own destiny. Watch Daro confront the limitations of his power, and smile as Jalni finds love. Does it last? Read the sequel, "Sword of Honour" to find out.

"The Tapestry of Tten", a gripping series of Fantasy Fiction novels by Julia Caesar is published by Arima Publishing. To order, please visit our website: **www.arimapublishing.co.uk** or write to us at:

Arima publishing
ASK House
Northgate Avenue
Bury St Edmunds
Suffolk
IP32 6BB
UK

RNIB Talking Books - A message from the Author.

A proportion of the purchase price of this book, is being donated by the author to RNIB, The Royal National Institute for Blind and Partially Sighted People, and will be directed to their National Library Service which runs the Talking Book Service and the Learning and Skills Library. These provide visually Impaired people with an accessible source of entertainment and education through the conversion of books into an audio format, known as DAISY (Digitally Accessible Information System) a unique system that allows navigation of audio books.

The resulting CD's dropping through the letterbox are a powerful tool in the battle for equality, giving blind and partially sighted people access to thousands of books which were previously not available. This lifeline service is invaluable to some tens of thousands of people across the UK.

"You have already supported this significant service simply by buying my book, but if you want to help further the aim of making it possible for all books to become accessible to Visually Impaired Readers, or need information about the RNIB, please call their helpline on 0303 123 9999 or visit www.rnib.org.uk

Thank you for your support

Julia Cæsar

www.ingramcontent.com/pod-product-compliance
Lightning Source LLC
Chambersburg PA
CBHW071138260626
47162CB00003B/839